THE MAKER SERIES

MAKING DEALS

Ivy Charles

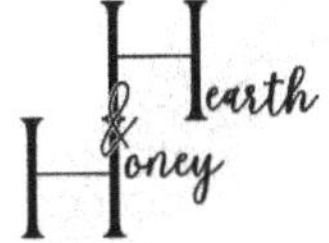

Making Deals

© 2025 by Ivy Charles

This book is available at special discounts when purchased in quantity for use as premiums, promotions, fundraisers, or for book clubs. For inquiries and details, contact the author at ivycharles.com.

Published by Hearth and Honey, LLC

Arkansas

Cover Design by Jennifer Stimson

Library of Congress Control Number: 2025912104

Paperback ISBN: 979-8-9989275-0-8

eBook ISBN: 979-8-9989275-1-5

To the love of my life, thank you for being my home.

Prologue

The hospital's antiseptic stench invades my nose, a stark contrast to the earthy smell of horses and fields I'm accustomed to on the ranch. Despite the familiarity of injuries and doctor visits that come with ranch life, nothing prepared me for the idle helplessness of sitting in this uncomfortable plastic chair. The shitty thing about hospitals is that they give you nothing to do but sit, wait, and stare. Dad, motionless and somehow looking small, feels like a punch to the gut. This stillness, this smallness, I've only witnessed once before—the day we lost Mom.

Dad is a shadow of the man who seemed invincible a week ago. His skin, weathered from years of working outdoors, appears sallow under the harsh fluorescent lights. Pain and fatigue deepen the rugged lines etching his face.

Relentless sharp, synthetic chirps from the machines surrounding him slice through the room's silence. Every tone carries an undercurrent of tension, confirming that he's still alive, as if the answer could change in a single second.

Heavy footsteps in the hall interrupt the rhythmic monotony, growing louder as they draw closer. A quiet knock, followed by the slow swing of the door, illuminates two figures, my younger brothers—Statler and Lincoln.

I pull Statler into a tight hug. "How the hell did you get here so fast? You were in California two days ago." My hoarse voice betrays the exhaustion I feel all the way to my bones. I haven't slept, hell, I haven't left this damn room in two days.

Statler manages a strained chuckle. "Don't act like when you call, we don't all know it's not a request." He observes me with concern. "Besides, you look like shit, big brother."

"He's not wrong," Lincoln joins in with a warm, teasing tone.

"I've never been happier to see that both of you assholes actually do listen. I'm grateful you made it. There's some stuff we need to talk about."

The weight of the impending conversation looms over us, a necessary confrontation that Dad, above all, will resist. He'll resist on principle, but I'm right to insist. Not to mention, I've already put the solution into motion, so there won't be anything to argue about.

Lincoln's voice drops to a whisper, "How's he doing?"

"Well, look what the cat dragged in," Dad grumbles, his voice breaking into our conversation.

"Hey, pops, you don't look so hot, old man." Statler moves to his side, gripping our father's hand.

"Don't get any ideas, I can still take you." Dad's response comes with a chuckle, though it quickly devolves into a cough.

I interject, "Dad, chill." The fatigue and tension of the past two days have worn me thin, leaving me raw and on edge, my voice sharper than I intended, but I can't seem to stop it.

"Being tired always has made you a bit of a hard ass," Lincoln teases with a smirk.

Ignoring Lincoln, I lay out the stark reality of Dad's health. "The doctors said it was a heart attack, a mild one, but it did require them to put in a stent. He's going to need medication, some changes in his diet and stress, and he'll need regular follow-ups."

"I don't need to change anything. These things happen. Everything's going to be fine," Dad stubbornly maintains, echoing his denial from the moment he regained consciousness yesterday.

"No, Dad, it's not fine, and yes, you do need to change," I counter, my patience fraying, tired of this conversation. "Riot needs you, and you can't keep running the ranch and the business entirely on your own while we're all out."

"Wyatt, what are you thinking?" Lincoln inquires, his gaze probing for answers before I even speak.

"Statler's got three years left, maybe more if he chooses, and you just passed the bar and are starting your practice. I've won two world titles. I already keep my base at the ranch. I've had this plan in my mind for a while now. I've always known what I wanted, even if the timing is sooner than expected." I pause to catch my breath. "I'm retiring from the circuit to join Dad at the ranch and run the business."

"Absolutely not," Dad protests, attempting to rise but collapsing back, his frailty more evident than ever. "You're not quitting anything, Son. I mean it. You're talented, better than me, at the prime of your career—"

"Dad." My voice comes out more like a low growl reverberating through the air. I lock eyes with him. "I refuse to tell Riot that yet another person she loves is gone, missing the most important moments of her life. This decision is final. I retired yesterday. The public will hear by tonight. A few sponsor obligations are still on the books, but then this chapter of my life is over. We'll be partners as soon as you're home and Lincoln drafts the papers. Your days on the road are over, at least for this year. Gary's already agreed to oversee the livestock at the upcoming rodeos." My hands betray me, trembling with the force of anxiety and worry building inside. My vision starts to blur at the edges. Breathing out hard, I turn to the door.

"I won't bother asking if you're sure," Dad concedes, his voice tinged with a mixture of resignation and frustration. "I've never been able to stop you from doing what you thought needed doing. Just don't regret it, Son." The room falls silent, my brothers' eyes fixed on us, questions hanging in the air. It's a rare sight, Dad and I at odds.

"I don't." As I close the distance to the door, I can think only of a shower and fresh air. "I'll be back in a few hours." With nothing else to be said, I walk out, shutting the door behind me. My decision is made, and it's as immovable as the mountains of Wyoming.

CHAPTER 1

Time

Five years later . . .

"Well, looks like just another day in paradise for you, Charlie." I barely hold back a laugh. There's Charlie, planted on the ground with his ass in a pile of cow shit, all thanks to a sick heifer.

"Honestly, Wy, I'm getting too damn old for this," he grumbles, picking himself up. He's a sturdy guy, not too big, not too small—kinda like Chris Stapleton if he'd seen a few more winters. Give Charlie a shot of whiskey on a long night, and he might even sing you a few bars.

"You're not that old." I gotta admit, I can't quite recall his age. He's been part of the scenery since I was a kid, and he seemed old back then.

"Son, I'm about to turn the big six-two next year. Sammy's doing his best to take over more of my load at the clinic, but if I really am going to retire, I'll be getting serious about finding another vet to help him. I put out some feelers with a few friends, seeing if I can get someone in here before foaling season kicks off in earnest."

"How does your better half, and the best woman I know, feel about that?"

"Annie's ready for retirement and less middle-of-the-night emergency calls. Says she wants to go on a cruise in Alaska."

"That's a far cry from Wyoming." Scratching at the scruff on my chin, I'm reminded I forgot to shave again.

"You're not wrong. It's another step in life. But look at you, you took over for your daddy and it all turned out great. I imagine Sammy will grow and do new things and adding a vet should allow him to do that," he says, sounding like he's got one foot in the grave already.

"Tell me you'll stick around for the fun stuff?" I can't cover the laugh as I point to him covered in cow shit.

"You'd be lost without me, Son," he retorts with a grin.

"Blasphemy. I'm just not looking forward to breaking in a new vet." I'd really miss him if he up and vanished, but I'm not telling him that.

"I imagine I'll be just like Shep, Wy, registering opinions no one's asking for and giving out sage advice," he muses.

My laughter booms through the air this time. Dad fought tooth and nail against retirement. Eventually he came around just enough to slow down, but he hasn't quit telling me what to do.

"You and Dad are painting quite the picture of retirement—bossing folks around without any of the responsibility. Next thing we know, you'll have your own 'Old-Timers' table at the diner. God help us all!"

"I can picture it now. We'll claim the corner booth, start our own little council," he says, as we head to his truck. Sure enough, I can see them holding court, spinning stories like they're the cowboy versions of King Arthur and his knights. More likely, they'll be swapping town gossip, not that they'd ever call it that.

"Tell Cathy I'll be into the office tomorrow to settle up." I flash a grin as we reach his truck.

"You got it." He snags a towel from the backseat and tosses it onto the driver's seat of the vet clinic truck.

As he climbs in, I yell, "Hey Charlie!" When he turns around, I add, "if you really gotta leave, try to pick someone we're all going to like. No assholes."

He grins while climbing into the truck. "Son," he says, "Statler has the market cornered on assholes. I'm not sure I could find another."

"I may be known for being stubborn, but at least I'm not known as the asshole brother." Shrugging, I lean on the hood. Stat's not really an asshole, he's just quiet and doesn't tolerate a lot. "Maybe you should introduce them to Lincoln first, come to think of it. He's never met a stranger."

"Now there's an idea. Or maybe Riot. When's she back next?"

"Not for a few more months. You might miss out on that. Besides, she's the wildest of all of us."

"Now who might be responsible for that?" Charlie teases, sticking his head out the window as he starts to back up the truck.

"I have no clue what you mean." I feel the grin tug at my mouth. Dad likes to say Riot's wild because she's the youngest and was raised by four men, but I like to think it means we raised her not to take any shit. If we didn't give her anything else, we made her tough as hell, and that's not nothing.

Ought to be interesting to see a little new blood in town. It's not that people don't move here; it's that to stay, you've got to be built for this land. Sure, there are plenty of vacation spots popping up, but at its heart, the town still revolves around the ranches. We made a smart move a while back, getting into direct-to-market beef sales. It's a grind, especially with the marketing and shipping, but it's given us a chance to show off our feed program and grow the ranch in new directions.

My phone buzzes as I watch Charlie's truck roll away. Meredith's name lights up the screen.

"What's up?"

"Good morning to you too, boss," Meredith's voice comes through.

"Alrighty, fancy social media manager," I reply. Still feels like the weirdest thing to say ever. "How can I help you?"

"Can you swing by today to check out this month's special boxes? We need to discuss the spring marketing campaigns too, and if I could snag a video of you packing boxes, it'd be a hit on socials," she says, a bit too fast, probably hoping I'd let that last part slide.

"Meredith—"

"I know, I know. You're not a fan of the camera, but trust me, it's a *fan* of you," she interrupts, her laughter clear through the phone.

"Fine. I'll be there in thirty minutes," I grumble.

"Check." She hangs up. Taking pictures and social media used to bug the shit out of me—they still do—but I understand their purpose. Businesses are built online these days.

Meredith runs a tight ship with her team at the warehouse, handling all the shipping, logistics, and media for the ranch. I was surprised when she applied for the job. She said she wanted a job that made her happy and allowed her to be with her kid, and turns out, she's damn good at it.

Dad had his way of doing things, and it worked for him. But times change, and so do we. Adapting wasn't easy, but you can't just ignore the shifts happening all around you. Sometimes, I find myself missing the rodeo days when all I had to focus on was the next few seconds. But now, we're the ones supplying the circuit with stock. Mom and Dad started the business, and I've taken it further, using what I learned on the circuit to improve our bull and bronc lines. Now, five years down the line, we're the top pick for rodeo stock. The beef sales, which Riot jokingly calls our side hustle, bring in steady cash, but the real profits are in stock contracting. When one side dips, the other usually picks up the slack. It's a balancing act, but it keeps things interesting.

The number one lesson I've learned in this life is that change is constant, so either you grow or die.

CHAPTER 2

Opportunity

Six weeks later . . .

I hate packing. I hate packing. I hate packing. I hate packing. I hate packing. It's like being reminded you own an absurd amount of stuff, yet somehow, can't get it all to fit into boxes. What if I just threw caution to the wind and packed a single bag?

"Okay, now you're just being dramatic, Parker," I say to Cooper, my service dog, who tilts his head as if to agree. I've managed to pack about ninety percent of my belongings into the moving container, set to be hauled off to Wyoming tomorrow. All that's left is the kitchen, and what we're taking on the drive.

"Parker!" Dad's voice echoes through the house.

"In the kitchen, Dad!" I yell back.

I hear his footsteps in the hallway and spin around as they grow louder.

Greg Mason is fit in his mid-forties, with a tan and a hint of stubble threatening to become a full-fledged beard. His eyes are warm, chocolate brown, and he stands just over six feet, a few inches taller than me.

"Thanks for saving the kitchen packing for me." He grins and pulls me into a hug.

"You're welcome. Besides, who am I to argue with a Michelin star chef when it comes to the kitchen, right?"

"Dang skippy!"

I'm meticulous with most things, but packing? I usually end up shoving things into boxes haphazardly. But not the kitchen. The kitchen is different—every item has a memory attached. These things deserve to be packed with care.

"What have you started on and what's left?" He looks around.

"I haven't packed a single item, scout's honor. I just assembled some boxes and tackled the junk drawer." I raise my hands as if swearing an oath.

"You were never a scout," he teases, eyes crinkling with amusement.

"Fair point." I turn back to taping boxes. We sink into a rhythm, the silence between us easy and familiar. I assemble boxes while he wraps the pots, pans, and dishes with care that speaks of years in the kitchen. It's moments like these when I'm acutely aware of the life I've been given, the life that began with loss and found its way to love. Adoption is loss, first and foremost. It meant that when I was adopted at ten, I had baggage and trauma and fears. My parents didn't even flinch. They immediately started us all in family therapy and my life changed forever in more ways than one.

An hour later, I tape the last box closed and scan the packed room. That's when I spot the photo on the shelf by the sink. It's us—Greg, Cameron, and me—wrapped in a tight embrace in front of a restaurant. I pick up the frame tenderly. We lost Cameron to cancer when I was seventeen, and the familiar ache still lives my heart.

"Do you remember this photo?" Slowly, I begin to wrap the frame.

Dad turns, his smile soft. "I always loved that picture. Our first restaurant in Chicago," he says, his arm coming around my shoulders.

"Cameron was larger than life, wasn't he? If you're the king of the kitchen, he was the king of the neighborhood."

"Isn't that the truth," he agrees with a chuckle. "He knew everyone. When I met him, he was bored with Wall Street and real estate, and he wanted something to call his own. Then, I came along," he says with a wink.

"And then me, right?" A familiar smile tugs at my lips.

"You got it, Snow. We had a great thing going in Boston, but we wanted more—a change, a challenge. We moved and we found you. Suddenly, it was three of us against the world," he reminisces.

"You were always in the kitchen, Cam was the face everyone knew, and I was . . ." I trail off.

"Buried in your books in some corner," he finishes with a laugh.

And he's right—I did love school.

"Alright, let's finish this up," I say, giving the photo one last careful wrap before tucking it among the cookbooks in a box. I can't help but steal glances at my dad. He's lost in thought, clearly worried about the move but putting on a brave face. He's been my rock. Cameron was all about confidence—walking into a room like you own it, facing challenges head-on with a defiant grin and a wink. Greg, on the other hand, taught me to be rooted, to dig deep. Cameron's gift was his courage; Greg's gift is his unwavering presence.

I slip under his arm for a hug. He pauses, wrapping me in a steady embrace, his chin resting atop my head. I inhale deeply, the unique blend of butter and smoke that's always clung to him fills my senses—a scent that's been my anchor for years.

"You okay?" His voice betrays the emotion he's trying to hide.

He's failing. So am I. Packing is emotional as hell.

"Yeah, it's just . . . it feels like the end of an era," I admit.

"It is an end, but that's not always bad. You're starting something new, and you deserve it," he reassures me.

"I know. Just feels a little final to leave Georgia. But it's a great opportunity." I'm trying to convince myself as much as him.

"Who would've thought, huh? Willa, Wyoming," he says with a light laugh, trying to ease the tension.

"Let's grab a bite, old man. I'm starving, and Cooper's itching for a walk," I suggest, eager for a distraction from all these big feelings.

"Don't go confessing to your future bovine patients that you enjoy a burger now and then," he quips with a straight face.

"Dork," I retort playfully, snatching my keys from the counter. I whistle for Cooper, taking my time to attach his leash, and we head out the door, ready for a break from the bittersweet goodbyes.

CHAPTER 3

Miles

PARKER

H our twenty-seven, and I'm officially dubbing this the longest drive of my life.

"How's it going?" Greg's voice crackles through the truck's speakerphone.

"I'm in Wyoming, so that's something. Remind me why I didn't just get a truck when I arrived?" I ask, half-joking.

"Debt, kiddo. What would Cameron tell you?" Greg's reminder is gentle but firm.

"Do the work to own it, so no one owns you," I recite the mantra Cameron drilled into me. He had a knack for finance, and when he learned about my need for security, he turned money management into my superpower. Those finance podcasts weren't exactly thrilling for a thirteen-year-old, but I'm grateful now.

"Got to go, Dad. Cami's on the other line!"

"Take care, sweet pea." The line goes dead, and I'm quick to switch calls.

"Hey, babes!" Cami's voice bursts through, loud and clear. Trust Cami to always dive into a conversation with all she's got.

"Oh, my gosh, Cami, this drive is the worst. I'm dying. Poor Cooper looks like he wants to murder me, and I'm not sure how, but my butt has never hurt this much."

"I can only imagine. Mostly, because I have no desire to torture myself with that drive when I could fly and have my bestie pick me up at an airport." She sing-songs the last part then busts up laughing.

"Yeah, yeah, yeah. So, how's LA?"

"LA's sunny, but the people? Not so much," she grumbles into the phone. "They're trying to turn this book into a television series, and all they see are clichés. They aren't grasping the depth of the story."

"If it feels wrong, walk away. There's a whole universe of streaming platforms out there. Or, hey, take the reins and produce it yourself," I suggest, absolutely serious.

"That's a big leap, but I'm already pushing to explore other options," Cami admits. "Do you think I need fake boobs?" she asks, out of left field.

I almost spit out my drink. "What? Why would you even think that?"

"It's LA. Everyone's got this . . . look. It's sort of like me but not and the key difference is their rack," she confesses dryly.

"You're not missing *anything*. What's this really about?" I press gently, sensing there's more to this story.

"Studio jerk suggested that because my character has a cochlear implant, she can't have any other *flaws*," Cami vents, frustration clear in her voice. She's had a cochlear implant since an accident left her deaf.

"That guy is a dickhead. If he gets the rights to that book, I'll be pissed at you. Also, your body is banging, and don't act like you don't know that. Also, I think we could bury his body somewhere in the never-ending landscape I'm staring at right now."

"Driving is making you quick to murder. You're usually the nice one. It's my job to be mean. You just save sweet furry little lives and leave the murder to me. I'll keep the idea in reserve and call you for disposal." Anything that makes her feel supported is a win in my book, even murder.

"Very funny. You know I'd kill. Only for you, Emmary, and Greg, but I would do it. Now, when is your break? Are you going to come out here and help me settle in?"

"I've got to finish this circus up and that's going to take considerable time. Then, I think I might come and hang for a while. I need . . . something," Cami's voice trails off, uncharacteristically subdued.

"Camilla, we've been friends for six years, you know you can tell me anything. Might as well start with what's really going on with you lately." I know something's been off with her. I can feel it.

"Truthfully, I'm not exactly sure, Parks. It's like my magic's gone out. I can't seem to tap into that part of me. It's more than tired. It feels like I'm burned out completely," she confesses, her breath shaky.

"You know I don't believe in magic. I believe in work. But if I were to believe in magic, you'd be the only one I know who has it." I pause, giving her a moment to digest my words. "No need to hurry. No need to sparkle. No need to be anybody but oneself."

"Virginia Woolf, always a classic," she acknowledges.

"I might not have the perfect advice, but I know you don't have to be anything other than yourself. And, I've got a spot for you here, whenever you're ready." I hear her sniffle on the other end. Cami's always been a whirlwind, but she only shows her vulnerable side to a few. To the rest of the world, she's ice, but to those in her circle, she's all heart.

To lighten the mood, I add, "And selfishly, I don't know what I'd do without you bossing me around and telling me what to watch. It's been six years of you running the show."

"I'll still be bossing, girly, don't you worry." Her laugh fades too quickly. "Hey, Parks," she adds softly, "I'm proud of you. I didn't get to say it before you left."

Her words hit me hard, and I blink back tears, the ache of missing her expanding through my chest. "I'm too emotional and utterly exhausted from this drive to take that in right now. You'll have to tell me face-to-face."

"Deal," she replies firmly.

Just then, my GPS chimes in, telling me I'm almost at my exit. "I've got to go, I'm nearly there."

"Love you. Send pictures and call me after you've caught up on sleep."

"Love you too." With a tap of the finger, I end the call. I look over at Cooper, my constant companion. "Cooper, we are loved and we're almost there. Everything is going to be okay. This is our next adventure. Wyoming's got nothing on us, right?" I can't help but feel a mix of excitement and nerves as we approach our new home.

CHAPTER 4

Groceries

PARKER

Six hours into my new life in Willa, and despite the lack of a bed or any semblance of an unpacked home, I'm buzzing with certainty that I've made the right move. Do I have a bed? Nope. Do I have furniture unpacked? Nope. *Am I asking myself questions like a crazy person? Yep.*

"Okay, Cooper, first things first, we need food. The movers are still a day out, so tonight it's just us. Let's hit the local grocery store. What do you say?" Cooper offers me a blank stare, the kind only a dog can give when you're laying out your plans. At least, it means I win all the arguments.

"Short trip this time, pal," I assure him as we descend the steps and hop into the truck. A five-minute drive later, and we're facing our first big adventure—cooking without any actual cooking equipment.

Pulling into the parking spot, I glance at Cooper. He's been my loyal companion for two years now, but not everyone's as welcoming as they should be to a service dog. "No worries, buddy. Small-town Wyoming's got to be friendly territory for a good boy like you." I secure his service harness, grab my wallet, and with a deep breath, set off to face the first real test of our new hometown.

Stepping into the grocery store, the tension I feel is palpable, but it's overshadowed by the practical need to stock up on essentials. As I maneuver my cart through the aisles, I'm drawn to the sight of three strikingly tall men in the produce section. I may not be in the market for a guy, but I can appreciate the male form. I'm a woman with a beating heart after all.

They don't look like they belong together. The first, Glasses, is the epitome of corporate. His deep navy suit that catches the light as he moves is a second skin. The glasses perched on his nose look navy like his suit. His build is lean, the kind that suggests not bulk but agility. He may be the shortest of the three, but still well over six feet.

Backwards Hat is the middle ground in height, a bridge between the others. His attire is a nod to the modern cowboy—the denim hugging his legs, boots scuffed from work, and the ballcap worn backward with a nonchalance. His physique is a testament to physicality; he's not sculpted like a bodybuilder but instead honed like a man accustomed to the weight of a saddle. His T-shirt, snug against his skin, is less of a fashion choice and more of a casual display of strength.

The tallest, Tattoos, is a living canvas. His black jeans and Henley are mere backdrops to the artistry of his arms. Though they lack vibrant color, the mix of landscape and flowers tell a story.

They're an odd trio. It's practically a "three strangers walk into a bar" joke. Their conversation drifts over to me as I select my fruits and veggies.

"Listen, Dad would love it," says Glasses.

"Dad would murder you for getting a cake like that," retorts Backwards Hat.

They are clearly talking about their dad, maybe three brothers?

"Maybe we should just get Dad hot wings, he loves those," suggests Tattoos.

"Listen, assholes, it's his birthday, and everyone's coming over. I've had the brisket on for twenty hours, so, no, Stat, we are not just buying hot wings. And Suits, we are not getting Dad a pin-up cake. He'd kill you after he died from embarrassment. We are here to pick up a normal cake that can feed all these people," Backwards Hat declares, clearly the one in charge. Glasses must say something in response because Backwards Hat smacks him on the back of the head, eliciting a laugh from Tattoos.

Just as I'm trying to be inconspicuous, Backwards Hat's eyes catch mine. My cheeks flush with heat—I'm totally busted. There's something about getting caught that's just mortifying, even though I find the ebb and flow of family interactions utterly fascinating.

Let's be honest, it's not a hardship to watch these guys. Hastily retreating from the produce section, I fix my gaze firmly on the linoleum and try to remember what I'm doing here. Tonight's about celebrating our new life. And if the welcome—or lack of a boot out the door—is anything to go by, Wyoming might just be the right kind of place for Cooper and me.

WYATT

As I wrangle the idiots to get back to the truck so we aren't late to the party *we* planned, my mind drifts back to her. She's not from here, clearly. She had a big-ass dog looking at her like she'd hung the moon. She was on the taller side, especially for a woman. She was heart-stoppingly beautiful, but that's not what I couldn't get out of my head.

Clicking the seatbelt into place, steering the truck out of the grocery store parking lot, we head back to the ranch. I must have been thirty feet away when I caught her looking over. Even at that distance, as soon as she locked those eyes on me, it felt like my heart stopped.

For the rest of my life, living rent free in my mind, will be her eyes—
vivid, piercing blue, like the endless Wyoming sky.

CHAPTER 5

Impressions

WYATT

Three days later . . .

Headlights cut through the rain like shards of glass. It's the vet truck, *finally*. These mares have a sense for drama, choosing a stormy night on a full moon to give birth. As a stock contractor, having a solid succession plan in bucking stock is critical. These horses won championships or broke men, sometimes both. The breeding program I started a few years ago means being selective about which mares get bred and how often. We need to balance having enough mature stock to buck while not being overrun with colts to train or feed. Of primary importance is to be intentional to breed in those championship qualities. Not every foal ends up as bucking stock in a rodeo, trying to throw a cowboy before eight seconds is up. We train and sell those for other rodeo events and various equine sports.

Foaling season sets my nerves on edge, even more so on a night like tonight. Storms and full moons don't always bring the best luck.

This year is the last we'll breed my mom's mare, Cinder. I've always been selective about breeding her, and every horse she's delivered has gone on to be a champion. Until last year, when her colt was stillborn. Though it happens, I'm not willing to chance losing her. After this foal, she'll live out the remainder of her life on the ranch in peaceful retirement, getting fat and lazy. Everyone around her sneaks her treats, yet no one seems to think I know that.

As the headlights dim and the engine cuts off, the door opens, and I see an unfamiliar pair of rubber boots matching a small form jump from the truck, followed quickly by a dog—a dog I recognize immediately. The woman from the store. The two figures make a beeline for the open barn doors. Once inside, she throws back her hood, shakes out the rain, and there they are—those sky-blue eyes that haven't left my mind since I first saw them.

As I look her over, she's wearing a T-shirt that reads "I have no shelf control" hovering over a stack of books.

That's a first.

Up close, she's even more beautiful than I remember. Those eyes of hers, I'm lost in them the moment our gazes meet. She's tall, almost to my shoulders standing this close. Her dark mahogany hair is pulled into a messy-looking knot on her head, exposing the perfectly smooth skin of her neck with little tendrils sticking out as if she did it in a rush. Her fitted clothes outline a figure that's both strong and soft in all the right places. I'm momentarily speechless, caught off guard by her presence.

Her dog, a service animal according to the vest around it, sits obediently by her side. Then the thunder cracks, reminding me of the night's urgency. I've got mares ready to foal. I need to focus, not get lost in a pair of beautiful eyes and perfect curves.

Get it together, Wyatt.

"Mr. Lochlan?" Her voice cuts through the storm's growl, a little tired and cautious.

"Yeah. Who are you?" I blurt out, immediately regretting my lack of manners. "I'm sorry, that came out wrong. My name is Wyatt. May I ask who you are?"

"Dr. Parker Mason. I'm the new vet Doc Cort Senior hired. I was hoping to meet you next week after I had a chance to settle in, but both Drs. Cort Senior and Junior got called out on emergencies, and when you called, they asked me to jump in."

I feel her confidence as she extends her hand for a shake. I take her hand, and it's like holding something precious—her skin unexpectedly soft, her fingers delicate.

"Listen, I appreciate you coming out." Dropping her hand before I make this awkward moment worse, I continue. "But—" I sigh, trying to find the right words. "You don't know the stock, I don't know you, and these mares are a critical part of our livelihood. I'd feel a lot more comfortable if Charlie or Sammy were here."

Her smile shifts from warm and kind to chilling, the air dropping by twenty degrees between us. Having a sister, I recognize that look all too well.

"Mr. Lochlan, you're right that you don't know me. If you want to kick me off your property and get Doc Cort Senior, feel free to call him yourself. In the meantime," she gestures to the barn behind me, "I'm going to check on your mares."

She sails past me, without missing a beat, and I'm left standing there, feeling a little stunned. Pulling out my phone from my back pocket, I punch in Charlie's number.

"Little busy here, Wyatt," he answers, his voice strained. "What do you need?"

"Doc, you have to switch. I appreciate you sending the new girl, but I don't know her, and these foals are too important to take a risk. You know what happened last season."

"Wyatt," Charlie grunts, and his tone shifts enough to tell me I'm about to get my ass chewed. "Not that I have to justify my hiring choices to you, but that *woman* graduated top of her class, has some of the best recommendations I've ever seen from her time in a clinic, and worked with a racehorse outfit for the last year *in addition* to clinic time. I'm an hour away, busy with another birth, and Sammy's even further. You needed someone there. I know what that horse means to you, but don't you dare insinuate that doctor isn't qualified. Stop being a dick."

The line goes dead.

Fuck. My. Life.

I didn't mean to make it sound like she wasn't qualified. Especially if it sounded like I thought that because she was a woman. I'd murder any man who talked to Riot like that, assuming Statler didn't beat me to it.

Turning on my heel, I head for the barn alley behind me. I've been through more than one foaling season, and she's a professional. I need to chill out and stop being an anxious asshole. Her dog is sitting on the outside of the stall door about halfway down the walk. Making my way to the stall, I peek in and see her checking our sweet little mare, Molly. When she finishes, she heads for the stall door, pausing at the latch, each of us occupying our own space on either side of the door.

CHAPTER 6

Second Chances

PARKER

"Feeling better?" My voice is a bit harsh, devoid of any real warmth. The irony isn't lost on me—Backwards Hat is the very person I'm here to assist. Here I am, fresh out of unpacked boxes, in the first clean version of scrubs I could find, no makeup, running on fumes from staying up late to unpack. And there he stands, still sporting that damn backwards hat, exuding an attitude that's grating on my nerves.

"Let's start over," he suggests.

"Oh, was our first start not that great?" I can't help the sarcastic smile that spreads across my face. I'm pissed that he'd even hint at doubting my capabilities. To hell with him. Raising his hands in a mock surrender, he flashes what I assume is his version of a charming smile—which, annoyingly, is quite charming.

"Probably doesn't qualify for a meet-cute," he admits.

I arch an eyebrow. "Meet-cute?"

"Yeah, my sister, Riot, says it's the best part of every movie, how two people meet."

I let out a snort at hearing that.

He smiles again, and this time, the smile hints at vulnerability. "Hi. My name is Wyatt Lochlan, and I'm sorry for being an asshole. I wasn't trying to imply you couldn't do your job. The other mare down there was my mom's. Last year, foaling went sideways, and it was stillborn. My mom passed away years ago, and the thought of losing that horse makes me . . ." he trails off.

His eyes hold a sincerity that's hard to ignore. I know I wouldn't be at my best if Cooper were in trouble. I step out of the stall, unable to hold a grudge, extending my hand.

"Hello, Wyatt. My name is Dr. Mason. You can trust me. I'm here to help." This time, my smile is genuine. He takes my hand, holding it a beat too long, his gaze fixed on me as if he's lost in thought.

"You okay?"

"Yeah, just a long night, and it isn't looking shorter," he replies, finally releasing my hand.

"You'll be happy to know that she's progressing nicely and seems to be on track." I point toward the entrance of the first mare's stall. "She's the one you're worried about?"

"Yeah, Cinder."

"Well, she's laboring a bit harder than I like, but so far, she seems to be doing okay. We'll keep our eyes on her."

"It's never boring around here. I can promise you that. How about some coffee? Least I can do for getting you out here at two in the morning." Wyatt's attempt at hospitality is clear.

"None for me, but I'd love a bottle of water if you have one."

"Of course, follow me." He turns, leading me down the alley and through a door into a small studio. It's a cozy space, with a mini kitchen to the left and a cluster of couches to the right. He points out the full bathroom behind a small black door on the far wall. The room feels lived-in, a comfortable space that's seen many late nights and early mornings.

He retrieves a water bottle for me and pours himself a cup. As I take in the room, my eyes are drawn to a wall adorned with photos and trophies—a testament to a family's legacy. The images span generations, from black-and-white snapshots to vibrant, recent victories. Among them, I spot Wyatt, his face alight with triumph.

But it's a particular photo in the center that captures my attention. It's a candid shot of a man and a woman in front of this very barn. Their embrace radiates joy, and even in the still image, their love is obvious. It reminds me of the kind of love my dads shared.

"This is quite a wall of success and victory," I comment, my gaze lingering on the central photo. "Who's this?" I ask, pointing to it.

"That's my mom. She passed fourteen years ago." Wyatt's voice is a mix of sorrow and pride. It's a tone I recognize—the sound of someone who has loved deeply and lost.

"She's beautiful," I say instinctively, moved by the emotion in his voice.

"Yes, she absolutely was. My parents built this place from the ground up. That's from the day this barn was finished." His words stir something in me, a familiar ache of my own. I turn away quickly.

Pulling my phone from my pocket, I set a timer for thirty minutes and glance back at Wyatt. "I'll check them again in thirty. Until then, we wait. You can stay or get some rest at your house. Just give me your number, and I'll keep you updated."

"I don't think I could sleep if I tried, Doc. You're stuck with me. But the good news is," he settles onto the couch and grabs the remote, "we have streaming to keep us busy."

I gesture to the TV. "Any particular favorites?"

"Action or comedy?" His offer is polite, and I can't help but appreciate it.

"Comedy," I choose. "Nothing like laughter to keep you awake."

"I couldn't agree more." A smile plays at the corners of his mouth. It's a small moment, a shared understanding that sometimes laughter *is* the best medicine—even at 2 a.m.

CHAPTER 7

Molly

PARKER

T ed Lasso's charm works its magic, and before I know it, the timer's ringing, pulling us back to reality. "That's our cue, Mr. Lochlan." I stand up from the comfort of the couch.

"Can we drop the 'Mr. Lochlan,' Doc?" Wyatt asks, a hint of sheepishness in his voice. "Just call me Wyatt."

"Sure." A small chuckle ripples through me. Men are so odd about the mister plus last name thing. Half think it ages them, and the other half get turned on. It's always interesting to find out immediately who is who. Because let's be real, they can't hide it.

Approaching the first stall, the paint's restlessness is a clear sign that she's close. I slip in quietly, not wanting to spook her.

"Hey, sweet girl," I whisper soothingly, letting my hands glide over her neck and shoulders, feeling the tension in her muscles. I believe in the power of touch, especially with animals as intuitive as horses.

After a few reassuring strokes, I don my gloves and move to her rear. She shifts, laying down, before I can check her. I'm careful to give her space, mindful of her powerful hooves. I check her and find what I'm looking for—she's ready. Glancing back, I see Wyatt hovering at the entrance.

"She's ready. You staying out there or coming in here?" Without hesitation, he's unlatching the stall and stepping inside.

"Why don't you go up there by her head."

He moves like a man who's used to command, to not being questioned, and who knows he's in control. He's also charming enough to get away with it. That's always a dangerous combination. I'm trying hard not to notice.

Years of celibacy aren't going in the trash because of one grumpy-turned-sunny tall, solidly muscular, dark-haired, bittersweet chocolate-eyed guy in a 49ers hat.

The mare whines softly, the sound quickly drowned out by a thunderous crack. The storm outside is raging, but inside the barn, we're in a world of our own, focusing on the life about to emerge. The mare's contractions are coming faster now, and it's time to get to work. This is what I'm here for—this moment, this miracle. Nothing else matters.

"I'll be right back, but stay with her. She's doing great, and we'll see those hooves soon. I need to look in on the black mare quickly."

"I got it," he nods, and I hurry off. These births can happen in a flash. The black mare is clearly uncomfortable, nipping at her hips. A quick check tells me she's not as far along. I jog back to the paint's stall, signaling Cooper to wait outside, and return to the mare's side.

"What's her name?" I slide back into position.

"Molly." Wyatt's attention never wavers from the mare.

I smile at Molly, spotting the hooves and a hint of nose. "Looks like we're doing this, Molly. Sorry, no birth mix, but you strike me as a classic rock fan."

Wyatt's laughter is a deep, rich sound reverberating through the quiet of the barn. Over the next half hour, I focus on ensuring a smooth delivery, letting nature take its course. When the foal finally arrives, the rush of adrenaline is both familiar and exhilarating. Wyatt has been a rock, his earlier anxiety nowhere in sight.

Molly stands, a good sign, and begins to clean up her newborn. I check the filly, healthy and beautiful with her distinctive black and white markings. "You have another healthy Lochlan filly. She's beautiful," I tell Wyatt.

"Thanks. She reminds me of a domino or those chocolate cookies with white chips," he says.

I see the resemblance too. "Domino's a good name." I pat his arm before turning to leave. Then I hear more pawing. The sixth sense flares to life between my shoulders. "Do you have any more mares in here close to foaling?"

CHAPTER 8

Violet

PARKER

"There's a storm in full motion tonight, all the vets I know are on farm calls, it's a full moon, and it's the thirteenth," Wyatt's voice carries a note of urgency, "meaning probably." His words rush out, tinged with anxiety. He strides across the alley to the stall of a breathtaking paint buckskin. I glance at my watch, realizing it hasn't been long since I arrived, but the night feels stretched, and my throat is parched.

"Can you grab my water from the table? I'll just go in here and do a quick check," I ask him.

"I'll grab it, but stay here." His tone is firm. "Violet's not a big fan of many people, and she could get irritated with you alone in there." I nod, understanding the unique temperaments of horses.

Approaching Violet's stall, I murmur softly, "You are the most beautiful lady I may have ever seen." She gazes back at me, her ears perking up as she steps closer, though not quite within reach. She's a vision, her creamy beige coat accented with bold white paint spots, black socks, and a mane and tail that weave black and white strands into a natural tapestry. It's hard not to wish she were mine. Not that I'd know what to do with her other than keep her alive.

"I know this is our first meeting, but I need to check you and see how you're moving along." I reach over the door to offer my hand for her to sniff. She obliges, stepping forward and turning to give me a better view. I gently run my hand along her neck and side, noting the fullness of her milk sac. I keep talking to her, introducing myself, sharing bits of my life to familiarize her with my voice. I tell her my name, that I moved just from Georgia, that I have a dog named Cooper.

Violet moves closer, greeting me with a gentle nuzzle to my shoulder, and I respond with soothing strokes along her face and neck. Wyatt's stunned silence from two paces away is almost comical, his expression is one of utter surprise.

"Something wrong, Wyatt?" I maintain a light tone even as I sense his concern.

He hands me the water bottle, and for a moment, our eyes lock—a silent exchange loaded with unspoken thoughts. I drink deeply, my eyes not leaving his, while my left arm continues stroking Violet. His eyes are so dark, you'd think they were black. There's a bigger story with this horse. After years of being around animals, it's a feeling you start to develop.

At Wyatt's nod, I unlatch the stall and enter, focusing on gently guiding my hands along her body to signal my intentions. When I reach her rear, the reality of her situation hits me—she's ready to deliver.

"Wyatt, she's ready. As soon as she lays down, she should deliver." My voice is steady despite the quickening pace of my heart as the adrenaline kicks in again. "I need to check the other mare. Yell when she lays down if I'm not back." A nod is my only confirmation he heard me; he's still staring and silent.

The other mare is restless, but no closer to delivering. Time seems to have flown by—it's nearly 4 a.m. now.

"Doc!" Wyatt's voice, edged with alarm, breaks through the hum of the rain on the barn.

Seeing Violet sends a jolt of urgency through me—the foal's hooves are turned upward, a clear sign of a breech or upside-down position. This complicates birth significantly.

"This isn't ideal, but we're still in the dark about what we're up against, so don't panic yet, Wyatt. Let's find out where we stand." I keep my voice steady, slipping into the professional mode Cami always teases me about. Wyatt nods as I mentally run through the checklist for this situation. Despite my usual disarray when it comes to packing, my approach to veterinary care is nothing short of meticulous. Because Wyatt seems a little stressed, I tell him what I know, hoping it helps keep him calm.

"Breech births are a little tricky. Instead of coming out nose first, this foal is coming out hind first, maybe even upside down. We need to act quickly." I pull on my long gloves and generously apply lube. "I need to reach in and figure out what we're dealing with here, Wyatt." He nods again, utterly still, the exact opposite of the acid churning in my stomach.

As my hand finds hocks instead of knees, I curse under my breath. "This foal's coming out backwards, but at least we've got feet. We can manage this, but we need to move and pull this foal before it suffocates."

My heart drums a staccato rhythm in my chest. I've successfully delivered ten foals in this position, and I'm determined not to break that streak tonight. I quickly instruct Wyatt on positioning the obstetrical straps and how to assist with the mare.

"When the next contraction hits, I'm pulling. She'll resist out of instinct. She's not going to be happy about it, so hold her steady. She's also standing, which means I'm going to catch this foal before it hits the ground. You with me?" I look up to meet his gaze.

"I'm with you, Doc." His eyes are a swirling storm of concern and determination, yet his hands remain unwaveringly steady.

As the mare strains with the next contraction, I pull with everything I've got. It feels like an eternity, and the pain is intense as her muscles clamp down on my arms. But in just a few minutes, I'm cradling a limp foal. Laying it down gently, I grab my bag, and start clearing its airways with a suction bulb, all the while rubbing vigorously to stimulate breathing. Time slows to a crawl as I wait for signs of life.

"Come on, big man," I whisper, urging him to breathe. Suddenly, the world narrows down to just the two of us. "You can do this. You're not going to be the first foal I lose, especially not on my first day."

Wyatt's voice breaks through my focus, quiet and resigned. "He's not breathing, Doc." He's right next to me, his hand on my shoulder. But I refuse to accept it. I've still got a heartbeat so I'm not quitting yet.

Rubbing vigorously, I continue talking to the colt, "Come on, big boy, help me prove this asshole wrong. Your heart's beating. Just breathe with me," I coax. I lean down, block one nostril, and gently blow into the other, trying to inflate his lungs. As the air comes back out, I feel up his left side where his heart still faintly beats. As I feel for his heartbeat, his chest rises on its own. I tickle his nose with hay, coaxing him to cough, to breathe, to live.

"Yes, big man, that's it!" I can't contain my excitement, not caring about the squeal in my voice. Wyatt's laughter joins mine.

"Asshole? Really? You had to insult me to get him to come around?" He's smiling, one dimple showing, and my heart skips a beat. *Damn dimples.*

"Some people just need the right motivation." Laughter bubbles out of me, causing me to snort in the least dignified way possible. I'm a mess, covered in birth fluids, but it only makes me laugh more.

"We've got one foal at 3 a.m., and now another at 4:12. If your other mare follows suit, we've got about forty-five minutes before the next one. Is that what you call a foaling hat trick?"

"I think you get your own trophy if that happens, Doc. Either way, let's see if we can't clean you up a little."

I linger for a few more minutes, watching Violet tenderly clean her newborn. The triumphant scene captivates me. Wyatt's hand finds the small of my back, guiding me gently out of the stall and back to the studio space in the barn. He fetches a few towels from the bathroom and tosses one my way.

"Thanks. Mind if I use the bathroom to clean up?" I point toward it. I really need a moment to myself. After taking care of the necessities, I open the door to find Wyatt waiting with a fresh shirt.

"I found some clean shirts in the dryer. I grabbed one for you." He holds out a shirt.

"Thanks, just a sec," I trade the towel for the shirt and duck back into the bathroom. I slip into the old, faded 49ers shirt—it's so soft, it's like wearing a cloud. It hangs down to mid-thigh.

When I step out, Wyatt scans me from head to toe. "It's a bit big on you," he observes, "but you're representing the 49ers well, Doc."

"The 49ers? In Wyoming? Who's the fan?" Maybe he can tell me who I plan to steal this shirt from. It's not stealing if I write them a thank you note, is it?

"Me," he admits, but before he can say more, loud whinnies from the barn cut him off. I rush toward the mare's stall, ready for the next challenge. But as I start to enter, I stop.

"Wyatt, call Doc Cort, Senior. Put him on speaker. Now." I'm realizing this round might not be a victory after all.

CHAPTER 9

Cinder

WYATT

The change in her tone reaches my ears before my eyes catch what's troubling her. I punch in Charlie's number and hold my breath, waiting for him to answer.

"Boy, if you're still upset about her being there instead of me, you can come talk to me tomorrow, but dammit, I'm tired, Wyatt, and I don't—" Charlie starts, ready to murder me, but Parker cuts him off.

"Doctor Cort, it's Parker. We've delivered two foals in the last few hours and are coming in on the third—a red bag. Who's closest, you or the other Dr. Cort? I'm going to pull this foal, but we need to get to the clinic immediately, and I don't have keys."

"Shit. Okay, listen to me. Wyatt, you there?"

"Yessir."

"Grab that old two-horse trailer and hook it up now. Once you pull that foal and Dr. Mason gets it breathing and hooked to an IV, you load them all up and head to the clinic. I just finished up here, and I'm at least an hour out, if not a little more. I'll meet you there. Be careful in this storm—it's pouring. But hustle."

"Thanks, Charlie." My gaze remains fixed on Parker as she accelerates, defying the limits of human speed. She's my only hope that both Cinder and the unborn foal survive.

"Wyatt!" Charlie's voice pierces through my racing thoughts, compelling me to re-engage. "Follow everything Dr. Mason tells you. If your dad isn't awake yet, get him up, or find Statler—just get someone else down to the barn."

"Yessir." I disconnect and shift my attention back to Parker.

"Go get the trailer now. We don't have time to wait for the hookup after. We can handle this, Wyatt. I can handle this. Trust me." Her tone remains steady, her eyes unwaveringly fixed on mine. I nod. Like a sprinter at the starting line, she dives back into preparations, fully immersed in her zone.

I bolt out of the barn.

The garage door slams behind me as I stride toward the key wall, just as my dad descends the stairs. The timing couldn't be more perfect—I won't have to juggle the phone, the keys, and the trailer simultaneously.

"Wyatt . . . that you? What's going on? Why are you slamming the door?"

"Yeah, Dad, mares are in labor. We've delivered two foals tonight, but Cinder's is red bag. Charlie's an hour away from the clinic, and Dr. Mason will need to move as soon as she delivers the foal." I hear Dad's footsteps hasten. Age hasn't slowed him down one bit. I toss him the truck keys. "Hook up the two-horse for me and bring it to the barn."

"Got it." He grabs his boots and jacket, and he's out the door as quickly as I am. He doesn't even stop to ask questions.

I sprint back to the barn, arriving drenched by the storm. Parker is busy strapping Cinder just like we did with Violet. She doesn't look up as she instructs me to check on the other mares and foals. I find the first foal standing and the second one stirring, ready to rise.

The storm outside rages with a life of its own. The wind howls like a chorus of wild creatures. Rain pelts the metal overhead, a relentless drumming. Thunder rumbles in the distance, a deep, ominous growl that rolls across the sky, punctuated by sharp cracks as lightning splits the darkness. It's a symphony of nature's power, a reminder of the forces at play beyond these walls, and I'm hoping it's not a warning for how this birth plays out.

Throwing up the bay doors, I spot the truck's taillights through the downpour. "Doc, you're about to meet the legend himself."

"Great, the more the merrier." Parker's voice is void of emotion; her face etched with determination. She's got a whole array of supplies laid out, ready for whatever comes next. She doesn't even glance up as Dad approaches.

"Nice to meet you, Doc," Dad greets her in his quiet way, his focus matching hers. "Where do you need me?"

"Stay by her head, keep her calm and standing." She instructs Dad, without ever looking up. Then she turns to me. "Wyatt, I need you back here with me. This time, you're going to catch the foal when I pull. I'll need to be quick to grab supplies as you lower it to the ground. Every second counts."

I watch her hands, precise and confident, as they slice into the placenta.

"Red bag births are dangerous," she starts explaining, and I can tell she's talking out loud, not necessarily to us. "The placenta's come away from the uterus too soon. The foal's been without oxygen, and we don't know for how long."

She moves past the outer sac, then carefully cuts through the inner one. Her arm vanishes inside, searching. I'm holding my breath, hoping for the best.

"Good news, gentlemen," she finally says, and I exhale in relief. "We've got two front legs and a nose. The foal's positioned correctly." She's calm, but I can hear the urgency in her voice. "Wyatt, get ready to catch on the next contraction."

I step closer, positioning myself where she needs me. This is it—the moment she pulls out a miracle—or we mourn our first loss of the night.

"Now," Parker commands, her teeth gritted, her voice strained with effort. Time seems to freeze, the world outside the stall ceasing to exist. The difficulty of the task is evident in her every movement, every bead of sweat on her brow. I'm already in awe of her skill, but if she pulls this off, if she saves this foal, impressed won't even begin to describe what I feel.

The foal slips into the world, a limp bundle of life falling into my waiting arms. Parker wastes no time—she's suctioning, stimulating, doing everything she can to coax breath into the little yellow body.

"Come on, baby girl," she murmurs, a soft encouragement amidst the storm's chaos. "Your buddy came back for me. Let's prove to him girls are just as tough." Her hands are a blur, searching for a heartbeat, her focus absolute.

A thunderclap shakes the barn, and her dog barks—a sharp, startling sound in the tense silence. She doesn't flinch, doesn't break stride. Whatever she's whispering to the foal, it's a private plea for life I cannot hear. Her hands pause over the foal's heart, and then, as if spurred by some unseen signal, she's moving again, her actions swift and sure.

"We have a heartbeat. Come on, baby," Parker's voice rings out with a mix of command and encouragement.

I'm focused on her every move, willing her the miracle she's demanding. She's breathing for the foal now, her hands expertly moving to its nostrils. One breath in, one breath out. I'm holding my own with each cycle until, miraculously, the foal's chest rises on its own.

"Yes! You got it, baby! Keep breathing!" she exclaims, her hands working furiously. She grabs sterile supplies, cleans off a small area of the foal's neck, and dries it. Then, with a swift motion, she reaches over me, grabs an IV kit, and sets a line as simple as tying her shoes.

As she sets up the IV drip, she looks up at my dad with a smile. "Wonders never cease, Mr. Lochlan. You boys have a third baby. Let's keep her alive, shall we? We need to get these ladies loaded up and, pardon my French, sir, but haul ass to the clinic."

She's already moving on to the next task, missing my dad's proud smile, but I catch it.

We work quickly to load up the mare and her newborn. Parker jumps into the vet truck with her dog. Dad and I climb in his truck. He takes the wheel, and I pull out my phone, shooting off a text to the ranch foreman and Statler, briefing them on the night's events and instructing them to call immediately if there's any change with the other mares. I tell them to move the rest of the mares closer to the barn for safety.

The rain is relentless, but we're on the move. Parker's headlights cut through the downpour right behind us.

"What's with the dog?" Dad's question cuts through the hum of the engine as he navigates the storm-soaked roads.

I shrug, keeping my gaze on the rain-lashed windshield. "Don't know. I thought about asking, but she didn't volunteer, and I didn't want to seem like a bigger asshole."

"Bigger?" Dad questions.

"I'll explain later." I wince, knowing he's going to feel the same about the situation, just like Charlie.

Dad nods, his eyes never leaving the road. "She's certainly had one hell of an introduction to the ranch."

I recall the night's earlier events, the successful deliveries, and the seamless way she handled everything. My respect for her grows, and a nagging question resurfaces, one that's been at the back of my mind since we met. What the hell is she doing in the middle of Wyoming?

CHAPTER 10

Cooper

PARKER

Relief washes over me as I pull into the clinic's parking lot and spot two trucks already there. I've only set foot in this clinic once before, and I don't have the keys or know the location of all the supplies we'll need. The adrenaline that's been fueling me is fading fast, leaving bone-deep exhaustion in its wake.

My eyelids are heavy, my body aches, and there's a gnawing emptiness in my stomach. It's as if every ounce of energy has been wrung out of me. Despite this, the lingering satisfaction from the night's successes and the quiet hum of contentment beneath the fatigue makes the weariness absolutely worth it.

Cooper had sounded his alert back at the barn and again on the way here. But between the filly and the rain coming down in sheets, I couldn't do more than check my app. If I get the mare and foal settled, I should have enough time to take care of it. Just a few more minutes.

I leap out of the truck, and the bay door rolls open to reveal both Dr. Corts ready to assist. We get to work unloading and situating the mare and her newborn filly. I brief everyone on the birth as we add antibiotics to the IV, hoping to stave off potential complications. Cooper has been waiting patiently outside the stall barking a few more times though not escalating his alerts yet. I glance at my watch, realizing we've spent nearly an hour getting everything sorted.

Stepping out of the stall, I see Wyatt, his father, and the two vets. The realization hits me—the night, or rather, the early morning, is finally winding down. I'm hit by a wave of hunger so intense it feels urgent. Food. I need food now.

"So, Doc, what do you plan to name her?" Wyatt's question catches me off guard.

"Excuse me?" I stop in my tracks. "Honestly, I'm going to need you to connect the dots for me here."

"We have a rule on the ranch, if you save an animal's life that doesn't have a name, you get to name it." His smile is both proud and a bit mischievous. His dad nods in agreement, and the other vets chuckle at the tradition.

"Have either of you gotten to name anything?" I turn to the father and son vet duo, curious about their experiences with this unique ranch rule.

"Oh yeah," Charlie chuckles, "but mine always seem to be cows. Named the last one Cheese because it goes with burgers." The humor is unexpected, and I laugh, a genuine, deep laugh that eases some of the night's tension.

"In that case, can I think about it?" I manage to say between chuckles, though I'm already thinking about heading to my truck to grab something from the cooler. That's when Cooper, ever vigilant, barks and starts pawing at me, drawing surprised looks from everyone.

I quickly check my phone, confirming what I already know—I'm experiencing a sugar drop, and it's teetering on the edge of becoming serious. The sudden alarm piercing the night from my phone confirms it, drawing Charlie's attention.

"What's with the alarm?" Charlie's eyebrows draw together in a frown, and there's a slight tilt of his head as he tries to piece together the situation. His eyes are focused, intent on me, searching for an explanation.

I'm suddenly the center of attention, all eight eyes and all four men entirely focused on me. I've not discussed the specifics of my condition, hoping to make a less dramatic introduction. But it would seem I'm not going to get what I want tonight.

"It's my glucose monitor." So much for drama-free, professional, first impressions. "I'm a type two diabetic. Cooper is my service dog. He alerts me when my levels are off. That alarm means I need to take care of this right now." I try to keep my tone matter of fact, wanting to handle this with as much grace as I can muster under the circumstances.

They all freeze, their stillness a stark contrast to the urgency of the situation. "I'm going to be just fine," I assure them, trying to inject a bit of humor to lighten the mood. "I need the red bag on the front seat of the vet truck. Cooper would have fetched it, but he's lacking in the thumb department." My attempt at a joke falls flat; they're too worried to laugh.

Sammy springs into action, heading for the truck as the others bombard me with questions. My vision blurs—a sure sign I've pushed myself too far. It's been a long night, after all: no food, not enough water, and too much energy spent.

"Men!" I snap my fingers, commanding their attention with my most authoritative voice. Sammy is already racing back to me with my bag. "I need to sit down. Listen carefully," I instruct, as my condition doesn't afford me the luxury of time. "My phone unlocks with my right index finger. The app you need is already open. I'm going to eat something to try and raise my sugar levels. It should take about fifteen minutes to see if that works. *If* I pass out, there's glucagon shot in this bag. Follow the instructions on the orange case and inject it into the back of my arm. If you're unsure, call 911. But we're not going to panic." My speech begins to slur. "We're going to stay calm . . . because it's going to be . . . just . . . fine."

I reach out for the red bag from Sammy, but as I do, the room starts to spin, and I brace myself for what comes next.

CHAPTER 11

Fifteen

PARKER

A curse slips out from behind me, and before I know it, I'm lifted into strong arms. "Keep your eyes open, Doc. Let me see those baby blues, okay?" The voice is firm, insistent.

I squint, trying to focus. "You're a bit blurry," I admit, the world tilting dangerously. "If I throw up on you, I apologize." I wait for a chuckle, but none comes.

"Doc, I know you think you're talking, but you're not making much sense." I can feel the concern as his grip on me tightens slightly. The warmth from his arms oddly comforts me. The motion of being carried brings a gentle sway, a rhythmic movement that I would find soothing under different circumstances. Resting my head against his shoulder, the steady thump of Wyatt's heartbeat against my palm anchors me to the moment. The faint trace of rain still lingers on him, mixed with the sterile tang of antiseptics.

"Okay," I say, trying to sound more coherent. I relent to the dizziness and nausea, closing my eyes for just a moment.

"No, Doc, keep your eyes open." The command snaps me back to attention.

"Back to being the asshole, huh?" I manage to say, my voice shaking. I'm aiming for light-hearted, but the strain in my voice is noticeable.

Wyatt sits with me in his arms. Though my memory of the clinic's layout is hazy at best, I think we're in the break room.

"I'm not going to respond to that." His voice is surprisingly gentle. "Now, tell me what you need." His hand pushes the hair back from my face, his eyes filling my vision.

" . . . Pepper." I reach for the soda, but my hands tremble uncontrollably.

His hands drop from my face and a second later I hear the fizz as he pops the can open. My shaking hands wrap around the cold aluminum, the chill a sharp contrast to the warmth of Wyatt's body. I shift so my feet hit the floor, ready to escape the spotlight and his lap. But his hands, firm and insistent, press against my hips, silently urging me to stay put.

I'm tingling from head to toe, the room around me a blur of shapes and colors. I take slow and deliberate sips. The sugary liquid is a lifeline, and I focus on the taste, willing it to work its magic. Cooper jumps onto the couch, nudging me with his head while my body continues to tremble.

Focusing on what I can feel, my first thought goes to Wyatt. His lap is an unexpected comfort, his muscular form a solid presence beneath me. His hand moves in slow strokes on my back, and I fight the urge to lean into the gentle touch. Trembling gives way to all-out shivers. Wyatt's hands gently pull me back against his chest, bracing his body against the torrent of twitching. It feels too close, too personal, and every instinct tells me to pull away, stand up, and walk right out of here. But I can't. The heaviness of my own head on my shoulders defeats the muscles in my neck, tilting, until it rests on his shoulder.

Closing my eyes, I focus on the steady rise and fall of his chest. He lifts my legs, pulling them across his lap, then wraps both arms around me as I shiver. His stubbled cheek grazes my forehead, a rough contrast to the smooth stroke of his hand on my arm. Gradually, the shaking and the tingling begin to fade, more of my senses rising to the surface.

Wyatt's belt buckle against my hip. The warmth and the heavy weight of his arm, draped almost protectively across my legs. The smell of leather and cedar. When the nausea mostly subsides, I risk opening my eyes. Pushing off Wyatt's chest, I turn, my eyes landing on the senior Dr. Cort's stern gaze.

"Sorry for such a dramatic morning." I try to infuse as much steadiness as possible into my voice, though it cracks slightly regardless. "I promise this isn't a regular occurrence. I'm meticulously organized and having Cooper ensures I catch things quickly. It seems tonight just needed one more unexpected twist."

Senior's response is immediate and authoritative, cutting through any attempt at self-deprecation. "Young lady, let's get something straight. Don't you dare apologize."

His tone reminds me of Greg, stern yet caring, stirring a mix of emotions into life inside me. Part of me wants to smile at the familiarity while another part wants to cry at the sincerity and some other part cringes at the total lack of professionalism I've got happening.

"We don't need or want an apology for something you can't control," the younger Cort says.

"Though I do expect a lesson for us on how to help you, especially in the event you can't tell us what to do." Senior's words are a command, but they're also a promise of support, a commitment from this new team that they're here for me.

"Are you insulin-dependent?" Sammy's question catches me off guard.

"That's a pretty informed question," I tease, raising an eyebrow at him.

"My best buddy from college is type one, but he has a pump, and I don't see one of those on you."

I take another sip of the Dr. Pepper, coming further and further back into my own body, the sugar doing its job. Feeling steady enough, I sit up a bit more, pulling away from Wyatt's chest. His hands simply slide back to my hips, his thumb rubbing a slow arch across my back.

"I'm not insulin-dependent," I clarify. "I do have a continuous glucose monitor on my arm, but a few years back, I realized I needed something more reliable. Given what this line of work requires, I don't always have my phone or notice when shifts in my sugar occur. Cooper is trained to detect changes, doing so often faster than my device." I gesture to my dog, who's been my steadfast guardian through all this, his head now in my lap.

I try to keep my tone light, not wanting to worry them or seem like I can't handle my condition, or worse, see me as though I'm fragile. "Cooper's my early warning system, and he's pretty good at his job," I add with a small smile, hoping to reassure them.

"Will he bark again?" Wyatt asks, and I can hear the genuine concern in his voice.

"He shouldn't. He has different alerts depending on what's happening, either high or low, and the severity of each. His discriminatory signals help me know what I need to do. He's also trained to bring me that cooler if he has access or get someone if he doesn't."

"Can you make us a list of what you find most helpful?" Sammy's offer is unexpected and kind. His eyebrows furrow slightly, and he leans forward, eager to understand and help. It's a simple gesture, but it soothes a fear I didn't know I was holding onto. Their immediate acceptance, their willingness to adapt for me without really knowing me, makes my throat tight and my eyes burn.

It's not the fear of starting over in a new place, the exhaustion, or the strange, tingling sensation from Wyatt's proximity that's getting to me or the feeling of being seen and accommodated without having to ask. Nope. It's all of it together.

"What do you call what we're doing right now?" Wyatt's dad inquires, calm and steady as he leans against the desk. He seems relaxed yet alert, his eyes observant, taking in everything.

"Sorry," I start, my face probably revealing my confusion. I can't help but feel a bit embarrassed about not remembering his name.

"Shephard Lochlan, but you can call me Shep, most do." His grin is infectious and warm. His own dimples are fully on display. What is in the water in Wyoming? Maybe it's just good DNA and charm freaking everywhere.

"Shep, sorry, thinking gets difficult when I'm like this," I admit, trying to explain the process I'm going through. "This is called fifteen and fifteen. I'm taking in fifteen grams of carbs and then waiting fifteen minutes to check my sugar again."

Wyatt chimes in, his voice laced with a mix of concern and encouragement. "By my count, you've got four more minutes. You should tell them about our hat trick. I believe we pulled the last foal within the five o'clock time frame." His smile is reassuring when I turn my head and take in his face.

I take the cue, grateful for the distraction. As I recount the events of the evening, the break room's atmosphere lightens considerably. Charlie's face softens to quiet understanding, with a gentle nod here and there along with a few smiles as he listens.

The men, now more relaxed, exchange knowing glances and chuckles, their laughter a mix of relief and camaraderie. Sammy teases Wyatt and their playful banter tells me years of friendship connect the two. Wyatt's hands are still warming either side of my hips, his slow strokes across my shirt a steady backdrop to the story.

The break room itself comes into sharper focus as the story unfolds. It's a cozy space, functional yet inviting. As each detail comes alive, it's easy to see this space is one of long hours and hard work. Framed photos of clients and life, capturing moments of triumph and joy, frame the walls. A sturdy, well-worn table sits at the center, surrounded by mismatched chairs.

The fridge, humming in the corner, is plastered with magnets of all kinds and a calendar marked with important dates. A coffee maker, its pot half-full, emits the comforting scent of freshly brewed coffee, and a microwave sits atop a small cabinet stocked with assorted snacks. It's a room that has seen many early mornings and late nights, a silent witness to the ebb and flow of life.

Though it isn't ideal, it's not the worst way to close out a night and bring in a new day.

CHAPTER 12

Naming

WYATT

Parker's recounting of the night's events draws laughter from everyone in the room. I can't help but join in, especially when she gets to the part where I acted like a complete asshole. Dad shoots me a stern look that sends a shiver down my spine, just like when I was a kid. She's sitting up on my lap now, her back straight, her voice clear. Relief begins to wash over me.

"I'll need to get back today at some point. I want to do a check on the other foal we pulled. Also," Parker glances over her shoulder at me with a hint of mischief, "I'm afraid we might not be able to save this shirt."

I can't help but smile as I look up from the app on her phone. "If it doesn't make it, it would be a worthy sacrifice to a helluva night. We owe you one, Doc."

"You know, Dr. Mason," Sammy says, a surge of pride in his voice, "I don't think Dad or I have ever delivered three foals in the same night, in consecutive hours. That's got to make you employee of the month, and on your first day!"

"If that prize comes with eight hours of sleep and a hot shower, I'll take it," she quips, and I can hear the exhaustion behind her humor.

"I think we can work that out," Charlie chimes in with his hearty Santa-like laugh, filling the room with warmth.

"What do those numbers you're staring at so hard say, Wyatt?" Parker's voice pulls me back to the present as I check the screen again. Guilt gnaws at me. I heard Cooper bark at the barn and when we got here. I should've checked on her, made sure she had everything she needed. She must've missed the first alert because of me.

After all she's done for us tonight, I failed to notice the one thing that mattered. Cooper's unusual behavior should've been a red flag.

"You're headed up, Doc. It looks like seventy-two." I'm relieved to see her numbers improving.

"Okay, that's good. Between seventy and one hundred is considered normal," Parker says, a note of relief in her voice as she points out the window to the dawn breaking. "The sun rises again. Hey, maybe that should be the filly's name—Sunny."

It's as if the air itself thickens, heavy with unspoken thoughts and sudden memories. I can see the hesitation in Charlie's eyes, a flicker of something like pain or perhaps nostalgia, as he averts his gaze. Sammy's mouth opens slightly, as if to speak, but no words come out. He simply exhales a slow, measured breath, his shoulders tensing then relaxing.

Dad stands motionless for a heartbeat, his eyes distant, reflecting a sea of emotions he usually keeps hidden. The name 'Sunny' echoes off the walls. Parker, sensing the shift, tries to retract her suggestion, her voice tinged with uncertainty. "Okay . . . maybe not a great name based on the reaction."

It's Dad who breaks the silence, his voice a low rumble that fills the room with surprising warmth. "No," he says, and there's a tremor there, a crack in his usual stoic demeanor. "I think Sunny would be a great name."

I feel a lump form in my throat and softly ask, "Are you sure?"

But he's resolute, his affirmation carrying a weight of acceptance and remembrance. "Of course. She would have loved that."

As understanding dawns on Parker, she turns to me, her eyes widening, a glimmer of realization reflecting in them. The words are heavy on my tongue. "Sunny was my mother's name."

The room remains quiet, the earlier lightness replaced by a shared moment of reverence for the past, a piece of our personal life that suddenly makes the name all the more significant.

"I'm so sorry. I didn't know." Parker's sudden apology slices through the room's newfound calm. She's on her feet in an instant, her discomfort palpable. "Completely forget I said it. It was just off-the-cuff." Her words stream out in a ramble that fills the room, each sentence overlapping the next. Her movements are a physical manifestation of her desire to undo the last two minutes.

I reach out, my hand finding hers, and I feel her pulse fluttering like a captured bird in her wrist. "There isn't any greater honor her name could bear than to represent the filly you literally breathed life back into. Naming rights are yours. The filly's name is Sunny." Her hand trembles slightly in mine before she pulls away.

"Okay. Well, umm," she starts, her voice a notch higher, betraying her discomfort. She avoids eye contact, her gaze darting from the window to the door, anywhere but our faces. "Sugar is back up, so I'm going to head upstairs, clean up, and take a nap." Her words are an escape route, a polite exit from the intensity of the moment.

As she turns toward the door, Cooper, her loyal shadow, leaps down from his perch and pads after her. The click of his nails on the floor marks their retreat. I watch her go, her squared shoulders carrying a tension that wasn't there moments ago. Just before she rounds the corner, she glances back, fixing her eyes on mine.

In that brief exchange, I see the layers of her worry, the desire to make things right, but she doesn't need to. The name 'Sunny' might have taken us by surprise, but it's a fitting tribute.

We owe her a debt for the foals' lives. *I* owe her. My family might label me overprotective, and Riot might call me a control freak, but in my heart, I know I'm just someone who takes care of things. Today, though, I can't shake the feeling that I failed pretty epically.

PARKER

As I turn the corner, leaving the tension of the break room behind, I can't shake the awkwardness that clings to me like second skin. The last thing I want is for them to associate pain with the name, especially one I suggested. I've shared that experience, being part of a club where memories are as sharp as glass, unwanted and intrusive.

Pushing through the apartment door, my mind is singularly focused on the prospect of a hot shower and something to eat. The clothes I peel off are stained and smelling of life and near-death.

The shower's spray hits me like a cascade of reality. Today has already been a day of extremes—life-saving acts performed with hands that now shake. I've blurred lines I intended to keep sharp; professional barriers have crossed into a space of intimacy.

Toweling off the last drops of water that washed away the remnants of the day leaves me clean but tired. After a quick snack, I slip between the sheets still turned down from last night.

Exhaustion pulls me under swiftly, and my dreams are a whirl of sensations—being held in strong arms, the brim of a backwards hat, rough stubble brushing against my forehead, and the steady thrum of Wyatt's heartbeat.

CHAPTER 13

Plans

PARKER

The blare of my phone's alarm jolts me awake, and I fumble to hit snooze, only to notice the time glaring back at me—it's well past noon. A night of sheer exhaustion and the unfamiliar comfort of a new bed had finally granted me a solid block of sleep. The only flaw? Apparently, my subconscious and my libido are teaming up these days because every dream was built around Wyatt.

I stretch languidly, arms reaching high above my head, and sit up, feeling the remnants of the night's tension ease out of my muscles.

"Hey, Cooper, want to go outside, buddy?" My voice breaks the silence of the room, and Cooper's head pops up from his oversized pillow nestled in the corner. He mirrors my stretch, before trotting over to the bed, eagerly thumping his tail.

"Oh, I forgot. How dare I?" My fingers sink into the patchwork of red and white fur. "You need morning scratches." His bright blue eyes stare up at me lovingly as I massage his head and shoulders in our familiar morning ritual.

Cooper isn't just a pet or a tool for my health; he filled a space in my life I hadn't realized was vacant. His presence ensures I'm never truly alone, especially on the days when solitude weighs heavily.

With a satisfied grunt, Cooper turns and makes his way out of the bedroom, signaling the start of our day. I reach for my phone, which rests on a chair that's found a second life as a bedside table. Unlocking the screen, Greg's message greets me.

DAD

How are you feeling? I noticed the drop early this morning though you seem to have levelled off. I'm giving you until 1pm your time then I'm finding the nearest plane. Answer me.

PARKER

Hi Dad. I'm fine.

She lives!

lol yes. I delivered three foals last night, and the last delivery was rough. I dropped but got it back up and I've been sleeping it off. Don't be a worry wart. You're listed as my emergency contact,
if i died, they'd call you.

Not. Funny.

I met someone last night. If you can imagine a combo of Andy Griffith and Cameron, that was him. He was the father of the foal's owner.

I want to hear all about him! I've got to open, but I'll call you tonight?

Yes. I'll tell you all about it.

I'll hold you to that. Love you.

Love you more.

Cooper bounds out the door, descending the steps with a purpose. I watch him for a moment before turning back to the kitchen. My blood sugar is a tad low, common after sleep, but nothing a quick protein shake can't fix. I'm not a fan of the taste, but they're convenient and have become a staple in my routine.

After starting up the blender, I step back to the door and let Cooper in. He knows the drill; he eats before I do. I fetch his bowl and fill it with his usual dry food, adding the supplements he needs. A handful of fruit and a dollop of yogurt complete his meal, and I set the bowl down, giving him the nod to start.

While he's busy eating, I pull out my phone and send a quick message to Cami.

PARKER

Awake? Video?

CAMI

Without hesitation, I tap the video chat icon. She answers immediately, her fair skin, dotted with dozens of freckles and delicate features, fills the screen. Cami may be petite, barely over five feet, and look like a fairy, but her presence is immense. She's all energy and strength, a force to be reckoned with. Her red hair is a messy crown atop her head, signaling the start of her day just as mine is beginning.

"I know why I'm just now getting around, what about you?" I ask Cami, as I prop up my phone on the kitchen island, gathering ingredients for my shake.

"I got up and worked out, pulled the deal from the studio, worked out some more, and then decided to shower off the creeps from said studio." Her voice is a melody of determination and annoyance as she meticulously applies her skincare products. Skin care is practically her eleventh commandment.

"That does sound fun." A hint of sarcasm bleeds through in my reply. "I had quite the exciting night, well, maybe morning, myself."

"Oh, do tell," Cami urges, her interest piqued as she continues with lotions and serums.

"Well, remember that guy I told you about from the grocery store the first day I was here?"

"How could I forget backwards-hat guy?" she chimes in with a laugh.

"It stormed like crazy here last night, and the clinic was swamped with emergency calls. They needed an extra hand, so Cooper and I stepped in. And imagine my surprise when I run right into the barn, through the pouring rain, into backwards-hat guy," I recount, still somewhat in disbelief.

Cami squeals, a high-pitched sound of excitement, urging me to continue.

"Okay, well, he's actually super rude—" I start to explain, but she cuts me off.

"Nooooo! I had such high hopes for him," Cami interjects, her face contorting into an exaggerated pout.

"He sort of redeemed himself." I dive into the story from the beginning, recounting every detail to her.

"Girl, I might love this man. You said he had brothers?" Her eyebrow arches with intrigue. Cami's enthusiasm is infectious, even through the phone screen.

I can't help but chuckle at her excitement. "I think so. There's one with glasses and one with tattoos, and of course, Wyatt himself. Seems like you could have your pick of all three."

She waves off the notion with a laugh. "Nope. I only get my pick of two. Seems like cowboy Wyatt is all you, babe. I mean, he forgets to drop your hand, carries you bride style, cuddles you in his lap, and lets you name his horse. I'm really hoping that last one also translates to a different euphemism." Her laughter rings out, clear and teasing.

I shake my head, dismissing her implications. "You're overthinking this. He was worried, and it was an intense night. That's all." I press the blender button, drowning out our conversation with its roar. Cami patiently continues her skincare, waiting for the noise to subside.

Once the blender quiets, she presses on. "Sounds more like you've already done enough overthinking for both of us, girly. C'mon, talk to me, what's rattling around in your head?"

I sigh, pouring the shake into a glass and grabbing a straw before settling onto the couch with my phone. "He's attractive, I won't deny that, but I've found men attractive before. It doesn't change anything. I need a plan to reclaim my professional distance. I need to build a life here."

Cami's response is gentle, yet firm. "Honey, we've talked about this. You need to get back out there. You don't have to be alone."

"I'm not alone," I insist, feeling that familiar constriction in my chest. "I have you, Emmary, Cooper, and Greg. That's enough for me, Cami."

"Parker, look at me," she commands softly, adding sign language to ensure I maintain eye contact.

"The fact that you're still standing after all that you've been through is proof that there's so much more inside you than you give yourself credit for. Moving on doesn't mean leaving her," she says, "it doesn't mean every man will turn out like him." Cami's words are meant to be a balm, but they sting with some level of truth, one I can't evaluate right now.

"I don't think every man will be him. I may not know much about love, but I do know that a person deserves to be loved fully, and I don't have enough of me left to do that. All of me belongs to her. Can we change the subject now?" My voice is a mix of resignation and defiance.

Cami huffs, her frustration evident in the darkening of her eyes and the line between her brows, even through the screen. "Fine. But I still think your thoughts around this are inaccurate, and you know your therapist would agree with me, and so would Greg."

"My therapist often agrees with you, but only I get to decide what my life looks like. And I've got a family, a really big one by my standards. And someday, you'll get married and have babies, and I'll get to be cool Aunt Parker and introduce them to smutty book boyfriends, which are the only acceptable types of boyfriends in my life."

She concedes, at least on the surface, if I know Cami. "Book boyfriends are quite extraordinary, so I'd say you have good standards at the very least. I do agree with one thing. You will be a very cool auntie someday. Though, there's the whole problem of finding a man that meets my standards, marrying him, and being able to have said babies."

I dismiss her concerns with a wave of my hand, teasing her. "Details."

"Okay, girl, my agent's calling, and I've got to go figure out a plan for this series. That said, I can't wait to hear more, and I expect all details on Wyatt and Wyoming when I call you later."

After our good-byes, I turn to Cooper.

"Cooper, what do you say we get ready and begin our second day of work? Hopefully, it's less exciting than the first." I scratch his ears affectionately and then prepare for the day. Despite everything, I really believe I'm going to love it here.

CHAPTER 14

Issues

WYATT

It's been twenty-four hours since we pulled off that hat trick, and all three foals are still standing, which is nothing short of miraculous, considering the dramatic way two of them came into the world. The sun has barely crested the horizon, and I'm already out here, hoping the rest of this year's foals will give me a breather before they decide to join us. A man can only take so much excitement and so many sleepless nights—thank goodness for the saving grace of coffee.

Sunny, the little fighter named after mom, is still at the vet's with Cinder. They'll be staying there for a while, but from what I hear, she's holding her own. The ranch hands have started calling Violet's colt 'Big Man,' a nod to the doc. My brother Linc found the whole thing hilarious, nearly choking on his coffee at the thought of someone finally calling me on my shit.

I haven't laid eyes on her since she left the office that day. Sammy swung by later to check on the foals, though. As I fill my thermos with coffee, headlights catch my eye. The way our house sits, you can see cars coming from a mile away. And just past the cattle guard, an electrical alarm lets us know when someone's approaching.

The alarm is one of Statler's additions; being retired special forces, he's kitted out the place with more security than a ranch probably needs. But it gives him peace of mind, and we all humor him. He can be an intimidating motherfucker when he wants to be, and that's not even mentioning his hulking guard dog, Gigi.

The monitor in the kitchen, usually a dull fixture, suddenly captures my full attention as an unfamiliar truck rolls into view. But the face behind the wheel? That's a face I've seen before—Parker. I find myself walking out the front door, casually leaning against a column as she makes her way up the drive.

The morning air is crisp, the kind that you can feel and almost taste, filled with the earthy scents of dew-soaked grass. The horizon is painted with the soft blush of dawn, a canvas of oranges and pinks. The wood creaks softly as I shift my weight.

Her truck looks like it's seen its fair share of farm roads. As it rolls to a stop, the engine's rumble gives way to the quiet of the morning. The sun, just a sliver above the land, casts a glow that seems to spotlight her as she exits the truck.

Every sense I have sharpens as she walks closer. I'm not one to mix business with pleasure, but I can't deny the obvious: she's beautiful. Admiration quickly replaced any initial attraction, given the circumstances and chaos of the other night.

But this morning, as she stands there in cargo scrubs that contour to her hips and thighs, the attraction is undeniable. She's paired them with a black shirt that complements her figure in a way that drives a punch of lust straight into my stomach. Her hair, no longer a silhouette against the stormy night, cascades down her back. It's long, flowing well past her shoulders, and for a moment, I'm caught up in the simple beauty of her.

Seeing her approach stirs a fleeting thought of what it might feel like to run my fingers through her hair, but it's quickly overshadowed by the tension I sense in her posture as she draws nearer. She stops at the bottom of the stairs, her spine rigid, her shoulders squared almost defensively. There's a tightness around her eyes, a guarded expression that wasn't there twenty-four hours ago. Cooper, her dog, is a wild contrast, staring up at her with nothing but adoration.

"Good morning, Wyatt." The way she says my name—it's different from the other night, distant and cool. Her voice lacks the warmth it carried during the storm. It's measured; each word enunciated with a precision that feels deliberate, almost rehearsed.

"Hey, Doc, out early this morning, aren't you?" I tease, trying to break the ice.

"I wanted to come check on the foals myself before my first full day at the clinic. If that's okay with you?"

It's as if we've reset, or worse, as if we're in the midst of an argument I wasn't aware we were having. The space she keeps is telling—she's positioned herself at the bottom of the steps, maximizing the distance between us.

"Have I done something wrong, Doc?" If I'm the cause of her discomfort, I need to make it right.

"I have no idea what you mean." Her smile, which seemed to come so easily just a day ago, now seems forced. It doesn't reach her eyes; it reminds me of a beauty pageant queen's practiced cool and detached expression.

"You sound like you're pissed at me again, or is that just me?" I probe a little further, hoping to understand.

"Wyatt, I'm fine." That's a line I've heard before, and it usually means the exact opposite. Sometimes, the best move is to step back, wait, and decide when to throw your rope.

"If you say so, Doc," I say with a nod toward the barn, inviting her to take the lead. She strides off, and I trail behind, taking in the sight of her. She's got her nose so far in the air I'd have to tilt her head down to see her eyes. Guess I'm throwing my rope now.

"You know, Doc," I start, my voice dipping into a drawl, "I'm not usually one for stirring the pot, but you're so tense, I feel the need to ask if there's a stick up your ass."

That stops her in her tracks. She whips around, and if looks could kill, I'd be vaporized.

"Mr. Lochlan, despite whatever your ego tells you, there is nothing wrong with me or the way I walk." She's facing me now, the color rising in her cheeks. Her eyes, previously flat, now seem to hold a storm behind them, crackling with lightning, focused with an intensity that draws me closer.

"Then, what is it? Just me, or the Wyoming air?" I close in, reducing the space between us to mere inches, my gaze fixated on her striking blue eyes as they darken.

"I'm. Fine." Her voice is steady, but there's a tension in her stillness, a coiled readiness as the muscle in her jaw flexes, her teeth clenched together just out of sight as she shifts her weight back to create some distance.

"How's Sunny?" Holding my ground, we stand face to face.

"The little yellow filly," she starts, a flicker of something crosses her features, "was doing beautifully when I checked her this morning. She's nursing well." The mention of the animal brings softness to her eyes, but it's quickly shuttered away.

"Does the name bother you?"

"I have no problem with her name." Her assertion is strong, but a flinch, a small, almost imperceptible twitch on her face betrays her, hinting at something behind her composed features.

"Your eyes say something different, Parker." I roll her name off my tongue, feeling its weight. It's personal, a challenge I want her to meet, but she doesn't. Instead, she steps back and away, continuing to the barn. It's a retreat, her gaze dropping as she walks.

CHAPTER 15

Instincts

I watch her closely as she finishes up with Molly and the little filly we'd named Domino. There's a part of me that's drawn to Parker's resilience, to the way she stands her ground. It's a rare mix, that strength coupled with a tenderness, a softness I've seen, though it's reserved only for the animals. When she approaches the stall door, I'm there, sliding the latch open for her. As she passes by, I reach out, lightly holding her elbow.

"You're used to getting what you want, aren't you?" Her question comes out flat, almost a whisper.

"Yes," I admit because it's true. But there's something about her tone, the way she's holding herself—it's like she's a puzzle, and I'm missing a crucial piece. The Parker I met a day ago was fiery, full of life. This version of her doesn't fit.

"Parker, I'm pretty sure after you nearly passed out in my arms, saved a couple of lives in front of me, and I told you about my mom, we're beyond cold or distanced professionalism." I can't hide the frustration in my voice. "For the record, I much prefer the fight you gave me a day ago than the freeze you're giving me now."

As I watch her reaction, hoping to break through, Parker pulls away completely, creating more distance between us. Losing isn't in my playbook but losing seems to be what I'm doing now.

"I'll keep that in mind," she says, her eyes a million miles away. The contrast of her doesn't sit right with me, so I switch gears.

"We named the little filly. Want to know what we settled on?" I watch as her icy facade cracks just enough for curiosity to shine through.

"Yes," she lets out a small, relieved sigh.

"Domino."

A genuine smile breaks free, and I feel a sense of victory.

"I liked that one. What about the colt?" She's moving again, heading towards Violet's stall, but at least she's engaged now.

"Well, Doc, turns out you named him too. The crew loved how you coaxed him out, so they've been calling him Big Man, and it stuck. They especially loved the asshole part."

She laughs, trying to hide it with her hand, but I can tell she's pleased. "He could certainly do worse. How are his feedings?" She stops at the stall door, and I sense an opening.

"Are we finally back to having a friendly conversation now?" I tease, hoping to lighten the mood further.

"Wyatt . . ." She exhales heavily, "I'll apologize for coming off coldly, I didn't mean to, but I'm a professional, not your friend, and it's better for it to stay that way."

"Is that the problem here?" I probe, sensing her retreat. "Here's how I look at it. We went through it the other night. You called me an asshole, we saved a few lives, I held you while you scared ten years off my life. I think that earns us professional *and* friend status."

She looks at me, her eyes wary and a little anxious, then she gives me the smallest nod, the corners of her mouth tipping up into a hint of a smile. It's a start.

"How are his feedings?" Parker's question pulls us back to the matter at hand.

"He seems to do okay, but I'll warn you before you go in there," I say, pausing her at the latch. "Violet hasn't let anyone near him without a fight. It's her first foal, and she's always been a handful. We've been keeping an eye on him, and he looks fine from a distance, but we can't get close enough to be sure. If you can't check him over, we might have to separate them, and I'd hate to do that."

She hums thoughtfully, pulling a peppermint from her pocket. I tried luring Violet with treats last night, all of them, with no success. I slide the latch open, watching closely as Parker steps inside, positioning myself in the doorway, ready to intervene if needed.

"Hi, momma," she whispers to Violet, the mint disappearing back into Parker's pocket. She doesn't venture further into the stall, just holds her ground at the entrance. I'm right behind her, close enough to feel the warmth of her back against my chest, close enough to smell whatever vanilla-scented product she puts in her hair.

In this standoff, I'm just a bystander, witnessing the silent battle of wills between Parker and Violet. It's a moment of tension and beauty, a dance of determination and care. If I could capture it in a photograph, I'd title it 'The Will of Two Women.'

"I get it." Parker's voice is a gentle murmur, like a calm stream flowing through the tension. "What does anyone but you know about keeping that baby safe? They don't see him the way you do. You're just being a good momma." Her words are soothing, meant to reassure but I hear something soft and knowing in her tone. "I'll make you a deal. You let me see him, and I'll make sure no one bothers you again for a little bit. I need to check his lungs and make sure we got all the fluid out." She speaks with an empathy that seems to transcend all God's creatures.

She steps forward, entering Violet's personal space, and the mare's head toss is a clear sign of her unease. My muscles tense, ready to move at the first sign of danger. My eyes never leave the mare as Parker steps closer.

"You can watch me," Parker continues, her voice steady, her presence unwavering. "If I do anything you don't like, you just tell me." Violet moves, a step that's both a challenge and a test, and I'm stepping into the stall before Parker's sharp command stops me.

"Do. Not. Take. Another. Step." Her words are quiet but fierce, a lioness asserting her territory. I freeze, respecting her command of the moment, a little terrified of the look on her face. Parker's attention returns to Violet as she navigates further into the stall.

"You're the boss," I concede, my voice barely above a whisper not wanting to break the progress of the moment. Watching Parker, I'm struck by the swift transformation she undergoes—nervous woman to confident professional to fierce protector, from vet to veritable horse whisperer. Violet, with her maternal instincts on high alert, keeps a watchful eye on Parker, but the tension has shifted as that subtle dance of trust unfolds before me.

Parker lowers herself beside the sleeping foal, her movements deliberate and gentle. As she listens to his breathing, Violet draws nearer, her muzzle almost resting on Parker's shoulder. It's a sight to behold. Parker Mason is fearless and absolutely incredible.

"He sounds good," she announces, her voice directed more to Violet than to me, as she rises to her feet. Violet responds by leaning into her, seeking comfort, or perhaps offering gratitude. It's a gesture of familiarity, a horse hug, one I've seen Violet share with only one other person.

The mare nudges Parker's pocket, and Parker offers her the mint. Violet accepts it with an unexpected gentleness, then nudges Parker back, reclaiming the space.

As Parker retreats, stepping back towards me, I can't help the grin that spreads across my face. She's managed to do what none of us could. I secure the stall door after Parker exits, still marveling at the sight.

"You know that horse usually hates everyone but my sister," I tell Parker, a mix of pride and wonder in my voice. "Riot brought her back from near death. We've been cautious about breeding her because of her temperament. She barely tolerates me and my brother Statler, and that's saying something."

Parker's response is nonchalant, a simple shrug, but I can tell there's more to her than meets the eye. She's got a gift, a connection with these animals that can't be taught.

"Sometimes, you just have to understand a mother's instincts and respect her boundaries," she says, her smile bright and unguarded. She's proud of her feat, and rightly so.

"You sound like you're speaking from experience there, Doc. Have you got kids?" The question slips out casually, but the impact is immediate. The air between us is charged, a heavy current, thick with emotion. She stumbles, and I wrap my arm around her middle, pulling her back into my chest. When she looks up, her piercing gaze is almost dull.

"Doc," I say softly, trying to meet her eyes, but she's quick to retreat, stepping back with a swiftness that puts distance between us.

"I'm sorry—clumsy moment. It's early, still waking up." Her words are tumbling out again rapidly. The lie hangs in the air. Her eyes reveal nothing, and somehow that makes me want to gather her in my arms, to offer comfort for something I know nothing about. Instead, I watch as she continues to retreat.

As she heads down the ally, her stride eats up ground, leaving behind the image of the commanding and confident woman. In her place the other woman, the delicate, almost breakable one.

Catching up to her is easy, but the heavy silence remains between us. Cooper trots alongside us, his eyes watching every move, but giving nothing away.

When we get to her truck, I reach for the door handle. The look she gives me could cut glass as she grabs the same handle herself.

"I am capable of opening my own door, Mr. Lochlan." Her voice is firm and heated with an edge of annoyance.

"You know, I can't decide if I love it or hate it when you call me that."

"Your preference isn't my problem," she snaps back, and the emptiness in her eyes recedes, a spark catching flame, drawing me in like a moth.

Pushed by a mix of concern, competitiveness, and an undeniable pull, I close the distance between us. "You know, every time you get that look on your face, and those little lines between your eyes, I wonder what it would feel like if I kissed you." The words are out, a solid step over the line of friendship.

I wait, holding my breath, to see how she'll respond.

Arrogance

PARKER

My mouth drops open, my hand instinctively releasing the door handle, curling into a fist. Did he actually just say that? He seizes the opportunity, opening the door without breaking our intense eye contact. A wave of desire surges through me, igniting every inch of my body. The air between us sparks to life.

We do not like arrogant men, Parker.

"You jerk!" I practically shout, unable to keep my voice down. He smirks, infuriatingly calm. "You are lucky that I'm not kicking your ass into the middle of next week for speaking to me like that. I am not some bimbo, and you are not as charming as you think you are."

"I'd agree on the bimbo part, and I knew I couldn't charm you into letting me open the door, so I pissed you off instead," he interrupts with rage-inducing smugness. "It worked. Which I suppose means point for me." He raises an eyebrow, challenging me.

A trick? He shocked me just so he could open a door! If he's look-ing for a fight, he's got one. "Of all the ridiculous, asinine, caveman, toxically macho cowboy behaviors—"

"—Get in the truck, Parker." His voice drops to a serious tone. There's no hint of teasing, only a sudden, inexplicable heat of frustration.

What right does he have to be mad?

"Fine," muttering through clenched teeth, despising the way my name rolls off his tongue, deep and rough. The infuriating flutter in my stomach is matched only by the racing of my heart. I hate that flutter. That flutter is a total bitch with no self-control. I command Cooper to hop into the truck, and he complies as if this morning's events are nothing out of the ordinary.

As I reach for the steering wheel to pull myself in, Wyatt's large hands suddenly encircle my waist, lifting me effortlessly into the seat. I spin around, ready to unleash a hell that could scorch the earth, all while ignoring the thrill zipping through me from his touch. It's rare to find someone who can handle my height with such ease, and despite my better judgment, I can't suppress the wave of raw attrac-tion that courses through me. But I'll be damned before I let him see even a hint of it.

"I can get in the truck on my own too, you know," I snap, my hand poised to slam the door—hopefully on his fingers.

"Oh, I have no doubt." That infuriating grin and matching dim-ples meet me.

"If anything changes with the foals," I muster every ounce of pro-fessionalism I possess, "call the office." Then I slam the door shut, a petty satisfaction blooming inside me.

I back out of the driveway, my mind racing as much as the engine. The T-shirt still lies on the seat beside Cooper, a reminder of the professional distance I failed to maintain. I wanted to see Wyatt, to convince him to choose a different name for the foal, to be the voice of reason. Instead, I yelled, avoided, then tumbled into his arms. *Great.*

"New plan," I declare to Cooper. "There are other vets, and other animal owners who need assistance. I don't need to see him unless it's strictly professional." Cooper gazes at me, his expression one of belief, and he should believe me—I'm in control. No more good deeds. They never go unpunished.

WYATT

I stand there, dust swirling around my boots, watching the tail-lights of her truck fade into the distance. Parker is a force of nature that's got me caught up in a way I can't quite explain. She's not the kind of woman I usually find myself drawn to, but damn if that seems to matter now.

Turning back to the house, I catch sight of Dad a few paces off, his stance firm, arms crossed—a sure sign he's got something on his mind.

"Morning, Dad," I call out, lifting a hand in greeting as he strides over.

"Son," he starts, and that tone, that particular inflection, is a warning bell. "What the hell was that?"

I can only offer a shrug, the image of Parker's fiery eyes still burning in my mind. "I have no fucking clue what that was. She got under my skin a little."

He harumphs, a sound that's more of a judgment than any words could be. "Charlie sees that, he'll kick your ass, and I'll let him. I see it again, and I'll kick your ass myself."

"Fair enough," I concede. "I'm not an asshole, Dad. She likes to argue, and something about that . . . it just makes me want to win the argument."

"Well, that's not shocking, Wyatt," he says with an eye roll, coming to stand beside me. "What started that argument in particular?"

"Well, she showed up today like I was a total stranger, and after we sorted that out, she had this moment with Violet. I asked an innocent question. At least, I thought it was, and she didn't say anything. Just tripped and then practically jogged to the truck. I tried to open the door, because you taught us manners, and she got pissed."

"So, let me see if I got this right, to prove that you have manners, you pissed her off on purpose?" Dad's words cut through the morning air, and I come to a full stop, watching him continue on without me.

"When you say it like that, I sound like an asshole."

"You're catching on, son." His voice carries a mix of amusement and warning.

Damn.

There's something about Parker that gets under my skin, and not in a way I'm used to. It looks like I'm in for another round of apologies; she might set a record at this rate.

Fate

PARKER

"Avoiding someone in small town Wyoming is not as easy as you think," I grumble to Cami as we settle in for our long-distance version of a Saturday night binge-watching party, complete with an array of snacks.

"I'm going to need more than that," she says, her curiosity piqued.

I sigh, frustration bubbling up. "How is it that he happens to be at the grocery store at the same time as me? I had to go twice this week because as soon as I saw him, I practically sprinted for the checkout lane. Then, I come downstairs on Monday, and there's his truck. I mean, I basically see that hulking navy blue, drool-worthy dually everywhere."

Cami bursts into laughter, tears streaming down her face. "Maybe," she hiccups, struggling to get the words out, "it's the . . . universe."

I cross my arms, my annoyance growing. "Then the universe is a total brat. I mean, who does this guy think he is, Cami? First, he pokes at me for not being friendly, then he argues with me over open-ing a door, and then he has the audacity to lift me into the truck. I was so mad, it's a wonder I didn't end him on the spot."

"Maybe you've just met your match, Parker," Cami suggests, wip-ing away her laughter-induced tears. "I mean, every man I've ever seen ducks for cover when you slip into the dragon slayer, which I'm deeply proud of, by the way. If your sweet nature couldn't convince heads of state into world peace, that pissed-off look could definitely do it. You're a force, babes. Maybe Wyatt likes that about you. That, or it's a cowboy thing, but since you haven't mentioned any other man treating you that way, I'm going to go with a Wyatt thing."

"I'm not that scary, Cami," I insist. "I was just trying to be professional."

Cami gives me a look that's part understanding, part exasperation. "Girlfriend, you are incredible, but you keep all that softness covered up by a confident and strong woman with the ability to switch to 'eff off' mode immediately. I admire that about you, I do. But you also use it as a shield, to keep people at a distance."

Her words hang in the air, and I can't help but feel a twinge of guilt. "It didn't work on you," I point out, secretly grateful for her persistence.

She smiles, a softness in her eyes. "Not for lack of trying. But I saw through it. You put up walls to protect that big, sweet, kind heart. I know what's really there, so I didn't mind."

The memories flood back, bringing tears to my eyes. "I'm sorry, Cami. If I was ever mean, cruel, or tried to push you away . . . I don't want to be that person."

"Whoa, babe," she cuts in, her voice gentle. "You never hurt me. You're not cruel. You've got a soft, gooey center. You just don't let people see it. But it sounds like Wyatt saw something, felt that shift, and was dumb enough, or smart enough, depending on how you look at it, to call you on it."

I huff, a mix of frustration and reluctance swirling inside me. "What if I don't want to be called on it? He's attractive, sure, but I'm not looking for that."

Cami leans back, considering my words. "What if you just co-exist with him? See where that leads. He might not be Mr. Right, but maybe there's a reason he's crossed your path. Greg always says to never underestimate the power of an unexpected ingredient, right?"

"He does say that." I chuckle, recalling the episode of *Knifed* where Greg triumphed with a bizarre combination of ginger molasses cookies and fish. "We should challenge him again. It's been too long since he's had a good culinary battle."

Cami's excitement is palpable as she squeals, "Yaaasss! When is he coming out?"

"I told him to give me a couple of months to settle in, but I doubt he'll wait that long. He's already demanding virtual tours and daily pictures of the place."

Her eyebrows dance with mischief. "What does he think of your little interaction with Wyatt?"

"He doesn't know," I admit, quickly covering my face, then peeking through my fingers at Cami's astonished look. "I don't want Wyatt to get murdered."

"You never keep things from your dad. Isn't that like a hallmark of your relationship? I mean, you even told him when you lost your virginity, didn't you?"

I nod, affirming our family rule. "Yes. We don't hide things. We face them together, even if they make us uncomfortable."

"Soooooo." Cami draws out the word, waiting for me to spill the beans.

"I don't know! It just feels like telling him makes it a thing."

"Mmmmhhmm, I think you don't want him to know you've got a little crush brewing. You are in Egypt floating along de-Nile," she teases, laughing.

"Okay, no more Wyatt talk. He's just another person that I happen to be actively avoiding. You are supposed to be picking our show. I suggest you do that, or I'm going to pick a *Die Hard* film to torture you."

"Don't threaten me with *Die Hard*," she warns, wagging a finger at me. "In honor of it being my turn to pick, I select—"

"Wait! Drumroll!" I interrupt, drumming on my legs with a wide smile.

"*How to Lose a Guy in 10 Days*!" she declares, and I can't help but roll my eyes. She always opts for the romantic comedy, but she has a knack for picking the good ones. We each cue up the movie and press play.

As the film starts, I can't help but wonder what I'd even tell Dad about Wyatt. That he's charming? That he likes to argue and get under my skin? That he's attractive? Someone else was all those things once, and the only result was heartache.

Avoidance

PARKER

The universe has apparently decided it's time to end my little game of avoidance. I kept the shirt, and I've been sleeping in it. Is this my cosmic retribution? Dad still doesn't know about Wyatt. Maybe that's why I'm being punished.

Regardless of why, here I am, stuck in the middle of nowhere with fate giving me the middle finger. It's midnight, and on my way back from a farm call, the vet truck starts smoking—because why wouldn't it? I should've taken my own truck. I should have called Dad. I should have returned the shirt, though I can't at the moment. Charlie's not answering, and Sammy's out on another call.

"Is this karma?" I whisper into the quiet truck illuminated only by dash lights.

The engine's still smoking, and the truck won't start. I rest my head on the warm steering wheel and meet Cooper's gaze. "I know what we have to do, but I don't have to like it, so stop giving me that look," I tell him. He just keeps staring. "If I'm right, we're a couple miles from the turnoff to his ranch. My phone's about to die, and no one else is picking up. We have no choice, Cooper." I'm saying it to Cooper, but really, I'm trying to steel myself for what I have to do next.

Exhaustion weighs on me. I've spent the past few weeks taking every farm call we've gotten so I could get to know the area. It was a good plan to ensure I don't get lost in the vast Wyoming wilderness. Tonight, I've jumped from call to call, and my cooler is now empty. My numbers were headed down the last time I looked at the app but with the truck engine dead, I can't charge my phone. All I know is I'm running out of time.

"Dang. Dang. Dang!" I mutter aloud, finding a shred of relief in voicing my frustration. "You know, Cooper, if I really think about it, this is his fault. If I hadn't been so busy avoiding him, I wouldn't be in this mess." I look at Cooper, seeking some sort of agreement.

"Decision made. Let's go for a walk, Cooper." He's unflappable, my sweet dude. I envy his cool demeanor. Through all the farms, animals, and people we meet, Cooper remains chill. I admire his ability to face any challenge. That's not just a huge feat for a dog; there's a life lesson buried in there somewhere for me. Maybe I'll learn it someday.

I hate the thought of leaving the truck here, with all its supplies, but options are scarce so I lock the door behind us, securing it as best as I can. "It's pitch black, so we're sticking to the road. I'm not anxious to meet the wildlife around here. Sound good?" Cooper just stares back in stoic silence.

"Maybe a car will come along, Cooper." The odds are slim. "I can't jog. My levels won't take it. But we're not taking a leisurely stroll here either. I'm not scared of the dark, but I'm also not ignorant of the fact that things that go bump often do it at night." With that, we set off, hoping for a stroke of luck or at least a safe passage to his ranch.

After what feels like an eternity, the familiar outline of the drive finally comes into view. "I might have been a little off about the distance," I admit, trying to catch my breath.

I navigate the cattle guard with caution, each step measured and deliberate lest I break an ankle and really top off this night. Cooper slips under the nearby fence with ease. We quickly walk up the drive and, really, was it this long before?

We're almost at the door when the lights come on suddenly, illuminating the porch. That's got to be a sensor, right? As I ascend the steps, the door swings open, revealing Wyatt. His hair is tousled, his appearance rugged and sleepy and undeniably appealing, even in the harsh glare of the overhead light.

Standing there, shirtless in the doorway, Wyatt is a sight that could make any heart skip a beat. His abs are defined, but not overly sculpted, a testament to natural muscle and hard work. The tan lines—or lack thereof—suggest a man accustomed to the outdoors, comfortable shirtless under the sun. His torso is a canvas of muscle and skin, with a cut of muscle over each hip, directing your attention straight to the promised land.

And then there's the tattoo, a floral design etched along his ribs, intricate and gorgeous. It's the kind of detail that makes you want to lean in closer to trace the lines and understand the story.

I catch myself, the corner of my mouth betraying my awe with an involuntary drool. The sight of all that exposed skin, in combination with a single button undone on the jeans slung low across his hips, is enough to make heat pool in my stomach and a soft ache come alive in my core. The glimpse of his underwear prompts a silent nod of gratitude to my dear friend Calvin Klein and his unbeatable gifts to womankind.

My eyes travel upward till they meet his. His expression is a mix of confusion and annoyance, his arms crossed defensively over his chest. It's clear he wasn't expecting company at this hour, who would be?

"What are you doing walking up the driveway at two in the middle of the freaking night, Parker? Do you know how dangerous that is?" Wyatt's voice is sharp, his glare intense. The softness I've seen before is absent now, replaced by an edge that commands attention.

"It's not by choice," I retort, my own frustration flaring up to match his.

"Explain." The word comes out like a bullet, and I can feel the tension radiating off him. If circumstances were different, I might have risen to the challenge, but right now I'm too tired.

"The vet truck broke down a couple of miles away. Charlie didn't answer before my phone completely died. Sammy's on another call. I don't have anyone else's numbers, not that it would matter at this point. I knew I was near your ranch. I didn't know what else to do." The words spill out, each one measured and deliberate. I can't help but feel a twinge of defeat, a weariness beyond being physically tired. Asking for help sucks, especially when I have to ask someone who has the power to unsettle me so deeply.

We stand there, gazes locked in total silence, until he abruptly turns and retreats into the house. The definitive closing of the door echoed through my own exhaustion. I'm left standing in the partial dark.

I glance at Cooper, considering our limited options. "I could take up space on a porch chair for the night. Surely one of the crew or Wyatt's dad will find us here in the morning and help us get back. That won't solve the sugar problem, but we wouldn't get murdered by a wandering serial killer or a bear, so that's something." It's not an ideal plan, but it's all we have for now.

I settle onto the porch steps, the vast night sky stretching above us. "The light pollution here is so minimal it's like you can see all the way through space. I've never admired stars until I got here," I muse aloud to Cooper, who seems content by my side. "Maybe I should get a telescope—that could be fun."

Sitting on the porch, I'm wrapped in the peaceful silence of the Wyoming night. Above, the stars twinkle to some unwritten musical rhythm, a shimmering river.

Clusters of stars form a few constellations I recognize, patterns that humans have traced and named over millennia, connecting dots to create heroes, beasts, and myths painted in light. Leaning back on my elbows I close my eyes and breathe it in.

Suddenly, the door behind me swings open. Wyatt appears, now dressed in boots and a shirt, keys in hand. "Let's go," he says, his voice firm.

I scramble to my feet, hurrying to keep pace with him as he strides around the corner of the house. "Go where?"

He halts so suddenly I nearly collide with his back. "Don't we need to go get that truck started?" he turns, looking as perplexed as I feel.

"Oh!" I can't help but giggle at the absurdity of the situation. "This little Abbott and Costello moment is kinda funny, but it's probably not possible to restart that thing. It was smoking when I left it, with all the dash lights on. I doubt there's much we can do in the middle of the night. If you could just get me and Cooper back to the office, I'll call a tow truck." Wyatt just stands there, his gaze intense and unwavering.

"Do you have to stare at me like that?" I whisper, his stare making me acutely conscious of every inch of space between us. I'm not sure why I asked, but it feels crucial at this moment.

"Yes." His response is firm, filled with a confidence that sends a shiver through my body. He turns away, heading toward the truck, and I'm left to follow, my heart racing with a mix of irritation and something else I can't quite name.

As we approach the truck, I roll my eyes when he heads for the passenger side first. "I want to fight you on this, badly," I admit as I catch up to him. "I want to open that door myself, but you're doing us a favor, so I won't because that would be rude." He opens the back door for Cooper, then the front for me, and despite everything, I feel a warmth spread through me at his consideration for Cooper.

"Up," he commands, and Cooper obeys, jumping into the truck. It's surprising, really; Cooper usually only listens to Greg and me. It's as if he's making his own judgment about Wyatt's character.

"Buckled up?" Wyatt asks, smirking as I nod, before closing the door himself. As he rounds the hood with those long strides of his, I can't help but feel a tangle of emotions—annoyance, gratitude, and an unsettling awareness of just how attracted to him I really am.

CHAPTER 19

Cinnamon

WYATT

Waking up to the sight of her on the driveway monitor was like being jolted from one dream into another. My hands in her hair, her mouth on mine, all blurred with her walking up the drive. Only the clench of my fists kept me from reaching for her the moment I opened the door, turning those dreams into reality.

Now, as I drive her home, sleep is the furthest thing from my mind. Her scent fills the truck, a blend of cinnamon and vanilla, sweet but sharp, reminiscent of Thanksgiving. It's a scent that overpowers the clinical antiseptic I've come to associate with vets, and it's maddening, especially at this ungodly hour. It makes me want to pull her out of her seat into my lap just so I can find its source on her neck. The twitch behind my zipper warns me away from that train of thought.

I haven't seen her in weeks. I've been on edge, so much so that even the crew has given me a wide berth. Lincoln said I was acting like a toddler who'd lost his favorite toy. It pissed me off that I'd upset her so much and hadn't had the chance to fix it.

"Where were you on call?" I break the silence that has settled between us, causing her to jump. She must have been lost in her thoughts.

"I was at the Neely's farm last, but in truth, I've been all over today." I notice the weariness in her voice as she answers. Her eyes looked a little glassy in the porch light earlier too.

"I haven't seen you around in a few weeks. I was hoping I would. I think I owe you another apology."

"You think?" Her voice drips with sarcasm, a sharp reminder of the distance currently between us. Definitely not friends, and I can't blame her for that.

"Yeah, I was a bit of an ass. *Again*. Though I do stand by the principle that you should expect a man to open a door, so we shouldn't have to fight about that."

"*Not* an apology then." Her lifted eyebrow is a challenge, questioning my sincerity. The sigh that escapes me is part frustration and part exasperation.

"I never can seem to get it right with you the first time, Parker. I'm also remembering why I don't apologize that often." The words are out before I can stop them, and I see her pinch the bridge of her nose.

"How about this, we call that one a draw. You don't have to be sorry, and I don't have to accept. Deal?" It's a truce of sorts, an acknowledgment of our mutual stubbornness.

"That sounds a lot like friendship to me," I smirk, the word 'friendship' hanging in the air, a tentative bridge between us. "I'll take that deal. Now, want to tell me why you have a headache?"

"I've been up for almost nineteen hours, Wyatt." It's a statement that explains the weariness in her eyes, the slight slump of her shoulders, and the tone of annoyance she's using perfectly.

"That's long, even for a vet. Why's that?" I probe, careful with our tentative truce but too damn curious to stop myself.

"I couldn't sleep. New place, new sounds, new everything, so I got up early, went for a run, cleaned the apartment, tried to unpack a few boxes." Her smile reaches her eyes, and it's a sight that eases some of the tension within me.

"Makes sense." As the drive stretches on, I find myself settling into the moment, the presence of Parker beside me. The dream may have been interrupted, but the reality of her is so much better. Even if she occasionally wants to throttle me, having her nearby is electric, a charge of energy that hums over my skin. Even if it means navigating the complexities of apologies and door-opening etiquette.

"Is right now the right time to make a request?" Her voice is so faint, it's like the words slipped out before she could catch them. She's not looking at me, her gaze fixed on the road ahead. Her hands are twisting in her lap, her shoulders square, the nerves rolling off her in waves.

"I'm driving you home in the middle of the night after being awoken by the driveway alarm from a very good dream," I say, trying to inject some humor into the situation, "I suppose now would be the best time to ask just about anything."

"So, not a coincidence," she murmurs, more to herself than to me.

"What?" I turn briefly to take in her profile, the glow of the moon highlighting the shades on her face.

"I couldn't figure out how you knew to open the door when I got there earlier—driveway alarm makes sense." She shrugs it off, but I can tell she's been turning it over in her mind.

"Statler installed security upgrades a few years ago. The alarm was non-negotiable for him. It goes off sometimes with animals so I was prepared to go back to sleep and ignore it but there you were." There she was, indeed, a vision given flesh, so unexpected that I had to blink twice to make sure I wasn't still dreaming.

"There I was," she whispers, her voice so soft it's almost lost in the hum of the truck's engine.

"About this question," I prompt, curious.

"Can you please pick a new name for the yellow filly?" The words come out in a rush, followed by a heavy exhale. She turns her head, looking out the window, and I can hear the plea in her voice.

The request doesn't bother me. It's the way she asked, the strain behind her words. She didn't want to ask, but she did—and that alone is enough for me to want to grant it.

Her refusal to meet my gaze tells me more than words ever could. "Look at me," I urge, my voice soft.

"No." Her voice is firm, her posture rigid.

"Give me something, angel," I coax gently, trying to bridge the distance her refusal put back between us. I've never been one to plead, but for her, I find myself willing to make an exception.

"Angel?" She turns to face me this time, her eyebrow arching in question. Her eyes are dark and deep. I'm quickly learning that her eyes are a formidable force, capable of disarming me with a single look.

"Feels like it fits," I say with a casual shrug, though there's nothing casual about the way my heart races. "What do you think?"

She hums, her head tilting slightly in consideration. "Aren't pet names reserved for people who are romantically involved or good friends?"

"We are friends. I thought our truce covered that. But if we aren't friends, then I think we need to look at this for what it is—our second date." Her laughter is a sound I didn't know I'd been waiting my whole life to hear.

"How do you figure this is a second date, Wyatt? When was the first one?" she asks, still laughing.

I wait for her to turn and face me. "The way I see it, hat-trick night was our first date since we spent all night together and I fed you in the morning. This is night two, I'm driving you home, and you're wearing my shirt." I noticed it the minute I opened the door, the sight sending a deep sense of satisfaction sliding through me.

She glances down at her shirt, then back up at me. A blush spreads across her cheeks. Her embarrassment is endearing and sweet in a way that makes her even more irresistible.

"I meant to bring it back the other day but," she begins, her voice trailing off as my laughter cuts through the night.

"You know what, I'm not sorry, and I'm not giving it back, laugh all you want," she declares.

"Keep it. I like it on you." The words come out more sincerely than I intend. That old shirt, once just a piece of fabric, is now something precious, simply because she's the one wearing it. "Tell me why you don't want that filly to be named Sunny *or* why you've been avoiding me for two weeks *or* admit we're friends. You pick."

She remains silent, her gaze fixed ahead, her arms crossed, this time protectively around her middle. She's retreated back into her own thoughts, cut me out again. But I'm willing to wait, to fight for the answers, for the connection that seems to be just within reach.

Finally, I pull into the vet parking lot.

The anticipation hangs heavy in the air. I want to understand the reasons behind her silence, her avoidance, and maybe, just maybe, hear her admit that there's something more between us than just a shared experience and a borrowed shirt.

CHAPTER 20

Memories

WYATT

Turning off the truck, I shift just as her voice, a ghost of a sound, breeches the silence between us.

"I know the pain of losing someone who means the world to you. I can't stand knowing a name I chose is causing your family pain." The weight of her words anchors me to the spot.

"Look at me, Parker." I ask gently, desperate to connect and understand her. She resists, a small shake of her head, keeping her gaze fixed on the world outside. I reach across the console slowly, my fingers gently guiding her chin until she's facing me. "Eyes." This time, she meets my gaze, and her eyes are full of fear and grief.

"Please." Her plea is a quiet storm, and it tears at me. I shift my touch, my thumb caressing the soft skin of her cheek as every part of me wishes I could erase the pain from her eyes.

"I'm afraid we can't take it back now. Paperwork is filed. It's done." The words are a gentle truth, delivered from a well of care I didn't realize was so deep. "If it helps, it doesn't hurt us. My mom would have loved it. She was fierce. You picked well, even if you didn't mean to. It was just a surprise. It squeezed a little at first, but not so much anymore." I let my gaze fall from her eyes, tracing the contours of her face, trying to understand.

As I watch a single tear escape, I feel a surge of frustration that I can't give her what she's asking for. I catch the tear with my thumb, a silent vow of apology. "These tears will bring me to my knees, Parker." Our eyes find each other again, and in that moment, I know I'd do anything to shield her from the ghosts swirling in hers.

"Does it really hurt less now?" Parker's question slices through the silence, her voice raw and rough with pain.

"No," I confess, the truth spilling out unbidden. "But time gives you a chance to balance the pain with joy, the grief with happiness, and that makes it easier, I guess." Parker's need for an answer, for some kind of understanding, pulls the words from me.

Slowly, I draw her closer, my fingers sliding to the back of her neck before I press a kiss to her forehead, meaning the action to soothe whatever's rising inside her. It's a stillness that feels almost sacred; it's a pause in the world where the only thing that exists is the two of us. The darkness outside presses against the windows. Parker abruptly pulls back, and I slide my hand from her neck, breaking the connection.

I sense she's not going to tell me more, so I grab my own door handle and step out of the truck. Her eyes connect with me as I round the hood, simply watching as if I'm something unexpected or foreign. I let Cooper out first, then open her door and step back to let her out. As she stands to leave, Cooper's bark pierces the night.

"Okay, Cooper, I hear you, buddy. Let's go inside." Her steps are quiet as she passes me, eyes down, and heads for the apartment steps. I close the truck door and follow her. I've ignored that warning once before. I won't make that mistake again. As she crests the third step, she sways and grabs for the rail. Instinct takes over, and I'm behind her in a stride, lifting her into my arms. Her face is pale in the moon-light as we ascend the steps.

"You have a habit of doing this you know, thinking I can't walk." Her voice is heavy, her eyelids fluttering shut, her head dropping against my shoulder. A wave of panic crashes over me, tightening around my heart with a vice-like grip.

"Don't close those gorgeous eyes on me," I urge her, desperate to keep her present with me. Her eyelids flutter open, and her gaze locks onto mine.

"I was closing them out of exasperation, not medical interference, Wyatt," she retorts, her breath huffing in annoyance. "And don't call me gorgeous." Her feisty spirit coaxes a smirk from me, one I know she detests.

"Keys." We've just reached the landing, Cooper trailing behind us, when she leans back in my arms, arching her body until she deftly fishes the keys from her front pocket. I'm honestly impressed she managed to do that. I set her down, snatching the keys from her hand and unlocking the door myself. Before she can step across the threshold, I've got her back in my arms.

I perch her on the kitchen countertop and pivot towards the fridge to grab her cherished Dr. Pepper. "Here. Drink. Now." I shove the can into her hand, then position myself between her open knees, my hands resting next to her thighs on the counter.

"You know you lose sentence structure when you're frustrated," she teases, a playful glint in her eyes.

"Not frustrated. Where's your phone?" I counter, trying to stay focused on the situation at hand.

"Oh, a whole sentence that time, cowboy." Her laughter bubbles from her lips.

"Hold tight," I tell her, my voice a low murmur. Her head tilts in confusion just before I wrap my hands around her knees and pull her to the edge of the counter. Before she can do much more than let out a small gasp, I wrap both arms around her, lifting her easily off the surface. Her legs wrap around my waist while she tries not to spill her drink. Her hand going around my neck to find her balance. The movement sends a thrill through me, as does the tiny shiver I feel run up her back as she arches just slightly. The smirk on my face is impossible to suppress now. I carry her to the living room, each step slow and intentional, my eyes not wavering from hers, enjoying the closeness.

"Caveman," she accuses softly.

"Drink." I hold out one hand, keeping the other wrapped securely around her back. She hands it to me and without putting her down, I set it on the table next to the couch. She unwraps her legs from my waist, but I keep my arm around her back, causing her feet to dangle off the floor. Slowly, I lower her down, until I feel her toes touch. I nudge her shoulder, and she drops back to the couch, sinking into the cushions.

"Phone charger?" I ask, finally breaking eye contact to scan the room for it.

"My room, chair beside the bed. First door on the left," she directs, pointing behind her to the hallway. I sidestep the couch and make my way to her room. The sight of her unmade bed and boxes lining the walls bear witness to a life in transition. I snatch the charger, then head back to the living room. She points to a plug on her coffee table.

After I plug in the phone, I sit down next to her. Reaching over, I pick up her hand gently. She turns to face me as I pull her hand across her body. Using her finger, I unlock her phone. It feels like a victory when she doesn't immediately pull it back, letting it rest where I place it on my chest. Her warm touch is the sweetest kind of agony seeping through my shirt.

"It's not that bad this time, Wyatt," she reassures me, sneaking a glance at the phone screen. "You can go. It'll come back up. I just ran out of snacks a while back, then had to walk a few miles to your house. It's not a big deal." Her head rests on the back of the couch, her legs curled up in front of her now that she's abandoned her shoes.

"Do those socks have cows on them?" Looking down at her feet, then back up, I see the smile start in her eyes before it makes it's way to her lips.

"Yes." Her chest shakes with silent laughter. "Don't judge."

"No judgement." I lift my hand in mock surrender, then settle it over hers on my chest.

"You really don't need to stay, Wyatt." Her eyes soften, along with her voice.

"Parker, I'm starting to understand that doing things yourself is important to you. But maybe I'm the one that needs to know you're okay. Friend or not, leaving you when I don't know for certain you're going to be okay would be a *true* asshole move. That said, I hear you, and I don't want you to be uncomfortable. How about some options? Option A, I can wait here with you. Option B, I'll go wait in the truck until you give me the all clear. Either way, I'm here just in case, but you get to choose where. That's a compromise. Personally, I'd like to stay in here with you, the couch is more comfortable than the truck. But only if that's what you want."

"That was tough, wasn't it?" she teases, a slow smile spreading across her face. "Compromise doesn't really strike me as your style."

"I solve problems, that's my way." I let my head fall back on the couch, stretching out my legs a little further to get comfortable, then twist my head to look at her. "It's my job to handle things, to take care of my people."

"And I'm 'your people' now?" Her voice wavers slightly, betraying her uncertainty.

"It seems to be heading in that direction."

"And if that's not what I want?" The furrow in her brow deepens, her eyes narrowing ever so slightly.

"Then that's that," I say firmly, yet gently. "I don't mind challenging you, Parker, but I'd never force you. If you want nothing to do with me when I walk out of this room, that'll suck, but I'll listen. I'd like to be your friend, though, if I can register an official request." I aim for a lighter tone, hoping to ease the tension from her shoulders.

"So the door thing, that's you challenging?"

"Something like that." My thumb rubs across the knuckles of the hand under mine.

"I'll consider it. For now, you can stay," she concedes, her eyes closing.

Soothing us both, I continue stroking her hand, periodically checking her levels. I've learned a lot after our last encounter, researching Type 2 diabetes for hours, not that I'd admit that right now. Most of what I learned told me that someone like Parker probably had a lot of processes and systems in place to manage her health, but knowing that doesn't seem to make me want to take care of her any less.

Her eyes stay closed, even as my touch wanders from the back of her hand to her wrist, down her arm and back. Her breathing slows, her body unwinding muscle by muscle. Her heartbeat slows to a steady rhythm. Ten minutes pass, her levels stabilize, and finally, she's sound asleep.

Careful not to disturb her, I lift her hand off my chest and stand. Sliding my hands under her once more, I lift her from the couch. As soon as she's in my arms, she exhales deeply, nestling her head on my shoulder, her face hidden in the crook of my neck.

Note to self: sleepy Parker is a cuddler.

A silent chuckle works its way free. I'm not usually one for cuddles, but I can't deny that right now, it's a pretty damn good feeling. As I carry her to her room, Cooper pads along behind us, his nails on the hardwood the only sound in the quiet space. Laying her down on the bed, I snag the nearest blanket and tuck it around her.

I place her phone nearby and check her levels one last time. Then, pulling out my own phone, I add her number.

Cooper settles on his pillow beside her bed, standing guard.

Satisfied that I've done everything I can for her, I exit through the front door, ensuring it's locked before closing it behind me.

CHAPTER 21

Regrets

PARKER

Therapy taught me the power of writing to untangle my thoughts. This morning, as consciousness seeps in, I reach first for my laptop resting on the floor. My thoughts are messy this morning, but all centered around one man. Nestled among the pillows, I open my ongoing log and let my thoughts flow onto the screen.

> *Is it possible to regret an entire evening even if it included no drinking and no sex? That has to be what I'm feeling, right? I almost cried. He didn't push; I'll give him credit for that. Perhaps he just assumed I was like a T-Rex and didn't make any sudden moves to avoid making me more emotional. Okay, he isn't that big an ass—not that I plan to tell him that. I awoke this morning in my bed, fully clothed, with Cooper on his bed. He locked my door when he left. He took me home in the middle of the night, wiped my tears, and then stroked my hand until I fell asleep. Okay, he'd pulled me off the countertop too. That was actually . . . . pretty hot. I mean, most guys can't exactly toss around a*

*woman like me, not that I'm a monster or anything, but I'm defi-
nitely not petite. He asked to be my friend. Friendship feels like
playing with fire though. I know what I saw in his eyes; it was
desire. I don't know if friendship with him will satisfy either of
us, and if I'm being honest, I want him too. I can say that here,
where no one will ever read it, but he does make me want.*

The buzz of my phone slices through the morning stillness.

UNKNOWN

It's Wyatt. Now you have my number.

I mean, couldn't get any simpler than that. He must have taken my
number when I fell asleep. The question for me is how to respond.

I look over to Cooper, "Am I supposed to thank him?" A silent
stare from Cooper. "He caught me off guard, that's all. I was tired
and feeling emotional and a little needy," I declare with a hint of defiance. Cooper, unimpressed, flops back down, feigning indifference.

The clock reads 7:00. I have one precious hour before the day
demands my presence downstairs. A shower beckons, and the thought
of breakfast stirs my appetite, but first, I need to deal with this lingering ache that two in the morning Wyatt seems to have left behind.

Rolling onto my back, images of Wyatt flood my mind. He's hot,
I can't deny that—just like I can't deny the way he creates an ache
within me. Thinking back, it's been awhile since I handled that particular physical need, which likely explains all the little tingles and
fires. I need to get this, and him, out of my system.

Closing my eyes, my hand trails down to my waistband. The scent
of Wyatt—leather and cedar—floods my memory. Instantly I recall
the feel of his muscles as he carried me up the stairs, solid beneath
me. His abs and that one undone button on the top of his jeans,
not to mention the tattoo . . . I picture his long fingers tracing my
cheek, then imagine them in place of my own. Arousal coats my fingers immediately. Already perilously close to the edge, I continue to

envision Wyatt's long fingers and rough hands until stars explode behind my eyes, his name on my lips. Slowing down, each spasm and shock pushes my breath to form jagged pants.

Wow. Just wow.

That has to be a speed record or something—only two minutes have passed. I must have had that one building for a while. That's the only explanation. It couldn't possibly have been the subject of my little fantasy. *Nope.*

Once my heart rate goes back to normal and I can actually breathe, I decide to reply. I'll just say thank you. That should be enough. Sweet. Simple. Friendly. My cheeks heat because nothing I just did falls in the camp of simple and friendly.

PARKER

Thank you.

WYATT

How are you feeling?

Fine.

Back to fine huh?
The truck is on it's way to you.

No. Just actually fine.
Also, you didn't need to do that.

It's what friends do.

Is that what we are?

You tell me.

Is that all you want?

That's up to you.

"What's the right response here?" I mutter, frustration lacing my voice. Cami's words echo in my mind, reassuring me that talking to myself isn't odd unless I answer back. Right now, though, the only other one to hold a conversation with is Cooper, and he's not helping. I'm drawing a blank.

Boundaries. That's what I need to focus on. No more daydreams about him. I'm crafting a new beginning here, amidst the vastness of Wyoming, and it certainly doesn't include the chaos of complicated relationships. With a firm nod to no one in particular, I sit up straighter.

I dive into the sea of pending messages and emails, answering one from Greg, assuring him of my well-being. He still receives alerts if my glucose levels falter, a safety net he refuses to remove. He claims it's a 'dad thing' to worry incessantly.

My phone buzzes and interrupts my thoughts again, but the number flashing on the screen is unfamiliar. I decline, rising and starting my day.

◇◇◇◇◇◇◇◇◇◇◇◇◇◇◇

After ten grueling hours, my muscles scream with a sweet ache, yet my heart swells with unparalleled love for my work. From the moment my feet touched the floor, the day's demands engulfed me. I thrive in this particular brand of chaos; it anchors me to the present, to the clarity of purpose. This aspect of my life is refreshingly straightforward.

I'd trade anything for a full-body massage, but aside from that, I'm riding a high. If I save this horse, I'll toast to victory with a tall glass of water and skip tomorrow's morning run as a treat.

It's not the joy of exercise that drives me to run or train; honestly, I despise it. But strength is essential in my line of work, and exercise is the dual key to managing my career and my health. My diagnosis taught me early on the immense benefits of a good workout, making the absence of it my preferred indulgence.

I'm determined to save this horse, and after that, I'll collapse. Both Charlie and Sammy are on duty, making tomorrow my first full day off. I've been on call non-stop, doing my best to settle in quickly. Now, it's time to step back, rest, and recharge.

"Okay ladies," I say, looking around the room of assistants who all happened to be female today. "Let's save a horse, so no one has to ride a cowboy tomorrow." The chorus of laughter is music to my ears. I press Play on my Cut It Up playlist, which predominately features Taylor Swift, and get down to work.

CHAPTER 22

Competency

WYATT

She didn't respond, and it's starting to get to me. I've been think-ing about her all day. I want to see that softness and sass. I want to feel her close. I want all of it. I am dying to know how much she's going to give me.

When I drove out this morning to track down the vet truck, I real-ized she had walked close to three miles in the middle of the night. The rush of fear rose up in me so unexpectedly, like a tidal wave, when I thought of all the things that could have happened. I wanted to chew someone's ass but there wasn't anyone to blame, so I called the tow truck instead.

I poured my energy into work, tackling every physical job on the ranch. There's never a shortage of tasks to keep you busy here. Today was all about preparing the beef sales—lifting, taping, boxing up orders. It's the end of the day, and I'm covered in sweat, but my need to see her hasn't faded with the work.

I've checked my phone too many times to count, but still no message. She hasn't turned me down, but she hasn't agreed either.

I want to see her, but I don't have a reason. Walking into the barn's studio, my reason sits, just waiting. Her T-shirt, clean, folded, and lying on the laundry basket, is precisely what I need. A plan begins to form. I need groceries first, then I need to convince her to have dinner with me.

◇◇◇◇◇◇◇◇◇◇◇◇◇◇◇◇

It's pushing seven on a Thursday night, and I'm expecting an empty parking lot, so the sight of trucks means I'm going to have an audience. Inside the clinic, it's quiet—no sign of patients, but there's a buzz of voices from the back. I've been coming to this clinic since I was a kid; its halls are as familiar to me as my own house. I head toward the voices and come across Charlie and Sammy, lingering outside the operating room doors.

Charlie catches sight of me and surprise flickers on his face, but he greets me with a firm handshake and a slap on the back all the same.

"Gentlemen, what are we doing standing outside the doors?" I extend my hand to Sammy too.

"Watching the new kid in surgery. Gotta admit, it's nice that someone else is looked at like the new kid these days," Sammy remarks, a touch of nostalgia in his tone.

"Is that music?" The sound filters through the door, catching my attention.

"Yep," Charlie responds, the 'p' popping sharply as he stifles a laugh. "She's got her own style, but I'll be damned if she doesn't have some of the steadiest hands I've seen in a very long time."

"Thanks, Dad," Sammy's chuckle fills the space, a sound of genuine appreciation.

Charlie's next words are laced with pride, "You . . . you know you're good at surgery, but you were always gifted with the science. Now me, I was just smart enough to hire you both." He laughs at his own humor.

"He's not wrong, Sammy. You've got a real talent for piecing things together, figuring out how to get an animal back on its feet. It's impressive," I add, happily giving credit where it's due.

Sammy's eyes twinkle with mischief as he looks my way. "Thank you, Wyatt. But I'm guessing you're not here just to sing my praises, are you?" He winks. "You bringing us the bill for the truck?"

"Mind your business, Sammy," I deflect, shifting my gaze back to the doors as he playfully nudges me.

The faint strains of Taylor Swift's "You Need to Calm Down" drift through the door, and I catch sight of her bobbing her head subtly to the rhythm. She's stunning. Her competence is sexy as hell. Cooper, ever the four-legged shadow, sits at the perfect distance, close but not intrusive.

Then the chorus hits, and the whole room's singing along, a chorus of "uh-ohs" that pulls an easy smile onto my face.

Charlie's voice is soft, almost reverent, "That's a moment right there." We're all captivated, watching her expertly finish up on a large horse I don't recognize.

"Colic?" I look to Charlie to confirm my hunch.

Charlie beams at me. "Good eye, young man. It's old Hank's granddaughter's horse. She's ten and was beside herself when he called. A man will move mountains for his grandkids. Dr. Mason's been on her feet all day, but she didn't hesitate. I wanted to see if she lived up to the surgical prodigy rumors, and from what I've seen out here, she does."

Watching her coordinate with the team, her movements precise and confident, is like watching a movie in real time. Finally, she turns, stripping off her gloves and gown, and heads for the doors. She stops, noticing us, one eyebrow arching as her gaze meets mine.

"Something I should know, Wyatt?" Charlie's voice is low, carrying that weight of authority, the same I've heard from my own father when he asks.

"I honestly don't know, sir," I reply, holding her gaze. She steps through the doors, breaking our staring contest to address Charlie.

"Sparky's going to pull through. He's still got to shake off the anesthesia and find his legs, but the colon impaction was straightforward. He should be back to his old self soon enough," she reports with a clinical detachment, as if she's just discussing the weather.

Charlie nods his approval. "Excellent work, Dr. Mason. You've more than earned a break for the rest of the night." His eyes flick to me, and I can tell he's already piecing together a story. He's got that same knack for gossip as my dad—I can almost hear the ribbing I'll get tomorrow.

"Are you sure? I don't mind staying." Her voice is steady, but Charlie's stern look cuts through any protest. Charlie and my dad ran herd on our crew of boys growing up. They don't fold and they don't bluff. I have to fight the urge to tell her to cave.

"I'd say a few weeks of farm calls, then having to walk to the Lochlans' place last night more than earns you a full twenty-four hours off. Get out of here." Charlie insists, and his tone leaves no room for argument.

"Thank you." Her smile could light up the darkest room, and it's all for Charlie. It's a look of pure joy, the kind that comes from a deep love of achievement. My girl likes to hear praise. And there it is, that thought—*my* girl. When did I start thinking of her that way?

"I agree. You were supposed to be off two hours ago, remember? Time to take a break," Sammy chimes in, his nudge sending her a clear message, and his wink thrown my way doesn't go unnoticed.

She laughs, a sound that's become a personal favorite, "If you need me, I'm just upstairs." Her words are casual, but they hang in the air, an unspoken invitation. She hasn't said a word to me yet, but that's alright.

"Doc." My voice is a low call as I step aside, pointing her to the clinic's hallway. She passes by, and I can't help but follow her lead, turning back to give a nod to the men. "Sammy, Charlie, good to see you both."

As I walk away, I swear I hear laughter behind me.

She doesn't pause or turn back despite being fully aware I'm there. I trail behind her into the office as she snags her cooler. Propping myself against the doorframe, I fold my arms, watching her. That raised eyebrow of hers greets me again, her silent code for "What the hell?" I love it.

"I came by to drop off your shirt. It's in the truck." My chin flicks toward the front, signaling outside.

"Oh." A flicker of surprise crosses her face, maybe a hint of disappointment too. It's a refreshing change, being the one springing surprises.

"Are you hungry?" I haven't budged from my post at the door. She's got room to pass by or stick around. "And just to be clear, I'm not asking you to go out. Just wondering if you're hungry."

She sizes me up, suspicion lacing her tone. "This feels like a setup, but I can't figure out the angle."

"Charlie and Sammy filled me in on your marathon day. I'm asking if you're hungry."

She exhales heavily, glancing at Cooper before meeting my eyes again. "Yes. I'm starving." It's like she's admitting to something monumental.

"I can help with that."

"See? A trap." She points an accusing finger my way. "How do you plan on helping me with that?" Her arms cross as she walks, borderline swaggers, stopping a couple of feet away. Her eyes, twin blue flames, searching and suspicious.

"You invite me up, like you would any friend." Her gaze sharpens. "I bring some of the groceries from my truck up and cook you dinner. If you're not up for that, I'll head home. Either way, you'll get your shirt back."

She scrutinizes me, her eyes wary. "Are you what you seem, Mr. Lochlan, or are you something else entirely?" She stands tall, like she's gearing up for a showdown, but I don't miss the slight tremor in her hands.

"Angel, I'm not sure what you're getting at, but I'm open to any questions you've got. I *am* going to need you to stop calling me that though. I'm trying really hard to behave, and that snotty tone mixed with that formal name really does something to me." She's a paradox, this woman—gentle yet fierce, sweet yet fiery.

"You can't talk like that *and* be my friend," she asserts, her voice firm, her shoulders square. This woman would fight to her last breath if she needed to, over the principle of just about anything.

"Let me cook for you, Parker," I offer, hoping to ease the tension.

Her arms cross protectively over her middle, her head tilting just barely to the side, and the line between her brows appears. I watch as she fights between confusion and surrender.

"If—and that's a big if—I let you cook, which I'm not even sure you're capable of, you have to stop with those comments. We reset: vet and animal owner. Deal?"

"No deal." Pushing away from the doorframe, I close the gap between us. "I can keep my thoughts to myself, but I've had your tears in my hand, Parker. I've had you in my arms. I've watched you fall asleep with your hand on my chest. I can't just go back. But," I find her eyes, "we don't have to dive into whatever this is. I stand by that. We can simply be friends. But this thing—" I gesture between us, "is there, Parker. And for the record, I can whip up a mean steak and sweet potatoes or a solid variety of breakfast foods."

The room is charged, almost crackling, with tension. I watch her weigh her options, her gaze probing mine for an answer. Her eyes soften, a single fleeting moment of quiet surrender before she speaks.

"I like steak. But you'll need to hunt down my pots and pans. And just so we're clear, I'm only agreeing to this because I'm hungry and tired." She lays a tentative hand on my stomach, pushing me back a step before walking past. She moves through the clinic and heads outside, straight for the truck.

"Where did you put the groceries? Do we need to refrigerate anything upstairs before it spoils?"

I hadn't considered that. "Passenger side. And yeah, putting some stuff in the fridge isn't a bad idea." I unlock the truck, and she swings open the passenger side door.

"Hold on a second," I interject as she reaches for the bags. There's no way I'm letting her haul the heavy stuff upstairs after her day. "Not everything in there is cold, and some of these bags are pretty heavy."

"You do know I'm not made of glass, right?"

"And you realize I'm not a *total* asshole, right?" I shoot back, matching her tone. I quickly sort the groceries, handing her the lighter bags while I shoulder the heavier ones. We move in a quiet rhythm, transporting the ingredients into her apartment.

CHAPTER 23

Dinner

PARKER

"Those boxes over there," I gesture to the four boxes perched atop my old, white-washed table. "They hold the last of the kitchen stuff. I've already unpacked the plates, cups, and most of the spices. They're in the cabinet next to the fridge, but the cutting boards and pots and pans remain captive in their cardboard prison. I need to take a quick shower and change, then I can help you find it all."

"No help needed. Go shower," he declares, not even glancing my way. He marches towards the boxes. He'll either sort it out, or I'll resort to my emergency stash of frozen dinners if he comes up short.

I retreat to my room, the soft patter of Cooper's paws echoing my steps. Glancing back before I cross the threshold, I'm captivated by the sight of him. There's an ease about him, a serene confidence that fills the room. His attire is a testament to his cowboy charm: scuffed boots, worn jeans that cling just right, and a dark-green T-shirt that complements his muscular frame. I catch a glimpse of a gold chain—a mystery hidden beneath his collar—that I've never noticed until now.

His hat is casually flipped backward, a silent nod to his style. His movements are deliberate, each motion precise as he sifts through a box. He concentrates on the contents, searching, evaluating—every bit the hunter.

Moving through the threshold, I focus on the task at hand. A shower is non-negotiable. My skin is stretched tight and parched from the endless assault of hand sanitizer. My makeup's probably a smeared mess now, and heaven only knows what's splattered on my scrubs.

I plug in my phone and give my monitoring app a swift glance before shedding my clothes and flinging them into a black hamper. Wrapping a towel around myself, I tiptoe across the hall to the bathroom. I crank up the shower to my favorite setting—blistering. The hot water cascading over my sore muscles is pure bliss.

As I move through my routine, I feel the tension melting away, muscle by muscle. I relish using all my cherished products, and I indulge a bit more than usual. "I'm not doing this for him," I assert to Cooper, who's sprawled in his usual spot beside the bathmat. "It's for my skin." I turn off the shower and step onto the mat. Glancing at Cooper, I quip, "Stop with the judgy eyes."

I wrap up my routine by scrubbing away the day's makeup—only a tad smudged around the eyes, thankfully. Score one for that brand. I comb through my damp hair, weaving it into two sleek French braids rather than drying it.

Crossing back to my bedroom, the aroma wafting from the kitchen makes my stomach rumble. The scent is promising; surely the taste won't be too bad. I throw on my most comfortable black leggings and an oversized T-shirt, then head for the laundry room.

I scoop up some dry dog food and supplements and fill Cooper's slow feeder bowl. Entering the kitchen, I catch Wyatt turning around, his expression one of surprise.

"What?" I challenge, having just checked my reflection—I know I don't look terrible.

"Nothing," he replies, pausing briefly.

"Clearly, it's not 'nothing.' What is it? Do I look terrible? You've seen me in the dead of night, once even splattered with afterbirth. Do I really look so awful fresh out of the shower?" I stride to the kitchen island, struggling to keep my pride intact and my insecurities at bay. I'm starving, so calling him a jackass doesn't bode well for eating whatever he's cooking.

"No, angel," he exhales with a hint of exasperation, "but I made a deal that I wouldn't say what's on my mind, and I'm sticking to my end."

"Oh." Now my curiosity is piqued, but I can't ask. Wyatt Lochlan can be such a frustrating man. He turns his attention back to the stove.

Turning my attention back to Cooper's dinner, I fetch a couple of containers from the cabinet. Wyatt's not asking for help, so he must be managing fine. I sprinkle Cooper's meal with freeze-dried blueberries—his treat—and a dash of pumpkin powder, then run it under warm water. It's only when I'm sealing the lids that I notice his gaze on me.

"Does he get that treatment every night?" he inquires, more curious than critical. Had it been criticism, I would've read him the riot act.

"It's crucial for him to have a balanced diet, especially when we're on call or in remote places. But I also insist on keeping his meals fresh and nutritious, so it's a bit of a balancing act. I jazz up his kibble with toppers and vital supplements to maintain his digestive health and overall fitness. He gets fresh food in the morning, like yogurt and eggs, and then more freeze-dried stuff and supplements in the evening. As a vet, it wouldn't be a great look if my service dog was overweight, misbehaved, or unhealthy."

He smirks at me, yet again.

"What, Wyatt?" I can't help but roll my eyes. "What's with that smirk?" I've never encountered a man whose gaze could say so much and yet so little.

"Nothing, just realizing you're not simple," he murmurs, the smile lingering, his eyes twinkling with humor.

"Is that supposed to be a bad thing? I don't know how to interpret that." I fold my arms across my chest.

"No, Parker, it's not bad—it's just true. There was a time when all I wanted was simplicity. Now, I'm starting to think that was where I went wrong. Doesn't seem to be what I want these days."

His words hang in the air, a silent admission made while holding my gaze. Unsure of how to respond to such a candid revelation, I opt for silence. I place Cooper's slow feeder in its stand, giving him the go-ahead to eat. Then, I retreat to a spot across the island, putting some distance between us.

"How much longer until dinner's ready?" I deftly change the subject.

"Sweet potatoes are baking. Given your half-hour shower, I'd say another 15 minutes or so. How do you like your steak cooked?"

"Medium rare. And as you've probably seen, there's a decent selection of drinks in the fridge." I move to open the fridge, ready to offer him a drink, but he stops me with a gesture. "What's up?"

"I got you a drink—actually, two." He nods to his side, and I circle around to find a glass of ice water and a bottle of root beer waiting.

"Thanks. I'll take the root beer. How about you? Want one?"

"No, I planned to take whatever you didn't. Water it is." He faces me as I lean against the island, opposite him. "So, you're into root beer and Dr. Pepper, you've got a dog, you're a vet, you prefer your steak medium rare, and by the book mountains around here, I'd say you're a reader."

"You've got me pretty much figured out. But it seems you've got the upper hand—I don't know as much about you."

"I can fix that. What do you want to know?" He turns back to the skillet, ready to sear the steaks.

I need to be careful or I'll end up answering the same questions I ask, so I think for a moment before jumping in. Favorite color?

Blue. Favorite food? Steak. Favorite sport? Rodeo. Second favorite? Football. I mirror his answers with my own. But as he serves our dinner, I brace myself for a confession.

"I actually don't know a thing about sports and," I inhale sharply, "I've never been to a rodeo." I blurt it out, then hide my face behind my hands. Silence falls. I feel his warm fingers gently prying mine away from my face, his eyes searching mine.

"You're a vet," he states, a serious edge to his voice. I nod in confirmation.

"You work on horses and cattle."

Again, I nod, but I don't break the silence.

"You live in Wyoming."

I give yet another nod.

"You're killing me, Parker." He groans, a sound of mock disbelief filling the space between us.

Unable to contain myself, I erupt into laughter that echoes off the walls of the quiet room.

CHAPTER 24

Disappointment

PARKER

"Honestly, it might sound absurd, but watching rodeos isn't a vet school requirement. I get the animal care part—how they might get hurt or need help—but I've never actually followed rodeo. School kept me swamped, and honestly, it never really kept my attention," I confess, laughter bubbling up as I try not to snicker at his utterly shocked expression. "Your face is priceless. Swear you won't tell anyone, Wyatt. Cowboys can be touchy about this stuff." I fight to keep a straight face.

"We'll have to ensure you've got the basics down if we're going to keep your secret safe from the cowboy world. You know the events, right?" His seriousness is endearing, and he's still holding onto my hands.

"I do. Bulls, bareback and saddle broncs, team roping, tie-down roping, steer wrestling, barrel racing," I recite.

"Good. That's a start. Do you know what folks like me do at rodeos?"

"You're the ones who bring in all the animals, aren't you?" His questions seem easy enough.

"Right. Stock contractors supply all the livestock, including the rough stock—the ones that buck. Now, what's the toughest event at a rodeo?"

Sucking in a breath, I'm about to guess when he cuts me off.

"Don't ever try to answer that, angel. Every cowboy will debate you till they're blue in the face over their event being the toughest."

"Understood," I acknowledge with a serious nod. "And which events did you compete in?"

"Professionally, I did team roping, tie-down roping, and steer wrestling. For kicks, I've ridden my share of broncs," he says with a wink, releasing my hands to retrieve the potatoes. The sudden chill on my skin that he had warmed leaves me feeling slightly disappointed.

"I can't wrap my head around that. I've never even ridden a horse, let alone considered mounting one that's trying its best to buck me off."

"Would you treat a dog that's known to bite?" He pulls out the potatoes.

"Of course, but you already know that. I'm having dinner with you, aren't I?" I tease.

"Ha, ha, ha. But my point stands. You're as much of an adrenaline junkie as any of us, just in a different kind of arena." He's got me there.

"Alright, enough easy questions. Hit me with a real rodeo challenge. I want to see if I can handle the pressure." I square my shoulders.

He chuckles. "How do they determine the winners in rough stock events?" He begins plating our food, his rhythm never breaking, even as we talk.

"That's simple. It's timing and scoring."

"And how is the score calculated?"

"I . . ." Pausing, I take a breath. "I don't actually know."

"Each rider and animal can earn points from two judges, assuming they stay on for eight seconds. The scores from both judges are combined. Highest total wins. Of course, there are ways to get disqualified, but we'll save that discussion for another time."

"Got it. I'm familiar with the common injuries animals sustain. I used to think steer wrestling would be the most distressing for me as a vet, but it turns out horses are more prone to injuries, whether in chutes and pens or during barrel racing, which is riskier for them than most people think." He hands me my plate, and I take it, grateful for the meal and the company.

"If you keep that up, you'll fool everyone. Except for me, of course—I'm in on your secret now."

"Don't use it against me," I warn him with a steady gaze, finding unexpected enjoyment in this playful banter, despite my initial apprehensions.

Without agreeing, he casts a glance at the dining table that's buried under boxes. "Where do we sit?"

"The couch is my go-to. My chairs are doubling as nightstands until I find some proper ones, and I don't have barstools for this island yet."

"Couch it is, then. Why haven't you got all your furniture?"

"To be honest, it's not been top of my list. I've gathered pieces I adore over time and all those are here. I have a thing for vintage finds, things with a story, so I'm patient until I find what I want." I settle into the couch corner, tucking my legs beneath me for a makeshift table. The first bite of steak elicits a moan of delight. When I glance up, his eyes are on me.

"Sorry," I murmur, a bit embarrassed. "It's good. And coming from the daughter of a chef, that means something."

"If you're aiming for friendship, maybe don't make noises like that. You're killing me."

"Sorry," I wince. Torturing him isn't exactly fair, but it does send a small thrill through me.

"What's with the scrubs? I've never seen Charlie or Sammy wear them." He asks while cutting his steak.

"A lot of vets opt for casual attire, but I've always been partial to scrubs. They're packed with pockets and save me the daily hassle of choosing what to wear. I've got a collection, mostly in darker shades, to hide the inevitable stains. Plus, I've got some festive ones for holidays like Christmas or Halloween. Not to mention it makes laundry a lot easier. Keeping my workwear separate from my personal clothes avoids any cross-contamination." I savor another mouthful of the delicious meal.

"Sounds reasonable," he replies, unfazed. We continue our meal in comfortable silence, both of us hungrier than I realized. Once we finish, I busily stack the plates and ferry them to the sink, setting up for a dishwasher load. He reignites the cast iron skillet, lending a hand with the dishes.

"Careful," he warns as he grabs the hot skillet, dousing it under running water to clean it himself. His familiarity with cast iron care doesn't surprise me. Seems like a thing a rancher would know.

"I'm going to take Cooper out for a quick walk," I announce, slipping into my most comfortable shoes.

"No rush," he responds casually, focused on the skillet.

Cooper and I step out onto the porch, and I watch him run around the grass. When we return, the dishes are neatly tucked away, and the skillet gleams on the stovetop. Wyatt's leaning casually against the sink, and I reclaim my spot across the small island.

"What's the deal with all the California team gear? The hat, the shirt I borrowed—did you live there at some point?"

"Borrowed means stole, right?" He shakes his head.

"Maybe." Laughing, I lean on the countertop.

"My mom's a California native. My dad, the cowboy, wasn't much for sports teams, but he'd often say he couldn't truly love anything my mom didn't adore. Guess that loyalty trickled down to us."

"Is that the origin of her nickname?" I inquire softly, not able to cover the hint of curiosity in my voice.

"No. In my mother's family, it's a tradition for the women to have floral names. My mom was actually named Sunflower. My little sister is Riot Rose. My grandmother was Lily, and the list goes on," he explains with a touch of pride.

"That's quite unique. Is that why you have the flowers on your ribs?

"Caught a glimpse, did you?" His eyes dance with a wicked gleam.

"It was dark, but I'm not blind," I retort playfully.

"Mmhmm," he hums, a soft smile in his voice, "yes, the women in my life are inked on the left side of my ribs, close to my heart."

"That's incredibly sweet." I feel warmth spread through me slowly.

"What about you? Any family traditions?"

I pause, gathering my thoughts. "To be honest, I don't really know. I never met my birth family. My mother left me at the hospital when I was born, and she overdosed a few years later. I was adopted at ten by Greg and Cameron. Being gay men, with unsupportive families, we made our own traditions, most of which revolve around food." I brace for a barrage of questions, but he simply gazes at me, his eyes narrowing slightly in thought.

"Which one's the chef?" he asks unexpectedly.

"Greg. Why?"

"Just making a mental note of who handles the knives profession-ally," he quips, and I can't help but laugh at his lighthearted response.

"Thank you, Parker," he says earnestly, his voice low.

"For what?"

"For sharing a part of yourself with me tonight. I sense that's not something you do lightly or often."

"You're welcome. Thank you for dinner. It was an upgrade from the frozen dinner I had planned." I appreciate the effort he put into the evening.

As I ponder our newfound friendship, a twinge of disappointment catches me off guard. Why does the idea of being friends suddenly feel so disheartening?

"Anytime," he replies, and then, takes a single step toward me.

He advances with deliberate slowness, and I can feel my heartbeat accelerating. His gaze is unwavering, fixed on mine, stirring that damn flutter in my belly. As he moves, the floorboards beneath his feet creak, each step punctuating the silence. It's a quiet dance, his boots against the wood, a gentle approach that seems to draw out time itself.

The kitchen island stands as a silent witness between us, its surface cleared of the dinner remnants. The only other sound is the faint hum of the refrigerator. It's a backdrop that fades as the distance between us closes, the world narrowing down to just the two of us. He approaches until we're standing face to face, and my heart steps up its rhythm.

"I told you I wouldn't share my thoughts, and I'm a man of my word, Parker. So I'm going to tell you what I want instead. I want to kiss you. If that's not what you want, tell me," he says, his voice a low murmur. Every instinct tells me to step back.

His hands rise to my face, thumbs tracing my cheekbones with the same tenderness as last night before he slides his hands back, cradling the nape of my neck. His eyes never leave mine as he leans in, tilting my chin upward with the gentlest pressure. I'm not sure what I anticipated, but when his lips finally meet mine—it isn't this.

I am irrevocably altered.

One kiss.

In that singular moment, it feels as though the very fabric of my reality shifts, a seismic realignment of my world's axis. A magnetic force takes over, and my hands, once lightly resting at my sides move to his hips, drawing him closer, obliterating any semblance of space between us. As he sinks in, his tongue runs over mine in light teasing strokes. A sound escapes, a soft note that seems foreign to my own ears. A feverish heat courses through me, and my skin blazes with a rapid flush.

The steady thrum of my pulse crescendos in my temples. His presence surrounds me as his hands glide from the nape of my neck down the length of my spine, igniting a trail of tingles in their wake. My hands find a home around his neck.

Suddenly, hands grip my thighs, lifting my legs. Automatically, I wrap them around his hips, locking my ankles at the small of his back.

The electricity of our connection hums just beneath my skin, his touch igniting wants long buried. Arching, desperate for the pressure of him, my hips roll. I'm acutely aware of the subtle vibrations emanating from his chest, an encouragement that resonates deep within my own being.

One of his hands slides up over my back, torturously slowly, until he tugs on the braid over my shoulder just enough to change the angle of the kiss, to take it deeper. The shift from teasing and tempting to worshipping pushes me beyond reason. Every instinct of self-preservation yearns to resist, yet I find the strength to do so utterly elusive. In a breathless moment of surrender, I yield to him entirely, to the electricity that exists between us, to the undeniable pull of shared gravity.

In this moment, all else fades into insignificance, eclipsed by the sheer liberation of being held in his arms. Kissing him is like stepping into a world where time ceases, where the noise of my mind is silenced. I lean back, giving myself over to the sensation, and he follows the curve of my spine with his hands.

His lips trace a path down my neck with reverence. Arriving in his own time at the intersection of my neck and shoulder, teasing nips and gentle kisses draw out a moan from deep within my chest. Though my hips continue to seek him, he seems content to hold me just far enough away to drive me to within an inch of reason.

He navigates the journey back up my neck with deliberate grazes of his teeth, a leisurely exploration that suggests he's in no rush to end this moment. Wyatt's teeth catch my bottom lip gently, a promise of passion laced with the softest touch, before he returns to my lips with a devotion that feels like he's committed to memorizing every contour.

His kiss is a study in contrasts—patient yet insistent, tender yet unyielding. He embodies a paradox that I can't unravel, a tornado that engulfs me with its intensity. Gradually, he retreats, our foreheads a whisper apart, sharing a single space of breath.

"If I keep kissing you," he whispers against my lips in between light soft kisses, "I'm going to haul you back in that room and act out every thought I promised not to say out loud."

His hands rest on my hips, squeezing lightly before urging me to unfold my legs. As my feet find the floor, I keep my hands clasped around his neck. Without really thinking about it, my fingers trace the fade at the nape of his neck. He hums a sound of contentment, his eyes fluttering shut.

His touch ascends from my hips, fingers dancing up my ribs in a slow caress that tempts me to cast aside all reason. But that very impulse, the look on his face, the buzz in my skin, jolts me back to reality, a surge of anxiety chilling my veins.

"We can't do this. It's too complicated, Wyatt." The protest is a battle cry against my own longing. My body screams for me to relent. My skin craves the warmth of his touch. My heart races in response to his intense gaze. My breath quickens, keeping time with the sudden pounding in my chest as I take two steps backward.

"It's not about can or can't, and yes, we could—but not tonight," he insists with a tranquility that stands in opposition to my inner turmoil. "I'm serious about being your friend, Parker. Tonight, that means telling you to get some rest."

"You don't know me, Wyatt. You speak as if this is some kind of eventuality, but that's not true. There are things about me you don't know, reasons why we can't, why this is impossible. Reasons I can't just say 'yes.' You don't know them," I gasp out, spinning away from him. A thunderstorm of frustration swirls within me. Anxiety tightens its grip. My gut coils like a relentless knot. My heart isn't just racing—it's sprinting, and the tingling in my hands isn't from the kiss—it's panic.

Air becomes elusive, each attempt to inhale more futile than the last. I'm suffocating from lack of air. My vision blurs at the edges, and reality smudges into obscurity. A part of me is acutely aware of this descent, yet it's beyond my control. It's always beyond my control.

In the swirl of chaos, a pair of dark chocolate brown eyes appear before me.

CHAPTER 25

Tears

WYATT

"Breathe," I command, my voice leaving her no room to argue. I draw her close, holding her tight against my chest. My hand cradles the back of her neck, the other wrapped firmly around her waist. She inhales sharply, her fingers clutching at my shirt, unwittingly pulling me in even tighter.

"Again," I instruct, demanding her body's obedience. Beneath my palm, her heartbeat is frenzied. Parker starts counting backward from one hundred by fours, her voice the only sound in the silence. I resist the urge to comfort; instead, I stand absolutely still, holding her against me, silently offering whatever she needs to find a sense of calm.

"I'm sorry," she whispers into my chest as her breaths begin to steady. I ease my hold ever so slightly.

"I'm the one who's sorry, Parker," I insist, regret like bile burning in my throat. Swiftly, I tilt her face up to meet my gaze. "I never meant to pressure you or make you uncomfortable—"

"No. No. No. It's not you," she cuts me off, exhaling deeply as she searches my eyes. "It's just . . . I'm not simple, Wyatt. I will never be simple on even the most basic of levels."

"I'm not interested in simple, remember?" I remind her gently, pressing kisses to her tear-streaked cheeks. The sight of her tears is enough to drive me through hellfire for her sake. "If I am the source of any of this, tell me. If my kiss brought this on, I apologize, Parker. Just say the word, and I'll do whatever it takes to fix it."

"You didn't cause this, not the way you think," she begins, her voice a fragile thread in the thick air of the room. "I just . . . " She falters, her struggle for words as visible as the tremble in her hands. "There are things I can't share with you. Can you accept that? Can you accept me and not push for answers?" Her eyes, wide and imploring, search mine for understanding.

"Are you in trouble? Did someone hurt you?" I ask, my muscles coiling on instinct. It doesn't matter what her role is in my life—friend, something more, or just my vet—no one will get away with harming her.

"No, it's not like that," she interjects. "I'm not in trouble," she assures me, but her careful choice of words suggests she's holding back.

"I find that hard to believe when a kiss, a pretty damn incredible one, just caused you to have a panic attack," I counter, my voice soft but firm.

"Your knack for reading me is alarming, Wyatt." She steps back, putting distance between us. "No one is hurting me now. It's been a while since I've been close to anyone," she admits, her cheeks coloring with the confession.

"Okay." The puzzle of Parker grows more complex with each word she utters.

"It's complicated," she says, her arms wrapping around her middle.

"I'll make you a deal," I suggest, hoping my playful smirk will bring some lightness to her eyes.

"Another deal?"

"Yes. If I ask a question you don't want to answer, just say 'pass,' and I won't press you on it." My offer hangs in the air, a bridge over the waters of her secrets.

"I get to pass, no questions asked? You want a chance at this that badly?" She attempts a laugh, but it's hollow, tinged with the uncertainty of her emotions.

"It's not about wanting a chance. It's about respecting you enough to listen. It's also about wanting to figure out what *this* is." I gesture to the space between us. "This thing, it's something. It makes me want to feed you and fight with you, kiss you, and challenge you and whatever we find in between. Despite the regularity with which I piss you off and have to apologize, I like you. I want to see what this could be if you do too." The words are my raw truth, offered to her without a filter to decide how she feels.

"Do I need to decide right now?" Her question hangs in the air, delicate as a spider's web.

I close the distance between us, drawn to her, my knuckles gently coaxing her chin upward. Her eyes, vast oceans of blue, pull me in, and I'm drowning in their depths, searching for a sign of her thoughts.

"No. But I'll be here when you do decide." I lean down, our lips meeting in a kiss meant to seal that promise. "Goodnight, Parker." I seal the farewell with another kiss, brief but brimming with intention, then I turn and step out.

From the truck, I catch her gaze at the window. I wink, and she shakes her head, a reluctant smile playing on her lips, and then she's gone from view. The thought of her surprise when she discovers the fridge's contents brings a smile to my face. I drive into the night, the image of her smile etched in my mind, reveling in the feel of her in my arms and the softness of her lips. Above it all lies the mystery of whatever she's running from.

CHAPTER 26

Wildflowers

PARKER

As consciousness seeps in, the first coherent thought that forms is a bewildered, 'What the hell have I gotten myself into?' It's been less than a month, and here I am, caught in a whirlwind of unexpected dinners and heartfelt declarations. Last night, after Wyatt left, it dawned on me—he hadn't taken his things from the fridge. When I opened it, ready to text him, I discovered he'd replenished all the snacks I keep in my cooler, right down to the Dr. Pepper.

A note lay there, casual yet sweet.

Thought you could use a re-stock. —Wyatt

Charm isn't a foreign concept; I've dealt with charm before. Yet Wyatt's brand of charm disarms me because it doesn't feel like an act. It's not the kind of charm used as a weapon or a tool of control. Wyatt offers me exits, respects my choices, and listens to me. His presence is a constant, his intentions always clear, his desires openly stated.

It's a blend of qualities that leaves me both unsettled and drawn to him—terror and intrigue in equal measure.

"Enough, Parker. No more overthinking about Wyatt," I chide myself, rubbing the sleep from my eyes and flinging the blankets aside. "Outside, Cooper." The dog ambles over, eager for his ritual morning affection, and my lips curve into a smile at our comforting routine. Rising, I stride to the door, ready to start the day. As I swing it open, I'm rooted to the spot, stopped cold by the sight that greets me.

Flowers.

A vibrant burst of color occupies the small porch, an unexpected gift at nine in the morning. They must have been dropped off while I was asleep. These aren't the clichéd red roses of a dozen courtships; they're a sprawling bouquet of wildflowers. Wyatt's not one for the ordinary, and he's proving it once again. How could he have known that wildflowers are my secret love? We hadn't spoken of my favorites, only the flowers inked on his skin.

As I gather the bouquet and let Cooper out, I'm transfixed by the wild array before me. My heart has always found a home among wildflowers. They were one of the elements of Wyoming that lured me here.

I place the mason jar, with its kaleidoscope of colors and shapes, at the center of the island. Cooper's paws patter back inside, and I secure the door behind him, my gaze returning to the flowers. A smile blooms across my face, as natural and wide as the plains outside.

The note, though—that's what truly unravels me. I feel myself melting like butter on a hot plate. It's a simple slip of paper, echoing a style that's all Wyatt.

Good morning.—W

It's straightforward, unassuming, yet it sends warmth cascading through me. It's not flirtatious, not sly, or pushy. It's just there. And somehow, that's everything. I reach for my phone, thumbing through to my messages with Cami.

I need backup. We need to talk soon.
Are you free? Video chat?

Explain. Do I need to bury a body?
You know I will.

If you were going to do that,
probably shouldn't put that in text.

Bitch, you can't convict without a body
– everyone knows that.

hahaha you're ridiculous

But you love me. 🖤
Can't video but can chat.
Tell me everything.

You're right about that. And no, no
bodies but remember Wyatt? We
sort of had dinner. Well he made
me dinner. Then we kissed.

STTOOOPPPP! I need every detail.
Now! It was amazing, wasn't it?

. . .

oh no, it was bad? that would suck for women everywhere.

it was incredible, felt like the earth-spinning incredible.

I knew it! So, what's the big deal?

He restocked my fridge with snacks from my cooler, and I opened my door to wildflowers this morning.

O.M.G. Please tell me you are not joking. Whomever raised this man should be thanked.

What do I do?

If there is even a small chance this guy could be good for you—take it Parks.

If I pursue this, but don't tell him about her, does that make me terrible?

You are without a single doubt the strongest, kindest, most incredible woman I've ever known. You could never be terrible. If he thinks you are at any point, there's a lot of land in Wyoming to bury a body. Greg will help.

You can let the walls down a little. I'm not saying tell him, but don't hold back on something that could make you happy. You deserve happy. Your V basically has cobwebs Parks. Dust that thing out and see if it still works.

You did not just say that?!

If the man kisses that well, I imagine he knows exactly how to do other things very well 😏🥒🐱💦

You're crazy, you know that?

Maybe, but I'm right.
Now, I want to see the flowers.

<IMAGE>

What does the note say?

<IMAGE>

I'm going to sign off. I hate you. I'll talk to you later.

Hate you too! Tell him I said hi!
TELL GREG.

I'm not answering her on that. I open my text chain with Wyatt.

PARKER

Thank you.

WYATT

YW. What's your plan for your day off?

Honestly?

Yes.

There are a million things to do but not sure what to tackle first.

What's on the list?

How about a deal? I'll tell you what's on my list if you tell me why you gave me wildflowers.

World-class flirting, Parker.

My head sinks back into the couch cushions as I let out a sigh. There's no taking back that moment. "I'm flirting about as well as an awkward thirteen-year-old," I confess to my dog, who seems more interested in his morning scratches than my love life. "This might just top the list of bad ideas, second only to that tequila-fueled birthday disaster with Cami." My phone's vibration interrupts my self-deprecation, and I see Wyatt's name flashing on the screen.

"Hello?" My voice betrays my confusion, making me sound like I've never used a phone before.

His laughter filters through the line. "You asked a question. Seemed easier to answer this way."

"Oh." I facepalm at my own awkwardness.

"Other flowers seem too fragile," he says, his voice soft yet certain. "Pretty but not strong. Wildflowers in Wyoming, though, they're survivors. They endure, no matter what the conditions. What I've learned about you thus far tells me they're the only flowers worthy of you."

His words leave me speechless, a rare occurrence. Warmth spreads through me; I'm torn between tears and laughter.

"Flowers make you speechless. Noted," he teases, and I can almost see the smirk on his face.

"No, not speechless. Just . . . " I trail off, still at a loss for words.

He waits patiently before prompting me again. "Just what, Parker?"

"I don't know what to say." I groan, then bury my face in my hands. I'm trying not to be embarrassed that flowers have turned me into a mushy pile of goo. "Honestly, my badass woman card is in jeopardy right now."

"Never." His voice is full of laughter, and I can imagine exactly what his smile looks like, wrinkling the edges of his eyes.

"Now what?"

"I believe you owe me a list of things you need to do today, according to your deal." Wyatt's voice pulls me back to the mundane and away from the edge of overthinking.

"It's just a normal list—groceries, bills, food prep for the week, working out. Hardly as impressive as your explanation. I think I got the better end of the deal." I can't help but wonder if I'm getting worse at this flirting thing.

"Nah. I'm still coming out ahead. You answered the phone." His confidence is infectious.

"Okay, cowboy," I tease, my cheeks aching from the smile I can't hide. "That charm works on everyone, doesn't it?"

"I don't know what you're talking about." The smirk in his voice is unmistakable. "How about this? Figure out what you can get done by say four, then let me come pick you up."

"I don't know if I'm comfortable going on a date in public," I confess, my honesty my only real shield at this point. "I just got here. I don't want to be part of the town gossip. I also haven't scoped out what places are comfortable with Cooper, and I hate surprising places with him because people can get upset and I don't—"

"Who said I was asking you on a date?"

"If it isn't a date, what is it?" I ask hesitantly.

"Dinner, just in a different location, not in town."

I exhale as my mind races back to Cami's words.

"Okay," I whisper, "Four o'clock. Cooper and I will be ready." I bit my lip, nerves settling in.

"Good girl."

The words send a shiver down my spine, and I hum involuntarily. Shit.

"Goodbye," I blurt out, ending the call immediately, praying he didn't hear me.

WYATT

I heard that.

CHAPTER 27

Lectures

PARKER

"I can't avoid this conversation any longer, Cooper." Cooper shows not a single ounce of empathy. I grab the phone and call Greg. With the time difference, it's one o'clock, and he should be between services. He answers immediately, just like always.

"Hello, Snow. How's the day off?"

"Productive so far. I've finished all my grocery shopping and laundry, now I'm just cleaning the apartment. What about you?"

"I found some amazing strawberries this morning, so I'm working on a special dish with them today."

"That sounds yummy." A minute of silence follows.

"Parker," Dad begins, "what's going on?" I sense the tension in his voice and quickly interject.

"I've been hiding something from you. You might feel the urge to fly out to Wyoming, but please don't. I'm an adult, and everything will be alright," I assert confidently.

"Okay, start from the beginning."

And so, I recount the story. I share the details about the three foals that I omitted initially, then our dinner, and finally, the kiss, and subsequent panic attack. I carefully skip the more intimate details; those are not for my father. He's my dad, not my best friend. I finish by telling him about the flowers and phone call this morning.

"What kind of flowers?" he asks, his calmness surprising.

"Wildflowers. He said they're the only ones tough enough to be worthy of me."

"I hate him," he declares, his voice flat and threatening, yet I can detect the sarcasm woven through it.

"Dad," I chide him playfully.

"Firstly, let's make this clear: we don't keep secrets. It's you and me, Snow. We're in this together, even through the worst. Remember that," he instructs, taking a deep breath. "Secondly, I like that you sound happy when you talk about him. You haven't sounded happy in awhile."

Tears stream down my face, silent but unstoppable, as I shudder, drawing in a shaky breath and wiping my face.

"Talk to me about the tears, Parker," he urges, always so in tune with my emotions, especially when they threaten to overwhelm.

"Dad, what if I'm incapable of love? What if I'm broken like my mother was?" I confess to one of my deepest fears, the ones I can only entrust to him. "What if this turns into another disaster like five years ago? What if what I am isn't enough?" I sniffle, dabbing at my face with my shirt sleeve.

"Parker," he says, using his lecturing tone. "No amount of love from me can convince you that what you perceive as damaged, I see as strong. What you view as broken, I consider healed. I made peace years ago with the idea that I couldn't fight your battles with loss, no matter how desperately I wish I could. I can't undo what happened five years ago or when you were born, and neither can you. None of it was your fault. So, when will you stop punishing yourself for it, sweetheart?"

"I'm not trying to," I insist.

Dad's voice, always a source of comfort, takes on a reflective tone. "You know, I remember that first year after we adopted you. We kept triggering all your fears and trauma. We felt so guilty." I feel my old wounds ache and catch my breath, but I don't want to interrupt. "I asked the therapist if we would ever stop feeling like the worst parents. She laughed. She said the person who thinks the worst of us is always us."

"You're not, you know? You and Cam were and are the best."

"I don't know about the best, but I know I've never given you anything less than my best. And you shouldn't settle for less than someone's best either. I hope you'll learn to accept your own best too. If this is an opportunity for you to do that, then good. Keep your boundaries. Come to think of it, don't do anything you don't want to."

"I won't." My laughter mixes with my tears, the depth of our conversation catching me off guard.

"Then take this for what it is, a chance to figure out what you want, then go get it. That's always worked for you in every aspect of your life. It won't fail you now." There's a familiar squeeze in my heart before it lightens.

"What are you going to do?"

"I'll start by looking him up on the internet," he says with a chuckle, deepening his voice to feign menace.

"Have you decided to visit sooner than we planned?" I tease him half-heartedly.

"Absolutely," he replies automatically.

"Are you going to grill him when you get here?"

"Without hesitation," he answers, the playful banter continuing between us.

"Will you tell me if you think I'm making a mistake?" My words tumbled out in a rush. "I didn't see it until it was too late. You have to promise to tell me if I'm wrong or just cursed to make bad choices."

"You're not cursed." Greg's voice is steady and sure. "But if it makes you feel better, I'll certainly let you know if I think he's no good. Now, the next question—our question," he prompts me.

"Do you love me?" This question has sealed every difficult conversation we've had since I was adopted. It began as a genuine inquiry, one I posed daily for nearly a year, then less frequently over time. Eventually, it evolved into a cherished tradition, a token of love, rather than a question of doubt.

"More than my own life, Snow. Always," he affirms.

"I love you too," I whisper back, my decision made. "Okay," I take a quick cleansing breath, "I need to finish cleaning and then get ready for my first not-date in years."

"I expect a report from you tomorrow." A hint of sternness tinges his voice.

"Yes, sir," I tease, ending the call and glancing down at Cooper.

"We handled that better than I imagined. I bet he's already googling Wyatt. Let's finish up our housework, then get ready. You need a bath, and I'll need one after you." I look down at Cooper who's already looking at me expectantly.

Just then, my phone rings, the same unfamiliar number as before. Again, I reject the call. No message follows. If it's someone I know, they'll follow up with a text. Shrugging, I block the number, then rub my hands together, ready to tackle the next task.

CHAPTER 28

Wranglers

PARKER

I've checked off every item on my list with surprising speed. I've managed to prepare for the week, wash two loads of laundry, balance my bank account, clean the bathroom, and even call Greg—all with enough time left to shower and choose an outfit.

"I wasn't hurrying," I assert to Cooper. "I was being efficient."

Everything has been running like clockwork, until now.

Standing in my bedroom, wrapped in a towel, I am utterly baffled by what to wear. "What if we end up somewhere fancy and I'm underdressed in jeans and sneakers? Or what if I overdress and we end up somewhere laid-back? This is ridiculous," I grumble. Cooper merely shakes off and settles into his bed, slightly miffed from his bath but thankfully not cowering underneath the bed.

This indecision is precisely why I avoid dating. Okay, maybe what to wear isn't the reason I avoid dating. I grab my phone and initiate a video call. Cami picks up instantly, her hands gesturing for me to wait. I watch as she attaches the external processor on her cochlear implant.

"Alright, girl," Cami speaks up, her hands mirroring her words. "Spill it. Why are you standing there in a towel?"

"He's on his way, and I have no clue what to wear," I admit to Cami, holding my towel in place. "Also, I've already called Greg, so no need for you to tattle."

"WOMAN!" Cami exclaims, her fingers spelling out the word for emphasis, her tone and expression underscoring the urgency. "Tell me everything."

"Here's the synopsis: I texted him to express my gratitude for the flowers and he called and we talked and somehow I ended up agreeing to be picked up tonight. It's a non-date, and we're going to eat somewhere, but not in town. Then, I called Greg and spilled the beans."

"We really need to work on your flirting skills," she chides, her voice rich with amusement, "especially if you managed to talk the man *out* of a proper date." Her statement, wrapped in the warmth of friendly teasing, pulls a laugh from deep within me.

"Okay, well right now, he's going to be here in forty-five minutes, and I'm naked."

"That could work. Go with naked." She deadpans, her expression as flat as her voice, but her eyes sparkle with mischief.

"Cami," I give her my most serious expression.

"Fine, fine," she relents. "Where's that cute summer dress you bought, the dark navy one?"

I rummage through a box and find the mid-length navy blue linen dress. "It's all wrinkled, and I can't find my iron."

"No worries," Cami advises. "Just dampen it slightly and toss it in the dryer on low for about ten minutes. While it's in there, grab your denim jacket. Oh, and do you still have those tan cowboy boots we picked up in Dallas?"

"Yes, I do," I reply, excited about the outfit coming together. "What about jewelry? It's not a date, so I don't want to overdo it."

Cami rolls her eyes at me and then exhales sharply. "Fine. No jewelry for your non-date. Just let that creamy fabulous skin do its job." She wiggles her eyebrows at me.

"Thanks, Cami." I sign *I love you* with one hand and Cami signs it back and offers a smile. I end the call quickly. I have just enough time to pull this off. I rummage for my jacket, searching through two more boxes to find the boots.

I throw the damp dress into the dryer and then race through my skincare routine, choosing tinted moisturizer, some mascara, and a neutral lip. I'm not applying date makeup because it's not a date. Besides, he's seen me covered in worse.

As soon as I finish, the dryer dings. I yank the dress out and dash back to the bedroom. Unwrapping my towel I reach for my favorite black bra. Despite my normal, practical, comfortable wardrobe, I do own a few things that could be deemed as sexy. Then, definitely not because he may see it, I choose high cut black lace underwear.

The dress feels like a second skin, cool and smooth as it slides over my body. The fabric clings gently, a whisper against my flesh, as if it's been tailor-made for this very moment.

Cooper remains silent about the evening's activities. He's sprawled across the rug, his head resting on his paws, watching me with those big, soulful eyes that seem to understand far more than they should. Every so often, his tail thumps against the floor, a soft drumbeat in the background, as if he's cheering me on.

Right as I finish getting ready, I hear a knock at the door.

I glance at my phone and turn to Cooper, his white fur catching the afternoon light. "The man is punctual, bonus points for that." I stride out of the bathroom, the boots hugging my feet with a familiar snugness. I snatch up my jacket as I head for the door. Once there, I pause to take a deep breath and fill my lungs with the subtle scent of vanilla from the nearby diffuser.

I can do this. This is easy.

Swinging the door open, a wave of anticipation washes over me, the same intoxicating pull in my stomach from last night. This man must be sent from the god of cowboys.

He stands there, sans baseball cap, his hair styled to casual perfection. His face, a canvas of joy, is open and inviting. As my eyes trail down, I take in the crisp white button-down shirt, the fabric taut over his broad shoulders, sleeves cuffed and rolled up to reveal forearms true to his life's work, corded and muscled. His tanned skin contrasts with the starched whiteness of his shirt, and I find myself unexpectedly captivated by the sight.

Continuing my gaze down, I can't help but admire how his jeans conform to his legs, the denim new, fitted, and hinting at the power beneath the fabric. I mentally applaud Wrangler for crafting jeans that so perfectly complement a man's form. He is perfection, down to the tips of the cowboy boots.

"Hello, Parker," he says slowly, each syllable a husky note that resonates through me, causing an involuntary shiver. I snap my head up to meet his gaze, finding myself lost for a moment in its depth.

"Sorry. Just trying to see if what I picked to wear matches the activity based on what you're wearing." I stumble through the words.

"You're a terrible liar. Anyone ever told you that?" His smile, with those irresistible dimples, delights me. He leans in, and his kiss on my cheek sends a wave of his now familiar leather-and-cedar scent washing over me. It's an odd combination, yet so distinctly him. My throat tightens as a parched sensation overtakes my mouth.

"The dress works perfectly," he declares, stepping back as if to get a better look at me. *Is this a silent duel of gazes?* He doesn't break eye contact, but his smile silently challenges me.

"I hate that smile—it's more of a smirk, like you know something I don't," I retort. My words carry no bite, only a bubbling frustration that I can't quite tamp down.

"You look beautiful. I would have started with that if you hadn't opened the door and immediately started drooling over me."

"I thought you weren't going to tell me what was in your head anymore?" I lean back and cross my arms, considering the bold move of shutting the door in his face, if only to avoid the throbbing in my core.

"That's not what's in my head. That's an observation of our current situation. If I were to tell you what's in my head, you'd hear about how your eyes haunt every dream I have. You'd hear about how that vanilla and cinnamon scent you wear drives me crazy. But I'm not talking about what's in my head. Instead, I'm going to say you look gorgeous, and what you're wearing is perfect. Are you ready to go?"

I glance at Cooper, my heart pounding like a drum against my ribs. His words freeze my thoughts, as a telltale warmth crawls up my neck, a blush I feel as it creeps across my face.

"Yes." I drop my arms and turn away from him, walking to the island to gather my purse and Cooper's leash, buying time to calm my racing heart.

"No cooler?" He sounds genuinely puzzled.

At last, I've managed to surprise him. It's about time.

"Oh, this bag is a cooler, just a cuter one."

"You're bringing the cute cooler? You do realize this isn't a date, right?" His voice is teasing, and I know it, but my muscles tense all the same; my hand freezes on the bag, as uncertainty floods through me. What am I doing? Why am I doing this? Have I lost my damn mind?

"Hey." His voice is a gentle murmur, like the soft rustle of leaves in the fall. I hear his footsteps approach, and I'm rooted to the spot. I can feel Wyatt's warm, inviting heat as he stops at my back. His hands land on my hips lightly before he spins me around to face him. His palms rest on my lower back, not pulling me closer, but not severing the connection either.

"Don't shut me out, Parker." As I look up at him, it's disconcerting how his intense gaze pierces my soul.

"I'm not a risk-taker, Wyatt. I hate conflict. I'm not impulsive and I . . . you . . . you feel like a risk laced with a hefty dose of chaos." I avoid his gaze, choosing instead to focus on the intricate pattern of the rug beneath our feet.

"Maybe so." He plants a kiss on my head, a soft touch that sends a ripple of comfort through me, my eyes closing involuntarily. "But you're not the only one risking something. I'm right here with you."

I tilt my head back and our eyes meet. "Why aren't you as nervous as I am?"

He sweeps my hair back and tucks it behind my ear, "In my profession, nerves mean you're after something that matters. The real question is whether you want it enough to push past being nervous. What if it turns out to be the best thing that's ever happened?"

"That's surprisingly logical," I whisper.

"I'm a pretty logical guy." He steps away, dropping his hands from my back, and the loss of his warmth is immediate, like the sun disappearing behind a cloud. He extends his hand in offering. "What's it going to be?"

Gazing into his eyes, I place my hand in his. "Okay." The word is barely audible, falling from my lips like a whisper or perhaps a prayer—I can't quite tell.

He remains silent, but his fingers weave through mine with a firm, warm grip. He pivots, leading me to the door. I pull out my keys, the metal cool against my palm. He steps confidently ahead of me at the stairs, placing the hand he's holding onto his shoulder as we descend.

"Is this a door thing?" Curiosity laces my voice.

"What?" He stops, his gaze meeting mine over his shoulder, a flicker of amusement in his eyes.

"This." I lift our intertwined hands, the motion drawing a subtle arc in the air. "You're holding my hand as we go down the stairs."

"Ah," a half-smile plays on his lips. He shrugs casually. "I suppose it's similar to a door thing."

"What's the premise?"

He resumes our descent, each step deliberate. "Safety, which has the added benefit of letting me hold your hand."

I shake my head, a snort escaping me. "It's neither practical nor logical. What if we were both carrying something heavy?"

"I'd still be in front, to catch you if you slip. Same reason I'm behind you on the way up, just in case."

As we reach the bottom, he adjusts again, so he's holding my hand. He leads me to the passenger side of his truck, opening the back for Cooper, then the front for me. I climb in, which is a bit awkward given the dress. He takes advantage and leans over to buckle me in himself. I can't figure him out. Wyatt isn't like anyone else, and yet he feels familiar. As he closes the door and makes his way to the driver's side, I just stare.

To break the silence, I go with the safest question I can think of, "Do I get to know where we're going?"

"Since it's not a date," he says while backing out, "I figured that means I can't take you anywhere alone, or in public, so the safest thing to do was take you to family dinner. We're headed to the ranch."

CHAPTER 29

Safety

WYATT

She's been silent, her gaze fixed on the passing scenery, quiet contemplation in her eyes. She doesn't seem frozen or uncomfortable, just lost in thought. The landscape rolls by, the bright afternoon sun bearing down, the visor in the truck casting a shadow across her face.

I can sense there's something she's holding back, a pain just beneath the surface, something that's turned the confident, dancing surgeon not afraid to call me an asshole into the panicked woman from last night. It's a contradiction. The confident side of her ignites a wildness in me, but her vulnerability captivates me and has claimed a part of me I didn't know was up for grabs. There's a craving that comes alive whenever she's near; it's an urge that's hard to ignore.

Her voice cuts through the soft hum of the engine. "It's beautiful here. That was the first thing I noticed when I drove through half the state to get here. It's like every view could grace the cover of National Geographic." She turns to face me, her stunning blue eyes bright and searching. "Do you ever get used to it?"

"Not if you're smart," I reply.

"What do you mean?" Her brows knit together in that familiar expression of confusion and curiosity, a small line forming between her eyes.

"This land isn't just a backdrop. It's a living, breathing thing. It's as beautiful as it is brutal. When you ranch here, you learn to respect it, to remember that your very existence hinges on its whims. If you ever lose that sense of respect, you'll find yourself consumed by it, burned out, and left with nothing."

"That's an interesting perspective." Her tone suggests she's mulling over my words, trying to gauge their truth. It's incredibly sexy to watch her mind work.

"Tell me about family dinner," she pivots, swiveling in her seat to face me more directly.

"It's dinner, with family," I quip, the sarcasm hitting its mark when she rolls her eyes in response.

"I got that much, smartass. Who's in the family?" she retorts.

The spark in her blue eyes, coupled with that playful, sassy tone and her smile, sends a surge of desire and longing through me. "My dad, whom you've met, and my two brothers, Statler and Lincoln. We make it a point to have dinner together once a week."

"That's nice. What do Statler and Lincoln do? Are they involved with the ranch too? Where's your sister?"

"Riot's training in Texas, she's an elite gymnast. Statler's a retired special forces guy. These days, he spends most of his time working with the horses. He's got a real knack for it and decided to come back home to put it to good use after he was discharged a few years back. Lincoln, well, he helps out on the ranch occasionally, but only when we're short-handed or when I make him. He's a lawyer by trade."

As I veer off the main highway onto the ranch road, her demeanor shifts, and she goes completely still. "You seem a bit tense all of a sudden. Is there something on your mind?"

"Nope." Her voice is quick, distant, almost robotic. "I'm fine."

"Fine," I echo her, steering the truck into the driveway and circling towards the garage before shifting into park. As she reaches for the handle, I flick the lock in place. She turns those blue eyes towards me, a storm brewing within them. "Someone once told me that a smart man knows 'fine' never actually means fine and a good man does whatever it takes to fix it."

"Who told you that?" Her anger is noticeable in her eyes, yet her voice remains measured.

"My mother," I confess softly. Yielding to the impulse, I reach across the console and pick up her hand. She doesn't withdraw it, simply watches me. "If this situation makes you uncomfortable, we can leave right now and head wherever you want."

"What if I'm not sure whether I'm uncomfortable yet?" She fixates on our now interlocked hands.

"I'll make you a deal. The moment you feel uncomfortable with anything or anyone at any point, just say the word, and we'll leave, no questions asked."

Her eyes meet mine, and I can see the wheels turning in her head, the suspicion.

"You'd really walk out on your family dinner, no explanation, just because I asked?" Skepticism tinges her voice.

"Yes." She relaxes slightly at hearing my response, a subtle nod and a quiet exhale betraying the breath she's been holding.

"What's the word?" Her gaze drops back to our hands, and I can't resist the urge to run my thumb over her knuckles.

"The word?"

"What is it with us and this routine? You said to say the word—what should it be?" she presses, a hint of amusement now mingling with her frustration.

"You want a safe word, angel?" I tease her, unable to help myself. It's a bit childish, sure, but the way she fights with me is too fun to resist.

"Get your mind out of the gutter, Wyatt." She rolls her eyes, but her voice regains its warmth and confidence. God, I love how my name sounds coming from her.

"It's a side effect of being around you," I say with a smirk, the one she claims to despise—or does she? That part's still a mystery. "Let's go with forty-two."

"Why forty-two? Is that some weird sex thing?" She withdraws her hand from mine and crosses her arms, her expression as grave as if she's facing a life-or-death situation. I try to stifle my laughter, but it comes out as a cough instead. Leaning back, I run my hands over my face, trying to compose myself.

"Baby," I groan, "I'm going to need you not to mention sex again if you want to keep my mind off it."

"Sorry." She doesn't sound sorry at all, though her cheeks are flushing. The corners of her mouth twitch upward, just like earlier when I caught her staring.

"Ronnie Lott was my all-time favorite football player. Can you guess his position?"

"What?" She's cautious, her eyes narrowing slightly. She finally relaxes her arms, letting down her guard just a bit.

"Safety."

She nods in acknowledgment. "Okay." Then she reaches for the truck door, pressing the unlock button. I quickly lock it again. She unlocks it; I lock it once more. This goes on until she's visibly frustrated.

"Wyatt," she says sharply, her irritation clear. "Let me out of the truck."

"I will. But I'm coming around to open the door, and you're not moving until I do," I declare, my voice steady despite the quickening thump in my chest.

"I'm not weak or powerless. I can open the door myself."

"I know," I respond, leaning closer, the scent of her skin filling my senses. My fingers graze her cheek, and she doesn't pull away. Emboldened, I thread my fingers through her hair, the strands slipping through like threads of silk, even better than my fantasies. "When I'm here, I'd like you to let me. It's not about doubting your strength or ability. It's my way of giving back a little of what you offer me by simply being here, trusting me with your time. Trust doesn't come easy to you, I get that. And I want to be someone you trust, Parker. I accept you as you are, and I hope you can learn to accept this part of me too."

Our eyes meet, and I see the flicker of a flame in hers, defiance and a hint of yielding just beneath. She leans back, her touch on my hand a silent plea, and I release her immediately.

"I can appreciate that, but—"

"Baby," I exhale, the word a mixture of exasperation and affection. "You need to know that being cared for, respected, and having someone want to do things for you, protect you, and please you—those should be your baseline expectations from any man. Including me. Don't lower your standards to assert your independence. Let me care, please." The last word, a plea, hangs in the air.

"I didn't mean I don't . . . I just meant . . . " Parker's voice trails off, her teeth clenching in frustration before she releases a pent-up squeal. "If I respond to that, I'll sound like a total—"

"Brat?" I can't help but cut in, a grin spreading across my face. "Are we going to keep hashing this out or will you wait patiently while I come around to open the door for you?"

In the backseat, Cooper has been a silent observer to our exchange. He's sprawled across the seat, his head resting on his paws, but his alert eyes follow every move we make. The thump of his tail and the strain of the leather under his shifting weight are the only noise in the cab while she looks out the window.

When she turns back to look at me, her surrender is written all over her face; her eyes soften, the hard line of her mouth eases, and she lets out a resigned sigh. "Okay."

I close the distance over the console in a heartbeat, planting a quick kiss on her cheek.

That's one battle down, countless more to go. I'm driven by this inexplicable desire to be someone she deems trustworthy. I have no intention of taming that fire in her spirit. In fact, I'm coming to realize that I'd take on the world to protect it—her—against any threat, past, present, or future.

CHAPTER 30

Introductions

PARKER

As we step out of the truck, with the cooler in one hand and Cooper's leash in the other, we make our way to the garage. Wyatt halts me at the door with a gentle touch on my arm and a challenging gaze, silently inviting me to revisit our earlier conversation. *Fine.* If he's so insistent on the doors, I'll let him have them all. Stepping back, I gesture to the door and roll my eyes, even though my insides are melting.

I stride in, and immediately the large laundry and mud room to my left captures my attention. It's an open space, a dream come true. A massive counter stretches before me, flanked by cabinets, a grand stainless steel farmhouse sink, two washers, two dryers, and what looks like a spacious dog-wash station. The floors boast large black tiles that contrast with the white cabinets and butcher block counter. To my right, there's an inset space with lockers built flush against the wall, ensuring a clear path.

A few steps further, I'm drawn to a wall adorned with photos—candid snapshots chronicling the various chapters of their lives. It's a busy display, yet it radiates intention and love, not chaos and clutter. Each photo captures a joyful emotion, and I can't help but feel this is the kind of wall that makes you want to belong. Beyond the lockers, an empty wall seems to await new memories. Wyatt approaches from behind, his hand gliding down my arm. But this time, instead of intertwining his fingers with mine, he guides my hand to point at a photo.

"That's my dad, as you know," he directs my hand to the next person, "that's Riot, Lincoln, and Statler. This photo is from last summer."

"You have a beautiful family." The words escape me, tinged with a sadness I hadn't intended. My voice betrays the ache of my own small, hidden collection of photos.

If Wyatt notices the sadness in my voice, he doesn't let on. Instead, he gently lowers my arm and leans in to kiss the top of my head. His presence behind me is a comforting warmth. And surprisingly, his hands resting on my shoulders feels good. It's a simple touch, a protective stance, yet it brings a sense of intimacy and a steady calmness.

"Bro, the hallway isn't that long, and we are dying to meet the doc!" booms a voice from down the hall.

"That's Lincoln," Wyatt comments with a dismissive shake of his head, as if their banter is an everyday occurrence. I have to admit, navigating family dynamics isn't exactly my forte. Greg and Cameron never brought another child into our home, so large family gatherings are foreign to me.

"Ready?" Wyatt asks with such genuine concern that I believe he would turn back if I asked. I simply nod, ready to face whatever comes next.

As we move further down the hall, the tantalizing aroma of food envelops me, and I suddenly realize just how hungry I am. Wyatt's hand guides me gently, taking up space on my lower back, leading me into a vast kitchen that takes my breath away.

Holy shit. I could spend my life in this kitchen and not regret a day. To my right, five large windows line the back wall, with a second, grand stainless steel farmhouse sink sitting proudly beneath the central window. Beside me, a massive six-burner stove paired with an elegant, white range hood, commands attention.

Light blue tiles grace the wall behind the stove and frame the windows, while pristine white countertops gleam in the light. Dominating the center of the room is an expansive island of stained wood topped with butcher block, surrounded by a mix of upper and lower cabinets, a large side-by-side fridge, and more storage space.

The lower cabinets echo the island's design, while the upper ones match the white of the range hood. Beyond the island and past the windows sits a large round table capable of seating ten comfortably. One side nestles into a bay window with cushioned seats, while the rest are individual chairs that, while coordinated, each boasts its unique design. Directly ahead, a tall vintage oval door with 'pantry' etched into the glass beckons.

"This kitchen is stunning," I sigh, not bothering to turn around. I can sense Wyatt's proximity, his nearness apparent in the warmth at my back.

"Thank you, Doc," Shep says, his voice resonating warmly in the spacious kitchen. He steps away from the sink, where the remnants of peeled vegetables float in the water, and wipes his hands on a towel slung casually over his shoulder. His handshake is firm, his palm roughened from work, conveying a sense of earnestness. The scent of freshly cut cucumbers lingers around him.

"You're welcome, Mr. Lochlan."

"Don't call him that, Doc. It'll go to his head. I'm Lincoln." Wyatt's brother introduces himself with a grin, his hand outstretched as his glasses catch the glint of the overhead lights. His grip is confident, and his laughter echoes off the walls, adding a layer of warmth to the room. Lincoln the lawyer—sharp, quick-witted, and with an aura that fills the space.

"And I'm Statler," another voice chimes in, deep and slightly rough, like gravel crunching under tires. His tattoos are a work of art across his arms, far more intricate up close than the day I saw them in the grocery store. A scar runs from his elbow to his hand. Statler, intimidating to say the least, stands an inch or two taller than Wyatt, his broad shoulders casting a sturdy silhouette. There's a softness though, in his eyes, when he smiles at me.

Surrounded by these towering figures, with Wyatt's presence at my back, I feel a momentary sense of claustrophobia. The kitchen's warmth, the rich aromas of roasting meat and simmering sauces, the laughter and banter—all of it closes in. Without thinking, I retreat a step into Wyatt's chest, his hands automatically coming to rest on my shoulders.

"Quit crowding Doc and let her actually finish walking into the damn room," Wyatt's voice rumbles with a growl, the playful tone replaced by a protective edge. They all step back, giving me space to breathe. A small tremble shakes my shoulders, Wyatt's hands tightening in reaction.

"You okay?" Wyatt whispers in my ear.

Nodding, I walk into the room, shoulders back, holding my breath.

"This is Cooper." I gesture to my gentle giant sitting quietly next to my legs. "He's my service dog. I can have him lie down out of the way, but he's never really been apart from me. He wouldn't understand being left outside or alone. Would it be okay if he stays here?" I venture further into the kitchen, swallowing carefully.

"Of course he can stay," Shep responds with such straightforward assurance that it seems my question was unnecessary. "He's a beauty, you know. One of the finest hog dogs I've seen in a long time."

"Thank you. You surprise me, Mr. Lochlan. Most people don't know his breed off hand." My smile spreads as I watch Cooper's nose twitch, taking in the scents of the kitchen, and I notice his ears perk up at the sound of sizzling and chopping. He's a towering figure, even for his breed.

"The kids' momma had a soft spot for them. Surprised Wy didn't tell you that." Shep smiles over his shoulder. "Though it's been a few years since we had one around here."

"Now we've just got Gigi, Stat's big-ass guard dog." Wyatt chimes in from behind me.

"What kind of dog? Will I get to meet her?" My gaze shifts to Statler. The corners of his lips lift.

"Great Pyrenees. She's not a big fan of the vet though, no offense."

"None taken. But I do make farm calls so if she's more comfortable here, we can make that happen. If she ever needs something."

"Appreciate that." Statler nods. "She's asleep on the porch, I'm sure you'll meet her before the night's over."

"You know," Lincoln interjects as they all drift back to their designated stations in the kitchen, "Wyatt's never brought a date to family dinner before."

I glance over my shoulder, lifting an eyebrow in mock surprise. "It's not a date." I hold Wyatt's eyes with mine to emphasize my point.

"Hey, I didn't tell them it was. They're just a bunch of nosy assholes," Wyatt retorts, his tone teetering between feigned innocence and outright mischief. I face the room again, the oven's warmth competing with the heat rising in my cheeks.

"Mr. Lochlan . . ."

"Call me Shep; Mr. Lochlan was my dad. Makes me feel old and put out to pasture." His laughter fills the room, warm and infectious. It's a sound that tugs at my heart, reminiscent of Cameron's own chuckles. A twinge of longing surfaces as I bask in the familiarity of that sound.

"Shep," I reply with a smile, "is there anything I can do to help?"

"We've got a mountain of veggies to chop for the salad. Think you can handle a knife?" He smirks, and it's clear the apple doesn't fall far from the tree. The same dimples, the same charm—it's all there in Wyatt too.

"I might just have the perfect skill set for chopping." Feeling more at ease, I claim a spot beside him at the island. He passes me a knife, and I'm greeted by an array of vegetables and crisp lettuce. With a task at hand, I focus intently on the chopping, the rhythm of the blade a familiar comfort as the conversation swirls around me. It's only when the chatter fades to silence that I realize all eyes are on me. I pause, knife mid-air, to find four sets of dimples smiling back at me.

"What?" I ask, a note of caution in my voice as I carefully set the knife down.

"I think you might be better with a knife than Stat," Wyatt remarks, his voice tinged with pride. The compliment sends a ripple of warmth through me.

"I feel like there's a story there, but my specialty is surgery, and my dad's a chef. If you were expecting poor knife skills—look elsewhere, gentlemen." I can't help but smirk back at them as I pick the knife back up. The ease with which I've settled into this dynamic surprises even me.

"You make a cute face when you're focused," Wyatt chimes in.

"Inside thoughts?" I challenge.

"Observations," he counters.

"Say, Doc," Statler interjects, stepping closer with a mischievous glint in his eye, "how about a race? Let's see who's faster."

"A man trying to finish before a woman, now why does that sound wrong?" I quip, arching an eyebrow. The guys, Wyatt included, erupt into genuine cackles. Statler's face turns as red as the bell pepper in front of me, caught between embarrassment and amusement. It's exhilarating, this playful banter, the laughter—it reminds me of Cami. She would adore this bunch, probably drawing endless inspiration from them.

"I take it all back." Statler's hands raise up in a gesture of playful defeat.

Wyatt's laughter fades as he regains his composure, the last chuckle leaving his lips as he wipes away a tear. He leans in close, his breath warm against my ear. "There's that smart mouth again."

The words send a shiver down my spine, and I'm acutely aware of the smile blooming on my face, unbidden and genuine. "You're very touchy."

"I'll work on that." Wyatt smiles. "I'm going to go grab the brisket. Be right back," he kisses the side of my head, winking before he exits the way we came.

In his absence, Statler returns to his post at the stove, stirring with a rhythm that speaks of familiarity, while Shep rummages through the fridge, the clink of bottles and rustle of produce filling the space. Lincoln, apparently taskless, approaches me.

"Tell us about yourself, Doc." He leans forward, resting his forearms on the island. He snatches a slice of bell pepper, the crunch echoing in the momentarily quiet room.

"That's a pretty open question. Can you be more specific?" I aim for a tone that's playful rather than evasive. As I glance up, there's a shift, a change from curiosity to something more penetrating, like a wolf homing in on a scent. A flutter of unease stirs in my stomach, my pulse quickening ever so slightly, my swallow almost audible.

"How about something simple? Where are you from?" he asks, a seemingly innocent question that's anything but simple for me.

"I spent most of my childhood in Chicago. But for the last eight years, I've been living in Georgia." I return to my chopping with deliberate slowness, using the task as a diversion from the probing eyes.

"Okay. What about family?" The question, like a splash of cold water, halts my hands for a mere moment, but it's enough for Lincoln to notice. When I meet his gaze, Lincoln's eyes narrow, a predator sensing weakness. It's a look I'm familiar with. Wyatt's absence feels like a missing shield as my stomach twists. The kitchen, once filled with the warmth of cooking and laughter, now feels like a stage under a spotlight, and I'm the reluctant performer.

"I have one parent in Chicago, my dad. I don't have any siblings." Not that I know of anyway. My best friends are mostly in New York now. That's about all there is that would qualify as family."

"Why Georgia? That's a ways from Chicago. Was it for school?" Lincoln reaches for another slice of bell pepper, his curiosity piqued.

"Suits, chill," Statler tosses out over his shoulder.

"I'm just asking." Lincoln shrugs, turning his eyes back to me expectantly.

Just then, Wyatt re-enters the kitchen, his eyes meeting mine. Whatever he sees on my face causes his gaze to narrow. "What are you doing, Lincoln?" His tone a mix of amusement and warning.

"Just asking questions," Lincoln responds with a roguish grin, not quite masking the intensity of his interrogation.

"You were grilling the doc," Statler chimes in, his tone lightening the mood.

"Lincoln." Wyatt sets his jaw set firmly as he places the brisket on the island, his eyes hard. The brothers exchange a silent conversation, and Lincoln nods in agreement.

"Sorry," Lincoln turns to me, his smile genuine. "It's a habit. Riot often tells me my questions sound more like an interrogation."

I manage a smile, feeling the tension ease slightly. When I glance up at Wyatt, he gives me a reassuring wink as if to say, 'I've got you.' In this moment, that small gesture is everything, and I nod back and exhale.

"Alright, dinner's ready," Shep announces, signaling the end of the questioning and the beginning of a new, more relaxed chapter of the evening. The kitchen fills with the sound of dishes clinking and the savory aroma of brisket, a reminder that, for now, I'm just a guest here to enjoy the meal.

CHAPTER 31

Confessions

As everyone bustles around, preparing plates and marveling at Parker's perfectly diced salad, I watch her unwind, her shoulders relaxing incrementally with each shared joke and story. I can't help but reach out with a few casual touches, a silent message that I'm here and she has the power to end this night whenever she wishes. She called me touchy, but her reaction says she relies on those moments.

We swap stories, delve into the quirks of ranch life, and even coax her into a sports team debate. Her admission of indifference to football sends a mock shockwave through my brothers, but her laughter, her genuine, carefree laughter, is the highlight of my night.

It's addictive; the more she lets it loose, the more I revel in it. My brothers spare no expense sharing my most embarrassing tales, but it's a price I'd gladly pay again for the joy of seeing her so entertained.

Dad begins the ritual of cleaning up, wrapping up leftovers with a precision born of years of practice. Linc and Stat take to the dishes with a well-oiled efficiency, the sound of running water and the clatter of plates a familiar backdrop to ongoing banter. Per my mother's long-standing rules, the kitchen is slowly cleaned and reset.

"Take a walk with me." I extend my hand, an invitation hanging in the balance. For a fleeting moment she hesitates but trusts me enough to slip her hand into mine.

"Thanks for joining dinner tonight. It was great to have you, and you're welcome anytime, Doc." Dad's voice is warm as he pulls Parker into a side hug.

She returns the gesture, a move that catches me off guard with its naturalness. "You can call me Parker. We've saved a life, and we've had dinner. I think that means we're friends now." Her smile is genuine and bright, directed at Dad. I can't pinpoint why, but I'm grateful she's at ease with him.

"What about us?" Lincoln's plea echoes like a puppy's whine, but I'm quick to remind him of his place with a playful smack to the back of the head.

"Brother, you haven't earned the right to drop the formalities. She's still 'Doc' to you."

Parker's laughter fills the room. She glances at Lincoln, her shrug conveying a mix of amusement and acceptance. "I guess that's the new benchmark. If it makes you feel better, you're the only company I've had for dinner since arriving here, so you're all well ahead of the game," she says, her words bridging the gap between stranger and friend.

"It was nice to meet you," Statler chimes in while drying his hands.

"Likewise. Thank you for inviting me," Parker replies, her gratitude genuine.

I acknowledge each of my brothers with a nod, share a quick hug with Dad, all while keeping Parker's hand tucked in mine. As we make our way from the kitchen, I shift her hand to my elbow, causing her to chuckle as we exit the garage door.

"Where are we headed?" Her curiosity is obvious in her eyes as she glances up at me.

"To the barn." I point with my free hand.

Outside, the world is in transition, living in the unique color of twilight, the kind that settles just before dark. The sun hovers just behind the silhouette of the mountains, its light fading into a blend of purples and oranges. The air is crisp, the kind that only exists in spring. The distant sounds of the day's end—cattle lowing, the wind whispering through the grass—create a natural soundtrack.

"Why?" she asks, her mind always seeking answers, driven by that unique blend of curiosity and suspicion.

Parker's warm hand on my arm highlights the slight chill beginning to settle. The energy between us is real, an electric current continually pulsing. I take in her face, illuminated by the last rays of the sun, her eyes reflecting the whole of the sky.

"To cap off our non-date, I thought we could dance. I know a place that's pretty empty this time of day." I wink.

"Dance?" She halts, her gaze lifting to mine.

"Yes." I lift her hand to my lips for a gentle kiss on her knuckles. "Taking you out to dance would make this a date, and we can't have that. So, we dance here, where it's just us."

She regards me with a dry humor. "Your logic has some holes this time."

With a nod toward the barn, she resumes walking, and I can't help but pull her back gently as she reaches for the door. Her annoyance is fleeting, and she relents, allowing me to lead her inside. The barn lights flicker on, and I pull out my phone, syncing it to the barn's Bluetooth, setting the stage for a dance I hope will be anything but ordinary.

"You have music in here? I never thought to ask that first night," Parker's voice floats over from where she's exploring, her figure framed by the stalls.

"Yeah, and I'm still curious about that birth mix you mentioned. Your surgery playlist was impressive, so I bet the birth mix is just as fun," I reply, watching her move with a grace that's as natural as the horses that usually occupy this space.

Her laughter rings out, her voice teasing. "You'll just have to listen and see. It's mostly songs about how terrible men are." She turns a wicked grin over her face. "What song are you picking?" She makes her way back to me, trying to look over my hands at the screen.

"I've got a few ideas, but I'm open to suggestions."

"Let's see how you do first," she says, smiling.

I scroll through my playlist. John Hiatt's "Have a Little Faith in Me" fills the space as I take her in my arms.

I pocket the phone and extend my hand, which she takes without hesitation this time. I draw her close, our bodies aligning as if they were made to fit together. With one hand at the small of her back, the other covering the hand resting on my chest, I begin to move slowly around the room.

The barn, a sanctuary of shadows and soft light, becomes our dance floor. Parker's gaze is fixed on our intertwined hands, yet a heavy silence hangs between us. I remain quiet, giving her the space she clearly needs. The truth is, I've been falling for her since the moment she called me an asshole, maybe from the first day I saw those eyes in the damn produce section.

"Is this song a message?" she asks, her tone laced with only the slightest hint of sarcasm.

I look down into Parker's face, upturned to mine, and see it is etched with the softest smile. The way she fits against me, feels like finding a missing piece—a sense of rightness that words can't capture.

"It depends. Does it sound like one you want to hear?" I feel her breathing deeply against my chest. She doesn't answer, but she doesn't need to. Her continued presence in my arms, moving gently with the music, speaks volumes.

As we sway to the music, our shadows merge on the barn floor, two figures becoming one in the dance. The barn's interior, with its high rafters and the lingering scent of wood and straw, shelters us from the world outside.

The music shifts seamlessly from one melody to another, and we continue to dance, lost in the rhythm and each other. It's during the fourth or fifth song that Parker surprises me, her forehead coming to rest against my chest. The gesture so small yet so intimate. As the final notes of the song fade, she falls still in my arms.

"I can't seem to find it in me to fight wanting you," she whispers, her voice a fragile thread in the vastness of the barn. She looks up at me, her eyes a storm-tossed sea. "I can't make you any promises, Wyatt. I can't attach any strings to this. I can't afford to."

Her words, meant to set boundaries, only draw me in further. "You make being with me sound expensive." The quiet of the barn settles around us, punctuated only by the quiet movements of the horses and the steady rhythm of our breathing.

I cup her face in my hands, searching her eyes for the words I need to hear. "Tell me what you want, Parker," I urge, needing her to give voice to the desire that I can see simmering just beneath the surface.

"Take me home, Wyatt. And stay."

CHAPTER 32

Wow

PARKER

Those words were simple, yet they feel profoundly complicated. I expected a wave of worry or a surge of regret to wash over me as I said them. I should have been tallying up every ghost and fear, every logical reason. Instead, there's only a sense of liberation in giving those words to him, like a dam bursting, loosening the knot of anxiety in my stomach. I trust him, as much as someone like me can trust anyone.

The rules—no promises and no strings—might seem unfair, one-sided, or even unrealistic, but they're necessary for both of us. For me, falling in love isn't an option. He hears my words, then takes my hand and leads me out of the barn and back to the truck. I don't resist when he opens the doors this time. I simply watch when he calls Cooper to jump in and secures my seatbelt.

When he climbs into the truck, I brace for him to speak, but he remains silent. He simply reverses the truck, then pauses, his gaze fixed on me. He squints slightly, as though he's searching for signs of fear or regret. Apparently satisfied with what he does—or doesn't—see, he lifts my hand from the console and brings my knuckles to his lips, which lightly graze my skin.

His eyes hold mine, and his smile generates a cascade of sensations across my skin—thousands of tiny sparks igniting at once. I expect him to let go of my hand once we reach the highway, but he doesn't. Instead, he keeps it firmly in his, his lips continuing to brush against my skin—my knuckles, the back of my hand, my wrist—each touch light and sweet. My mind falls silent. His touch shuts out the world around me and quells the chaos within me.

Pulling up to the apartment, he's out of the truck and rounding the hood before I even realize I'm anticipating his approach. When he stands before me with that lottery-winning smile, my heart jumps, squeezing my lungs. If he keeps looking at me like this, with pride and a little arrogance dancing across his features, I may never open another door.

Moving from the truck, we make our way up the stairs. We enter the apartment in silence, one that seems to be loud and uncertain but inevitable.

"Could I be any more awkward right now?" I mumble, my eyes closed, hands massaging my temples where a headache threatens to bloom. *Stupid nerves.*

The click of the deadbolt echoes through the room, his steps even and calm as they move closer to me. Even with my eyes closed, I can feel his presence in front of me. His rough calloused palm slides across my cheek, threading into my hair before cradling the back of my neck.

"There's nothing awkward about you." His words surprise me. I hadn't realized he'd heard my self-deprecating mumble. "Give me your eyes, Parker."

My breath catches as I lift my head, slowly opening my eyes to meet his, where the desire is almost palpable. Closing the remaining distance, his eyes stay locked onto mine until he kisses me. It's a slow, tender gesture, melting through the worry as his fingers use just enough pressure to pull me forward into his body.

I yield to his kiss, pushing out every last bit of resistance. He pulls back, only a fraction, his breath playing across my lips.

"Are you sure this is what you want?" His question is a gentle nudge, as his lips float across my cheek. Voiceless under his touch, I can only nod. "I need to hear you say it, baby."

His words bring me back to the precipice of resistance, but as I open my eyes, the restraint I hold dear falls away.

His presence is all-consuming, and I give myself over fully. "Yes."

Immediately, his lips crash into mine, the shift in intensity shocking my senses. It's not the slow, tender dance of before, but a fierce, enthralling collision. My fingers wrap around his wrists. Rising onto the balls of my feet, unchecked yearning pushes me to close every sliver of space between us. His kiss resonates through my chest, causing a tremble to snake down my spine.

This is an inferno, a blaze, claiming every part of me with a hunger that's as exhilarating as it is terrifying. Raw desire heats my blood. My history offers only pale shadows of this feeling, whispers of memories overshadowed by the brilliance of his tongue dancing and teasing mine.

He runs his hands from my face and down my back, placing one at each hip and lifting me with ease. Wrapping my legs around his waist, I tilt my head, giving his mouth free reign to move across my skin. From my lips to my jaw, he trails warm kisses, pausing just below my ear before continuing his journey down my neck. Arriving at the junction between my neck and shoulder, his teeth lightly scrape across my skin. My toes curl as my thighs clench against the sensation.

Only when he slides me slowly down his body, over his hardened length, do I realize we're in my room. After years of celibacy, my need washes over me. My hands tremble as I attack the buttons on his shirt until I can slide it from his broad shoulders, exposing a mass of golden skin. Hungry for his kiss, I pull his mouth down to mine.

Dazed and breathless, I mumble, "There's a zipper under my right arm." Pulling back, his movements slow, his mouth moves to my wrist. Torturously, as though time doesn't exist, his mouth journeys from my wrist to my shoulder, the only noise a combination of my unsteady breaths and the sound of my zipper slowly being lowered.

"This dress," he growls. "I've wanted to take it off you all night." My knees weaken, the heat in my core turning molten.

"Nothing stopping you now." My voice emerges, strange to my own ears, each word laced with the ragged edge of desperation.

A playful smirk appears on his face as he gracefully crouches to gently slide off my boot and then my sock, sending warmth up my thigh. He turns to the other leg and repeats the action, each movement etching itself into my consciousness—a vivid, indelible memory of him on his knees before me.

He slides his hands up, disappearing under my dress, floating along my calves and the outside of my thighs, until he finds the lace that rests high on my hip bones. My lungs burn. He's moving so slowly I might burn up entirely before he ever touches me.

With the same mix of tenderness and fire as his kiss, he guides my underwear down my legs, the lace rough against my skin. He doesn't rise, simply slides his hands back up my legs, his stroke light, leaving my skin pebbled in his wake. When those hands shift to the inside of my thighs, grazing my center, my breath escapes in a sudden, forceful torrent, a pent-up storm breaking free.

Looking up from his knees, desire flashes through his eyes as he strokes and circles, teasing me before backing away.

"Wyatt," I breathe out, the name a fusion of desperation and command as my hips roll forward.

"What, baby?" he murmurs, his hands pushing up my dress while his mouth places soft kisses on my thighs.

"You should know . . . it's been . . . a long time." The words feel clumsy, inadequate, as he nips at my thigh with his teeth, his touch adding enough pressure to tease.

"Define a long time." The deep timbre of his voice makes me quiver. A powerful tide of lust surges within me; it overwhelms my senses and renders speech nearly impossible.

He shifts away suddenly and, taking advantage of my lack of balance, he grips my waist and settles me on the edge of the bed. My head drops on his chest as he pulls my legs apart further, my dress pooled around my waist.

"I need to . . . to . . . " My jaw clenches as my nails dig into the warm skin covering his ribs.

"Answer me, Parker. How long?" His fingers tease me and my body twitches in response, but he stays just out of reach.

"Five years," I confess, the words burning in my throat. His reaction is immediate, and he stills his hands. Embarrassment and shame begin vying for dominance inside me, forcing my eyes shut so I don't have to face him.

Despite my embarrassment, a tremor courses through me. His hand gently brackets my jaw, tilting my chin up, silently commanding me to obey. With a slippery and tentative grasp on my courage, I force my eyes open. They look into the deep abyss of his gaze, a wild, untamed darkness.

"Is that supposed to make me want to stop?" Even in the dark room, the muscle twitch in his jaw, the tension in the lines of his mouth, are obvious.

"I was just trying to . . . manage your expectations."

"Manage my expectations?" He repeats it back to me slowly, as though he's full of rage at each word.

The sudden prickle of goosebumps erupts across my skin. It's as if each tiny hair is standing on end, a miniature army at attention, reacting to an invisible current flowing from him, dancing over my flesh.

"Yes," I mumble, "I haven't done this a lot and certainly not recently and I probably should have said that sooner but I. . . " Turning away, the heat of humiliation and mortification are too much to bear. I try pulling back, but he simply flexes his grip on my thighs, holding me in place.

"Eyes." His intensity threatens to unravel me, as he stands statue-still, waiting for me respond. My last shred of self-preservation vanishes as I look up, meeting his gaze.

"That doesn't make me want you less, Parker," his eyes darken, "it makes me want to claim every inch of you over and over until the only thing you know is my name."

I swallow hard, a cascade of sharp tingles erupting from my fingertips, surging through me like electricity. My hands tremble as I lift them to his chest, the powerful thunder of his heart below my palms.

"I have no idea what to say to that," I whisper.

"You don't need to say anything, it's not a test, there's no right answer." His hands begin a slow and lazy movement up and down my body, betraying none of the vast hunger I see in his eyes. "Tell me if I do something you don't like or you need me to stop. Understood?"

"Yes." I nod slowly.

His hands and mouth go back to tormenting my neck and arms and skin. My head falls back without permission, giving him more access.

His appreciation rumbles through my skin as his hands slide under me, pulling up. "Arms up, baby."

Complying immediately, the sensation of the dress sliding up and off my skin is enough to make me whimper. His hands settle against my face, followed by his lips.

His kiss is gentle, no longer teasing or challenging, almost soothing until I melt against him, my body held up only by the strength in his arms. Only then does he travel down, dragging his lips across my neck and shoulder while reaching behind me to unclasp my bra. Exposed, entirely at his mercy, I reach for his belt but he steps back.

"Let me take care of you for a little while, Parker." His voice carries an unexpected plea, a strange blend of authority and agony. I find myself responding with a silent nod.

His hands skim down from my neck seconds before he drops a soft kiss on my forehead. Then he's lifting me and pushing me back onto the bed, joining me instantly, his mouth lowering to my aching skin. His hands and teeth and tongue all blend together, competing sensations driving me to within an inch of my own sanity. Arching into him, my hands thread through his hair without thinking. He lifts his head, momentarily leaning into my touch with a hum in the back of his throat.

My body is electric at his strokes, his mouth covering every inch of exposed skin he can reach, alternating between kisses and tugs, sucking, and scraping. My hips roll into his hand, a low moan breaking past my lips.

The sound emanating from him in return is possessive and animalistic. Before I can take another breath, the pressure from the hand between my thighs increases, the fullness emptying my mind of any coherent thought. I moan, the sensations crashing and mixing, volatile and vicious, roaring in my ears until I don't even hear myself.

"Are you going to give me what I want, Parker?" he whispers, branding himself onto my skin. "Do you want to be good for me?"

"Oh . . . Wyatt . . . " my voice cracks under the strain of sensations as I clench my jaw.

"Let go, baby," he encourages.

Release slams into my body and every thought is stolen. Only the chorus of his name crosses my lips, and I feel him tremble next to me before he whispers, "Good girl."

Boneless, I collapse onto the bed, panting, lungs burning, aftershocks trembling through me with each beat of my heart.

"Watching you fall apart is now my favorite thing." His hands float across my skin, up my thighs, over my hips, until he finally rests his palm on my cheek, turning my head to face him.

He drops a series of sweet kisses across my face, and I feel my answering smile break across my face, utterly unable to be held back.

"I think I should get to see it again, don't you?" he says against my smile. The only sound I can make is somewhere between a laugh and whimper as white-hot pleasure rolls over me.

He shifts, moving down, hands sliding along my calves. It takes a full ten seconds for me to realize what he's about to do as his kisses trace closer and closer to my center. My breath hitches in my chest, and I feel him pause immediately, as though he's already perfectly in tune with my body. "Is this okay, angel?"

"No one's ever—" the words get stuck in my throat.

"Can I?" His voice is quiet, but the need in it is loud.

"Sure." The anticipation builds as he begins to move again, pulling me to the edge of the bed.

"Tell me if I need to stop." His words leave no room for argument, and in a breath, he closes his mouth over me.

"Oh god, Wyatt." My fingers sink into his hair .

My hips jerk, but his hand moves up to my hip, pinning me where he wants me. I fight to breathe, tightness gathering, muscles quaking at his every move. Finally, I break like a wave against the shore, thinking only of him. The mattress shifts beside me, and I wrap my arms around his neck, letting him steady me.

He nuzzles my neck, even as his arms wrap around my back, holding onto me, letting me take what I need. When I finally loosen my hold, he lifts his head. His eyes meeting mine, I am undone.

CHAPTER 33

Sunrises

WYATT

If I died right now, with my arms wrapped around her and her taste on my tongue, I'd consider it a life well lived. Her every sound blends into a symphony, heating my blood with need. Feeling her heart pounding as she tries to steady her breath, her body turned slightly into mine, sweet and warm, is a drug.

I want to know every inch of her. Like an addict, I want to own every sound, shiver, and tremble. My name called out from her lips for a lifetime wouldn't be enough to satisfy me.

"More," she whispers, before her arms uncurl from around my neck.

Smiling down at her, I see her eyes clear and bright, dancing with happiness. Pushing back from her, rising to stand, I take her in. Smooth skin, miles of leg, long dark hair forming a halo around her, face smiling and relaxed, eyes closed.

The sound of my belt buckle clanging against the floor interrupts the silence, and she opens her eyes slowly. Moonbeams light the darkened room, but they are enough to let me to see her eyes widen as I tear into a foil packet. I catch the worry that flashes in her eyes.

"Doing okay, Parker?" I ask, making my way back onto the bed beside her.

"Okay feels like an understatement," she whispers, stretching up to kiss me.

Dropping down, I lose myself in her kiss. The soft feel of her lips, the lazy slide of her tongue driving me crazy. Straining my control, I break the kiss, choosing instead to stroke and explore, learning what she likes with every little response she gives. Running across the left side of her ribs, I feel the raised skin against my lips. A tattoo, the room too dark to make it out entirely. Something about discovering this hidden piece of her excites me.

Settling into the cradle of her hips, aligning us, I push forward slowly. She tightens around me, her thighs quivering against my hips. I move back, then forward again, fighting my own need to be seated fully inside her.

"Wyatt," she moans, her voice strained, rasping.

"I love that sound," I whisper in her ear.

"More," she whispers, her breath warm as it floats across my neck.

Moving slowly, inch by inch, her nails dig into my shoulders. "You're taking me so well." I feel her clench at the words, heat building at the base of my spine in response.

"Don't stop," she whispers, relaxing her thighs and wrapping her arms around my neck.

I kiss her cheek and continue to move against her. I feel her breath catch, her arms tightening around my neck.

"Talk to me, baby," I whisper against her ear, stilling my movement until she tells me otherwise.

"Just adjusting," she mutters, her lips press against the skin of my shoulder, and I feel her take a deep breath, her ribs expanding against me.

"You're so beautiful." I kiss her cheek, then her nose as she continues to move against me. "Do you have any idea what you do to me?"

She glides her hands through my hair. I open my eyes to see hers already looking deeply into mine, the blue almost as clear as glass. "Show me."

The words snap my control, and as I move, she arches with pleasure. I watch her mouth fall open, her head arching back with pleasure. The pressure builds at the base of my spine as I drive us both to the point of no return.

"That's it, you're right there, be a good girl for me, angel." She tightens almost instantly at the praise, clamping around me, release bursting through her.

"Wyatt," her voice strains, cracking slightly as I move, pulsing around me until my own release finds me.

Lowering to my elbows, my breath burning in my chest, I bury my face in her neck right over the source of vanilla and cinnamon. Her arms wrap around my back, pulling me down to her.

"I'll crush you like this."

Her head shakes against my shoulder, and she lets out a faint whimper when I try to pull back, which tugs at my heart. Turning my head, I trace her cheek and her ear and the crown of her head with quick kisses until she relaxes enough for us to separate slightly.

"Hold on, angel."

Her nod a silent answer, her arms wrapping tightly around my neck. Sliding my arm under her, I roll to my side, keeping her tucked tightly into me, her head resting on my arm.

My hands glide up and down her back, and I can feel the tension melting away at each pass, relaxing her into my hold. Her breathing slows, finding an easy cadence that matches the strokes of my hand. She's cuddled into the curve of my neck, her hand curled into a small fist just beneath her chin, a contented, smug smile gracing her features—a look of pure, unspoken triumph that satisfies me from the inside out.

"I'll be right back." Kissing her forehead, I slide my arm from under her and she protests, the cutest little pout on her face as I settle her head on the pillow. Swinging my legs over the edge of the bed, I rise and head for the bathroom.

Returning with a warm washcloth, the heat radiating from the fabric into my hands, I see her curled onto her side. Her eyelids flutter open as I get closer, light spilling in from the hallway to reveal eyes that sparkle. Her smile, gentle and intimate, beams up at me, and it's as if time itself has stopped, rooting me to this spot at this moment.

"That's *my* smile," I declare, my voice deepening instinctively, exactly like the damn caveman she calls me. "I love all your smiles, but that one . . . that one is mine." I claim it, and in this instant, I embrace it without reservation. A blend of satisfaction and joy illuminates her entire face, reaching her eyes and making them glow. I close the gap between us, drawn to her as she watches me, tracking my every move.

"How will I know which smile it is?" Her voice tinged with genuine curiosity, as if the answer matters deeply to her.

"What are you feeling right now?" I probe, seeking to guide her to her answer.

"Sort of a loaded question, Wyatt," she pauses and takes a slow breath. "I guess I'm feeling a bit self-satisfied and relaxed and happy." Her soft sigh fills the silence between us as her lips tip up even further at the corners.

"That's the smile I want—the one you use when you feel exactly like that." I lean over, parting her legs, gently cleaning her up, her eyes watching me with a mixture of surprise and confusion. Tossing the cloth toward her laundry basket, I settle on the edge of the bed.

"Do I get to claim something? Or is that just a caveman thing?" Her question is tentative and a little teasing, but her gaze is direct. To an outsider, she might appear bold, but I catch the little hitch in her tone that betrays her uncertainty.

Pulling the blanket up, I drape it over her, ensuring she stays warm before I respond. "Anything you want." My fingers weave gently through her silky hair. I can't seem to stop touching her like this; tenderness isn't my default, but for her, I find it easy.

"A kiss," she says after a moment's pause. "It's slow, almost gentle, where your hands are in my hair like now." Her request settles with significance inside me; and the gravity of her asking for anything at all is not lost on me.

"It's all yours." I press a kiss to her forehead. "Can you check your level for me?"

She rolls her eyes, shaking her head slowly before she says, "You worry too much."

"Not worried at all," I counter, lying through my damn teeth. "Just making sure I know, so I can plan the rest of the night accordingly."

"Is that so?" she laughs, her fingers tracing lines across the back of my hand. "I'll need my phone."

"Be right back." Winking, I make my way back to living room, grabbing a bottle of water and her phone. Returning, I plug her phone into her charger, then pull mine from my jeans pocket. She sits up, checking the phone with a little nod, before setting it back down.

"Normal," she declares, eyebrow raised in triumph.

Before she can lie back down, I lift her arms, one at a time, looping them around my neck. The blanket falls away, leaving my hands to roam her skin.

"I have a request." I draw her close. "Think of it like a door thing."

"Okay," she chuckles, curiosity dancing in her voice. "What could that possibly mean right now?"

"You're on the wrong side of the bed." Leaning in, I drop a kiss on her lips.

"That's the side farthest from the door," she observes, looking behind her, a hint of skepticism in her squint.

"Exactly." I lower my head to the soft skin of her throat, to a place that she seems to enjoy.

"I don't understand." She tilts her head back, inviting me to continue as she arches slightly into my hold.

"If an intruder came in, they'd reach you first on this side. If you switch, I'm first," I explain.

She halts my advances by pushing back and cupping my face in her hands. "That's dumb. No one's breaking in," she states confidently, her practicality drawing a chuckle from me.

"It's a door thing." Shrugging, I watch her ponder the logic.

"If I refuse?" she asks, her head cocked to the side, like she's weighing all her choices. I love the way her mind works. I love it when she pushes back. Arguing with her is my third favorite pastime these days.

"Then the answer is no. Your voice will always matter to me."

She releases my face, shaking her head in amusement.

"I don't understand why you'd take my no on this but fight me on doors. It's confusing, Wyatt."

"I don't mind making you angry, Parker, but I wouldn't ever make you uncomfortable. I'll happily fight you over something small like a door, but I wouldn't push against you on something that has the potential to make you feel unsafe."

"Interesting. Not entirely sure I understand, but I suppose I appreciate that there is some kind of logic to it, rather than just caveman instincts."

"There's probably a fair amount of caveman as you call it, but hopefully slightly more evolved."

"I need my phone on my side. Move the charger over here, and the spot is yours," she concedes, with a slight eyeroll.

"Deal," I wink, sealing our agreement with a swift kiss.

With everything in its place, I flip back the covers and slide in beside her. I slip an arm under her shoulders, gently rolling her towards me until she's snug against my side. She shifts hesitantly, as if gauging how I'll react.

"Closer, Parker," I tease. Her hand slides across my chest. "More." I challenge.

She wiggles forward, until her head is on my chest and her leg is hooked over my thigh.

"Better?" she asks sarcastically.

"Yep." I squeeze her hip lightly.

"What now?" she murmurs, her voice tinged with lightheartedness. "I'm a little rusty." A giggle erupts from her, and I can't help but join in with a soft chuckle of my own.

"Now we sleep, until I can't hold myself back from wanting you again. If that's good with you."

"That works."

I feel her smile against my skin.

"I might have gotten condoms today." Turning her head slightly, she buries her face in my chest. If the lights were on, I'd see the blush of her embarrassment work its way up her neck.

"How'd you know what size?" I ask, not the least bit shy and more than willing to play this conversation out if it makes her smile.

She looks up and clears her throat. "I'm a doctor. I made a proportional estimation based on your height." Her clinic voice is even and unemotional until she says, "Then hoped I wasn't wrong." She slaps her hand over her mouth, holding in her next laugh as it trembles through her body.

I grab her hand, pull it away, and tilt her face up to mine. "That's rather presumptuous of you, planning to end up in bed with me. Now I feel used."

"Liar." She rests her hand on my cheek, her thumb tracing my lip.

"Got me there. I'm curious though about whether you were right. Where are they, should we find out now?" I move to sit up.

"No!" she squeals, wrapping her arm around my chest to pull me back down.

"I'll find out soon enough," I tease. "Better sleep while you can, Parker." Stroking my hand up and down her side, tracing each curve, I feel her breathing start to even out.

"Did you see Cooper?" Her voice is soft, laced with the weight of impending sleep.

"He's half-hidden in your closet," I reply, my lips brushing her hair as my hand continues its path along her skin.

"Hopefully, we didn't traumatize him for life."

My fingers glide over her shoulder, tracing the line of her neck. Slowly, I become acutely aware of a series of scars. Each time I near them, she tenses, so I carefully alter my movements to keep her comfortable.

"Parker, why so long?" I ask, the question hanging between us.

She stiffens, her relaxation evaporating instantly. "Pass," is all she offers.

Gently, I lift her chin with my free hand, needing to see her eyes. "You know," I stroke her lips, hoping to convey sincerity, "if you ever decide to break our deal, I'll prove you can trust me."

"Noted." Her response is simple, but it's the slightest edge of pain in her eyes and sudden shortness of her breath that truly catch me off guard.

She settles against me again and, bit by bit, she relaxes. I feel her start to drift when she whispers, her voice thick with sleep, "Don't break me, Wyatt. I won't survive a second time."

When I glance down, she's asleep.

Slowly, I drift off, wondering who broke her the first time and just exactly how I'd make them pay for it.

CHAPTER 34

Calling

PARKER

"Wyatt. I can't . . ."

"You can," he croons. "Give me another one." Every inch of me feels like an exposed nerve, every touch from his hands magnified as he glides across my body. His fingers dig into my hips, his teeth scrape across my neck, guiding me over him. Everything pulls taut inside me, an invisible thread stretching so tightly my muscles clench.

"Don't hold back, baby." My body locks up as waves of pleasure cascade through me. He doesn't stop, drawing out every ounce of pleasure slowly, methodically. Before I can collapse, muscles trembling, he reverses our positions.

He picks up his rhythm, a man unleashed, until he's falling over the edge. I feel him shudder and exhale quickly as I roll my hips one more time.

He collapses next to me, pulling me in tight, letting my body curl into his. He kisses my cheek before leaving the bed. When the mattress dips beside me, blankets sliding over my skin, he pulls me close, his front to my back, my head cradled on his arm. He runs his fingers through my hair and within a few strokes, I'm almost asleep. That's when I hear him whisper, awe in his voice, "Best night of my life."

◇◇◇◇◇◇◇◇◇◇◇◇◇◇

Dawn creeps in, and I'm awake, my body's internal clock pushing me, along with Cooper's restless nudge, to go outside. Carefully, I extricate myself from Wyatt's arms. In the semidarkness, my fingers find the fabric of his shirt on the floor. Slipping it on, buttoning it slowly, I can't help but watch him.

His chest rises and falls steadily, his sleep deep and undisturbed. I can't decipher my feelings. The faint light is enough to highlight the contours of his face. Memories of last night and all the ways he used his mouth start to flood my mind. Every square inch of my body has been worshipped, exactly like he said he would. No matter what happens from this point forward, this night will remain one of my greatest treasures.

Feeling cherished and desired with his every move was intoxicating. I shiver, thinking about his low and gravelly voice praising me. Before I climb right back into that bed, I force myself to focus.

I tiptoe through the bedroom door, easing it shut with a soft click. Making my way to the front door, I release Cooper into the cool pre-dawn air. As I stand in the doorway, in the absence of Wyatt's warmth, doubts—unwelcome and persistent—begin to seep in, turning the silence into a cacophony of 'what-ifs.'

What if it was so good because it had been so long?

What if it wasn't as earth-shattering for him as it was for me?

What if he simply decides he's gotten me out of his system?

What if I just made the second biggest mistake of my life?

181

I steal a glance at the clock—five in the morning means seven in New York. Once Cooper is back inside, I check my level and prepare a quick snack. Reaching for my laptop, I initiate a video call to Cami. True to form, she's up with the sun. When her face appears on the screen, I gesture for sign language only. Cami's eyebrows arch in silent inquiry, her expression sharpening with curiosity at my request.

"What are you doing sitting in the dark, Parker?"

"It's early," I reply with a nonchalant shrug.

"Are you wearing a man's shirt?" Her grin is practically audible even though only her hands are moving, her eyes filled with teasing and knowing.

"Yes," I confess, feeling a mix of embarrassment and defiance as I bury my face in my hands, only to peek through my fingers at Cami's flurry of signs.

"Spill it. Was it amazing? How many times?"

I hesitate, feeling a blush creep up my cheeks even in the dim light. *"It was incredible, and I don't think I should share that."*

Cami, playful and persistent, begs. *"Come on, girl. Two? Three?"*

"Five!" I cave, the admission sending a wave of heat across my face, turning it a shade of red I'm sure even the darkness can't hide.

"Damn! Are his brothers single? Because honestly, honey, that's above average."

"I think so, but that's not why I'm calling. Focus, Cami."

"You got banged into oblivion and are currently occupying a man's shirt, forgive me for being distracted." Cami's face on the screen is a blend of sternness and empathy. *"Tell me why you're calling me instead of sleeping."*

I sigh involuntarily, the weight of my fears pressing down on me. *"I swore I wouldn't get attached, but I am and it's just going to get worse. Continuing this is a bad idea."*

"Parker, stop," she chides gently. *"You deserve to be happy."*

"I'm still broken. I can't talk about her. I think about her every day. I don't want to forget her." The words hang heavy in the air between us.

"Oh, sweetheart," Cami's eyes soften, "*we will never forget her. Don't let that fear hold you back.*"

The tears start to fall, and I brush them away hastily. "*I can't tell him, Cami. I can't bring myself to say it out loud.*"

"*You don't give yourself enough credit,*" she signs. "*But for now, just take things one step at a time. You're spiraling into some future place that might not even happen. You don't have to tell him about her, but that doesn't mean you can't enjoy time with him. It doesn't need to be all or nothing, Parks.*"

A throat clearing suddenly interrupts the silence. Looking up, I see Wyatt, his silhouette framed by the hallway light, arms crossed, standing in his black boxer briefs, an unreadable expression on his face.

CHAPTER 35

Friends

WYATT

"Parker!" The shout, a woman's voice, grabs my attention as I circle the kitchen island, holding Parker's gaze. I position myself behind her, shielding against my lack of a clothing.

"Oh, my. My name is Camilla." The red-haired woman on the screen signs as she speaks, and I can't help but watch the flurry of her freckled hands.

"Good morning, Camilla. I'd apologize for my lack of attire, but it seems Parker needed my shirt more than I did," I say with a grin, watching Parker sign along to my words.

Camilla's eyebrows dance suggestively at Parker, and she signs something back—something that causes a sweet blush to bloom on Parker's face.

"I'm going to go, Cami!" Parker interjects abruptly.

"Wait!" Camilla calls out. "What's your name?" Her smile is loaded with mischief.

"Wyatt. Nice to meet you, Camilla," I respond with a nod.

"Call me later, Parker!" Cami's voice follows us as Parker snaps the laptop shut.

I spin Parker around gently to face me, my hands framing her as she leans back against the island. "Who was that?" I ask, hoping she'll open up just a little.

"One of my best friends," she answers quietly.

"How did you two meet?" I press a kiss to her forehead, eager to learn more about her and uncover the layers of her past.

"In college. I never really had a best friend besides Greg and Cameron. I knew people, liked them, but I've never been great at making friends. Cami just decided we were best friends and made herself a part of my life." She chuckles. "I didn't have much choice. Eventually, we moved in together. She's in New York now, but we still talk almost every day."

"Is that when you learned to sign?" I kiss one cheek and then the other as her hands moved to my chest. I hold back, gripping the counter at her hips, willing myself not to take her right here.

"Yes. I never wanted her to feel isolated or like it was a chore to communicate with her." Parker shrugs.

I stare at Parker, profoundly struck by the depth of her compassion for others. "You are an extraordinary woman, Parker."

She stares back silently, eyes wide with surprise, as if such praise is a foreign language to her.

Note to self: remind her how incredible she is every single day.

I lean in, brushing a kiss over her lips. "Why did I wake up without you?" I ask, my voice barely a whisper against her skin.

"Cooper needed out," she whispers back. "We're both used to getting up at five."

"What's the usual routine?" I inquire, feeling her hands slide from my chest up around my neck.

"We wake up, he goes out, I check my level, work out, shower, and get ready, the usual stuff," she explains, a hint of routine in her voice.

"Hmm, we're awake, he's been out, that means level is next, then we can shower," I suggest, keeping my tone light and playful.

"Wyatt," she groans as I close my mouth over the spot below her ear. "I'm sore, the good kind, but I have to work today. My body might actually dissolve into a useless heap if you try what I think you're thinking."

Her whine is endearing and sweet; I can't help but chuckle softly against the skin of her neck in response.

"I'll make you a deal," I propose, kissing her temple and weaving my hands through her hair. I sense her yield into my touch, her body softening in my hands, causing something primal in me to roar to life.

"These are my favorite," she confesses, her voice quiet, her lips soft.

I sink in again, just to give her more of what she wants, because I can. Finally pulling back, I coax, "Open your eyes, angel."

She complies, revealing the deep blue ocean of her eyes. They're hazy, swirling with raw desire, sending a thrill through my blood.

"Hi," she breathes out, breaking the silence that has settled between us.

"Hi," I return her greeting with a smile, the connection between us palpable even in the simplest of exchanges. "Do you want to hear the deal?"

"We're making a lot of deals. I'm going to need a notebook."

"I'll get you one." I settle my hands against her hips. "I won't take you again in the shower if you let me come back tonight."

Her face is an open book. I find myself captivated by the way her thoughts seem to play out right before me; I can see the gears turning, weighing every possibility before settling on a path. Her face tenses, a silent confirmation of her internal struggle.

"I'm on call tonight." She catches her lip between her teeth in a clear sign of apprehension. She's always bracing for impact, always preparing for the worst. Some day, I'll find out why and who's responsible for that.

"That's okay, baby. When's your next free night?" I ask, trying to soothe her worry.

"Tuesday." A hint of wariness laces her voice.

"How about I come over then? I'll even bring dinner," I offer.

"I've already got dinner planned, but if you want come over, I'd like that." Her body language shifts, a visible release of tension in the lowering of her shoulders, her hands relaxing against my chest.

"Is that so?" I probe, keeping my voice casual, tucking away my excitement at her agreement.

"Yes. I meal plan for the week," she shrugs in the most adorable way. "If I don't plan ahead, I end up eating crap because I'm too tired to cook after work most days."

"What's on the menu?" I pull her closer.

"You'll have to let me go to check. It's on the fridge," she says, attempting to step away, but I hold her close, using her hips instead to turn her, pulling her back against my chest. Before she can read the schedule, I start massaging the muscles in her neck, and she groans, relaxing into my touch.

"Taco bowls," I read aloud from the fridge as her chin drops to her chest when I dig into the muscles on her shoulders. "I've never had a taco in a bowl before, but I'm definitely interested."

She glances back at me, a small smile on her lips. "Lots of protein, veggies, complex carbs with a little kick. All I have to do is assemble when I get home."

I whisper close to her ear, "I'm starting to think the way to your heart might be through your stomach."

She laughs, a sound that vibrates against me as she rests fully into my chest. "That would be a new and untested strategy," she admits, the tension easing from her muscles under my touch as I knead her arms.

Noted.

"Let's stick to the plan then. I wouldn't want to disrupt the doc's well-oiled routine," I tease.

Her smile, the small shake of her head, eyes still closed, snaps the last shred of my restraint. I lift her into my arms, carrying her towards the bathroom, as her laughter rings out and she lets me join her for the next step of her morning routine.

CHAPTER 36

Wisdom

WYATT

I saw her wipe away tears during the call with her friend, but I chose to stay silent until the despair in her eyes became too much to witness. The instinct to erase that pain was visceral, an uncontrollable force within me. Even in the shower, surrounded by steam and water, her body revealed stories she hadn't voiced.

The scars I felt on her shoulder and neck extend down her back—nearly perfect circles now visible in the light of the shower. They stand out starkly against her skin, igniting a fury within me as I considered a million possibilities for how she got them. Her tattoo, a series of dots, dashes, and Roman numerals, is small, about two inches. When my fingers grazed it, her body tensed, telling me how important it is to her.

Balancing my desire for answers with the possibility that she may never open up is a challenge. Without knowing her past, I might inadvertently hurt her, and my stomach twists just thinking about it. I don't know how to fend off ghosts and demons I can't see, even though my heart is screaming at me to protect her.

Back in the ranch house, the clock ticks toward six thirty, marking a later start to my day than usual, but I don't mind. Entering the kitchen, I'm met with the amused looks of my brothers and dad, their grins wide and knowing.

I'm in dire need of coffee; Dr. Pepper is not a passable substitute. I pour myself a cup, gulping down half in a single, satisfying swallow. After a refill, I take my place at the table, ready to face whatever these assholes have in store.

"Where you been, big brother?" Statler's voice, laced with mischief, cuts through the symphony of morning chatter, his smile spreading wide across his face.

"Fuck you," I retort with a grin I can't suppress. The joy bubbling inside me is too potent, too precious to let anything dim it. This woman has an uncanny power over me—her thoughts can level me, her sounds leave me speechless, and her touch drives me to the brink of sanity. And damn, it feels incredible.

"Boys," Dad's voice, firm yet affectionate, gently reprimands us. "Cursing isn't for the kitchen table." The rule is old, one of mom's, but it's etched into our family's fabric, as much a part of us as the land we work.

"Sorry, Dad," I chuckle, shaking my head at the memory of past scoldings. "I don't think I've gotten in trouble for swearing in years."

"For real though, man, I've never seen you quite like that with a woman before." Lincoln, ever the observer, joins the conversation with a seriousness that catches me off guard. His observation hangs in the air, heavy with implication.

"Like what?"

"You were staring at her all night like a lost puppy," Statler adds, his tone teasing yet kind. "You and her dog matched expressions."

I grinned and sipped coffee. "It would seem so." If looking at her like a sappy motherfucker means waking up with her in my arms, then so be it—I'll wear that label proudly.

"Wyatt, are you sure about her? There's something off, something she's hiding." Lincoln's words are a match to kindling, igniting a blaze that burns away the morning's the easy conversation.

"Don't go there, Lincoln," I grit through my teeth.

"It's not a judgment, Wy. It's just true. She was too calculated, too evasive. Answering questions partially but not fully, diverting attention back to you. Noticing those kinds of inconsistencies is what I do, Wyatt." Lincoln's face is neutral, but his eyes are hard.

My grip on the coffee mug tightens. "Do your job somewhere else and leave Parker out of it." I slam my cup down. "Don't question her or dig into her past or push her for answers. She is off limits. Do you understand me?"

Lincoln's response is calm, but it doesn't quell the storm of anger inside me. "I understand," he says quietly. "I just don't want you caught by surprise. I don't want you to get hurt."

"Fine. Consider your concern heard." Grabbing my cup, I walk to the sink and dump the remaining contents before turning out of the kitchen.

He means well, but my heart has already chosen its path, and there's no turning back. I'm in too deep, and I'll shield her with every fiber of my being, even if I don't know what I'm shielding her from.

◇◇◇◇◇◇◇◇◇◇◇◇◇◇◇◇

Dust swirls around my boots as I heave another bundle of wire onto the bed of the fencing truck. The sun is climbing higher, and I can feel the heat on the back of my neck when a familiar voice cuts through my thoughts.

"Wyatt."

I pause, a half-smile tugging at my lips. "You know, I could always tell I was in trouble when you said my name like that," I say without turning, focusing on the task at hand.

"Then it communicated exactly what I intended." Dad's voice is steady, his presence as solid as the land we stand on as he leans against the truck.

I let out a sigh, the weight of the supplies in my hands matched only by the weight of the conversation this morning. "I know, Dad. I know he was trying to help, I know he loves me, I know everything you're about to say. It doesn't make me less pissed." The words tumble out, a mix of frustration and resignation.

"Wyatt." His voice drops, a softness that stops me in my tracks. I turn to face him, meeting his gaze. "Son, Lincoln hasn't figured this one out yet, but there's a difference between a person with secrets and one with scars."

I swallow hard, the lump in my throat rising unexpectedly. "Dad, she's . . . " Words fail me as I try to articulate the delicate dance of trust Parker and I have been navigating. "Her past is complicated. There are a lot of things she hasn't told me. But she's just starting to trust me. She may never tell me the whole story. I won't force her, and I won't let anyone else either. She asked me to accept her, without knowing, and I have. She deserves that request to be respected."

Dad nods, understanding and pride etching his weathered face. "I agree, my boy. I didn't come to tell you what I saw as a warning, I came to tell you not to screw it up." His words hit me like a gust of wind, leaving me momentarily stunned. Weaving wisdom and experience into his tone, he continues. "Strong women aren't with you because they need you, Wy, but because they choose you. Being chosen, well, there's nothing in this world quite like that."

A surge of curiosity washes over me. "Why haven't I heard you talk like this before?"

"Because you didn't need it before, but it sure seems like you need it now." He closes the distance between us, his arm coming to rest across my shoulders. "I came to give you some unsolicited advice your mother gave to me years ago." The warmth of his arm, the sincerity in his eyes, and the timbre of his voice—all take me back to being a ten-year-old kid again.

The dust settles around us as I sit on the tailgate, the weight of Dad's words still hanging in the air.

"Go ahead," I urge him, my curiosity piqued.

"A strong woman doesn't need a savior. She needs a home. Your job is to be the place she feels safe enough to do whatever she needs. It isn't easy, Wy. Loving a woman like that means knowing when to act, when to wait, and when not to act at all."

I can almost hear the echo of Mom's voice in his advice.

"Don't you think it's too soon to talk love, Dad? I've only known her a little while, and she avoided me for a chunk of that." The question slips out before I can stop it.

"I don't know, Son, is it?" Dad's lop-sided grin is a challenge wrapped in a simple question. He pats my back and walks away, leaving me to mull over his words.

"Dad," I call out, the word carrying across the distance between us. "How did you figure it out? How'd you learn to love like that?"

"I made it my life's work, Son." With those words, he turns and strides away, silhouetted against the sun.

I'm left to reflect, my own puzzle slowly piecing itself together. Before I can complete it, Statler's voice breaks through.

"You look confused, big brother." He joins me on the tailgate.

I can't help but chuckle at Statler's statement. "Not confused," I clarify, "Dad just said some things I've never heard before."

"Like what?" Statler prods, leaning back on his arms, his curiosity piqued.

"Advice about strong women."

Statler nods, his gaze thoughtful. "I'd say from my observation, that's exactly what you have. Is she what you want?"

I pause, letting the question sink in. Reflecting on my past relationships, I realize they pale in comparison to what I have with her.

"A few months ago, with any other woman, I might have made myself pull back. But the idea of waking up with her like I did today," I confess, "sounds pretty fucking perfect."

The memory of her this morning flashes before me—her eyes glancing up over her shoulder, her body leaning back against my chest, the way she moved as she got ready. A smile spreads across my face, unstoppable and genuine. "I just have to figure out how to get her to agree to let me."

"You're a stubborn son of a bitch," he says, his smile mirroring my own. "I've rarely seen you lose. If I was a gambling man, I'd bet on you."

"Good, because I think I'm going to end up betting it all on her." With a newfound energy, I hop off the tailgate. "Want to help me build some fence?"

Statler's response comes with a grin. "Not particularly, but I won't tell you no."

CHAPTER 37

Homemade

PARKER

"Come with me to family dinner this Sunday," Wyatt whispers into my ear, his arms encircling me from behind. It's been two weeks, and my stomach still flutters every time he touches me.

"I can't finish the dishes with all your PDA." I spin around within the circle of his arms, lifting my soapy hands in a mock threat, but he just laughs, unfazed.

"I'll take over the dishes," he offers, pressing a kiss to my neck that sends a shiver down my spine.

I can't help but lean into him, tilting my head to give him more access, and I'm rewarded when he sucks lightly on the spot where my neck and shoulder meet.

"Say yes, Parker." His plea, spoken against my skin, sets off a dozen sparks humming through my body.

"Only if you let me cook," I counter, my wet hands finding their way under his T-shirt sleeves to settle on his solid warm biceps. He doesn't even flinch, just continues lightly kissing my neck.

"Deal," he agrees, pulling away with a suddenness that leaves me leaning into the space he's left. I open my eyes to his self-satisfied smirk.

"No more kissing while we're negotiating," I scold, playfully swatting at his abs, which is about as effective as a gnat against a horse.

"I can do a lot with my mouth that doesn't involve kissing," he retorts with a growl, making my toes curl. "What are you making?"

"Tofu," I lie, turning back to the sink with a hidden smirk.

"I really hope you're bluffing." His hands find my shoulders, thumbs pressing in with a skill that makes me drop the plate I'm holding. Thank goodness it's plastic.

"Don't stop." I sigh, gripping the sink's edge as his hands work magic across my back.

"If you give up on those dishes and let me handle them, I'll keep going," he bargains, his teeth scraping across my neck.

"The dishes are all yours." I lift my hands from the sudsy water and dry them on the towel.

"That was easy," he laughs from behind me. "I would have started with that thirty minutes ago if you hadn't been so adamant about the dishes."

"The rule that those who cook don't clean seemed important," I admit, "until you started doing . . . this." I can't suppress a groan as he works out a particularly stubborn knot near my shoulder blade.

His arm, strong and warm across my waist guides me backwards in a slow dance of steps until we make it to the couch. The chaise offers a perfect perch as he eases down, and I find myself settled in front of him. He lifts my shirt over my head, and then his hands return, strong and sure, their warmth seeping into my shoulders and back. His fingers glide across my skin, deliberately and tenderly kneading away the tension.

"What kind of marathon did you run at the clinic today? Your back's practically stone," he murmurs, his breath a soft caress against my rapidly heating blood.

"Big dogs," I sigh, the words muffled as my head dips forward, succumbing to his touch. "All of them afraid of the exam table. Every single one."

"Am I hurting you? Your skin's red," he says, concern lacing his voice as he pauses.

"If you even think of stopping, I swear I'll actually make tofu." My threat, delivered at a whisper, is sincere.

"No need to fight dirty." His laughter fills the air around us, comforting me, and I feel his lips graze my neck, his breath warm on my skin.

"Seriously though," I breathe in deeply as his hands travel lower, prompting an instinctive arch in my back, "What's off limits for your family? Anything you all can't or won't eat?"

"Tofu," he replies, his hands tracing comforting strokes up the length of my back.

"Spaghetti and meatballs?" I murmur, barely able to keep my eyes open under the spell of his touch.

"Perfect," he affirms with a soft kiss on my shoulder. "Turn around."

I rotate to face him, my eyelids heavy. As he begins to work on my shoulders and collarbone from this new angle, I melt into him involuntarily, my body overriding my mind. I'm resting against his chest, his heartbeat against my cheek. He reclines, bringing me with him. Gradually, his firm pressure gives way to gentle strokes. With my head resting on his chest, his body warm and that unique blend of leather and cedar surrounding me, I'm on the brink of slipping into a deep sleep.

"What would you have done without me? How do you take care of yourself?" His voice is a gentle hum, laced with a hint of concern as his hands continue stroking.

"I'd be like everyone else, I suppose," my voice soft in the quiet of the room. "A hot shower, yoga, or sleep."

A playful grin tugs at my lips as I lift my head from his chest, finally allowing my eyes to open. He's reclined, head tilted back, eyes closed. "You know what this back rub has earned you, Wyatt?" I tease.

His head tilts down, eyes meeting mine, a smile playing on his lips. "What's that, angel?" The flicker of desire in his gaze is unmistakable.

"Not what you're thinking," I say with a laugh, shaking my head. "However, I will make spaghetti from scratch."

"Deal," he agrees. "Can I stay tonight, Parker?" he asks, his voice soft yet earnest, a tone I've never heard him use with anyone, as though I'm the only person he softens for.

I hesitate, the words catching in my throat. "I'm on call tonight . . ." I hesitate, my words trailing off, the invitation hanging in the air.

Despite every reason to maintain a certain distance, he's impossible to resist, my body craving him against my will. "If you want to," I continue, his immediate smile telling me everything.

"Why don't you go get ready for bed, I'll finish up in the kitchen and meet you there." He sits up, taking me with him.

"Okay." Pushing off his chest, I stand. His hands run up the backs of my thighs before he stands, leaving us chest to chest.

The domesticity of the moment wraps around me, like a quilt meant to be comforting but sewn with threads of panic. It's an odd sensation, this internal tug-of-war—seventy five percent of me yearning to sink into this feeling, while the remaining twenty-five can only think about all the ways this could go wrong.

I make my way to the bathroom, the click of Cooper's paws a familiar soundtrack as he assumes his usual post outside the door as I wash my face.

When I look up, I catch a glimpse of Wyatt, relaxed and framed by the bathroom doorway. His arms are folded, a smile on his face.

"I got you something." My voice cracks slightly betraying the uncertainty that flutters in my stomach.

"Oh?" He straightens, stepping into the cramped space of the bathroom, his eyes lit with curiosity. I reach into the drawer, the simple act feeling somehow monumental, and hand him the gift.

"It's a toothbrush." I feel the heat rise up my neck as he examines it, his gaze shifting between the object and me. His smile unfolds slowly, like the first rays of dawn. "Do I get to keep it here?"

His question is tentative, hopeful, as he draws me close, our chests pressing together in a silent conversation as his hand rests at the small of my back.

"Yes," I whisper, my gaze dropping. But his fingers are gentle as they lift my chin, forcing my gaze up.

"Thank you, Parker." His kiss on my cheek ignites a different kind of heat, one that is slow, steady, radiating out from my heart, settling deep into my bones.

I nod before slipping past him. In my bedroom, the ritual of preparing for sleep is a comfort against the heart-racing intimacy a simple toothbrush brought about.

Minutes trickle by, and the bed dips as he joins me, the sheets softly rustling. His presence is a feeling, so I remain still while anticipation builds within me. Then, with his signature brand of tenderness, he slides one arm beneath my head, a pillow of flesh and bone, and drapes the other over my hip.

Pulled back against his chest, surrounded by him, my muscles unfurl, anxiety and tension seeping away like sand through an hourglass. His heartbeat is a steady drum against my back, my own quiet lullaby. I'm adrift in the harbor of his arms, and as sleep beckons, the world fades until there's nothing but the warmth of him.

◇◇◇◇◇◇◇◇◇◇◇◇◇◇◇◇◇◇

The kitchen is washed with the golden glow of evening light, casting long, warm shadows that dance across the countertops thanks to the expanse of gorgeous windows. I roll the pasta dough, transforming it into delicate ribbons on the island.

"I doubt any of us will be satisfied with boxed pasta again." Shep's voice, rich and hearty, fills the space.

"My dad likes to say, if you have eggs, flour, and ten minutes, you don't need a box," I share, my hands working with familiar ease, shaping the pasta into tiny nests that await their transformation in boiling water.

"And the sauce?" Shep inquires, his forearms resting on the island, his smile as inviting as the aroma filling the room. "Is the recipe a secret, or might you be persuaded to share? Because it smells like heaven, and I guarantee it'll be better than the jar."

"I'll write it down for you."

His Wyoming charm sways me as easily as a key turns a lock, and I can't help but return his smile.

"I was prepared to haggle more for that secret," he admits with a chuckle, his eyes twinkling with mischief.

"You make it hard to resist. You remind me of someone who would have given you all of Greg's recipes without a moment's hesitation, much to Greg's annoyance," I say, a fondness in my voice.

"Who's that?" Shep's voice gentles.

"My dad, Cameron." Swallowing, I push down the lump in my throat.

"What about me reminds you of him, sweetheart?" His voice holds a somber note, yet it's filled with empathy.

"He was charming and funny, characteristics that seem to be a staple of the Lochlan gene pool. But beyond that, Cameron was a pillar, always ready with a shoulder that seemed tailor-made for holding whatever you needed it to. A trait I get the feeling you share. You hug like him too. The kind of hug that just reaches right down into the soul," I confess, my voice cracking as a surge of emotion rises within me. I turn away, blinking rapidly to keep the unexpected tears at bay, swallowing hard against the feeling.

"I'm honored," Shep says quietly, his voice understanding and reverent. "I'm always here, if you find you ever need one of those hugs, Parker."

"Deal," I reply, lifting my gaze to meet his, a smile breaking through the emotional cloud.

He nods just as the door swings open, and the rest of the Lochlan men make their entrance. Statler is the first to reach me, his fist raised for a bump—a gesture I've easily come to return. Wyatt follows, his arms wrapping around my waist from behind, his lips pressing a fleeting kiss to the crown of my head.

"I really want to say that you didn't have to do all this for us but I'm one step away from drooling over the smell," Wyatt whispers in my ear.

"I'm glad to hear it." I turn to offer him a smile, which he seizes as an opportunity to plant a quick kiss on me. "PDA, cowboy," I warn with laughter.

"Need me to do anything?"

"Nope. I've got it. But you do have to let me go," I tease, matching his playful energy.

"Damn," he feigns disappointment, and I roll my eyes at his theatrics.

"Hey, Doc," Lincoln greets as he enters the kitchen, and I feel tension creep into my shoulders. It's probably unfair, but the nerves take over anyway, leaving a bitter taste in my mouth.

"Hey," I manage, offering a nod in his direction.

"Wyatt, did you mean to leave the arena pen open because you've got a herd in it if you didn't." Lincoln's smile is easy, but it doesn't quite reach his eyes.

"Shit. No." Wyatt releases me. "Be right back. Stat, let's go push them out."

"I'll give you a hand," Shep chimes in, ever the helpful one.

And then it's just Lincoln and me. *Great.*

"Parker, I've got to ask," Lincoln starts, leaning against the counter with a look that's both concerned and a touch sad. "Did I do something wrong?"

His question catches me off guard, and I pause, knife in hand. "No, Lincoln. You didn't," I assure him, setting aside my task to give him my full attention. "I'm sorry I made you feel that way. It's just . . ." The words are difficult, the admission even more so.

"As long as it's not something I did, you don't need to tell me," he offers kindly, and I'm struck by the sincerity in his voice.

"If I tell you that, in my experience, lawyers tend to not be exactly what they say, can that be enough?" The words are heavy with a million unspoken memories, fears, and failures. Swallowing carefully, I wait for his answer.

"Of course. I can understand that experience." His expression genuine, he nods. "To some degree, I'm whoever my family needs me to be, so you're not wrong, but all those versions are still me. Being me means I can't overlook the little moments where I know you hold back, or the instinct that tells me you have a story, but I hope I can prove that being me also means all I want is you and my brother happy. I don't want to make you uncomfortable, not here. You're safe here, Parker, in case no one has said it that directly to you yet."

He speaks his words quietly and sincerely as I watch the emotion swirl in his eyes. "You Lochlan men are certainly cut from the same cloth." I swallow. "And, as odd as it feels to me to say, I think I believe you, Lincoln."

A smile breaks through my reserve, tugging up the corners of my mouth. He returns the smile, and once again, it's pure Lochlan charm. "Good. Let me know if I step outside the lines, Doc."

"Deal." I laugh shaking my head. "You are all far too charming for your own good. You know that?" I laugh, shaking my head as I turn back to the sauce, stirring the rich, red blend.

"Dad claims the charm is all from mom," Lincoln playfully teases as he rounds the stove, his fist raised in a gesture mirroring Statler's.

"Well," I respond, meeting his fist bump with my own, the contact a brief affirmation of our tentative connection, "Considering your dad's charm, I'd say he's being modest. No offense to your mom, of course."

He chuckles, conceding the point with a nod, then urges me, "Put me to work."

"You can be on bread detail." I direct him towards the fridge. "I baked it yesterday. There's a sparkly blue container in there with compound butter. Just slather each side and get them on a baking sheet."

"Yes ma'am," he replies, his tone light, giving me a playful salute before heading to the fridge.

I watch him from the corner of my eye and let out a small breath I hadn't realized I was holding. One by one, these men dismantle my defenses, showing me that they are unlike any others I've known.

Boots on hardwood signals the return of the others, and I'm struck by the realization that I've just spent fifteen peaceful minutes with Lincoln.

Every day with the Lochlans is a revelation, each moment better than the last. As I glance over, my gaze connects with Wyatt's, and in that silent exchange, I spy an open offer to join his world.

CHAPTER 38

Poetry

WYATT

I zip up my bag, my mind wandering through the past few weeks. On the nights she's let me stay, I find watching her answer the call line and slip seamlessly into her role as a vet undeniably sexy. She's not slept over at my house yet; she was visibly uncomfortable the last time I brought it up, so I've let it drop for now.

Slowly, cautiously, she's lowering barriers, letting me learn more and more about her. As it turns out, the way to Parker's heart is through a well-stocked kitchen, so I do my part to make sure her fridge is never empty. While some women might desire diamonds, Parker treasures snacks.

My conversations with Camilla—or Cami, as Parker calls her—have been enlightening. Cami ignites a boldness in Parker that's fascinating. Their friendship is complex, grounded in something I don't understand, and unshakable. However, I sense a nagging familiarity about Cami that I can't quite place.

Over the last few weeks, we've built a comfortable routine. Some mornings we run together; other times, I watch her move through her workout as I get ready for the day. My clothes haven't found a home in her closet yet, but my toothbrush standing next to hers on the sink is a small victory. The most significant gesture she's made was to purchase a single-cup coffee maker, complete with various coffee pods. I demonstrated my appreciation repeatedly in the shower.

Her image in my kitchen still lingers, even two weeks later. Parker's spaghetti and meatballs left us in awe. I was worried she was making it too difficult, but she was adamant that her way would be better, and she wasn't wrong. It easily ranks as one of the best meals I've ever eaten. The battle for leftovers was fierce and decided by rock-paper-scissors, which left Parker genuinely mortified. She vowed to make enough for everyone to share leftovers next time to avoid future arguments. She was serious when she said she hates conflict.

Even though the food was incredible, it's the image of walking in and seeing her standing there smiling at me that I review over and over. Day by day, she gives me more of herself. She's taught me basic sign language, shared her love for the color blue and preference for sunny days, and her excitement to experience her first snowy Wyoming winter in the months ahead.

I even know her comfort food—mac and cheese—which I discovered when I came over and found her, eyes rimmed in red, making it. When I asked what was wrong, I found out she had to put down a family pet. The little girl who owned the dog sobbed in the office, which led to Linda crying, then the techs, then her, and eventually even Charlie teared up. I swallowed a laugh when I turned her into my arms, squeezing her tight as tears spilled from her eyes.

The situation wasn't funny, but Parker was absolutely crushed at breaking that little girl's heart. About the time I opened my mouth with a circle-of-life cliché on my lips, she looked up into my eyes and the devastation in hers stopped me cold. Remembering my dad's advice, I chose not to say a word. I finished making the mac and cheese, then kept her wrapped in my arms the rest of the night.

We've had one official date out in the world. It should have been two, but after a night spent on a call, she dozed off in my truck on the way to dinner. Rather than wake her, I drove her back home and suggested a movie on the couch. She was asleep on my chest before the opening credits finished. She didn't even stir as I stood with her, carrying her to bed. She simply curled into me and stayed there until sunrise.

Regardless of how she feels about public displays of affection, in the quiet of the night, or when we're alone, my girl is a cuddler. Waking up, finding her tucked into me, her body's heat has become my personal sunrise.

The knock at the door pulls me from my thoughts, and I glance up to see Lincoln standing in the doorway, his posture relaxed against the frame, like he's some sort of model.

"Suits!" I greet him, the brief tension that flared between us weeks ago already gone. "What can I do for you?"

"Looks like you're packing a bag again. Parker off work tonight?" His inquiry is casual, but there's an undercurrent of curiosity.

"Yep." The finality of the zipper's closure punctuates my response.

"She's really the one for you, isn't she?" Lincoln's voice carries a note of wonder, a rare thing for him.

I can't help but smile. "I'm thinking so but trying to take it slow."

"Ugh, look at you. Just a sappy love-sick idiot. You told her yet?" He teases, but there's a genuine interest behind his ribbing.

"You'll figure it out someday too, buddy, and I'll love watching you fall on your face."

"Maybe. I've never met anyone who could keep up with me, so I'm not too worried about it. But . . ." He saunters in and perches on the dresser, a habit from childhood. "Don't beat me up here, I just . . . how do you know if you don't *know* everything?"

I face him, taking a seat on the edge of the bed. "Lincoln, you like answers. It's what makes you a damn good lawyer. But this last month confirmed what I've felt all along. I *know* her, even if I don't know all her stories. Knowing comes from the mornings waking up with her in my arms, the small concessions she makes, like letting me open doors. It's how she outplayed Statler in poker. It was the moment she literally breathed life into that foal. All of that is her, and there's never been anyone like her."

"That was almost poetic," he admits with a smile, then hops off the dresser. "I'm happy for you, big brother."

"Thanks." I feel contentment that only family can bring spread through me.

Lincoln's departure leaves a silence in its wake, pushing what I don't know to the forefront of my mind. None of them are deal breakers, but I pray someday she feels safe enough to tell me about each scar I've found on her skin. From the small one over her right hip bone, to the twin scars on her abdomen, or the jagged line etched into her left knee. I want to know where the burn marks, those faded battle wounds, across her hands and wrists came from.

Until she's ready to tell me, I choose a different path. I opt for my actions, my touch, to speak all the words I can't. The joy I feel when her body no longer tenses under my fingers, her tattoo no longer a trigger for withdrawal, is unmatched. So, I'll keep touching, soothing, proving she's safe in my hands.

The thought of confronting the source of her pain flickers through my mind, an instinct I can't act on, so I temper it. For now, my mission is clear: to be the home she needs, the person who proves she's not alone, no matter what she's facing.

I glance at my phone, seeing her name light up the screen.

Jogging down the stairs and out the door, I deposit my bag into the truck, then hustle to the barn to get ready for her.

CHAPTER 39

Lady

PARKER

Somehow, I've been persuaded that learning to ride is a critical skill. I've been bribed with trails and wildflowers. I have no clue how he managed it, and I have nothing but doubts.

"I work with horses every day. Surely it can't be that hard to learn. Right?" I muse aloud, seeking affirmation from Cooper, who gazes back at me with his tail rhythmically drumming against the seat. He's as smitten with the ranch as I am.

Pulling up to the barn, I step out with Cooper by my side, and a flutter of nerves causes my stomach to turn over. This occasion feels monumental, and I can't pinpoint why. I stride into the barn and catch sight of him grooming a solid white horse, more petite than the others I've encountered these past months. I take the moment to observe him. The barn is filled with the strains of slow, easy country music, stirring memories of our first dance here. As the day's light wanes, it casts long, amber shadows across the hay-strewn concrete.

Wyatt's movements are a blend of confidence and grace. He murmurs to the horse, his voice hushed, so I can't quite catch what he's saying. Yet, I can easily conjure the timbre in my mind. He opted for a baseball cap instead of his cowboy hat today, and it sits backward on his head, oozing quiet confidence. He's clad in a fitted white T-shirt that showcases his bare arms. His jeans are darkened from the day's work, his boots scuffed and well worn.

I'm intimately familiar with the feel of his body, the way his muscles contract under my touch when I trace his tattoo. His voice, saying my name in the stillness of night, stirs undeniable emotions in me. He is a force that even my deepest doubts and fears can't withstand. My demons and ghosts alike surrender to him.

The moment he senses my presence, our eyes lock, and the intensity of his gaze ignites a fire somewhere deep, a force so potent that it convinces me I can conquer any challenge. In his eyes, I find a strength that bolsters me and a softness that draws me in.

Impulsively, I stride towards him. Using his shirt, I tug him down to meet my lips, pouring into the kiss every unspoken word, every tangled emotion. He responds in kind, his touch a language of its own. Warm strong hands wrap around my thighs, lifting, my legs gripping his waist. When he pulls away, his eyes mirror my soul. He leans in, his forehead against mine—a gesture that's become a cherished favorite of mine, even though he doesn't know that.

"Hi, angel. Everything okay?" he asks softly.

"Yes." I wrap my arms around his neck, resting my head on his shoulder, inhaling his scent. His hand moves up to cradle the back of my neck while the other circles around my back, holding me close to him. In this position, I imagine I look like a bear clinging to a tree.

Suddenly, I hear someone yell, "Get a room!"

The shout startles me, and I instinctively try to disentangle myself from his hold, but he keeps me anchored to him, both hands now under my thighs. I glance over my shoulder to see his brothers approaching, a playful smirk on their faces, and I can't help but feel heat coloring my cheeks.

"Suits, say another word, and I'll have Statler whip your ass," Wyatt calls out, his voice echoing down the alley with a mock sternness.

"What, can't do it yourself anymore, old man?" Lincoln retorts. His approach is casual yet deliberate.

"I know when not to let go of what's in my hands. I delegate accordingly." His grip on me tightening just a fraction, a silent reassurance.

Statler's hand lands on Lincoln's shoulder, his tone serious yet amused. "I accept all responsibilities delegated to me. Remember that."

"No fighting," I say sternly, looking each of them in the eye.

"Yeah, no fighting." Lincoln feigns seriousness, eliciting a laugh from me.

"That includes no poking at your brother, Lincoln," I quip before I can stop myself. The moment of relaxed banter surprises me just a little. Wyatt's comforting laughter vibrates through me, and then he plants a soft kiss on my cheek.

"I'm hurt, Doc." Lincoln's playful objection echoes through the barn, his hand dramatically placed over his heart.

"What do you two want?" Wyatt inquires, his tone light but curious.

"We came to see if you wanted to hang out before the doc got off work, but she beat us here," Lincoln explains, his eyes glinting with a mix of mischief and brotherly affection.

"Want me to finish up with Lady so you all can head out?" Statler's offer is sweet.

"Nope," Wyatt replies with a smile that reaches his eyes. "The doc is going to ride tonight."

"That remains to be seen." I make another attempt to escape Wyatt's hold. But he responds with a gentle squeeze, his touch commanding and possessive.

"You'll do great, Doc," Statler encourages, before turning to Lincoln with a conspiratorial grin. "C'mon, little brother. I feel like beer and pool at your house is on the menu tonight."

"We don't get to stay and watch?" Lincoln protests, only to be pulled back by Statler's firm grip on his collar.

"No," comes the simultaneous response from Statler and Wyatt, a united front against any further teasing.

As they retreat, I face Wyatt again. "Can I get down now?"

"Maybe. Answer me this first, do you want to learn to ride? You don't have to, Parker. I can get you to that field without it." His voice is a blend of concern and sympathy.

"Put me down, and I'll answer," I negotiate, and with a gentle ease, he lowers me down to the ground. I turn to the white mare, running my hand along her soft coat, which grounds me.

"I want to try, but that's not why I'm nervous," I confess, my voice cracking just slightly.

"Okay. Is why you're nervous the same reason you kissed me just now? I'll never complain about it," he says, his smile disarming and genuine. "You just don't typically initiate public displays of affection. You doing okay?"

"I don't know why I did it really, and I don't know why I'm learning, so I suppose the answer to your question is yes. I guess that's why I'm nervous," I finally admit.

"That makes sense," he responds, tenderly brushing hair off my forehead and tucking it behind my ear. "You love information. You're like Lincoln that way. Probably doesn't feel great to feel like you're missing a piece."

"How do you do that?"

"Do what, angel?" he replies softly, stepping closer and wrapping me in a comforting hug.

"Understand me." The statement hangs between us like a delicate thread.

"Let's just say I'm a quick study," he states, a knowing look in his eyes that only deepens my confusion. "For now, kiss me anytime you want and let me know if I can help you feel less nervous. Deal?"

"Deal." I nod slowly, the agreement settling in my heart.

"Good. Now, introductions," he says, taking my hand, lacing his fingers through mine. "This is Lady. She's fifteen, calm, and easy-going. She'll take good care of you."

"Hi, Lady, nice to meet you," I greet the mare, stroking her neck.

Out in the small working pen, Wyatt patiently explains the saddle's components, answering my questions until it's time for me to mount. As soon as my feet leave the ground, the world shifts. Suddenly, I am part of something larger, a tradition as old as time. The saddle creaks beneath me; I feel the leather warm as I get comfortable. Lady's muscles ripple under my palms, a living being of power and grace.

We move together, Lady and I, a slow dance in the setting sun. My nerves settle into a rhythm with her gait, and the world narrows down to the beat of her hooves, the tenderness of Wyatt's gaze, and the vast sky above. I can see why riding is so addicting. The session ends, but the feeling lingers—a sense of accomplishment, of belonging to something bigger than me.

As we leave the barn, the image of Lady turning out into the field, free and graceful, is a mirror to the potential life I could embrace—a life filled with simple joys, with sunsets and sunrises, and Wyatt. It's a vision that beckons with the promise of hope and a future as open as the fields stretched out before us.

CHAPTER 40

Interrupted

WYATT

The anticipation of her weekend off sends a current of excitement through me. I'm dying for two uninterrupted days, a stretch of time where she's mine alone, away from the demands of the world. As I pack my bag, a task that's become as familiar as the lines of my own hands, my phone lights up. The buzz of the notification is like a race's starting bell, and I'm ready to run headlong into the weekend.

ANGEL

Good news & bad news. Which first?

WYATT

Bad.

You can't spend the weekend here with me.

I fail to see what good can come after that.

Cami surprised me and flew in. You get to meet her.

I mean I'm glad but . . . not as good as having you naked for 48 hours in bed with me.

I didn't say you couldn't have me, just that you can't sleep here 😅 and I'm sorry. I'll make it up to you.

I take it all back.

Cami wants to go out tonight. Want to round up your brothers and take us dancing? Cami said a cowboy bar is required.

We could just send her with the guys and stay back.

ha ha no, no one counters Cami's plans once she makes them. Give in, it'll be faster.

Let me check.

I switch text threads to my sibling chat.

WYATT

Hey assholes. Parker's best friend surprised her by flying in. The girls want to go out dancing and wanted to know if you wanted to join.

RIOT

I hate that I don't get to be a part of this stuff.

LINC

I'm in.

STAT

Same.

Even if you were here you couldn't go to a damn bar Riot.

STAT

Agreed.

LINC

Wait... is her friend hot?

OFF LIMITS. You do not get to mess with Parker's friends.

LINC

Fine. But is she hot?

Ignoring that . . . You should know she's deaf. She wears a device that lets her hear and she can read lips but just look out for her at the bar okay?

STAT

10-4

RIOT

Take a pic or something . . . no one has shown me what Parker looks like yet. Please!

We'll see.

LINC

Pick the girls up at 830 and meet us at the bar.

I switch back to my texts with Parker.

WYATT

Guys are in. I'll pick you all up at 830 and they'll meet us at the bar.

ANGEL

Which bar?

Now, I just have to avoid killing every guy at the bar who looks at her tonight.

Easy.

◇◇◇◇◇◇◇◇◇◇◇◇◇◇◇◇◇

PARKER

"The guys are in. Wyatt's coming to get us at eight thirty," I tell Cami as she meanders through my apartment, her footsteps echoing softly on the hardwood floor. The bright afternoon light filters through the sheer curtains, the room awash with the oranges and pinks of the sunset.

"Great, that gives us," she glances at her watch, "roughly three hours for you to spill all the secrets you've been keeping."

"I have no idea what you're talking about." I whirl around, busying myself in the kitchen to avoid her probing gaze.

"Parker, you're the worst liar ever. Out with it, or I swear I'll drag Greg into this."

"You wouldn't dare!" I spin back to face her. Instantly my heart races; it feels like a fluttering bird trapped in my chest.

"Try me. Start talking," Cami commands, hands on her hips, the doorway framing her silhouette. The eyebrow arched in challenge is as clear as the determination in her stance.

"I . . . I'm overwhelmed, Cami." I throw my hands up, frustration bubbling in my chest. The motion releases the scent of cedar from the shirt I'm wearing because it's his.

"I can't stop feeling all the things or waiting for the other shoe to drop. I'm worse than a moth chasing a flame when he's around, but he never demands more than I'm ready to give. Oh no," I wave my arms again, my anxiety rising as I pace before the sink. "He persuades, requests, bargains, negotiates with his stupidly adorable deals but never demands. Except he insists on eye contact when I look away, though I don't think that counts. I know I'm holding back and I know it's not fair to him. The longer I withhold, the more it feels like I'm ashamed of her or hiding something, and the guilt is killing me Cami."

I slump onto the new barstools—Wyatt's recent addition—and rest my head on my folded arms atop the island, the cool wood beneath my skin offering a stark contrast to my heated cheeks.

Cami's hand finds my back, her touch soothing. "I think it's time you tell him, honey." Her concern is palpable, as tangible as the comforting weight of her hand on my shoulder.

"I don't know how. When I try, the words get stuck, and I can't breathe."

"Parker, this man, what you're experiencing, I understand," she says, her hands framing my face with a gentle firmness. "You've never really opened up about it, but that doesn't mean you're not capable."

"Did I ever tell you about my last conversation with Cameron?" I whisper.

"No. Would you like to?"

I nod. Shutting my eyes, I inhale deeply. "He asked me for a favor actually." Cami's hand slips over mine in a comforting gesture, and I let the memories carry me back to that sterile room in the hospital, the beeping monitors the only break in the silence.

"Snow, can you do something for me?" His voice is weak, a mere whisper, each word straining as if he's lifting a stone.

"Anything," I whisper. Hot, relentless tears carve rivers down my cheeks. I'm not ready to close the book on our story, but the final page is being turned without my consent. Fate doesn't yield to desperation, a truth Cameron has etched into my heart in these two weeks.

"Be brave, baby girl." His hand trembles as it reaches for mine, and I feel how cool his once-warm hands have become. I clasp it, and a surge of memories floods through our joined hands. We look at one another in silent acknowledgment of a looming goodbye. He's been my rock, my confidant, my cheerleader.

"I'm scared," I confess, a truth I could only share with him. Together, we've dissected every nightmare, every trauma, every secret.

"That's the best part. Bravery isn't about not being scared, it's about having the determination and the courage to keep going even when you are scared. Life is scary. You have to choose to live it."

"And if I mess up?"

"You will, countless times. It isn't about the mistakes you make; it's about the memories. It's about adventure in the face of adversity. It's about love in the presence of loss. It's about belief in the magic of life, even after you've faced the harshest realities. You were my magic, Parker. Don't ever lose your magic, baby girl."

His arms open wide, an invitation I accept without hesitation, climbing beside him on the hospital bed. As we lay there, the world outside fades—a symphony of beeping monitors and hushed

I dab at my tear-streaked cheeks with the sleeve of my shirt.
"When I'm with Wyatt, Cami, it's like a tornado, all tangled up and
nameless. But there's one thing I'm certain of—Wyatt makes me want
to be brave. He makes me want to do what Cameron asked. It's just
. . . I don't know how. What if it changes everything?"

Cami exhales sharply, her own eyes glistening as she mirrors my
actions. "Something tells me when the moment's right, you won't
have to wonder how. And from what I know so far, I can guarantee
it'll change things, but I think it'll make it something stronger, Parks."

I let out a sigh, the weight of our talk pressing down. "Can we
change the subject?"

Her grin is a sliver of sunshine. "Yes. Let's tackle those red-
rimmed eyes and get ready. I've picked out the perfect ensemble for
us. Tonight, we embrace boldness, and tomorrow . . . tomorrow you
can wrestle with bravery. If you decide to tell him, I'll be right there
if you want. You don't need to do it alone."

Taking a deep breath, I resolve to put aside my worries. "Tomorrow,
Parker will deal with that. Tonight is about letting loose."

Cami's smile widens. "Exactly! Let's find me a cowboy tonight,
shall we?"

CHAPTER 41

Bars

The knock resonates in a familiar rhythm that sets my heart racing. The hours spent with Cami since her airport arrival have been like rediscovering a lost piece of myself. The outfit she's chosen for me, while initially surprising, now feels like a second skin—I can't deny it—I look hot.

As the door swings open, Wyatt's reaction is everything I'd hoped for. Desire dances across his face, a look I've grown to recognize and crave. His gaze lingers on me, taking in the bold statement of my black knee-high boots, the leather skirt hugging my curves, and the cropped vintage tee. Tonight, I'm shedding the usual attire for something that screams "wild," and it's exhilarating. My hair falls just right, my makeup is a masterpiece of intentional imperfection, and my lips are blood red.

"Damn. That's exactly how I want a man to look at me," Cami declares, her voice tinged with approval. Wyatt's attention snaps to her, and I savor the moment of surprise before his eyes find mine again.

"Good thing I can hold my own in a fight with you dressed like that," he teases, a playful glint in his eye. I throw my head back, laughter spilling out, light and carefree.

"No fights," I sign as I speak the words, but my attempt at sternness undermined by the distraction of his gaze. It's a look that kindles a need, my body knowing exactly what happens when he follows through on that look, the ache in my core is difficult to ignore.

As Wyatt turns toward Cami and and deliberately shapes his fingers, his voice accompanying the signed words, "My name is Wyatt."

I can't help but feel a swell of pride. Cami's smile is radiant, reflecting the joy I feel inside. Wyatt's determination to master this new language, to bridge the gap between worlds, is more than just learning—it's an act that demonstrates his desire to be in my world.

His back is to me, but I move to stand beside him. He glances my way, a silent conversation passing between us for me to sign his next words. He's not ready to do it himself, but I know with time, he'll get there.

"If you're ready to stop a few hearts in this small town, ladies, let's go," Wyatt says with a confident grin.

Cami is already on the move, clutch in hand, as I fasten Cooper's leash. It's a necessity in public, even though we don't use it in the clinic or at the ranch. Wyatt patiently waits as I secure the door, his anticipation for the evening palpable. He slides up behind me, his hand venturing slowly up my hip to rest just below the hem of my shirt, covering the sliver of my exposed skin.

"I may not be able to sleep here tonight, but you should keep this outfit, so next time you wear it, I get to take it off you." His breath is warm as his lips trace the shell of my ear.

"I was hoping you'd say that." Maybe it's the outfit, but I feel a surge of confidence that pushes me to press my hips against him. The hand on my waist squeezes gently.

His lips find my neck briefly before he lets go of my waist.

As Wyatt turns to go downstairs, his hand hovers just above his shoulder, an invitation for me to take it. My hand finds his, a dance we've perfected. Cami leans casually against the truck, her eyes lighting up as she begins to sign with an infectious energy.

"Did he just hold your hand on the way down? He's like a book boyfriend come to life. Who taught him that?" Her grin spreads.

"I'm not sure," I reply with a laugh, pausing by the door, not yet reaching for the handle. *"Just remember, they don't know about your job. These guys are sharp, though, so watch your words."*

"Got it," she responds with a playful wink.

"Not that I mind being left out, but we should go if we want to make it on time," Wyatt interjects, his voice pulling us back to the present. He ushers Cooper into the back seat, then holds the door for Cami. Once she's settled, he moves to my door.

Sliding past him, I pull myself in. He leans across to buckle me in, his movements deliberate, the faint scent of his cologne invading me. His fingers skim across my thighs where my skirt has ridden up, leaving a trail of prickled goosebumps in the wake of his touch.

Cami's voice cuts through the night, a mix of surprise and curiosity. "Wait, did you just let him open the door for you *and* buckle you in?"

Wyatt chuckles, a sound that rumbles through the quiet cab. "We have an understanding about a few things. I'll let Parker elaborate," he says, a hint of pride in his voice. The arrogance flickers across his features, urging me to pull him close and kiss him, but I roll my eyes instead.

"He's got some caveman tendencies, and after a small discussion, we came to an understanding —or rather—we made a deal. He opens doors. The seatbelt, I'm pretty sure, is just a side effect of the short skirt."

Wyatt's smirk, complete with those charming dimples, seals our little pact with a wink as he closes the door with a soft thud. Circling the hood, he's oblivious to Cami's theatrical fanning.

"Oh, honey," she exclaims, "this man is something else. You do see that, right? I mean, this is the stuff of novels."

I can only muster a soft confession. "I told you. He's genuinely good."

Wyatt slides into the driver's seat, unaware of our exchange, so Cami doesn't respond.

"Wyatt, who schooled you in the art of being the ultimate book boyfriend? You've got the moves down to an art." Cami's curiosity is piqued.

Wyatt's brow lifts as we pull away. "Not sure what you mean by 'moves'?"

"Going down the stairs first. Opening the door. Looking at her like a snack." Cami lists them off on her fingers, and Wyatt's laughter—that infectious sound I adore—fills the cab once more.

"Parker's not a snack, Cami. Respectfully, she's a whole damn meal. And the way I look at her, that's a bit beyond my control. The rest? That's table stakes. I've got a baby sister, and any guy who doesn't live up to those standards isn't going to be around long enough to learn them."

His hand finds mine, a gesture as natural as breathing, and he presses a kiss to it, a silent reminder that the truck doesn't count in our public affection deal.

Cami's teasing voice breaks through. "You're setting the bar high, Wyatt. You're going to have to crank the A/C in this truck though if you keep kissing her hand like that."

He laughs, then flicks on the A/C before winking and reclaiming my hand.

"Tell me, are these the Lochlan standards? Do your brothers also abide by them?" Cami's eyebrows arch in playful inquiry.

"Absolutely not, Cami! His brothers are off-limits," I assert, a bit too quickly perhaps, my voice firm over the hum of the engine.

"I'm sorry, what was that?" Cami teases, feigning deafness. I can't help but laugh, shaking my head at her antics.

As we pull up to the bar, the scene is straight out of a classic Western film. The building stands solitary against the backdrop of the open sky, its wooden façade weathered by time and elements, telling stories of countless sunsets. The sign above the entrance, outlined in flickering neon lights, spells out the bar's name, *Woody's*, in a rustic font. The neon buzzes and hums, a beacon in the twilight.

The parking lot is a patchwork of gravel and dust, with trucks and motorcycles scattered about. The bar's windows are tinted, and the soft strumming of a guitar and the muffled sound of laughter bubble out from inside. The door, heavy, solid, and black, is etched with scars and chips that speak of years of patrons' comings and goings.

Together, the whole place is oddly charming. It's the kind of place that feels like it could be home to outlaws and heroes, a spot where tales are spun and legends are born.

Cami reaches for the door handle, but Wyatt, with a click of the lock, playfully denies her escape. She looks up at him, a mock glare that quickly dissolves into laughter as she throws her hands up in surrender. Wyatt's small act of chivalry, his respect for Cami, doesn't go unnoticed. As we step out of the truck, after Wyatt opens the doors himself, the scent of smoked wood and fried food drifts out to greet us.

As he shuts the doors, his brothers stride across the lot, their effortless swaggers commanding attention. The night sees them dressed in casual attire, yet they wear it like armor, each piece telling a story of the men beneath that I've come to know.

Wyatt stands out in his navy blue button-down, the fabric hugging his shoulders just right, hinting at the strength that lies underneath. The shirt is unbuttoned just enough to reveal a glimpse of the gold chain he wears, one I often find myself tracing when we're together. The contrast speaks volumes about the man he is—grounded yet unafraid of a little shine.

Lincoln's choice of a light blue polo shirt is no accident. It's the color of the summer sky just after dawn, and it makes his eyes—a matching shade of blue—all the more striking. The clear-rimmed glasses perched on his nose add a touch of intellectual charm, a counterpoint to the raw physicality of his brothers.

Statler looks no different than normal, clad in his signature black henley tee. The sleeves are pushed up, revealing the canvas of his arms. I've come to learn a lot about him, the most quiet of the three, but he keeps the stories behind his ink to himself.

Together, they're a vision of rugged charm. They move with confidence that's as natural to them as breathing, a trio that doesn't just walk into a room—they own it. And tonight, as they approach the bar, it's clear they're about to own this one too. The women inside don't stand a chance.

A twinge of annoyance pricks at me, an emotion I shouldn't be feeling. I'm not exactly the jealous type. *Something to overthink about later.*

With Cooper's leash securely in hand, I voice my concern. "Are you sure the bar will be okay with Cooper inside? It's not like the grocery store. People here might not be comfortable." The thought of potential conflict makes my stomach churn.

"Yes, ma'am," Lincoln says with a lawyerly precision that's both intimidating and impressive. "I made sure to clarify the policies regarding service animals—"

"—He scared them with big lawyer words." Statler's interpretation is more succinct.

I can't help but feel a twinge of embarrassment as heat creeps up my neck. "Thank you," I murmur, not wanting to be seen as a troublemaker in my own town.

Statler's introduction breaks through my thoughts. "Hi, I'm Statler." He shakes Cami's hand firmly, his smile genuine. Then Lincoln steps forward, "I'm Lincoln," he says, his smile reaching his eyes.

Cami's signing is swift, her humor not lost in translation. *"Holy gods, girl, do they grow all the men in Wyoming like this?"*

I shake my head, amused. *"Nope. Just these three, as far as I know."*

"They are panty-melting. The glasses are killing me. I want to take a bite out of him."

Lincoln's laughter is light. "I suddenly feel the urge to learn sign language, so they can't talk about us without us knowing."

"Sorry! I'm Camilla, or Cami. It's nice to meet you. And don't be afraid to tell us to knock it off with the signing—it's a habit." Cami's introduction is warm and inclusive. "Depending on the noise, I might have to disconnect the external transmitter. Just make sure to look at me when you speak or touch my arm to get my attention. I'll keep up."

The brothers nod, a trio of understanding. Lincoln offers his arm to Cami, a gentlemanly gesture, and she accepts with a playful wink in my direction. Statler hangs back, a silent guardian, as Wyatt's fingers intertwine with mine. It's his way of silently supporting me, just like he does every time we go somewhere new with Cooper. The night is alive with the sound of boots on gravel, the anticipation of the evening palpable in the air.

"Do I want to know?" Wyatt leans closer, his breath warm against my ear, his words laced with a playful secrecy.

"Just how panty-melting the three of you are." My smile blooms naturally as I tilt my body into his. The fabric of his shirt is soft against my chin as I pull him down a bit further before continuing. "You should know," I add quietly, "you can't melt what isn't there."

"Is that for me?" He kisses the tip of my nose playfully.

"Maybe." I wink.

"Good girl." His fingers tighten around mine, a gentle but knowing pressure.

Biting my cheek, I focus my eyes forward, trying my best to ignore how much I want to leave Cami to the guys and take Wyatt to the closest private location and let him act on everything his eyes just promised.

Focusing on the task at hand, each step toward the bar's entrance causes my heartbeat to quicken, a staccato rhythm that echoes my mounting nerves. Wyatt, ever attuned to my feelings, shifts his hand to rest reassuringly on my hip, guiding me through the doorway protectively, a silent communication that eases the tension from my frame. It's a trust that has grown slowly and steadily, rooted in countless small assurances. And now, without knowing exactly when it happened, I find myself depending on it.

CHAPTER 42

Drinks

PARKER

The bar houses a dance floor surrounded by tables, nestled beside a stage alive with music. The first thing that strikes me is the colorful glow of neon signs, casting a rainbow of lights over the polished wooden surfaces. The walls are adorned with memorabilia, likely the stuff of local legends.

The wooden dance floor has well-worn planks, a testament to countless boots that have tapped, twirled, and twisted on it. Strings of fairy lights crisscross the ceiling, adding a touch of whimsy to the otherwise rugged-looking room. The stage is a focal point, small but mighty, where the live band currently commands the room. It's nothing like the city bars that try too hard—it's relaxed and even inviting.

Around the dance floor, the tables are an eclectic mix of high-tops and booths, each offering a view of the night's festivities. The bar itself is a masterpiece of craftsmanship, with rows of gleaming bottles reflecting in the mirror behind it. Bartenders move with a grace, their hands deftly pouring and mixing to the musical cadence.

It's early, not quite nine, and the crowd is a generation or two ahead of us. We find a table on the quieter side of the dance floor, near the back. I admire how the guys communicate without words, their silent agreement leading us to a spot where we could enjoy the night without shouting.

Cami and I take our seats, the brothers positioning themselves protectively around us. Wyatt chooses to stand, his shadow a comfort behind me. His hand finds its way to my neck, fingers dancing lightly beneath my hair, sending waves of calm down my spine.

Wyatt taps Cami's shoulder, leaning in to ensure she hears him over the music. "Drinks?"

"Yes!" Cami says enthusiastically. "Whiskey and Coke for me, and Parker will have a whiskey straight up, over ice, with a water on the side," she declares confidently. Wyatt gives me a questioning look, one eyebrow arching in silent inquiry.

"Whiskey's perfect—distilled, no sugar. I could go for vodka, but—"

"Vodka turns her into a daredevil!" Cami jumps in, her voice bubbling with mischief. "Dare her to do anything when she's got vodka in her system, and she'll do it. In college, I dared her to climb up on the bar and—" Her tale is cut short as I clamp my hand over her mouth, her grin betraying her delight. I shake my head, silently pleading with her to stop.

"Please, do go on, Cami," Lincoln urges, a playful glint in his eye.

Wyatt's voice, low and intimate, brushes my ear. "I'm cashing in on that vodka knowledge at some point," he murmurs, a hint of promise in his tone. Then, with a final squeeze on my shoulder, he strides off to the bar.

Cami's voice cuts through the hum of the bar, playful and teasing. "Is this about as wild as Wyoming gets?" A smirk plays on her lips.

Statler's laughter is a rich sound, one I've scarcely heard, and it envelopes our table. "No ma'am, give it about an hour or so. This is the early crowd. The rowdy ones come later."

I watch Wyatt navigate the crowd, nodding to familiar faces. He returns, balancing our drinks with ease. He passes three dark amber bottles to the guys, followed by Cami's drink, and then mine. Her eyes sparkle with mischief, her fingers wiggling in anticipation. I nod back in silent agreement.

She counts down on her fingers—three, two, one—and then it begins. Our drinking handshake is a choreographed dance of fists tapping, palms sliding, and elbows bumping. It ends with our drinks raised high and slammed back in unison, the table echoing our satisfaction with a solid smack. We seal it with a high five, the sound crisp in the air.

"It's been forever since we've done that!" Laughter bubbles up from within me. I catch Lincoln and Statler's amused expressions, their smiles a mix of fondness and disbelief. Turning to look at Wyatt over my shoulder, I see his smile, full and bright. *Those dimples make my heart skip a beat.*

Cami's laughter mingles with mine as she addresses their astonishment. "What?"

"Did you two just slam back those drinks after a practiced handshake?" Lincoln is clearly impressed, his voice laced with a hint of wonder.

"Yes, sir! Back in college, Parks didn't have Cooper, and my transmitter couldn't always be on—so we adapted. The shake, which we definitely can't do trashed, is how we know if we're drinking too much." Cami's eyes dance with pride.

Statler nods, his voice warm with admiration as he says, "Kinda genius."

"We can do anything anyone else does. We just have to find our own way to do it," I say, my voice steady and sure.

"The real question is, can you dance, Doc?" Statler's challenge hangs in the air.

"Are you asking, Statler?" I can't see Wyatt's face, but the smirk on Statler's tells me all I need to know—Wyatt's not thrilled.

"Yes, ma'am, I am." Statler rises, offering his hand. Without a backward glance, I take it, letting Statler lead me onto the dance floor. He sends me into a spin, then pulls me back against him. I can't help but laugh, feeling completely at ease.

"You're only doing this to make him mad, aren't you?" I ask, finding my balance in Statler's arms. He's built like a fortress, and while it's a comfortable fit, it's not the same as being held by Wyatt.

"Of course I am. I never pass on a chance to rile him up, though it's not usually this easy," Statler admits with a grin. "I give him one song, max." Statler spins me out and back in time with the beat, then guides me through the paces of a two-step.

"Relax a little, Doc," Statler teases.

"Sorry, I'm not used to this. Being an only child, it's odd to suddenly have a person and then inherit all their people." My confession surprises me; I suppose the whiskey is to blame for that, but the sentiment rings true.

"Fair enough," Statler says, spinning me around and pulling me back. "You know the best part about finding your people, Parker?"

"What's that?" I look up into his eyes, so like Wyatt's yet so distinct.

"They stay your people, no matter what. I don't think my brother will mess this up, but even if he does, you'll still have a family here that will keep you safe," he assures me, his words wrapping around me like a promise.

"All of you have said something like that. Tell me, why do you think it's safety I need?" I challenge, my voice steady despite the uncertainty rising like a burn in my chest.

Statler's gaze softens, and he looks at me with a depth that feels too revealing. "Of all the things the military taught me, one of the most significant was how to spot someone with ghosts."

"What if it's me that screws it up, Statler?" The question slips out, a whisper of my deepest fear.

He smiles, a flash of confidence in his eyes. "Your specialty is surgery, so I imagine you'll stitch it back together just fine," he reassures me.

"I appreciate the confidence." I shake my head, trying to dispel the doubts. He turns me, pulling me around behind his back, making me laugh.

As the song nears its end, I feel Statler's laughter vibrating through him, his attention shifting to somewhere over my shoulder. "What can I say, Doc? I'm never wrong," he boasts, spinning me out one last time. But this time, he releases me completely.

Panic flares briefly as I lose my sense of balance, but then my hand is caught—captured by a touch that sends a familiar tingle across my skin. Spun back into place, I'm pulled into arms that feel like home.

Wyatt.

"Hello, angel." My body fits into his as if we're two pieces of the same puzzle. It's intoxicating, and at this moment, I'm exactly where I want to be.

"I never really noticed how I did or didn't fit into anyone's arms until now." The words tumble out and I cringe. Clearly, it's been a while since I've had whiskey if it's loosening my tongue this much.

"Have you figured out why that is yet?" Wyatt's voice is close and steady; my confession doesn't faze him.

"No." I meet his gaze, catching a fleeting shadow of pain before it's gone.

"Then, enjoy it," he says, dipping his head to kiss my cheek, flinging my thoughts to the four corners of my mind.

I try to gather myself, but it's hard. Statler's words echo in my mind, mingling with the music and the rhythm of our dance. It's everything I've ever longed for and everything I'm scared to lose. Wyatt, as if tuned into my sudden turmoil, leads me through a complex spin, his movements sure and steady before he pulls me back to him, his smile wide. I can't help but reflect it back to him.

The song ends and he leads me off the dance floor just as I watch as Cami and Lincoln take our place.

The night unfolds with laughter and stories, each dance with the brothers a fresh new story as they banter easily with one another. Wyatt keeps finding ways to reclaim me. Cami and Lincoln, too, seem drawn together, their steps in sync.

The fun and camaraderie are a welcome respite from the demands of work and the weight of worry. The proverbial saying about all work and no play echoes in my mind as the DJ takes over, the band's farewell hanging in the air.

Cami, breathless and glowing, collapses onto the stool beside me. "How is it that you all know how to dance this well?" she asks, her question directed at the brothers, her eyes still shining from the dance with Lincoln.

Lincoln's grin is infectious as he exchanges a knowing glance with Statler. "Well," he begins, the corners of his mouth twitching with amusement, "we learned early that women have a strong appreciation for a man that knows how to dance."

"Translation: you learned you could pick up girls." Cami's retort is quick and laced with sarcasm.

"I plead the fifth," Lincoln declares, his slow, sly smile aimed like an arrow straight at Cami. They're in their element, Olympic champions in the art of flirtation and facial expressions.

I'm on the verge of offering Cami another drink when the opening chords of a beloved anthem fill the air. Our reaction is immediate and instinctive—we scream. We leap to our feet, our hands clasped, our bodies moving to the beat as we make our way to the dance floor.

The bar transforms into a vibrant canvas of motion as Taylor Swift's "Ready For It?" pulses through the speakers. The dance floor, once a calm sea of casual sways, erupts into a storm of exuberance. Women from all walks of life converge, forming a sisterhood of rhythm and revelry. Each one is a flashing silhouette against the strobe lights, their shadows dancing on the walls like carefree spirits.

Cami and I are at the heart of it, our hands intertwined, our bodies moving in sync with the beat. We're singing at the top of our lungs, the lyrics a shared mantra that binds us together. The chorus hits, and it's as if a current surges through the crowd, our collective energy reaching its peak. We're more than just patrons in a bar; we're a chorus of voices, a mix of stories, each one singing out for the world to hear.

As the song winds down, "Party Rock Anthem" takes over, the baseline a heartbeat that drives us to remain in the crowd.

CHAPTER 43

Education

PARKER

Cami and I are in the thick of the crowd, dancing with abandon, our bodies slick with the effort of keeping up with the music. Three songs deep, and we're riding that perfect buzz, the kind that makes you feel invincible but still sharp. That's when a group of guys from the bar sidles up to join the fray. At first, it's all in good fun, the more the merrier, right? But as they inch closer, a little too close, I shoot Cami "the look"—that silent signal understood by women everywhere.

We pivot, aiming to slip away without a fuss because, let's face it, avoiding conflict is just easier. But these guys are not reading the room. They block our path, encircling us, and one of them, with eyes glazed and red, makes the bold move of grabbing Cami's wrist.

Big mistake.

Cami's reaction is swift and practiced. Her hand arcs, breaking his grip, then twists his wrist in a swift motion. In the blink of an eye, he's down on his knees, his wrist contorted, his friends frozen in disbelief, the whole bar watching.

"It's not polite to touch what isn't yours," Cami snaps, her petite five-foot stature nothing compared to the force of her personality.

The guy's eyes bulge, a mix of pain and surprise. "You—" he starts, but Cami tightens her hold just enough to cut him off.

"Now, now, no name-calling. Just say you're sorry," she instructs, her tone firm.

"Sorry," he grunts out, the word forced between clenched teeth. Cami releases him and strides past, her head held high. I trail behind her, a smirk on my lips.

As we near the edge of the dance floor, our guys are there, having abandoned their table. Lincoln steps aside, his gesture grand, as if parting an invisible curtain for us. We glide through the opening, returning to our table. Cooper sniffs at my legs, but doesn't alert, just settles at my feet.

"Care to tell us about that?" Wyatt's tone is cool but the undercurrent of anger is palpable. These men have a code, and disrespecting women isn't part of it.

"That?" Cami's voice is sugar-coated innocence, but her eyes are dancing with triumph. "That's called an education. As a woman, you find it's frequently your responsibility to hand them out." There's a full ten-second pause before the brothers' laughter fills the space.

Statler's the first to recover. "Krav Maga?"

"Correct," Cami confirms, then turns to me, her hands a flurry of signs.

"Care to fill us in, ladies?" Wyatt asks, his curiosity piqued.

"Cami said the three of you are precious but she's worried you've forgotten we're not just any women—we're badasses raised in big cities. We're as tough as they come. But all's forgiven if there's food in our immediate future."

Lincoln's smirk is a thing of beauty. "Oh, we didn't forget," he says, his gaze locked on Cami, "we were just making ourselves available for delegation." His wink is conspiratorial, as his eyes lock with Cami.

"Very smooth, lawman," Cami shoots back, the spark in her eyes igniting in response.

"Let's get out of here and get you two food fit for badasses, then," Lincoln suggests, and the flirtation between them is as tangible as the night air.

As the night winds down and goodbyes are exchanged, a plan for brunch tomorrow emerges. Wyatt comes through with chicken nuggets and French fries on the way back to the apartment. Cami's quick thanks and retreat up the stairs to my place marks the end of an evening that's been anything but boring.

"I'll have to remember to thank her for giving us a few minutes alone." Wyatt's words float between us as he opens my door.

As I turn to step out of the truck, I find Wyatt stepping toward me. He catches my legs, his hands gliding over my boots to land on my thighs, pulling them apart gently as he steps between them.

"I know I can't stay, but," he leans in close, "I can't walk away without doing at least one of the things I've wanted to do all damn night." The space between us is charged, his lips a mere breath from mine, hovering like a promise yet to be fulfilled. I close the distance, my hands finding their way to his neck, fingers threading through chain he's wearing. The world tilts slightly as he closes the gap, his kiss demanding and desperate all at once.

The world around me blurs, my only focus is his touch, his taste, the feel of the heat from his hands. He swirls his tongue around mine playfully before tilting my head slightly, finding the exact angle he wants. My back arches as he sinks in, my chest pressing into his. Pulling away from my lips, he shifts, choosing to place soft teasing kisses on my neck as his hands slide under the hem of my skirt. Heat rolls over my skin, a flush from head to toe, as his fingers brush against my core.

"Do me a favor?" Each of his words is punctuated with a kiss to the column of my neck, his fingers continuing to stroke. My head falls back, his lips taking advantage to move around and up the other side of my neck.

"What favor?" I ask, breathless from his touch.

"Dream about me because I'll sure as hell be dreaming about you and everything, I plan to do the next time we're alone." He lifts my head, looking me in the eye as his fingers slide fully into my heat.

"Oh, god," I groan, his eyes holding me in place. His hands overtake my body—the darkness from the cab, his body blocking mine from view—pushing me to let go, to give in to the moment. Relentless fire burns, lighting me up from the inside, as his hands move across my body with an edge of possession I've come to crave.

"Don't stop," I beg, my voice more croak than groan. The breath backs up in my lungs. My hips roll, chasing the pressure. A loud whimper escapes when he increases the pressure.

"Shh, baby," Wyatt whispers, the laughter in his voice a counterpoint to the heat of his touch. He steps in closer, pushing my legs wider, my thighs trembling as he pulls me to the edge of the seat.

"More." I complain, my fingers curling in his shirt, tugging just enough to bring his lips back to mine. Kissing him, I pour out every ounce of desire coursing through my skin. I'm on the edge of pulling him inside and telling Cami to take a walk when he groans, or maybe it's more of a growl, but either way it turns my core, heat rolling across my skin.

"I've been thinking about this all night, Parker, since you opened that damn door. Dying to have you. Be a good girl. Give me what I want." His praise washes over me like a downpour of rain. He kisses my neck as his hands move across me. He knows the map to my body like he's the one that drew it. I'm teetering on the brink in less than a breath and over it in a heartbeat.

My release washes over me, the roaring in my ears the only thing I can hear for a full ten seconds. Every muscle is trembling when he wraps me in his arms, hugging me close, a flutter of light kisses on my head.

"You're going to hurt if you don't let me help you," I whisper against his neck as my hands glide down to his waist.

"I'll be alright." He kisses my cheek, pulling back, holding my face between his hands. "Go. Inside. Parker." He nips lightly at my lips between each word.

He leans back from my mouth, a whine of objection crossing my lips in protest before I can stop it. My eyes are still closed when he slides his hands around my waist, lifting me out of the truck and placing me softly on the ground in front of him. My eyes remain closed, refusing to end this moment.

"Eyes." The single word is a gentle caress wrapped in the velvet of authority. It's a tone unique to him, a blend of tenderness and command that speaks to something deep within me. His hands gently roam over my sides and back, the air thick with desire and full of promise. Finally conceding to his request, my eyes open.

"I love that look," he mutters, his voice a soft rumble that stirs the air between us.

"What look?" I tease, lingering in the moment, reluctant to break the connection.

"The one that says you want me. It darkens your pale blue eyes to the same navy of the sky right at dawn," he explains, his words painting a picture of desire and transformation.

"Wyatt," His name is a sigh on my lips. He speaks of me as if I'm precious, and I'm torn, wondering if his reverence would withstand the truth. A wave of guilt crashes over me—omission is a form of deceit, after all. My longing for him was just the beginning; now, the more time I spend with him, the more longing is changing into something else.

"Go inside, baby," he urges, his clarity tinged with empathy, as if he's glimpsed the turmoil behind my gaze.

I nod, and he steps back to let Cooper out of the back. When I reach the apartment door, I pause and glance back, catching Wyatt's gaze. He's the embodiment of desire, claiming me with a look that's as vital as the air we breathe. I send him a playful wink, a silent promise, and he shakes his head, a mix of exasperation and affection, as he settles back into his truck, his eyes not leaving me until I'm safely inside.

The moment I step through the door, there's Cami, dramatically fanning herself by the window, her laughter filling the room. "I couldn't see anything specific, but damn girl," she declares, still chuckling, her hands beginning to slow clap.

I can't help but roll my eyes at her theatrics. It's been an incredible night, one of those rare times when everything just clicks. But beneath the surface, there's a nagging sensation, a premonition that this peace is temporary. There's a shadow at the edge of my thoughts.

"Cami, what have I gotten myself into?" The words slip out before I can catch them, heavy and tired.

She grins at me, her smile confusing everything I feel. "I think it's called a mutually satisfying relationship, Parks."

"I'm not built for relationships," I confess, the admission tasting like a prelude to the overthinking I swore I'd save for tomorrow.

"Honey," Cami begins, her voice soft and soothing.

"You know I'm right!" I cut her off, my voice rising despite my intentions, my hands moving with each word, signing out my pain in sharp, punctuated gestures. "I. Am. Damaged. And scarred. And broken."

Cami watches me from the living room, her arms crossed, her expression unphased by my outburst. "As long as that's what you believe, that's all you'll ever feel, Parker."

"I'm sorry," I blurt out, the apology quick and earnest. "I didn't mean to yell at you. I'm not mad at you."

She shakes her head, dismissing my apology with the ease of long friendship. "Babe, I know that. You're my best friend. You can yell if you need to. But, Parker, you need to face this. You have to stop running. So, if you're not angry, then what are you?"

"I'm terrified." The words barely more than a breath.

"Good," she says with a nonchalant shrug. "What's the worst that can happen?"

It's a nightmare I've played over in my mind a thousand times. "The worst is he learns everything about me and decides it's a deal-breaker and he walks away. I'd have to start over—new job, new place—because staying here without him would be unbearable." I kick off my boots and draw my feet up under me on the couch.

Cami's gaze is steady, her voice firm. "You really think, after everything he's done, after all the trust you've built, that he'll turn into James when you tell him the truth?" She discards her shoes and drapes a blanket over us.

"I don't know," I admit, resting my head back. "I never expected James to become who he did. So, what the hell do I know?"

"What happens if you don't tell him?" Cami's question is like a stone dropped into the waters of my mind, sending ripples of what-ifs across the surface.

I can't help but bury my face in my hands as the possibilities tumble out. "He's the kind of man who might stay out of a sense of honor, just to prove he could. But then what? Resentment builds over time. He's patient now, sure, because we're having a blast and the sex is incredible, but what about a year from now, or five? Or when the conversation about kids happens?" The words are muffled behind my palms.

Cami's voice cuts through my chatter as she pulls my hands away from my face. "Deciding he's going to be anything other than who he has shown you he is, is unfair to him."

I push back, desperate for her to understand. "James was great until he wasn't," I argue, my signs sharp with frustration.

"No, honey, he wasn't." She counters with unwavering certainty. "James never showed you the basic courtesies, never made the effort to communicate with me. He was a selfish, self-absorbed bully with no depth. He was all about control. You were just too nice to notice all the little shit. Wyatt, on the other hand, is an ocean of depth and understanding. They're not the same, not even close, and it's unfair to compare them."

"I'm trying to be fair, Cami," I protest, feeling the sting of her words.

"No, you're not. You're trying to justify running. It's what you do." She's relentless, her voice a mix of exasperation and concern.

Her accusation hits hard, hurting and confusing me at the same time. "How can you say that? What are you talking about?" I demand, seeking clarity.

Cami's hands go up in a gesture of surrender. "Hear me out," she pleads. "When you left Chicago, you went as far as you could to escape the memories of Cameron. After James, and—"

"Don't say her name." I interrupt quickly, desperation flowing through me.

She nods calmly. "After everything, you buried yourself in school. You've been running from relationships ever since. And now, you're admitting that if things go south, you'd leave. You're incredibly strong, Parker, you've survived so much. But there's a difference between fighting *through* something and fighting *for* something. That's the brave Cameron was talking about, the kind that makes you fight to stay."

Her words leave me speechless, my gaze fixed on the floor as I grapple with the truth she's laid bare. "I don't know what to say," I admit, the silence around us heavy with the weight of her honesty.

"Don't say anything," Cami persists, her voice a steady stream of encouragement as she takes my hands in hers, "but don't run. Don't let your fears sabotage this—don't be the architect of your own heartache this time." Her grip tightens, a lifeline against the current of my tears, and she brushes my cheeks.

Her words make sense; they're a blueprint, a strategy to hope, but bridging the gap between my head and my heart, feels like crossing an abyss. She rises, moving to the bag of chicken nuggets, leaving me with only one question: what's it going to take to bring the truth to the light?

◇◇◇◇◇◇◇◇◇◇◇◇◇◇◇

Cami is lost in a deep sleep, breathing even and calm, the exact opposite of me. I'm restless, the bed a desert of discomfort, each toss and turn a futile attempt to escape the biting ants of my thoughts. With a sigh, I rise carefully, retreating to the living room. The couch beckons, a soft island in the darkness. Cooper follows, settling next to me.

The quiet of the room wraps around us. My mind, however, refuses to settle, galloping through the plains of introspection.

"You know, Coop," I murmur into the darkness, "when you lay my life out like that, Cami's not wrong." My hand moves to my chest, trying to soothe the ache that blooms there. "I'm tired of being wound up in knots of anxiety and fear."

"I don't want to keep running," I confess to the shadows, to Cooper, to myself. "I just don't know how to plant my feet and face it all. Cameron told me to be brave, but how the hell does bravery actually work?" A pause, a breath, an admission. "And yes, I know I should talk to a therapist." The words hang in the air, a step towards a truth I've skirted around.

CHAPTER 44

Borrowed

WYATT

She's likely deep in sleep by now, and here I am, wide awake and uncomfortable without her. I need her to figure out she loves me as much as I love her. I'd chase her to the ends of the earth for that truth, but I'm aiming for a smoother path, and holding back is killing me.

Impulsively, I reach for my phone. Even if she reads it in the morning, I need her to know she's on my mind.

WYATT

Miss you.

The response is immediate, those three little dots stirring a flicker of concern that she's awake still.

ANGEL

Miss you too.

Can't sleep? or still partying?

Can't sleep. There's a small woman in the place of a very large man in my bed.

I'd offer to remove her, but I've seen her fight. How can I help?

haha good point. The truth?

Do I want the truth? The ache in my heart intensifies with her question. Who wouldn't want the truth?

From you? Always.

The truth is . . . I can't get comfortable. Somehow, I've gotten used to you being here. You put off a lot of heat, and you don't smell like lemons.
So my bed doesn't smell right and it's not the right temperature. I realize it's probably dumb and clingy and you're cringing. I'll hate myself for this 1 a.m. confession tmw but I'm too tired to care right now.

I'm used to being next to you too. I can't solve that tonight, but I can fix the other problems.

Her words, candid and vulnerable, settle within me. It's not just comfort she's seeking—it's presence. No other motivation is needed.

Rolling out of bed, I grab my T-shirt from the floor. Snatching my hat from the dresser and yanking on my running shoes is quick. I stride into my closet and pick out a sweatshirt. I tiptoe down the stairs, the silence broken only by the buzz of my phone.

How??

I resist the urge to reply. Truck keys in hand, I slip out the side door. The drive to the clinic is quick. I kill the headlights early, keeping my arrival a surprise. I ascend the stairs, hoodie slung over my shoulder, and shoot her another message.

Open your door.

The click of the lock and the creak of the door are my cues. Her expression of utter astonishment is all the confirmation I need.

Note to self—surprise her more often.

"You're here," she breathes out, her voice tinged with disbelief, as if she's seeing a mirage in the desert.

"Always," I affirm, stepping closer but pausing at the doorway. Her gaze is fixed on me, unblinking, and I can't help but revel in the intensity of her stare. With a fluid motion, I pull the hoodie from my shoulder, sliding it over her head. I guide her arms through the sleeves, one by one. She seems stunned.

"Why?" The word hangs between us. Her eyes are pools of confusion, searching mine for answers she's not even sure how to ask for. I step over the threshold of the door and shut it with a soft click before erasing the distance that separates us.

"Because," I begin, my hand cradling the side of her face, a gesture as natural as breathing, "I need you to understand I'd do anything you needed, even at one in the morning. Because I want all of you, and I don't mind proving to you every day that you can trust me with all of you. Because I need you to know, without hesitation, mine is the hand you can always reach for. Because it's you Parker. For me, it's *only* you."

She exhales, a sigh that's heavy, as she leans into me, her arms wrapping around my waist, her head finding its home over my heart.

"You weren't supposed to fall for me," she murmurs against my chest, her words a feather-light confession, making me chuckle.

"We might have to renegotiate," I reply, pressing a kiss to the top of her head. "I don't think I can stop."

"I'm trying to figure out how to be as brave as you," she whispers, the weight of her worry barely allowing the words to escape.

"I can't promise you it won't be scary or that I won't mess up or act like an idiot caveman, but I can promise you don't have to feel any of that alone." My hands glide up and down her back, each stroke a silent pledge I'm praying she feels.

"Is that a deal? And this one's non-negotiable, Wyatt." She pulls away slightly, her eyes locking onto mine with an intensity that could outshine the stars. "I mean it. No matter what happens. Not even if—"

"—Deal," I cut in, not allowing her doubts to take root. I dip my head, coaxing her chin upward with a gentle nudge of my nose. She gives in, and our lips meet, sealing our pact with the softness of a kiss.

"You're doing it again," she accuses, a hint of exasperation lacing her words.

"What's that?" I prod gently, inviting her to reveal her thoughts.

"It's hard to put into words. It's like—" She pauses to collect her thoughts. "Every one of my senses becomes you, like every weight and worry, every bad memory, disappears. Even the relentless noise in my head is quiet." Her eyes squeeze shut, a dam holding back the tide of tears.

"You say that like it's bad," I tease lightly, my thumbs gliding across her cheeks.

"You don't think it is?" She searches my gaze, seeking the truth.

"No," I confirm with a nod. "Now, go to bed." I step back, releasing her from my embrace.

"You're leaving?" Disappointment and shock etch her features, her arms crossing defensively.

"Yes. You need rest. Plus, Cami's visit is important to you—you should spend time with her." I brush a stray lock of hair behind her ear.

"If I'm grumpy and tired tomorrow, it's your fault. Just so you're aware," she retorts, her feigned annoyance masking the affection underneath.

"Noted." I grin. I turn to leave and pull the door closed behind me, its soft click a temporary goodbye.

CHAPTER 45

Struggling

PARKER

The click of the lock marks his departure. For a moment, I stand enveloped in the stillness of my living room. Drifting back toward the couch, my fingers brush against the hoodie. The fabric is soft against my skin, and it carries the unmistakable scent that is uniquely Wyatt.

The hoodie is clearly a favorite, its frayed edges regaling stories of daily use. It's oversized on me, the hem reaching below my butt. I curl up on the couch, drawing a blanket around me. Its warmth is a poor substitute for his arms but will have to do.

In the dim light, the room is a canvas painted with traces of him. The coffee pot, the barstools where he sits and recounts tales of his day with animated gestures, even the little hook by the door he hung for Cooper's leash and my keys—all of it proof of his existence in my life. The room hums with a silent melody—the scent of him, the soft snoring of Cooper from his spot on the rug, they all weave together into a lullaby that finally pulls me under.

My phone's shrill alarm pierces the morning stillness, rousing me from the cocoon of the couch. The rich aroma of coffee wafts through the air, a scent that instantly conjures images of Wyatt in my mind. I stifle the flicker of disappointment as my eyes land on Cami bustling in the kitchen, not him.

"You okay?" Her eyebrow arches in that all-too-familiar way, a silent probe for the truth.

"Yeah. Just a restless night," I reply. "Didn't want to wake you."

"Try again, sister." Cami's expression is a mix of skepticism and concern, her no-nonsense demeanor firmly in place.

"Honest. I just couldn't get to sleep, so I camped out here."

"And . . . " she urges, not buying the half-story.

"And, Wyatt texted, swung by with this hoodie, and then . . . I finally slept," I confess in a rush, as if speed could blur the details. I rise, stretching languidly, and head to the door to release Cooper into the light-filled morning, the sun already claiming the sky.

"I'm going to need the full story, Parks," Cami demands, settling onto the couch with her coffee, her posture expectant, her eyes alight with anticipation.

"Fine." I relent. The story pours out of me—a deluge of confessions, revelations, and the raw honesty of last night's encounter.

"Oh," she exhales, a soft sound of wonder. "I'd think he was a figment of your imagination if I hadn't witnessed all this unfold." Her finger points to the hoodie, now a symbol of something more.

"Please elaborate. What's happening now?" I press, seeking clarity.

"Oh no, no, no. I'm zipping it. You're on your own to figure this one out, sweetie." She mimes sealing her lips and tossing away the key playfully.

"Fine. Then I claim first dibs on the shower—and all the hot water," I declare, a mock threat hanging in the air.

"You do that," Cami responds, her smile hidden behind the rim of her coffee mug.

CHAPTER 46

Brunch

WYATT

Light spills across the ranch as I begin my morning routine with the horses. The earthy scent of hay and the musky aroma of the animals fills the crisp morning air. I move among the horses with a familiarity born of countless days just like this one, my hands automatically filling their troughs with feed, the grains falling softly.

I run my hands along their necks, offering soft words of greeting; in turn, I get gentle snorts and nuzzles. It's peaceful, just me and the horses, and the comforting routine of my life.

The sounds of the day starting up carry over from the distance—the low murmur of voices from the ranch hands as they begin their day, the occasional burst of laughter, the jangle of tools, and the creak of gates swinging open. It's a symphony of daily life here, one that's as familiar to me as the back of my hand.

As I finish tending to the horses, my phone buzzes.

Hey, it's Cami. I'm going to lay it out for you. You just might be the first guy who seems like he could actually be worthy of her. Handle with care, okay? Be the guy I think you are. And just so we're clear, if you hurt her, there's not a place on this planet where you could hide from me.

WYATT

Thanks for the vote of confidence— and the heads-up. If I ever mess up, I'll personally recruit Statler to your cause.

Deal. 😉

Shaking my head, a smile pulling across my face, I return to the chores at hand. Cami doesn't have a thing to worry about from me. I'm already in this forever.

◇◇◇◇◇◇◇◇◇◇◇◇◇◇◇◇

Later that morning, we converge at Mel's—the town's crown jewel of diners, mostly by default. There's only one true diner, after all.

The diner is alive with the clatter of dishes and the clinking of silverware. Waitresses bustle from table to table, their voices a blend of friendly banter and efficient orders. The grill chef calls out ready orders with the same cadence he's had since I was a kid. The jukebox in the corner plays a selection of classic hits, the low volume allowing it to be a backdrop rather than a distraction.

The decor is a throwback to a simpler time, with red vinyl booths that invite you to slide in and stay awhile. The walls are covered with black and white photos of the town's history, and the counter stools are occupied by regulars who discuss the day's news over steaming mugs of coffee. Typically my dad and Charlie make up members of that band.

I'm there with the guys when Parker and Cami make their entrance, fashionably late by just a few minutes. Lincoln's hand goes up, beckoning them over. If Parker's look last night was a knockout punch, today's is a heart-stopper. She's the embodiment of sunlight—ripped jeans, my hoodie, a braid over her shoulder, and those striking blue eyes. We rise as they approach, gesturing for them to take the inside seats of the booth. They exchange a glance, their hands moving in silent conversation, leaving us out of the loop.

"Parker, this is a door thing," I tell her, half-teasing, half-serious. "You can argue all you want, but odds are against you with all three of us here. Want to give it a shot? If you win, we'll switch."

Cami's eyes dance with amusement, and Parker's head shake and accompanying eye roll is all in good humor as they slide in. Cooper claims his spot beneath the table, snug under Parker's legs.

"So," Cami signs, her curiosity clear, "why the inside seats? This one's new to me."

I glance at my brothers, giving Lincoln the nod to field this one.

"Ladies," Lincoln begins, the lawyer in him taking the floor, "if trouble walked through that door, we'd be hard-pressed to shield you from inside this booth. Anticipating your resistance to the idea of random crime, let's say, hypothetically, someone takes a spill—any flying food or glass would hit us first, sparing you. Plus, Stat never sits on the inside. All aforementioned scenarios at play, it is because we honor you and your immense and incredible power that we seek to ensure your safety."

"Wow," Cami responds, her tone dry as desert air. "Quite the comprehensive case, counselor."

"Thank you," Lincoln says, a touch of pride in his voice.

"It's mostly bullshit, but I do appreciate your willingness to take a plate of biscuits and gravy on our behalf. As I have no desire to do so myself, I am willing to allow the current placement to stand."

Camilla's retort is delivered with such precision, it almost feels rehearsed. She then casually flips open a menu, signaling the end of that discussion. Lincoln, ever the inquisitive one, leans in, eyes glimmering with challenge.

"Are you a lawyer?" he asks, curiosity piqued.

"Nope. Not at all," she replies, then pivots the conversation to Statler with a question of her own, accompanied by a disarmingly sweet smile. "You never sit on the inside. Care to explain?"

Statler's response is low and matter-of-fact, "Old habits. I'm retired special forces." He says it with a detachment that always catches me by surprise. We've all learned to respect his space and quirks, understanding that his service left marks that aren't as visible as the scar on his arm.

Cami doesn't linger on the topic, quickly moving on with a hint of mischief in her voice. "Interesting. I think I'm going to have to ask an imposing question." Her gaze shifts to me, and I can't help but chuckle.

"Well," I say, "I'm not sure if I should be intrigued or wary. That's quite the lead in."

"Go with intrigued," Lincoln interjects, his eyes fixed on Cami.

She leans in, her voice dropping to a conspiratorial whisper. "I'm an author, among other things. But I do not write under my own name, so I'm trusting you to keep that to yourselves."

The revelation clearly shocks Parker, who quickly moves to show her support, her hand resting reassuringly on Cami's shoulder as she issues a stern warning to us all.

"I can only count on one hand the number of people who know that truth, until now," Parker states with a calm intensity that leaves no room for doubt. "If you betray her, no one will ever find your body." Despite her hatred for conflict, her protective nature is clear, and I understand it completely, even if I'm a little surprised. I cover the fist she's unconsciously formed under the table with my own hand, drawing her focus to me.

"I appreciate the threat, baby," I assure her, my voice steady and sincere. "But you won't need it. You have my word, Parker." She gives a small nod of acknowledgment. Cami's slow smile and the subtle wink she sends my way tell me she planned this and she approved of my response.

Lincoln's encouragement is a gentle nudge for Cami to continue. "Go on," he says, and Cami dives back into her thoughts.

"As I was saying, I write. The landscape of Wyoming has sparked something for me, and I'm hoping to channel that into my next book. I'm looking for a quiet place to work, off the grid. Any chance there's a spot at your ranch I could use for a month or so? I will pay for it I just need it to remain off the radar," Cami proposes, her eyes scanning our faces for a reaction.

I exchange a quick, wordless conversation with my brothers. It's a brief ten-second exchange before I respond. "We've got a space not being used for anything, about the size of Parker's apartment. You're welcome to it anytime." I decide to leave out the part about not accepting payment; that's a conversation for another day.

Cami's face lights up with a victorious "Yes!" and a celebratory double fist pump. But it's Parker's reaction that catches my eye—her face is aglow, a silent admission of how much having Cami close by means to her.

With the matter settled, Parker shifts the focus to more immediate concerns. "With that business out of the way, I'm starving," Parker declares. The waitress arrives just in time to take our orders, and Parker, after a quick glance at her phone, decides on a loaded omelet.

The banter around the table is easy, as if Cami and Parker have been part of our group for years. Lincoln's attempts at flirting with Cami are met with playful rejections, while Statler remains mostly an observer, chiming in now and then with a story or joke.

Under the table, I feel Cooper stir at Parker's feet. He's quiet, no barking this time, but Parker is attentive to her phone, checking it once more before casually taking a sip of Cami's coffee. It's a move that doesn't seem to surprise Cami in the slightest.

"Parker," I start, my concern slipping through despite my best efforts to keep it in check.

She cuts me off with a reassuring smile. "It's fine, Wyatt. Really, I'm just playing it safe until the food arrives." The table falls silent, all eyes on Parker, but it's Cami who breaks the silence.

"Stop staring at Parker. She doesn't like it, and she's got everything under control. Don't be dicks and make her feel awkward." Cami's words slice through the air with a fierceness that rivals Parker's earlier warning. Her tone leaves no room for argument.

"You two are quite the duo, huh? A bit of a wolf pack?" Lincoln, ever the charmer, tries to lighten the mood.

Cami shoots back with a grin, "We're a trio, actually. But yeah, a badass wolf pack sounds about right. We have no problem ripping out throats when necessary, and we are beautiful."

"You can't blame us for admiring beautiful women. That'd just be cruel," Lincoln responds.

"Smooth save, counselor," Cami retorts, her eyebrow arching in mock disapproval.

Before the banter can continue, Parker interjects with a practical observation. "Besides, the food's here."

CHAPTER 47

Surprise

WYATT

"I'm just trying to figure out why food snatching seems to be such a common thing among women. Is it coded in your DNA? Is there some secret pact about swiping fries off our plates or sipping from our drinks? Our sister does it too," Statler interjects as the waitress starts distributing our food.

I spot Parker's order on the tray and without hesitation, I take her plate and set it in front of her. "Eat," I urge. She doesn't argue, just starts eating with an appetite that makes me smile. Food is truly the way to my girl.

"That's sexist," Cami declares as her own plate lands in front of her. She points accusingly with her fork, then, quick as a flash, snatches a piece of bacon from Lincoln's plate as it's set down.

"Yes, Cami, you're welcome to my bacon," Lincoln responds, his tone dry as he deadpans over to her.

"How's that sexist?" Statler jumps back in, confusion in his eyes.

Cami takes a hearty bite of her pancakes, then explains with a flourish of her hands. Parker looks up to translate for us. "She's saying if men had to watch their diet as much as women, they'd be swiping food too. It's not about gender. It's about hunger. And apparently, it's men's fault women are always hungry," Parker translates, a chuckle escaping her as she returns to her eggs, shaking her head.

"Exactly," Cami confirms, triumphantly raising her fork. "What do you have to say to that, lawman?"

"Woman," Lincoln replies, feigning exhaustion though we all know he thrives on argument. "I know when to pick my battles."

I feel Cooper shift and settle back under the table by Parker's feet. Curious, I hold up a piece of bacon to her. "Will he take this from me?"

Her smile softens as she shakes her head. "No, he's trained to only take things from me. If you fed him, it would distract him from his job. But thank you for the offer. I can give it to him if you're okay with that." Her gratitude is genuine, and I nod, passing her the bacon for Cooper.

Parker covertly feeds Cooper bacon under the table, issuing a swift command in a language that's foreign to my ears.

"That wasn't English like some of his others. What was it?" I ask, dissecting the pancakes before me.

"Not all his commands are. It helps prevent accidental commands from other people. That was—"

"German." Statler and Parker chime in unison. She glances at him, her head cocked curiously.

"Is that one of those special forces things?" Cami inquires, setting her fork down.

"Maybe," Statler answers, a small grin on his face.

"Know any other languages?" she probes further.

"Yes."

"Going to share which ones?" Cami teases.

Statler grins at her, then declares, "Not a chance."

Our laughter fills the air, echoing Cami's feigned dismay. "How am I supposed to craft a character after you if I'm clueless about his abilities?"

"You don't," Statler retorts, his voice losing its playful edge, his shoulders rigid with tension, his smile gone.

"Stat—" I begin, ready to make him apologize for being rude, but Cami cuts in.

"No, it's okay, Wyatt. I can be overly curious quite easily. You should know though, I have a deep respect for personal boundaries. I'd never violate them intentionally. You have my word, no characters like you. Though I can't quite promise no cowboys, no lawyers, no tattoos, or no brothers—those are sort of a staple in my genre." Cami smiles, then winks at Statler. Statler's posture softens slightly as he acknowledges her with a nod.

I notice Lincoln's muscles remain coiled, his gaze fixed on Statler with an intensity that suggests a brotherly brawl, not foreign to the three of us over the years. Lincoln's gaze connects with mine and I subtly signal him to hold off; this isn't the moment for confrontation. He acknowledges with a nod, and all returns to normal.

As we near the end of our breakfast, a young girl, maybe ten, dashes up to our table. "Doctor Mason!" she exclaims, her voice bubbling with gratitude. "Thank you so much for saving my horse. He's doing great! Grandpa says I'll be back in the saddle soon, but only at a walk for now."

"I'm thrilled to hear that," Parker responds, her smile radiant as she addresses the girl. "I can't wait to see you riding again. Remember to take a picture for me, and have your grandpa bring it to the clinic. I love displaying pictures of all the animals we help." She connects with the girl effortlessly, her usual defenses nowhere in sight. It's a rare glimpse of Parker entirely unguarded.

A man approaches and recognition dawns on me—it's Hank. He scoops up his granddaughter, offers Parker a heartfelt thanks, and they head for the cash register. The normalcy of the moment, the kind I could easily get used to, settles in my chest. Rising from our seats, my attention is drawn to a man in the corner. His gaze has been fixed on us since his arrival. Clad in a three-piece suit, he looks distinctly out of place in the diner.

"Statler," I begin, ready to alert him to the observer.

"I've got him," he murmurs, his voice a low thrum that the girls, preoccupied with exiting the booth, fail to catch. As we stand, the suited man strides towards us. Statler intercepts him with a shift in his stance. I reposition myself, instinctively shielding the girls, every nerve standing on end as I take him in.

"Can we help you?" I challenge, my voice sounds oddly cold, even to my own ears. The strangers gaze skims over me, stopping on Parker with an unsettling familiarity.

"Hello, Parker." The man's voice carries a deceptive silkiness, a veneer of smoothness. His words flow with an artificial ease, each syllable dipped in sugar, which fails to mask the bitter undertones of resentment in his eyes, simmering just below the façade of calm. It's a careful performance, a studied act of civility.

I twist my head to look back at Parker, but don't dare to move from my spot between her and the man, my instincts screaming to keep him away from her. The diner's hum fades into the background as Cami's eyes, once pools of warmth, now burn with true violence and unfiltered rage. Cami's jaw sets, a clear sign of her resolve, and her hand grips Parker's. Her body is tensed for battle, every line and curve ready to defend, compounding my belief that this man is a danger to the woman I love.

Parker stands in stark contrast—fear and pain on every feature. The color drains from her face, leaving only a ghost-like paleness that speaks volumes of the shock coursing through her. Her breath, usually steady and sure, now stutters in her chest. Her hands, the knuckles white from their grip on Cooper's leash, tremor slightly.

"You would summon me all this way wouldn't you, darling? Had you responded to my calls, this could've been avoided," he states, rooted to the spot, neither advancing nor retreating.

"You need to leave, James. Now." Cami is the first to confront him.

He dismisses Cami with a glance, as if she's invisible. "Where is my daughter, Parker?"

With my eyes still on Parker, I watch the words slam into her at full force. The fear and devastation in her eyes, her breath catching as her lips tremble, her body rigid with shock.

"Parker," Cami's voice cuts through the tension, loud and clear, snapping Parker back to the present. "It's time to go."

The sight of Parker's face, etched with terror, the wreckage and destruction created by this one moment already pushing a single tear down her cheek, ignites a fury within me. As the man in the suit reaches out towards her, I step in front of him, an unyielding wall.

"Lay a hand on her and lose it," I growl, the words slipping out between clenched teeth. My mind races to make sense of the chaos, but my priority will always be her safety.

"Let's go, Parker." My tone is harsh, usually reserved for moments of command, to pull her back from the edge of panic. Her body responds, but her eyes avoid mine this time. As the girls begin to move, we form a protective circle and usher them out. The man in the suit remains stationary, his smile chilling as if he knows exactly what he's doing and enjoys it. Parker's hand darts into her bag, retrieving her keys as she and Cami make a beeline for the truck. They're in and speeding away before we can reach them.

I turn to my brothers, both of whom are waiting for instruction, their anger as clear as my own. "Let's go."

◇◇◇◇◇◇◇◇◇◇◇◇◇◇◇

Parker and Cami's voices clash in the apartment, echoing concern and confusion. As we burst through the door, both women whirl around, prepared to fight. Though when they take us in, their expressions shift to a mix of frustration and relief.

"What's happening? Who was that?" I ask carefully, struggling to keep my voice steady against the mix of emotions raging inside me.

Parker's eyes are pools of anguish as she faces Cami. "I can handle him myself, Cami. He's after something, he's always after something, I just need to figure out what it is."

"The hell you will, Parker. I'm not leaving you to deal with that abusive asshole alone."

"Cami!" Parker's sharp, piercing, shout cuts through the conversation with command and urgency, conveying a clear message, halting Cami's next words in their tracks. It's a verbal manifestation of her desperation to control this situation.

"Parker, he's not getting anything more from you, and he's not getting near you. Not anymore, not again. I'm calling Greg, and you need to tell them," Cami points to us.

"No!" The word is a visceral cry from Parker, laden with pain. "Please, Cami, don't . . . just give me a moment to think, to make a plan." Tears carve tracks down her cheeks, and I'm torn between the anger pushing me to confront this mysterious man and the barrage of questions in my head.

Cami yields, her resolve softening. "Alright. But I'm not going anywhere until he's gone. I won't stand down this time, Parks."

"Okay. Okay." Parker's hands tremble as she faces us, hastily wiping away her tears and donning her stoic mask with whatever shred of control she has left.

"I'm sorry. I owe you all an explanation, but I can't right now." Her voice is a fraction of its usual strength.

"Parker, are you in trouble? No matter what your answer is, we *will* protect you. We take care of our own, and that includes you both." Lincoln's voice is unexpected, gentle yet firm.

"I'm not in trouble. I just need to understand why he's here. James never acts without motive," Parker manages, her voice breaking, hands shaking, as she fights the tears.

"Parker, baby, hand Lincoln a dollar from your wallet," I instruct.

"What?" She turns, bewildered, her confusion evident in the line between her eyes.

Cami steps in, her touch soothing as she caresses Parker's arms. "Sweetheart, he's making Lincoln your legal counsel. Pay him, and let's deal with this asshole. It's long past due."

"No," Parker asserts, pulling away from the embrace. "I can't involve you all in this mess. He destroys everything, I won't let him destroy you too." Her eyes brimmed with fresh tears. "I'm capable of handling this. Please, I need you all to leave. Now. He probably knows where I work. He could be here any minute. He'll come after you. Please, go."

The pain and fear radiating from her is a living thing, her complexion no less pale, and it's unbearable to witness. I can't resist drawing her close, wrapping my arms around her, as her body shakes almost violently. Glancing at my brothers, I receive silent nods of understanding.

"We're not going anywhere," I declare, gently coaxing her face away from my chest to meet her gaze. "None of us are leaving. You don't have to explain anything right now, but you're not facing whatever is happening alone. If you think I'm stubborn about something as simple as opening a door, trust that I'm immovable on this. I won't leave you."

Cami's soft voice interjects, "He seems serious, Parks." A silent exchange seems to pass between them, triggering a torrent of tears from Parker.

"Cami," Parker breathes out, her plea almost a whisper, her eyes darting between all of us in the room rapidly, her breathing quickening as if seeking an ally and finding none.

"Parker, you can't run from this, not anymore. And right now, next to three men that look like they'd kill for you seems like a pretty solid place to make a stand. Tell them," Cami urges, her voice steady. Parker's breaths pick up speed, her eyes move from frantic to wild, her pupils blown wide. Her mouth gaps, but no sound comes out.

"Baby, just breathe," I soothe, pulling her close once more, feeling her arms tighten around my waist. I press a kiss to her hair and exaggerate my own breathing until she starts counting backward, this time in groups of six. As she fights for control, I find Cami over Parker's head, her eyes glowing golden, a tear running down her face. "Cami, take Stat and Linc and head back to the farm. Use my truck. Parker and I will follow shortly."

"What a touching picture." The moment shatters with the sound of a voice. Twisting over my shoulder, I see Parker's demon, her ghost made flesh, standing in the still open door.

Parker's body pulls taut, her jaw clenched, braced and waiting when the man known as James validates her assumptions from just a moment ago.

"You didn't actually believe I wouldn't find you, did you, Parker?" he taunts.

CHAPTER 48

Eat

PARKER

He's here.

"I'll ask one more time, and only one, dear, where is my daughter?" He doesn't enter the room, but his presence tries to.

"*Your* daughter?" I break away from Wyatt's arms, stepping around him. "I will *never* let you have her."

"Oh, I think you will, Parker, or did you forget that I know you? You like to believe you're a fighter but you're not, darling. I don't enjoy proving my resolve to you, but you know I will if you force my hand."

I feel small. The urge to flee is overwhelming, and a silent scream builds within me.

Cami's voice slices through, fierce and defiant. "Do your worst, asshole."

Lincoln steps forward, his tone measured but firm. "I'm not sure who you are, but threats to my client won't be tolerated."

James's eyes light up with a twisted joy. "Oh dear, I think you've grown a bit over-confident in your time away," he chuckles joylessly. "I will so enjoy reminding you of who you really are, beginning with this." He brandishes a folded paper like a weapon.

As James advances, Wyatt's arms circle me, pulling me back behind him. Statler has moved too, flanking Lincoln. Together, they form an impenetrable wall between James and me.

James raises his hands, feigning innocence, as Lincoln accepts the document. Silence descends as Lincoln scans the contents.

"It's a petition for full custody," Lincoln states, his eyes lifting to meet mine.

"I must say, you've hidden her from me well. I didn't think you had it in you. Now, I know you wouldn't put her in foster care, Parker, which means you've hidden her somewhere. I want her back. Now. Deny me access, and I'll—"

"Be very careful what you say next." Wyatt interrupts, his voice a low growl of barely contained fury. The room seems to shrink, my breaths become shallow.

"Never." My voice trembles, even through my determination.

"I planned to be reasonable, darling. But if you're going to hold this line, the consequences will be great. I found you. I'll find her."

Tears blur my vision, a searing pain tightens my throat, my chest constricts. I can't draw a full breath. With heart-wrenching resolve, prepared to rip through my own soul with this single confession, I steel myself, meet his gaze, and let the truth fall from my lips. "You won't find her, because she's dead."

"With all your might and connections, seems like you overlooked the most crucial detail." Cami's voice is low and venomous as she steps beside me, her hand a comforting weight in mine.

"What have you done?" James's voice is stripped of any pretense, raw anger bleeding through.

"That's not your business. But I'd wager," Wyatt glances toward Lincoln, seeking confirmation, "that any custody claim is moot if the child . . . isn't here anymore."

"Yes," Lincoln affirms, his voice clear but with a dangerous edge I've never heard before.

"You wretched little—"

"That's enough." Wyatt cuts him off with a calm that's almost terrifying. Then, for the first time, Wyatt's eyes find mine. I'm deaf to James's ranting; only Wyatt exists in this moment. "May I?" he asks softly.

I nod, granting permission because the only thing I feel is the swell of pain threatening to grey my vision.

"You're done," Wyatt tells James, each word a final nail. "Not another word to her. Not ever." With a firm hand, Wyatt ushers him out and slams the door. James's fury is audible even through the wood barrier.

"I'm so sorry," I whisper, my gaze sweeping over them, my grip on Cami's hand tightening. "I'm so, so sorry."

"Parker," Wyatt begins, but I can't face them, not now. I raise my hands in a silent plea and flee to the bathroom. Cooper pads in behind me as I close the door. Sliding down to the floor, I yield the contents of my stomach. When there's nothing left, I surrender to the burn of tears in my throat, shattering as the pain tears free from my soul, leaving only numbness in its wake.

◇◇◇◇◇◇◇◇◇◇◇◇◇◇◇◇

A gentle tap on the door pulls me back from the darkness of sleep, my eyes crusted and sore, the cool tile beneath my cheek.

"Parker, honey, let me in." I rise, my limbs heavy and foreign, unlocking the door, before collapsing back against the tub. Cami enters quietly, shutting the door behind her. She wets a washcloth and, sitting beside me on the floor, begins to wipe away the tears that seem to have dried on my face. Her kindness is a tide of warmth in the cold sea of pain I'm drowning in.

"Should I have told him? Did I owe him that?" I whisper, the weight of the past heavy on my shoulders.

"You owe that monster nothing, Parker." Cami's voice is a fortress against my doubts.

"Was all of this my fault? Am I a horrible person?" The tears breach my defenses once more, a relentless flood.

"Parker, hear me," Cami's voice is firm, her face unyielding. "You did everything you could for her. You were far more kind than he deserved, and in the end, he chose his path. He had no right to her life, however brief, and he has no claim to her memory."

"What if he comes back?" The question is a specter, haunting the edges of my mind.

"If he comes back, you let people help you this time. You have an attorney, and those men, they care. Deeply if how much badgering I had to do to get them to leave is any indication. I'm not exactly a pushover. Statler and Lincoln practically had to drag Wyatt away."

"How do I face him? He has questions, and he's entitled to answers. But that story . . . I've never managed to tell it, not even in therapy," I confess, my hand instinctively clutching at the ache low in my abdomen, where I used to feel her move. "I can barely say her name, Cami. James is right, I'm not a fighter. I'm not strong."

"Parker, that piece of shit isn't right about a single thing. Now, let's focus on the immediate. Let's get off this floor, okay? One step at a time."

"Okay." Each movement feels like wading through thick sludge. Cami guides me to my room, and I change into fresh clothes, clinging to Wyatt's hoodie. I want him, yet I can't bring myself to ask for him, not after today. Today, reality collided with fantasy, and the message is clear. He deserves so much more than me. As I change, Cami's voice drifts in from the doorway, but the words are muffled.

Cooper's weight settles beside me as I sink into the bed. Cami enters, a plate in her hands.

"Wyatt brought food. Said he wanted to make sure you ate." Her words are a gentle nudge. "Why don't you eat while I swoon over here," she teases, taking a seat beside me.

"I need to end things with him. He deserves more than this . . . better," I say quietly, while studying the lines and creases on my hands.

"Parker, it's not about deserving, but even if it was, you'd deserve happiness and love more than anyone I've ever known. Right now, you need to eat. It's steak and a sweet potato," Cami insists, her voice a mix of comfort and command.

"What?" I'm taken aback as I glance at the plate.

"What's wrong?" Cami asks, placing the plate beside me.

"It's the same thing he made the first time we had dinner together," I say, a mix of nostalgia and surprise warring inside me.

The moment is shattered by the buzz of my phone. An unfamiliar number flashes on the screen, sending a jolt of tension through me. Cami and I exchange a glance, deciding wordlessly to ignore the call. But then, a text message arrives, stark and ominous.

+1 (456) 456-4556

This isn't over.

The words are a cold whisper across the room, and I feel Cami's hand tighten around mine.

CHAPTER 49

Empty

PARKER

The morning light creeps in, and I find myself cocooned in the warmth of Wyatt's hoodie, the scent of him lingering. I rise, careful not to disturb a sleeping Cami, and tiptoe across the room. Cooper, with his tail wagging, greets me at the door.

I let him out and punch in Greg's number, my heart pounding against the walls of my chest. His fury burns through the phone line, a hurricane held at bay by the thin thread of my assurances. James is gone, and that's the only anchor I can offer Greg to keep him at bay in Chicago.

Cami's time here is ticking away, and I'm torn between gratitude for her presence and the need for solitude. I need to gather the fragments of my life and figure out how to live it and protect everyone from whatever storm is coming.

Settling on the couch with Cooper, I confide in him, "I don't know how to figure out what his next move will be or how to stop it." Cooper's gaze holds mine lovingly as if he doesn't care about the outcome, only me.

"I think I do." Cami's determined voice slices through the silence. "He's running for office. Following in Mommy and Daddy's footsteps. His opponent's wholesome family image is winning hearts. James is behind in the poles and getting desperate. He needs to repair his image of the young, privileged playboy."

Her words echo in the hollow chamber of my heart. "Why does that make me feel worse?" I murmur, the void expanding with each breath. "I feel empty, Cami, like I just woke up with nothing. I thought I'd never have to feel like nothing ever again. Yet here I am."

Cami tosses a blanket over us both as she settles next to me. "We'll get through this together, Parker. You have more than you think but you'll only see that if you face him this time." Her hug is the reassurance of a one-woman army.

"You'll have to leave soon," I whisper, the words heavy on my tongue.

"I'm not going anywhere. I'm here for you." Her resolve is fierce.

"You can't stay. You have your own world waiting. I've only ever asked you for one thing, and now, I'm going to ask for another." I hold her hands, seeking strength in her touch. "Please, go home."

"That's not a fair thing to ask, Parker," she says, her head shaking with a mix of defiance and understanding. Cami's protest is a gentle storm, her words laced with care.

"It doesn't have to be fair," I reply. "But it's what I need." With that, I stand and retreat to the sanctuary of the shower, letting the water cascade over me, hoping it can wash away the shards of brokenness. The thought of being whole seems like a distant dream, one I've foolishly allowed myself to entertain with Wyatt. Wyatt, with his unwavering kindness and the love of his family, deserves a life untouched by this kind of chaos and darkness.

Stepping out, the world hasn't changed, but Cami's expression has. Her smile, usually a beacon of comfort, now puzzles me. "Why do you look like that?" I ask, unable to decipher the joy in her eyes.

"Come and see," she beckons, her voice a trail of breadcrumbs leading me to the living room.

The sight that greets me is breathtaking—a meadow brought indoors, wildflowers in jars everywhere. There must be a dozen, with colors and shapes of every kind.

"Read the note, Parker," Cami urges, handing me a small paper.

I'm not going anywhere. I'll be here when you're ready.
—Wyatt

The words are a balm and a burden, and I close my eyes to steady the swell of emotions. Handing the note back to Cami, I leave the room in silence, the only way I can, allowing the words written to simply hang in the air.

The drive to the airport is a journey of silence and simmering frustrations. Cami's anger is palpable, a justified response to my insistence I suppose. I can bear the weight of their anger; it's a mantle I deserve to carry for putting her and anyone else in the path of James's destruction. Hugging her tightly, I tell her goodbye, and watch as she walks inside.

Returning home, I see Wyatt's figure waiting on the steps. I draw in a deep breath, steeling myself, locking away the need to be wrapped in his arms and let him surround me. If all I can do now is protect him, shield him from the storm that always seems to surround me, then so be it. As I step out of the truck, he descends the steps, and we meet at the bottom.

"Hi," he whispers, and the world narrows the way it always does. The warmth of his voice blankets the disarray of my mind, soothing the sharp edges of chaos.

"Wyatt, I—" my words falter. His hands cradle my face with a tenderness that threatens to shatter the thin glass of my resolve.

"I'm not here for words," he says, his eyes searching mine. "I'm here for something far more important."

"What?" The word is barely a breath, a fragile sound in the thickening silence.

Slowly, he allows his actions to answer, his arms enfolding me, drawing me into his chest. For a fleeting moment, I surrender, a precious pause in the tidal wave of destruction. I allow myself to be weak, to melt into him, to be surrounded by his strength, his warmth, the steady rhythm of his heart.

But reality is relentless, and I do what must be done—I push him away. "Goodbye, Wyatt," I say, each step away from him a battle against the gravity of his presence. A pain that rattles my bones in every move.

Five more steps, Parker.

"Stop." His voice halts me, and I brace myself for the onslaught of emotions I expect to see mirrored in his eyes. But there's no anger, no hatred, no sense of betrayal—only a smile, warm and unwavering.

"You think you need to do this alone, that somehow you're protecting everyone. But you don't need to protect us, angel," he says, his smile bright, even through the blur of tears gathering in my eyes. "I meant what I said. I'm not going anywhere. If you need me to prove it, I'll do that. I'll prove you're more than he could ever comprehend, more than even you see. I'll see it for both of us until you see it too."

He turns, his steps carrying him back to the truck, and I watch him, as he waits for me to enter the safety of my home. Inside, I reach for a protein shake, the routine motions a distraction as I care for Cooper. Then, I climb back into bed, the echoes of Wyatt's promise lingering as I drift into a restless sleep, the uncertainty of tomorrow whispering in the dark.

◇◇◇◇◇◇◇◇◇◇◇◇◇◇◇

Seven sunrises have come and gone. Cami's calls punctuate the days, a persistent rhythm I've chosen to mute. James's silence is a void, its emptiness as loud as thunder, ominous and dark. My replies to Greg are brief, confined to text. Even Lincoln's voice has tried to break through, filtered through legalities and options. But I know the course I need to stick to.

Wyatt's been the hardest to hold out against, each day revealing some new proof of his promise.

The first day, I woke up to a case of Dr. Pepper with a note attached.

What kind of doctor is Dr. Pepper. A fizzician.—Wyatt.

I saved the note with the others in my keepsake box in my closet. Day two I didn't wake up to anything, but when my day was over, there was a big container of piping hot mac and cheese with another note.

You should know, I can get cheesier.—Wyatt

Day three was a T-shirt with wolves howling at the moon.

I thought the wolf pack needed a mascot. Cami is terrifying btw.—Wyatt

Day four, a giant bag of Cooper's favorite chew sticks.

I couldn't leave him out.—Wyatt

On the fifth day, the calendar granted me a reprieve—a day off. Yet, curiosity buzzed in my mind like a persistent bee, wondering how Wyatt would manage to leave his daily token unnoticed. The afternoon stretched on, and an unexpected call pulled Charlie away to an emergency. Despite the promise of rest, I found myself donning the familiar cloak of duty, stepping into the breach at the clinic and working alongside Sammy.

Returning upstairs later, a surprise awaited me—a box adorned with an extravagant bow, as if it were a gift meant for celebration rather than consolation. I brought it inside with a mix of trepidation and anticipation. Nestled within was a blanket, plush and comforting, carrying his scent. Beneath it, a stack of books lay like hidden treasures, each one plucked from the depths of my Amazon wish list.

I'd sent a text off to Cami to ask if she was helping him.

Her only response:

CAMI

Going to keep helping.

I didn't answer. The note?

*Abibliophobia: The fear of running out of books. Which will never happen to you, that wish list is long, angel.
—Wyatt*

Day six came with a text halfway through the day.

WYATT

Since mix tapes would make me seem old, here's a playlist instead.

He'd named it Songs That Remind Me of Parker.

Today unfolded like a paradox, the best and worst entwined. I woke to a kaleidoscope of sticky notes, a vibrant collage plastered across my front door. Each one bore a fragment of something he adores about me—a spectrum ranging from the way I say his name, to the way I feel in his arms, my eyes, my dancing, even how I put him in his place when we first met.

As I absorb each handwritten confession, a startling realization dawns on me, no armor I forge will be strong enough to keep him at bay. Wyatt's determined to be by my side, to uphold our deal, and I'm not sure how much longer I can fight it. Each day chips away at my determination not to need him.

My phone vibrates in my back pocket.

911 Answer your phone. Now.

The phone's sharp ring slices through the silence, a harbinger of urgency. We reserve 911 for life's most dire moments, my pulse quickening as I answer.

"Parker, James played his next card during a debate last night," Cami's voice comes through, a calm in the brewing storm. "He spun a pretty story, painting himself the hero and victim. It's all over the news now, his narrative twisting to his advantage. I don't know what his endgame is, or how it will involve you, but I didn't want you surprised."

A tide of disconnection engulfs me, submerging my senses and smothering every nerve until my eyes blurred.

"Thanks, Cami," I choke out, my voice a stranger to my own ears. My mind races for the off button, for escape.

"Parker—" Cami starts, but my mind is already retreating.

"It'll be okay, Cami," I assure her, though my voice trembles. "I've got to go—vet call." The words are a lifeline, pulling me away from the edge. I end the call, my heart a drum line moving out of my chest and into my throat.

Then, the phone rings again, the unknown number all too familiar this time.

I answer and before I can say a word, Jame's voice slithers through the speaker, "Parker, listen carefully. I'm on the path to victory, and I won't be stopped here, not by you, not by anyone. Here's what's going to happen next. You're going to join me for interviews, play the part of the grieving mother, and then I'll release you free and clear."

Rage builds within me, a tidal wave, an uncontrollable tsunami. "How dare you!" I spit out the words, finally finding a well of strength, my voice firm with resolve. "I will *never* help you."

"Your choice, darling. But do remember, we could have done this an easier way." His unyielding threat hangs in the air like a guillotine.

My gaze falls to the sea of notes before me, each a testament to a different choice, a different path. This is the choice before me, not of two men, but between a tyrant and the memory of my daughter. Hell itself couldn't forge a flame fierce enough to make me side with James.

With a voice from somewhere deep within me, one I don't fully recognize, I declare, "Fuck. You. She will never be yours."

Slowly and seductively, with an air of cruelty, I hear his final taunt. "Enjoy tomorrow, darling."

My stomach heaves as the line goes dead.

CHAPTER 50

Plans

WYATT

Day eight dawns with a promise I've made to myself: I will see her tonight. I've been cautious, leaving things for her when she's not around. Not out of reluctance to see her, but to make sure she didn't feel uncomfortable. But the ache to see her has grown too insistent, too raw to ignore. It's selfish as hell, I admit, but I need to see her. The day starts early, with the sun barely cresting the horizon as I tackle the downed fence, working tirelessly under the sun's steady climb.

As dusk approaches, I step back into the house, the murmur of hushed voices greeting me. In the kitchen, the worried faces of my family are the first hint of trouble. Dad approaches, his voice steady, "Son, I need you to stay calm."

Anxiety grips me, "What's happened?" I demand, feeling a chill crawl up my spine.

"He did an interview. He released Parker's full name, where she lived, everything, he implied the baby's death was her fault. He must have called her too because he has a recording of her. He's painted her as the villain."

Rage tunnels my vision, every thought narrowing to one singular goal: *Parker.*

Turning, I head for the door but Dad blocks my path, concern etched deep in his eyes. "Wyatt," he says, "Charlie called. He and Sammy said the clinic was getting bombarded with calls and reporters. Charlie had to call the sheriff to get them to leave the parking lot. He sent Parker to the apartment but she's surrounded."

"I have to go." My heart races with the thought of her trapped, alone, and in pain.

"Wait, Wyatt!" Dad's voice is a command, but I'm beyond hearing.

Statler's grip on my arm is iron, but my glare is steel, "Let. Go."

"You can take a swing if you need to, big brother, but you need a plan. You can't just barrel in there, Wyatt," Statler challenges.

"Don't be a hero, Son. Be a *home.*" My father's words cut through the fog of my anger.

I draw a breath, but it is shallow against the tightness in my chest, "Dad, I have to get her out of there."

He meets my gaze, his next words a guiding light. "You do, but the way you do it will define exactly what kind of man you are to her. Choose, Wyatt, between the kind of man that demands she bend to your will, or the kind that helps her stand on her own two feet."

"Dammit," I grit out. "Plan." The word is an anchor in the chaos. "We need to give her time to pack her stuff in the truck. And we need time to leave. If we can keep them off the property, then we have time to pack but leaving will be harder." My mind races, piecing together a strategy on the fly.

"Lincoln," I look over quickly locking my gaze with his, "care to distract reporters with an implication of an official statement?"

"Love to." He grins, the thrill of the hunt alive in his eyes.

"Statler, if we take the long way, can you make sure we aren't followed?"

"Consider it done." He nods, a silent vow of support, and releases my arm.

With the plan taking shape, a surge of resolve courses through me. "Let's go remind my girl she has her own army." We split into two vehicles, Statler riding shotgun with me, Lincoln trailing in his own car. Dad stays behind, prepared should anyone follow or beat us back to the ranch.

◇◇◇◇◇◇◇◇◇◇◇◇◇◇◇

The clinic lot is a chessboard, and we're the pieces. Cloaked in the guise of official vet business with the help of Charlie and Sammy, we pull in and circle the back of the building. As soon as the truck halts, I'm out of it, taking the stairs two at a time. Stat and Lincoln are right behind me.

I knock, but I'm greeted with only silence. "Parker, baby, open the door. Please." My please is a blend of desperation and determination. "I have a plan. I want to help if you'll let me. Even if you don't, at least hear me out. Let me see your face."

The lock clicks, a sliver of hope blooming as the door cracks open. I step in, expecting to see her in front of me but she isn't. I turn and seek her out, and find her behind the door. Her eyes, usually so bright, are dulled by tears, their redness spreading an ache through my own chest. Her cheeks, flushed with the heat of emotion, are the only signs of life in her otherwise ashen face.

"Baby," I extend my hand, an offering of choice. She takes it without argument, and as she steps into my hold, the weight of eight days' worth of worry crashes into me. I hold her close, her tears a silent language of pain seeping into my shirt. Her tears are not the loud cries of the overtly dramatic; they are the quiet, frustrated tears of a strong-willed woman shattering.

"Parker, we need to get you out of here," I whisper, kissing her head. "They have this place surrounded. They can get to you too easily. I want you to come to the ranch. It's easier to protect you from there, and it gives us time to come up with a way to deal with this fucker."

"I won't have anything left after this," she murmurs, her voice a broken whisper, her defeat a tangible presence in the room. "He found a way to take her from me, Wyatt. I was supposed to protect her from him, and I failed. I failed all of you. I wasn't strong enough."

"You didn't fail, Parker, not even close," I assure her, cradling her face. "Look at me. Accepting help, wanting help, doesn't mean you aren't strong. It means you're smart. Your only mistake has been thinking you had to do it this way. You don't, baby. Together, we can deal with this. Please, please let me help—let us help."

"You don't realize what you're bringing to your family. He'll come for you. That's what it means to be with me, Wyatt, destruction." Her voice is a tremor that sends ripples through the tense air. I watch as the emotion flickers like a shadow across her face, her gaze dropping in some silent admission of shame or guilt.

"Eyes, Parker." My voice is firm, a lighthouse calling her back to me from the sea of darkness she's battling. She hesitates but lifts her eyes to mine. "You don't understand the strength of the people who stand with you. Let me prove it. Let me show you this story, our story, because it ends differently. Say yes."

Her breath hitches, a quiet gasp that fills the space between us, and for a moment, she leans into my hands. When her eyes open again, there's a glint of defiance, a spark that refuses to be extinguished, igniting my own hope.

"Your sister is supposed to be here next week. Make her stay in Texas." Her statement is unexpected, pulling me from the moment.

"Why?" I answer, my confusion clear in the furrow of my brow.

She steps back, her gaze sweeping over us, taking in the collective strength we offer. "Do you trust who's with her?" Her urgency is palpable, her voice a crescendo of concern that cuts through the stillness.

"Yes," I nod, my response immediate and sure.

"Call them. Tell them to watch their backs, to say nothing to any-one about me or you, or your family. Keep her away from social media if possible but make her stay in Texas. Do that. Protect her, and I'll come with you." Her hands are a flurry of motion, twisting together in a dance of anxiety.

"Deal. Stat, call in any favors you have and put someone on Riot to manage any pressure from the press."

"Done." Statler, phone already in hand, his back to us, steps into the role of the shield against the storm for Riot.

"Here's the plan. We're going to load up the truck with as much of your stuff as we can. Lincoln's going to talk to the press as a dis-traction. Then we're going to leave, and Statler's going to make sure we don't get followed. Pack what you need, I'll grab Cooper's stuff, Lincoln, you start on the kitchen."

Her voice halts me, a soft but strong tenor, "Wyatt." I pivot to her, every fiber attuned. "I'm sorry."

"Don't," I say, my words a simple truth. "Don't apologize. Trust me. Let me stand beside you."

She nods, a silent acceptance, and then she's a whirlwind of action.

I navigate the familiar path down the hall, the laundry room a capsule of her life. Cooper's food is in a large rolling plastic bin. I grab it as well as a labeled basket, and then a leash and second body harness. I toss the basket on top of the bin, snap the lid closed, and cart it all to the truck.

Returning, I find two bags sitting outside the bedroom. Lincoln's packing up her fridge. I start loading bags in as they finish filling them up. Statler joins after concluding his conversation with Riot.

"Riot?" I query, as we balance the weight of her life in our arms.

"Handled. I called Will. He's sending his personal security." Reassured, together, we pack the back seat, a jigsaw puzzle of Parker's existence.

"Parker, we're out of time," I yell down the hall. "The clinic's clos-ing, and the trucks are going to look suspicious. Let's go."

I watch Parker emerge, her movements quick and decisive as she slings her backpack over her shoulder and snatches up the bag from the floor. "Let's go for a ride, Cooper," she declares, her overly upbeat voice entirely out of context for the situation.

She ushers Cooper out the door with a swift gesture, then spins to secure the lock behind me. I'm trailing, arms laden with groceries, as Statler makes a beeline for his SUV. Parker and I are synched, our strides matching as we head for her truck.

I navigate to the passenger side, hoisting the groceries into the back before calling up Cooper. Parker's already settled in the driver's seat by the time I swing the back door shut.

"Angel, I don't want to seem like an asshole right now but get your ass over here." I can't mask the urgency in my voice. I motion to the passenger side. "We're taking a road you won't know so we can avoid being followed back to the ranch."

"Right, sorry," she concedes, and with a fluid motion, she climbs over the console. I can't help but admire her agility. The door slams shut with finality, and I dash around to the driver's side. Once I'm behind the wheel, I pull up alongside Lincoln, rolling down the window.

"Go make a ruckus," I instruct, and he responds with a nod that's all the confirmation I need. We give him a minute's head start—it's all he'll have to create a diversion.

"Ready?" I ask Parker. She nods, a visible swallow betraying her nerves.

I ease the truck out of the parking spot, every movement calculated to avoid drawing attention. But the moment we're spotted, I slam the accelerator. We've got a two-minute window before they can get loaded up, and I intend to use every second. We weave through the town, down familiar streets and then onto a dirt road.

Yeah, it's the long way home, sure, but it buys time—time I'm hoping will coax the full story from Parker. The truth, finally, unvarnished and honest.

CHAPTER 51

Moving

PARKER

The truck's interior has become my sanctuary for the last hour, the world outside blurring past as we drive. Wyatt tells me Statler's out of sight, and I should feel safe, but the tension doesn't leave my shoulders. I'm lost, gazing out the window, knowing this brief respite will only last a day at most. Tomorrow, the media will be on our trail again. The Lochlans' identities will be revealed, especially with Lincoln boldly stepping forward as my attorney. *How can it be that this still haunts my every moment?*

"Talk to me, Parker," Wyatt's voice is soft, a nudge rather than a shove.

Turning to face him, I study the man who's become my unexpected lighthouse in the storm. His profile is a study in rugged beauty, from the strong line of his jaw to the hint of stubble. His powerful arms strain against the fabric of his black shirt. Our eyes meet, and in those eyes, I find a depth of understanding I hadn't anticipated.

"Please don't ask right now, Wyatt, I don't have anything left, it's an unfair advantage." The words barely escape, and even I feel the heavy weight of unspoken truths.

"Okay," he nods, and I see the struggle in his eyes.

He wants to ask; he wants to understand. He's entitled to the truth, and I owe him that much. But laying bare the fragments of my past, the pieces I've kept buried even from my therapist, is an insurmountable task. Trauma is a shadow that lingers, no matter how much time seems to pass. It's a battlefield I'm not ready to step onto. I yearn to offer him something—anything—but the full extent of "her" remains locked away. So, I find a compromise, a sliver of truth, and I hope it's enough.

"If it helps, I can tell you one thing," I begin, the words tumbling out. "I don't think you'll hate me or judge me when you find out. I was worried you would at first—absolutely certain, actually. But I don't think I've misjudged you that badly. Then I was worried it would compromise you, put you in harm's way. Now, if I could find the words, Wyatt, no matter what it cost me, I swear I'd give them to you. I lived this story, but I've never been strong enough, brave enough, to put it into words. Now, I realize that makes me a coward."

"I don't agree with that," he grumbles defensively.

"I know. It's why I didn't want you to fall for me. I don't deserve you, and selfishly, I didn't want to lose you. No matter what happens next, the last few months with you have been some of the best of my life." Turning back to the window, I wipe away the tear that's managed to escape. I'm surprised. I didn't know I had any left.

I can feel his intense gaze without looking. "Am I allowed to ask more questions?"

"Pass." I cling to our agreement, seeking refuge in the scenery. I had hoped that this place might become home someday. Now, I'm left to wonder if it will still feel that way when all is said and done.

We continue our journey, the Wyoming landscape unfurling in a tapestry of beauty as the sun begins to dip below the horizon.

Abruptly, a gated entrance appears ahead. Wyatt springs into action, opening the gate before circling back to drive us through. He secures it once more, and we proceed down what seems more like a well-trodden path than an actual road. Cresting the hill, the ranch house comes into view, a beacon of safety in the encroaching dusk. Relief washes over me. Although I'm aware that I'll have to leave eventually, for now, this place is a haven.

As we near the house, I ask, "Is there a spot in the barn or a garage where we can hide my truck? It's likely they'll have long-range telephoto lenses, so we need to keep it out of sight as much as possible."

Wyatt looks over, and instead of steering towards the house, he veers off towards one of the barns, guiding the truck right up to the towering overhead doors. He leaps out, his movements swift, and punches in a code that sends the door trundling upwards. Returning to the truck, he fills the silence with an explanation. "This is our indoor arena."

"Whatever spot you had in mind for Cami, I can make do with," I suggest, trying to keep my voice steady.

"It's right here. There's a keeper's apartment inside—no one's lived here since Statler when his place was being built just down the road," he says, his voice betraying a hint of disappointment. "I wasn't expecting this, Parker. I thought you'd be staying in the house. With me."

A wave of nausea hits me, my stomach twisting into knots. "Wyatt… I think I need some space for a little bit if that's okay. I'm not shutting you out, I heard you at the apartment. I just need . . . time." My eyes are fixed on the floorboards, but I can feel the weight of his stare.

"If that's what you need, then we'll set you up here," he concedes softly. "Just know, whatever story you have to tell won't change one simple fact. As real and as true as gravity, I'm going to keep being here for you." His assurance wraps around me like a warm blanket.

I glance his way and find his knuckles white against the steering wheel, his face a mask of calm. He's holding back a thousand wild horses worth of emotion, all for my sake. For a man who claims patience isn't his virtue, he embodies it now. For me. And in this moment, my heart tumbles deeper into love with him.

"Okay." The word slips out, a soft surrender as I reach for the door handle.

"Shut. That. Door." His command slices through the air, each syllable a deliberate beat. He's not raising his voice, but the shift from being patient to pissed couldn't be clearer. I catch a glimpse of his expression, and seeing the hurt etched there, I instinctively look away.

"Eyes." The word is a quiet demand, pulling me back. I hesitate, swallowing against my own fears, praying I don't see disappointment. Eventually, with a shallow breath, I lift my gaze, and I'm met with a swirl of hurt and unwavering determination but no disappointment.

"We're in the middle of a chaos I might not fully understand yet, but it doesn't alter the dynamics between us, Parker. My emotions—anger, frustration, exhaustion—they don't change the way I treat you. They will never change who I am to you. Doors are mine. That's our deal. You are mine. Whether that notion pleases you or fucking infuriates you, I'm open to discussing it later, but those are the facts. Don't expect less from me, not ever. Do you understand what I'm saying?"

Emotions tumble through me, colliding with a force that leaves them unidentifiable. Yet, amidst them all, I can identify one. Hope.

"Okay. Doors are yours, even when you're angry." He acknowledges my consent with a simple nod, then exits the truck, swiftly moving to my side to open the door for me. We work in silence, unloading the truck, the only sound the crunch of gravel as Statler arrives to help.

We draw near a modest door, and Wyatt, after a deft input of another code, nudges it open with his foot. A chill greets us, the darkness of the space only slightly lessened by the faint light that filters in. We're standing in a narrow hallway leading to a more expansive area, a room that seamlessly blends kitchen with living space. Wyatt deposits the groceries onto the central island.

A flick of a switch, and the room is fully lit. "I'll get the thermostat going again after I grab the rest from the trucks." His voice is steady and sure, the earlier tension seems to have evaporated. "Up those stairs, you'll find two bedrooms and a shared bath. Don't hesitate to open the windows. They overlook the rear of the property, no media to worry about. Down here might be bare, but upstairs, you'll find a bed in each room. The closet under the stairs holds sheets and blankets."

His demeanor is composed, his confidence unshaken, a stark contrast to the flicker of anger I witnessed before. It's clear he's not thrilled about my presence in the apartment as opposed to the house, yet he's not coercing me into following his script. He's honoring his promise, standing by me, not as a warden but an ally.

Turning to Cooper, I muster a half-hearted jest, "Well, Cooper, we've found ourselves in the river, it seems. Time to paddle, wouldn't you say?"

CHAPTER 52

Offense

Three days have passed, and her name is now viral. Reporters are camped at the ranch's entrance, like vultures waiting to attack their dying prey. Lincoln has made several trips to the apartment to check on Parker, with limited success, which leaves him jumping on the edge of legality with this James asshole.

Every day, as Parker heads to the clinic, she's greeted by a sea of reporters, their cameras and questions a barricade she has to push through. Statler bolstered our security with more cameras and an automated gate that's being installed today. The first night Parker stayed here, we caught a reporter trying to sneak up the road. Watching Statler's behemoth of a dog, Gigi, chase the intruder was a moment of comic relief we all needed.

The second night, the crowd grew bolder, attempting to breach the fence rather than the road, only to be met with the same deterrent. Our names, alongside hers, are plastered all over the media, and this James Perkins has become a regular feature on the news. Sammy and Charlie have halted Parker's farm visits due to the relentless paparazzi.

Each evening, I make my way to her door, knocking and waiting for the sound of her footsteps. When she opens it, I kiss her forehead and remind her I'm still here. She thanks me, hugs me tightly, then lets go. Cami tells me Parker's responding to messages again, a small victory. Greg and Cami are flying in tomorrow, a surprise we worked out, leaving Parker in the dark, in the hopes that their visit builds her up. She needs her people around her, a familiar circle of safety. If I can't breach her walls, maybe they'll have better luck.

The press hasn't spared my family, my career, or our ranch either. Riot's been dragged into this too, but they've had to tread lightly since she's so beloved in her sport and across social media.

I pull out my phone, thumbing through to my thread with Parker, ready to reach out once more but trying a different tactic today. She's feeling pressure from everywhere. It seems like today she could use a little laughter.

WYATT

What do you call an alligator in a vest?

ANGEL

What?

An inVESTigator.

You're dumb.

How does dry skin affect you at work?

You don't have any elbow grease
to put into it.

ha. ha. ha.

Why do seagulls fly over the ocean?

Why, baby?

Even if it's a dumb game, she's talking to me. Her responses are
quick and simple. I'll take it. Even if I had to search the internet for
dumb jokes.

Because if they flew over the bay,
they'd be bagels.

Not bad for a rookie.

I have a funny dad.

Tell me about him.

He's been all over the news, I think you
know him now.

Got me there. He seems pretty cool.
You didn't tell me he's a Michelin star
chef. Now my steak compliments mean
even more.

They don't leave anything out do they?

Doesn't seem like it.

I have to go back to work.
Animals can't help themselves.

That's true, they don't have thumbs.

LOL

Thanks for the laugh cowboy.
I needed it.

See you tonight.

Feeling the weight of progress, or at least the semblance of it, I'm roused from my thoughts by a knock on the door frame. Lincoln's there, a question in his posture.

"Got a minute?"

His casual lean doesn't match the urgency I sense. "Sure, what's up?"

"We need her story, Wyatt. Without it, I can't pin defamation on this guy, and he's treading just within the law. She's answered my basic question, letting me push a little, but it's all coming to a head. Without all of it, we're shooting blanks," he says, frustration lining his words.

"Fuck." I exhale deeply, the day's stubble itching against my palms as I rub them over my face. "I won't force her hand, Lincoln. Let's give plan A another day. I think having her dad and Cami here might be what she needs to take that step, but if it isn't, then you better work on a plan B."

"Okay. But remember, we're playing defense here. We need to switch gears, and fast," he replies, his usual jovial demeanor replaced by a rare seriousness. I know beneath that easygoing exterior is a man who'd go to the ends of the earth for his family.

"I get it," I assure him as he departs. Twenty-four hours. That's the window I'm hoping gives her what she needs to muster enough strength to make her stand. If it's not, then we'll think of another way. No matter which path we follow, we need to act soon.

Forced

PARKER

The clinic has become a fortress, with everyone banding together after the initial chaos. Each evening, I have to brave the main roads, enduring the flash of cameras as I make my way back to the ranch. The brink of exhaustion looms over me, threatening to pull me under.

I've gone dark everywhere I can to stem the tide of scrutiny. Greg's been bombarded with calls, and his restaurant has become a stage for unwanted media encounters with reporters asking about my childhood. Even Cami's not immune, with reporters swarming her in New York.

And then there's Wyatt. Logic has no place in this; I crave his presence. His hoodie has been my nightly comfort, his scent soothing my frayed nerves. I long to open up to him, to share the whole story, but the words clump in my throat as soon as they form, stuck and unspoken. Each night, he arrives, his hug a silent promise, and I find myself holding on, wishing the words would tumble free.

The buzz of my phone alarm snaps me back to reality, signaling the end of lunch—a meal I couldn't stomach. Despite the gnawing hunger, nausea is a relentless gatekeeper. With a resigned sigh, I pack away my untouched meal.

Cooper's steady gaze meets mine, a silent reassurance in the midst of chaos. Sleep has become a stranger these past few days, my body and mind at war with each other, leaving anxiety and my unsettled thoughts to run the show. The temptation to hide away, to let the world fade behind closed doors, is a siren call.

But that's not the choice I want to make. I'm fighting—for her, for Wyatt, for a future that seems to be slipping through my fingers like sand. Each plan I conjure up dissolves before it can take hold, leaving me back at square one.

Stepping out of my makeshift sanctuary, I force a brightness into my voice as I address Cathy, the linchpin of our office. "Hey Cathy, who's up first?" I ask, hoping to mask the weariness that clings to me.

"We've got a bit of downtime. Charlie and Sammy wanted a word when you got back," she replies. I feel the floor drop away beneath me. I knew this conversation was inevitable. The clinic's atmosphere has shifted; the reporters lurking outside are like a storm cloud over our heads, driving patients away, disrupting the calm we once had. My role here has become untenable.

Sinking into the exam chair, I bow my head, trying to stave off the nausea that threatens to consume me. Charlie and Sammy enter, a united front, and Charlie takes a seat before me. I can't bring myself to meet his eyes as the wave of sickness rolls through me.

"Honey, I'm gonna tell you something, and I need you to hear me out," Charlie begins, his voice heavy with a gravity I recognize all too well.

"Go ahead. I already know you're about to fire me. The business has been turned upside down, and I'm at the center of it—like a ringmaster in this jackass circus. I'm aware of the incessant calls, the 'no comments' from Cathy. I understand, and I'm not even upset with you for it. Just do it—rip off the Band-Aid, please," I say, bracing for the impact of his words.

"We are *not* firing you. Not over something you've got no control over," he asserts with a firmness that leaves no room for doubt. "I may not have any clue what the hell really happened, but I'd like to think I know you well enough to know what's being said isn't true." Charlie's voice cuts through the fog of my anxiety, a commanding echo that oddly reminds me of Greg and, strangely enough, Wyatt.

Sammy chimes in, his stance and expression mirroring Charlie's intensity when I finally look up. "Agreed."

"That said, I do think you need a break. Your sleep is non-existent based on the circles under your eyes. Your health is erratic—if Cooper's alerts mean anything—and this harassment isn't going to stop."

"I can go back out on farm runs or be on call. You need me—that's why you hired me." Desperation seeps into my voice as I clutch at straws. It's a plea wrapped in the guise of negotiation.

"You can't, and deep down, you know it. They'll trap you with fake emergencies. And if I let that happen, do you have any idea what Wyatt would do to me?" Sammy's calm response is a reality check.

I'm taken aback. "What the hell does Wyatt have to do with this?" I folded my arms defensively.

Charlie's head shakes in disbelief. "That boy blows our phones up checking on you every day," he reveals.

I'm floored. Sammy's slight smile only adds to my shock.

"Did you really think he wouldn't be checking on you?" Sammy's question is rhetorical and his amusement clear.

Charlie's laughter rings rich and warm. "For a smart woman, you're missing a big part of this picture. Pack up, go back to the ranch, make a plan with Lincoln, and fight this asshole. We'll hold your place here. I'm not losing the most talented surgeon I've had in years over this." His words are a directive, pushing me toward resolution.

As he exits, Sammy offers a comforting touch—a slight squeeze to my shoulder. "You can trust Wyatt. He's as stubborn as they come, maybe even more than you, Parker. He won't give up. You won't be alone in this, even if you wanted to be." With that, he leaves, and I'm left grappling with the realization of Wyatt's silent vigil and the depth of his care. Emotions swell in my throat, forming a knot I can't swallow.

The world shrinks to the space of my cluttered thoughts as I retreat to the back, my hands mechanically gripping the cooler. I move through the motions, exiting the back door, circling to my apartment. The climb upstairs is automatic; I gather more odds and ends and pack them away. An invisible force demanding to be felt forms a weight on my chest, and it is suffocating me.

Anger would be a welcome reprieve from the relentless exhaustion of searching for a path forward. The world blurs at the edges, tears welling up unbidden, as I usher Cooper into the truck and take my place behind the wheel.

And then, like a cruel twist of fate, my past spills out from the radio speakers—my name, the one that belonged to another life, echoes in the confined space of the truck. The sealed chapters of my history are laid bare for all to hear, each word a dagger to my already battered spirit. Though the journey is a blur, I drive, the truck seemingly guided by an unseen hand. My only coherent thought is Wyatt—I must find Wyatt. My skin is slick with sweat, and Cooper's barks are distant, muffled by my pulse pounding in my ears as I turn up the ranch driveway.

◇◇◇◇◇◇◇◇◇◇◇◇◇◇◇◇◇◇

The ring of my phone is a distant chime, barely piercing the fog filling my mind. Through the haze, I see Wyatt approaching the truck, his figure a beacon in the narrowing tunnel of my vision. I'm paralyzed, the weight of an unseen elephant crushing my chest, the air thinning around me. I watch helplessly as Wyatt opens the door, his lips moving, but the sound is lost to me, drowned out by the silent roar in my ears.

Cooper's frantic pawing and barking are a blur in the periphery of my collapsing world. I'm gasping for breath. Each inhale requires Herculean effort, burning against an invisible opposing force. Then, suddenly, Wyatt's familiar scent surrounds me. His hands cradle my face, and his voice finally reaches me, a distant plea urging me to breathe.

I cling to his shirt, drawing air into my lungs with all the strength I have left, my eyes closing as I surrender to the tremors racking my body.

Shep's voice cuts through the din, a command that carries the weight of authority. "Get her inside, Son." Other voices join the chorus, but they're just echoes to me now.

Wyatt's whispers are a mantra, his warm breath soothing against my ear. "Just keep breathing, baby. Just breathe." I'm aware enough to know I'm seated on his lap now, my head resting against the steady rhythm of his heart while his hand traces soothing patterns on my back.

Cooper's barks are sharp, insistent, as he leaps onto my legs. "Where's her phone?" Wyatt's voice is tense, urgent.

"I've got it," comes Statler's reply, and I feel Wyatt's grip on my hand, grounding me.

"This is way lower than the first time, Parker—baby, tell me what to do." His eyes look into mine, pleading for guidance. "Tell me, Parker."

My teeth chatter uncontrollably, and my world shrinks to the space between Wyatt and me. It's overwhelming, suffocating. "Cooler. Shot," I manage to slur out, the words heavy and distorted. "Don't call . . . 911," I force the command out just before darkness claims me.

Fear

WYATT

Panic grips me. I call out for the cooler while my hands frantically warm her face, her arms, every part of her, trying to elicit any response from the limp form.

"I've got the cooler," Statler confirms, swiftly positioning himself on the coffee table in front of me.

I plead with her. "C'mon, baby, open your eyes. Look at me, Parker." Her heartbeat is faint under my fingers, but she's unresponsive, lost somewhere I can't reach.

Statler's voice cuts through my fear, "What do I do, Wyatt?" His tone is unnervingly calm.

"Look for an orange case. The injection goes in her arm." I watch as he retrieves the orange tube, the instructions inside prompting him into action.

"This kit says we should have called 911 already," Lincoln interjects his concern.

But then, Parker's phone illuminates. "Dad" is calling. I answer without hesitation.

"Parker!" The voice is frantic with worry.

"Sir, this is Wyatt Lochlan. She's passed out in my arms right now. She told us to give her the shot but not call 911. What do you want me to do?"

"Okay. Okay. Follow the instructions on the kit exactly, hold the needle like a pencil, stick it in the arm without her glucose monitor at ninety degrees." The instructions come rapid and clear. "She has fifteen minutes to wake up. Parker has a phobia of hospitals. That's why she didn't want to go. How far are you from a hospital?"

"Ten minutes if I ignore all the laws."

"Good. If she is not awake in the next five minutes, at five minutes and one second, you get your ass in the closest vehicle and you get her to a hospital. Take the glucagon shot with you. Call them and tell them you're coming. Do you understand, Wyatt?"

"Yes sir," I affirm, my voice trembling for the first time.

Statler's voice is focused, all business. "I've got it. Going in." The urgency is palpable.

"Start the timer." Her dad commands. "Is her phone unlocked?" he asks, and I realize the gravity of every second ticking by. The chaos is deafening, Cooper's bark a frantic soundtrack to the crisis unfolding before me.

"Yes, sir." I squeeze Parker's hand. Cooper's barking is relentless, but at Greg's command through the speaker, he settles down. The now silent guardian rests his head on his charge's lap. "I've got the app up already."

I can't tear my gaze away from her. Statler's fingers monitor her pulse, his eyes on his watch, and I'm counting every heartbeat with him.

"Now, we wait," I say to myself. The memory of her arrival is seared into my mind—the lack of color in her skin, the dark circles like bruises under her eyes, her body trembling.

"C'mon, angel, open your eyes, yell at me for carrying you in the house because you're perfectly capable of walking," I coax her, desperation pushing me. My thumb caresses her cheek, willing her back to consciousness.

"Four minutes," Lincoln states, keys in hand.

"Stop being so damn stubborn about every damn thing and open your damn eyes. Right now, Parker. I'm going to put you in that truck and take you to a hospital in sixty seconds if you don't open your eyes. Call me a caveman asshole all you want, but I swear I'll do it." Her eyelids flutter, and hope surges through me.

Her whisper is faint, a thread of sound that barely reaches my ears. "Did you just threaten me?" Her eyes remain closed, veiled from the world and from me.

"Hell, yes, I did." Pressing a kiss to her cheek, then her forehead, saying a silent prayer for her to continue her way back to me. "Sometimes, you just need the right motivation, remember? You taught me that. Now, open up those eyes and let me see those gorgeous baby blues I dream about." Relief begins to seep in as her eyelids flutter open, revealing the familiar oceans I've missed.

Her father's voice, a distant tenor, reminds us of the practicalities. "What's her glucose level?"

I had almost forgotten his presence on the line.

Statler efficiently consults her phone and relays the number.

"Daddy?" Her voice is laced with confusion, a lost child seeking reassurance in the chaos.

"I called, Parker. The nice man whose lap you're sitting on answered. Apparently, he dreams about your eyes. Don't think we won't be chatting about that later." Her father's voice is a mix of concern and mocking, or at least I hope that's mocking.

She groans, and I can't suppress the smile that breaks through my worry.

"Where's Cooper?" She stirs and searches for her companion. Cooper responds, nuzzling into her lap. "Hi, buddy. Good job. Good boy," she praises, her hand weakly petting his head, while Statler continues to monitor her pulse.

"Dad, they got my files. I heard it on the radio. They know my birth name, they know about the hospital abandonment, about my foster families. All of it. How did they get that?" Her voice cracks, the strain of the day, the weight of her world, collapsing into me as she folds into my chest.

"I don't know, sweetheart. I'm so sorry," her father sighs. His voice has surrendered to frustration and helplessness.

"I've already called in a few favors to figure out who's responsible," Lincoln chimes in.

"Am I to assume you're the lawyer?" Greg's voice rings out from the speaker, slightly amused.

"Yes, sir," Lincoln says quickly.

"Cami was right," Greg chuckles. "You found a whole crew out there, Parks. That's like a 500 percent increase in friends for you."

"Very funny," she whispers. Suddenly, she stirs, a surge of motion as she lunges up. "I don't feel so good." She tries to stand and sways, covering her mouth.

I rise quickly, my hand on her back guiding her down the hallway, just in time for her to yield her stomach's contents.

My father's voice echoes down the hall, Parker's phone in hand as he approaches the bathroom. I gather her hair back, keeping it clear. "What am I doing here?" I call out, seeking guidance from her father. Fear threatens to rise inside me.

"Don't panic, Wyatt, it's just a reaction to the shot," he reassures me. "It's partly why she hates the thing. Give her a few minutes and it should pass. Start with saltine crackers and ginger ale if you have it, then we can figure out what her glucose looks like after that."

"Got it." My dad answers, then hands me the phone.

I set the phone on the sink and dampen a washcloth with cold water. Returning to Parker's side, I drape it over her face as she lays her head on her arm that's resting on the toilet.

"I'm sorry," she whispers, her breaths labored.

"Don't piss me off by apologizing, Parker," I chide gently, settling beside her. Cooper squeezes in next to us.

"You know, Son, if you weren't dating my daughter, I think I might like you." Greg laughs.

"Be nice, Dad." Parker groans.

"I'm pretty sure it's written in the fine print that he gets to hate me a little," I laugh. "If you want to keep talking to her, sir, I'd love to let you, but you'll have to do it in front of me because I'm not walking out of this room until she does."

"I'm catching onto that," her father responds, a hint of humor lightening the atmosphere. "Parker, you still there?"

"How did you know to call, Dad?" she asks, her voice weak.

"The app alerted me," he admits, and she groans.

"You *still* have that thing on your phone? I thought we talked about that weeks ago." Annoyance tinges her words.

"You talked. I chose not to listen. As long as you're my daughter, this stays on my phone. If you want to fight about that, I suggest you get your health under control. Then, I'd be more than happy to discuss it with you," her father states firmly.

"Damn," I say, impressed by his resolve. "I think I'm in love with your dad." A faint smile graces her lips, which calms my racing heart.

"Of course you are," she mumbles. Lifting her head from her arms, she turns, surprising me by laying her head in my lap. I adjust the cloth on her head, soothing her with gentle strokes along her arm and back, the way she likes when she's falling asleep. "You're both stubborn pig-headed mules," she declares, but there's a warmth in her words that speaks of love and exasperation intertwined.

"Where do you think you learned it, Snow?" Her dad's voice is a mix of amusement and pride, and I can't help but raise my eyebrows.

"Snow? Please, sir, tell me all about whatever story earned her that nickname," I urge eagerly.

"Well, she was about twelve," her dad begins to recount the story. Despite her exhaustion, Parker's smile tells me she's okay with me hearing it. "And suddenly, we weren't allowed in her room, not even to put away laundry. We were worried she was hiding something serious or maybe embarrassed about getting her period."

"Dad!" Parker's mortification is palpable, and she buries her face in the washcloth.

"Periods are a part of life," I reassure her, gently moving the washcloth aside to look her in the eye. "I'm a rancher. It takes more than a period to embarrass me. Please continue, sir." Her head shake is resigned, but there's no real protest as her dad continues his story.

"What he said, Snow. Anyways, after about a month of this secrecy, we hear a tiny squeak from her room. She tried to shoo us away, but I insisted on entering this time. What we found was the last thing we expected. She'd turned her room into a makeshift animal hospital. Baby birds, a squirrel, a turtle with a cracked shell. She'd built cages and was nursing them back to health."

I can't suppress my smile; it's such a Parker thing to do. "Cameron just looked at her and asked why she thought we'd be mad that she was Snow White, and the name stuck. We did have to lay down a rule, though—no more animal rescues without telling us."

Her father's story paints a picture of a young girl with a heart as big as the outdoors, a trait that's clearly followed her into adulthood. It's a glimpse into the past that makes me appreciate the woman she's become. "Snow," I repeat, the nickname now taking on a whole new meaning for me. "It suits you perfectly."

"As fun as this trip down memory lane has been, I think I need to find some food." Her words sound tired, but I detect determination underneath them.

"Wyatt, keep taking care of my girl. I look forward to talking to the man behind the sticky notes more. Parker Lorraine Mason, you and I are going to talk later. I love you." The love in his farewell is a stark contrast to the formality of using her full name, a signature parental move.

"Love you too, Dad." She smiles.

"Bye, sir," I add before hanging up. "He full-named you," I can't help but comment, a light tease to ease the tension as I help her to her feet.

She's unsteady, like a sapling in the wind, but she finds her center leaning against me, her cheek a soft pressure on my chest.

"I owe all of you an explanation. Might as well give it now," she murmurs, but her body tells a different story—one of fatigue and a need for rest.

I can't suppress the protective surge within me. "Parker, you may have just taken about thirty years off my life," I admit, half-joking, half-serious. "But no one here is going to push you to talk about something you don't want to, not ever."

"I know." She tries to pull back half a step, and I simply step forward, tightening my hold.

"We do want to help. I want to help. I know you're trying to come up with a plan that protects all of us, but you don't need to. Let us protect you this time."

Her gaze lifts to mine, eyes glistening with unshed tears. And in that moment, with a simple, "Okay," she grants me the permission I've been seeking—to stand guard and be her shield.

CHAPTER 55

History

···

PARKER

His family surrounds me, their eyes quietly taking me in as I regain my composure. I catch the flicker of emotions across their faces—curiosity mostly, mixed with concern—but they hold their questions. They respect my silence, choosing not to pry the story from me. Clutching the ginger ale, I realize the depth of Wyatt's words; they're here to support, not judge. They don't see me as an outsider or a damsel in distress. They embrace me as one of their own, just as my dads always have.

"Lincoln," I call out, and he immediately turns to me. "As my attorney, if I share a story with everyone here, does it stay under attorney-client privilege?"

He ponders for a moment before answering, "No." He exhales heavily. "However, I consider their presence here confidential, and I'll do whatever it takes to keep them silent, if that's your wish."

I nod, inhale deeply, and let my guard fall, hoping the words will follow. "I don't think I've done anything illegal yet, but I suppose moral is for you all to decide. You all know I'm adopted. I'll skip over that part for now if that's alright."

They respond with understanding nods.

"During my third year at university, I had my path set. I was so determined, and I wasn't going to let anything stop me." I sense Wyatt gently shaking with laughter next to me, his comforting hand on my thigh. "Cami insisted on dragging me to a party. She still blames herself for that. She was adamant about getting me out of our apartment, fearing I'd implode without some fun. That's where I met him—Mr. Charming, Funny, and Smooth. After a few casual weeks, we decided to date." Unable to meet Wyatt's gaze, I turn to the window, watching the clouds move across the open blue sky.

"Cami noticed the red flags right away, and looking back, they seem more obvious to me now than they did at the time. I think that's how abuse works. He was never physical with me, but he thrives on power, control, and manipulation. It started small, just little digs at my intelligence or appearance, my parents, my friends. He chipped away at me, knowing my insecurities. It was like he was in my head. He leveraged my discomfort with conflict, often disguising a verbal punch as a joke. Eventually, I was isolated from everyone, and he shifted into more obvious tactics. By then I didn't see them. I didn't believe I was worth much. When I did push back, he'd find ways to punish, demean or degrade me—whatever suited him at the time. One day, he insulted my dads, said it was 'workable' that my parents were gay because one was dead, so he could spin the grief angle. That was it, that was the moment the glass shattered, and I saw him clearly and what I'd become. I packed my bag, leaving behind anything I didn't consider critical and showed up on Cami's doorstep."

Wyatt's hand floats up and down my back, and knowing where this is going, I feel my breath catch. The words stick to the roof of my mouth, so I lean into him.

"Just breathe," he whispers in my ear. "You're safe. I'm not going anywhere."

Nodding, I inhale, close my eyes, and force the words free.

"Two weeks later, I found out I was pregnant. It was completely unexpected. I couldn't imagine tying my life to his. All I could think was how cold and awful it would be—what a child raised with that kind of person would have to endure. So, I lied."

I swallow the guilt, keeping my eyes on the mountains through the window before I continue.

"His mother is the governor of Georgia, so despite Cami and I moving, changing our numbers, going full no contact, trying to hide my pregnancy as long as possible, he found me. By then, I was showing, so I told him it wasn't his."

I replay that night in my mind, eerily silent as if frozen in a painting. Then, chaos erupts, like pressing play on a paused video at full volume.

"He spewed his normal venom of cruel and vicious lies. Words that would have broken me before, but all I could think of was to show him what he wanted to see so that I could keep her safe. It was the first time I'd felt strong in a long time. He threatened to make me abort her or give her up, and he told me I wouldn't embarrass him by having some other man's child when he'd made me. In the end, it was like I finally felt the steel in my own spine, and I told him he could go to hell."

Gazing out at the horses grazing peacefully, I realize how much the normalcy of their world contrasts sharply with mine. I'm uncertain of how long it will take, but I'm compelled to finish my story now or risk never sharing it at all.

"I might have sucked at defending myself back then, but I wasn't going to let her down. Cami called it my 'momma bear' era." A small smile breaks free as I think back on the good parts—the sunrises and the joy.

"I was going to keep her. No one was going to take her from me. Cami and I moved again, into a bigger place, and then she and I, along with her sister, Emmary, decided this was going to be our life.

We were going to raise this baby, and only us, plus Greg, were ever going to know the truth about her paternity."

Lincoln's voice broke through my thoughts. "I knew I liked her." His simple declaration of approval makes me appreciate the men around me all the more. Their honor is uncomplicated yet profound. They stand as a united front, and they had welcomed me into their fold without hesitation, simply because it was within their power to do so.

I inhaled deeply and turned to Wyatt, who's sitting quietly, letting me absorb his warmth, his strength. His expression is tense, the hand not on my back clenched, but his eyes—there's no judgment, only an understanding I've come to cherish.

"I thought I'd done the hardest thing I'd ever have to do. I was wrong. About halfway through my pregnancy, at my twenty-week anatomy scan, I learned how much worse it could really be. We were ten minutes in and the tech excused herself. About thirty or so minutes later she came back, with my doctor, and a laptop." I take a deep breath. This is the hard part.

"Immediately, I knew something wasn't right. Basically, without all the medical jargon included, her heart had developed incorrectly. As long as she was attached to me, via her umbilical cord, she would live, but as soon as she was born, she'd die. There would be nothing they could do. Essentially, the damage would be irreversible—incompatible with life." I wipe away the tears as they fall, trying to pull in as much air as I can.

"Baby, slow down," Wyatt says quietly. "Take a second and breathe."

"I'm sorry." I pull in a breath, hands trembling.

"Stop apologizing." His voice hardens.

"Right," I breathe out. "Not sorry."

The room around me chuckles collectively.

"I remember sitting and staring at the laptop screen as she explained each detail. I don't remember everything she said. I kept thinking this was my payback—I lied, and this was my punishment. I don't know how I got back to our place, but when I did, Cami called Greg. They both asked me what I wanted to do, and suddenly, I felt her move. I told them right then; we were going to love her. I wanted to love her for as long as I possibly could because eventually, I wouldn't be able to. My only living blood relative, and I would lose her."

Shep approaches, his footsteps a soft echo in the room. He extends a tissue towards me, a silent gesture of comfort.

"The rest of my pregnancy was normal, which somehow made it worse. I went into labor early, at thirty-eight weeks. I labored for about eight hours, and then it was time. Greg and Cami were both there when she was born. I asked Cami to hand me my phone, and we all took a million pictures of her. She deserved to be loved for however long she lived by everyone who could love her. I held her as she took her last breath." Tears cascade down my cheeks, blurring the world into a watercolor of emotions. Amidst the haze, I sense Wyatt's movement. He leans in, his hands cradling the back of my neck with a tenderness that rips open the door of my soul, the pain pouring out freely.

Wyatt gently lifts my chin, locking eyes with me. "You don't need to keep going, Parker."

"I do," I insist. "I owe everyone here. I owe you all the truth." The pain is tangible, as if releasing a festering wound, allowing the toxicity to seep out. For her, I'll endure this.

"Parker," Statler interjects, his voice firm yet kind, "you don't owe *us* shit. And while I'm sure my voice is one of many, this wasn't your doing, it wasn't your fault. Maybe the person you owe this story to is yourself."

Shep crouches before me, his presence quiet and steady. "After Sunny passed," he begins, "I insisted on therapy for all of us. The therapist . . . she said something profound. She told us that only by collecting our shattered fragments can we hope to see what they might become." His grip on my hands is both gentle and firm. "If you need to collect this fragment, allow us the honor of holding it with you, then keep going because I have a feeling you'll be able to do something beautiful with it."

His words tear through the last of my heart's defenses. A guttural cry of deep, agonizing anguish escapes me. In a fluid motion, Wyatt draws me into his arms, and I bury my face in the safety of his neck. It's a maelstrom of pain that ravages my being. The ache spreads quickly to my heart, my bones, my skin. Breaking, piece by piece, is all I can feel—until the scent of cedar and leather seeps into my consciousness and the sensation of warmth from his arms and the steadiness of his hands as they hold me prevent me from giving in to my own devastation.

Slowly, indescribably slowly, my skin and bones release the hurt. Held tightly against his chest, the tide of my torment begins to settle until I draw my first truly clear breath in five years. I feel as though the wounds themselves have finally been cleansed.

Lifting my head from Wyatt's chest, the oppressive and unyielding weight is somehow smaller. He loosens his hold, but the strength of his support remains unyielding. Looking around, I see every man in the room just as steadfast. I realize that Shep is holding my hand, Statler's got his hand on my knee, and Lincoln's hand is on my shoulder. I realize I am surrounded by a new circle of support.

Not a single person walked out or showed the slightest hint of discomfort. They endured the searing pain alongside me, their silence a statement of solidarity. Grasping Wyatt's hand, I press his palm to my cheek, drawing in a lungful air that tastes like hope. With newfound clarity and a sense of empowerment rising from the ashes, I shift, letting go of Shep. I set up and square my shoulders.

"She graced us with thirteen hours and twenty-seven minutes of pure existence. In that fleeting span, she was fully loved. Her passing fractured something inside me, and grief seeped into every part of me, every wound. I couldn't eat. I couldn't even leave my bed. I was slipping away. Greg and Cami tried to nudge me toward therapy, but I wouldn't go. One day, they made me get up and shower. They didn't tell me but drove me straight there. Then they threatened, cajoled, pushed, and basically dragged me through the door. Eventually, we all went, sometimes together."

Wiping my face, I sit up further, my breathing taking a more measured pace. Wyatt adjusts, too, simply wrapping his arms around my ribs and pulling my back to his chest. Closing my eyes, I find his hand, covering it with mine and matching the rise and fall of his chest. It's a wordless affirmation of him giving me his strength, letting me pull it into me without restriction.

"During one of those sessions, my therapist tapped into my scientific curiosity and introduced me to the concept of Fetal Maternal Microchimerism. It's a complex phenomenon, the essence of which is the enduring presence of a child's genetic material within the mother. That revelation was a turning point. I had her DNA. She wasn't just a memory, she was with me, etched into my cells. Knowing that, I quit therapy. I threw myself into school. She lived, as long as I did, so I wasn't going to waste a single second. I was going to be someone she would be proud of, so I worked to excel. And I did. I found my voice, my strength, and my skill. I never expected James to resurface in my life. And until today, I never imagined telling anyone her story, because I couldn't."

"What was her name?" Wyatt poses the question softly, the question that always grips my heart.

"I couldn't say it for the first two years. Cami created a sign so I wouldn't have to. Even now, sometimes I can't get the sound out, it gets caught in my chest. It's the reason I couldn't bear to name your horse Sunny—I couldn't inflict that pain on you. So, I opted to keep her close, in a place visible only to me." Rising on trembling legs, I face Wyatt, my left side toward Statler. "Can you, please?" I look at Statler, revealing the tattoo etched under my left arm—a mirror location to Wyatt's own.

Statler's eyes widen in recognition. "Morse code," he murmurs with a small smile, and with a nod from me, he speaks her name with reverence, "Stella Lorraine." I lower my shirt, reclaiming my seat, facing the room once more.

"For years, I've carried her with me. She has been mine, my sole responsibility. But I don't know how to guard her—not now. If I admit she's his, I am everything they say I am, and there's probably some legal repercussion. If I don't, then I'm the harlot. I can't figure out how to tell the truth without revealing the entire story."

"He claims that you won't tell him where she's buried. I understand completely, but it does mean he could try to have her exhumed." Lincoln says it quietly, trying to soften the blow.

"He can't." I shrug. "I didn't bury her. I tried, but when I saw how tiny the casket was, I . . . " my voice breaks and I shake my head.

"Where is she now?" Lincoln's voice is curious but gentle.

"I had her cremated. The wildflower field you took me to," I look back at Wyatt. "I planned to see if you'd take me back. It finally felt like the right place to let her rest." Tears spill over, gently this time.

"Anytime you want," he whispers, kissing my forehead.

"Okay, as far as anyone in this room is concerned, you heard her say that she spread the ashes already and there is no DNA evidence." Lincoln says firmly. Everyone in the room nods.

Wyatt's voice is soft when he says, "We can figure this out, if you'll let us help."

"Yes, please." I leaned in till our foreheads touched. We remain in that shared stillness for a moment before he pulls back, then looks toward his brother.

"Lincoln, you mentioned he's toeing the line with defamation yet hasn't quite crossed it. That's fine. What if we don't engage him in a legal battle? What if we go straight to the source of his influence— the court of public opinion."

"That could work," Lincoln nods.

"Good. You reach out to Cami. Given her status as a renowned author, she must have connections in the media world. Let's tap into that network. Statler, I think we need to tighten security. If my idea works, we'll need to be able to get people in and out of here discretely. Dad, I need you to run the ranch for a bit and pinch hit on anything else that comes up. We'll iron out the specifics once we assess our resources with Cami and everyone gets some rest."

Lincoln's fingers fly over his phone, likely messaging Cami, while Statler's voice is a low hum, already coordinating with someone. Shep just nods. No questions from the family's patron. Wyatt stands at the helm, his leadership undisputed. He turns to me, his hands gentle as he wipes away my tears.

"What part of the plan do you have, Wyatt?" I lean into him, breathing him in, letting his scent and touch soothe my over-stimulated body.

"I've got *you*," he states firmly. I let my eyes fall shut, the sound of boots scuffing against the hardwood, signaling the others' departure. I'm certain Wyatt gave the signal, but I'm too drained to chide him for being rude.

"Look at me, angel," he urges, his hand tracing a path from my back to my face. I resist the pull to meet his gaze.

"I told you I wasn't simple. I'm sorry for not being open earlier, for concealing so much. I know what it makes me sound like—what my willingness to hide a child from her father probably says about me as a person. I'm so sorry, Wyatt—"

"Eyes," he commands with a firmer tone. His words coax my eyes upward, slowly, until they meet his, where I find only acceptance. Tears blur my vision anew, surprising me with their persistence.

"I'm . . . you don't have to . . . we haven't discussed . . . " My words falter, tripping over themselves as I offer him an escape. But he silences me with a gentle hand over my lips.

"I'm here—it doesn't matter if it's messy, chaotic, complicated, or one in the morning," he assures me. "Our deals may have brought us together, but they aren't what's holding us together. You're mine, Parker."

CHAPTER 56

Promises

WYATT

Rendering her speechless is a rare feat, yet here she is, silent. I patiently wait until I see the realization dawn in her eyes.

"What does that mean?"

"It means I'm not a quitter," I tell her, tucking a stray lock of hair behind her ear, then cupping her face just how she likes. "It means I want to see your eyes every day. It means blue became my favorite color the moment I met you. It means I want all of you, everything, the things we know and the things we don't. It means you and me first, and everything and everybody else second."

The timing may not be traditionally romantic, but it feels right. She's my entire focus, my everything. Life's been a series of gambles, but she's the risk that's worth it all. She's the prize at the end of the struggle. I'm certain of that.

"Wyatt, don't. Don't say what I think you're going to say. This is a mess, and it's about to get loud and emotional and—"

"Stop."

Her eyes widen slightly in surprise. I can't help the anger that flares within me. "I've got more than enough backbone to withstand whatever happens next, Parker."

"I've never doubted your courage, Wyatt. I . . . I need you to be sure. For what amounts to the second time in my life, I want to believe in a promise. Whatever promise you make, I want to believe it more than I want anything else."

"And what was the first time you wanted to believe a promise, Parker?" I ask quietly.

After a moment's hesitation, she says, "When Greg and Cameron promised me I'd never have to return to a foster home because they loved me, and I was theirs to keep." Her voice is strained, but mixed in with her vulnerability, I see a flash of hope. I plan to turn that spark into a full flame.

"Do you understand, Parker, that I'll earn that trust from you every single day? I will not let you down."

Parker lifts her hands to rest on either side of my face, and a small smile threatens to break through on her lips. "You don't have to earn it. You already have it. I just need us to make it through this. Give me time. Please."

"Alright, baby. I'll make you a deal. No more going at this, or anything else, alone. We're in this together. Agree to that, and I'll keep my thoughts to myself a little longer." My hands slide from her face down to her arms, a gentle touch before resting on her hips.

"You should know—I probably need to go back to therapy. As you've witnessed, I struggle to talk about things. I mean, I'll make the deal, but I could be really bad at this, so just be patient." Her eyebrows lift, that familiar crease forming between them.

"If you mess up, we'll fix it together. I watched my parents for years, and I came to understand that if it's done right, partnership makes facing life easier, not harder. Besides, I could be the one to mess up. You might need to have patience with me. Think you can do that?"

"Deal." Her voice is a soft murmur as she curls up in my lap, head against my chest. "I'm really tired."

A chuckle escapes me as I rise effortlessly, her body cradled in my arms. Her squeak of surprise is music to my ears. "I've got a remedy for that too. C'mon, Cooper." We pass by the kitchen, where my family pauses mid-conversation. "Be right back," I announce without breaking stride, ascending the back stairs.

"Where are we going?" Her words are heavy with the weight of fatigue.

"Just wait," I reply, a hint of mystery in my voice. We reach my room, a place she's not yet seen. Gently, I set her on the bed; her eyes scan the room, taking in pieces of me. "I'll be right back," I promise, heading toward the bathroom.

CHAPTER 57

Sleep

PARKER

Wyatt's world unfolds before me, each detail a piece of the puzzle that is him. My gaze wanders to the dresser, where a 49ers hat lies casually along with a jar brimming with coins and a childlike clay bowl cradling a watch I've never seen him wear. The array of hats on the rack—baseball and cowboy—speak of facets of his life I've yet to discover.

Black and white photos of Wyoming's vast landscapes decorate the walls and hint at a depth and complexity mirroring the man himself. The bed, grand and unmade, with its dark wood and contrasting linens, makes me smile. It's so him—imposing yet inviting. His bookshelf, a testament to past victories and passions for buckles and vinyl records, stands meticulously organized.

Here, in the heart of his sanctuary, I sit, absorbing the essence of Wyatt.

As he reenters the room, the subtle scent of his cologne prompts me to pivot and meet his gaze. I recognize him in both familiar and new ways as the sunlight streaming in from the window casts a halo around his silhouette.

"What's that look for, Parker?" he inquires, his voice a comforting baritone in the quiet space.

"I realized something," I begin, the words flowing with newfound clarity. "There are other things I haven't told you. Questions I haven't asked because I didn't know how to answer them myself. Maybe that's not the same as what you want to say, but it could be a good place to start. Let me practice a little."

"Alright, what do you want to tell me, angel?" His voice is soft, the light in his eyes clear and bright as he walks toward me.

"I've spent weeks bracing for the moment I'd realize our relationship isn't what it seemed. Instead of finding that, I found myself anticipating you being there. Needing you to be there. My drive here today was foggy. All I knew was that I needed to find you. That if I did, I'd be okay."

I step toward him, close enough to feel his warmth but without making contact. He looks down at me, his eyes softening in that familiar way reserved only for me.

"I'm glad to hear you're starting to figure that out," he says, his smile blooming to reveal the dimples that I adore. I reach out to brush his stubbled cheek with my fingers. My thumb traces his lips, lingering as I explore their contours, while my other hand settles on the firmness of his hip. I indulge in the moment, my touch taking in every contour of the landscape of his face.

"How did you get the scar here?" My fingertip traces the line above his right eye.

"Bull dogging. It was muddy. I slipped as I came down and took a horn to the face."

"And this one?" My touch follows the jagged path near his temple.

"One of the rough stock mares didn't take well to being loaded into a trailer, kicked back and hit the loading panel, which popped me right in the face." His hands find my waist, and he pulls me closer.

"Your turn, angel. Where did the scar on your knee come from?"

"First year of vet school," I recall, the memory as vivid as if it were yesterday. "Kicked by a stud horse. That lesson in appropriate distancing was learned swiftly."

He chuckles and nods with a knowing empathy. "And the circles on your shoulder and back?"

The circles, those are some scars I wish I could forget. I feel tense, but he stays steady, his hands reassuring. "I was with a foster family, and they weren't cruel, just . . . negligent. They had this ornate metal trivet hanging near the stove. One day, I was trying to cook, and without thinking, I set it on the burner. It got hot, really hot. In a clumsy moment, I knocked over the pot, which sent the trivet flying. I was wearing a tank top, and the metal seared my skin before I even knew what happened. Needless to say, I didn't stay with them much longer after that."

He furrows his brow, concern etching his features. "How old were you?" His voice is feather-light, his touch on my back tender as his fingers run over my spine.

"Seven." I feel the tension in his frame immediately. "Don't be angry. They weren't monsters. I was actually quite fortunate. My first foster family cared for me for four years. They were older, and when their health failed, I had to move on, but they cherished me. They took photos, documented my milestones so I'd have something to hold on to as I got older. After them, there were others—some kind, some indifferent, but none were abusive or cruel. Many kids in the system aren't as lucky as I was."

He draws me closer, and his lips delicately brush my forehead before asking, "And the scars on your wrists and hands?"

I chuckle, shaking off the shadows of the past. "You try having a father who's a chef and see if you can spend that much time in the kitchen without getting burned." I grin. "That damn pizza oven always got me, but I also mastered the art of a perfect hand-tossed crust."

"I'll have to build you a pizza oven then," he declares with a smile that lights up the room. "But how about I handle all the taking in and out?"

"Deal." His offer warms my heart, and I nod. "The one on your knee looks like an ACL repair surgery. Is that right?"

"Very good, Doc." He smiles down at me. "Year before my first national championship win."

"And the tiny scars on your shoulder?"

"From arthroscopic surgery for something called a SLAP tear. What about the scar on your hip and the two on your stomach?" he asks, curiosity dancing in his eyes.

"The two on my stomach are from having my gallbladder removed—turns out it's not essential. Who knew?" I say with a shrug. "My hip . . ." I pause; my memory is still tinged with embarrassment. "Let's just say it was a lesson in youthful ignorance."

"Were you a rebel?" His tone is playful, an attempt to keep the atmosphere light.

"Far from it. I was a quiet, book-loving, science-obsessed kind of kid. You wouldn't have given me a second glance."

I laugh, dispelling any myths of a wild past.

He looks at me, a smirk playing on his lips. "I disagree. I would've noticed these eyes, even if I was young and stupid." He leans in and kisses me, showing me another facet of desire, educating me on how many ways there are to want someone.

"Now," he says, in between soft kisses, "strip."

"Wyatt," I pause, "I don't think—"

"Get your mind out of the gutter." His laughter erupts, a spontaneous outburst that fills the room with its rich timbre. "You're taking a bath."

"A bath?" I draw back slightly, my gaze lifting to meet his.

"Riot claims a bath is the best remedy for anything. The only thing I've got here, though, is Epsom salts. I figure that'll have to be a good enough substitute for all the girly stuff."

With a fluid motion, he pivots us, his back now shielding me from the view of the bathroom. He steps backward, guiding us toward the door. There's a subtle hesitance in his movements, a vulnerability that he rarely shows. The man would face down a killer animal, a drunk idiot, the media, and all my demons, but gets nervous about running me a bath. As he halts next to the tub, I close the remaining distance between us, wrapping my arms around his waist.

"Thank you."

"Arms up, baby." Without a word, I raise my arms, my eyes locked onto his. Slowly, with a level of care that threatens to bring forward a flood of fresh tears, he slips the shirt over my head.

His eyes, warm and intense, leave mine to roam every inch of my skin. Beneath his gaze, my body ignites, a live wire of sensation that sends a cascade of shivers tumbling down from the crown of my head to the tips of my toes. Hooking his fingers under the edges of my sports bra, he pulls it up and off.

His hands, rough and calloused from years of hard work, glide from the slope of my shoulders down to my wrists. With deliberate care, he lifts each wrist, draping my arms over his broad shoulders, creating a bridge between us. With my arms out of his way, his hands move to my hips, thumbs tracing the skin above the line of my pants. After a moment, dipping his hands under the waistband, he pulls down my scrubs and underwear all at once. Dropping himself down to one knee, he works each leg free. Before standing, he runs soft kisses across my hips and abdomen.

When our eyes meet once more, the desire I find contained in his gaze is as deep and fathomless as the ocean itself. His eyes, nearly black in the low light, reflect an inferno that burns solely for me. The yearning for him is so potent that it robs the breath from my lungs.

"Get in the tub." The deep husky tone of his desire greets me in the words.

"Alone?"

"This time," he says simply. "Not next time." The grin that spreads across his face can only be described as predatory, a lion with prey in its sight. Nodding, I turn, his hand taking mine as I step over the side of the tub and sink into the deep, hot water.

"I'll be back in just a minute." Quietly, he backs out of the room, eyes locked on mine.

Cooper, ever on duty, claims his spot beside the tub. The soft click of his nails on the tile is the only sound that pierces the silence of the room before he settles on the bathmat.

The warmth of the water soothes me, and it's all the more comforting because Wyatt thought of drawing it for me. He listened to my entire story, offering nothing but unshakable and unwavering support. It's strange to think that the number of people I trust implicitly has doubled in just one day.

Recounting my life's tale in one breath was exhausting. My former therapist would be overjoyed with the progress. She once likened Stella's story to a flower that would eventually push its way to the surface when I was ready, like a bud breaking through the soil. She'd be pleased to know she was right.

I should probably reach out to her.

I lean over the tub's edge to address Cooper. "If you had asked me three months ago if four men I barely knew would be the first to hear her story, I would have thought you were out of your mind. But it feels fitting somehow. For the first time, talking about her doesn't leave me feeling empty. It's like the words gave her life shape and weight and meaning."

Cooper eyes me, brimming with what I swear is pride.

Settling back in the tub, I let my eyes consider the bathroom. Undeniably, this is Wyatt's space. The black hexagon tiles, the large wooden vanity and white sink, a soap dispenser, an electric razor, and a neatly hung towel—all centered against a large, frosted window. The tub, the centerpiece of the room, sits adjacent to a spacious glass-enclosed walk-in shower. Across from me is a door, likely leading to a toilet. Everything is meticulously organized and spotless. Guess that means his cleanliness wasn't just for me—good to know.

"There are a million things to think about, Cooper," I say, resting my head against the tub's rim. "I'm just going to lie here for a moment and start our list." And with that, I drift off to sleep.

CHAPTER 58

Healing

WYATT

Stepping back into the bathroom, the sight of her sleeping calms me. I had dashed to the apartment, thinking she could use the comfort of her own things, but the peaceful rise and fall of her chest tells me her body is already taking what it needs. I can't imagine how exhausted she must be, not simply from the shot but also the story. I quietly gather her clothes from the floor, careful not to disturb her, and carry them out to the laundry basket.

My bed, unmade and chaotic, is a witness to how shitty my sleep has been without her. I use the time to strip it down and replace the linens.

As I head down the stairs with the laundry, I can hear my family greeting me from the kitchen. They pause their conversation as I approach; their expressions are a mix of curiosity and concern, silently asking for an update. Fading daylight darkens the typically sunny kitchen, but the aroma of brewed coffee brightens the air.

"Just a minute," I tell them. "I'll be right back."

Lincoln's laughter breaks through the tension. "You only need a minute?"

"She's asleep, asshole," I reply, the sound of their laughter a welcome reprieve from the day's heaviness.

"Damn, dude. If you're going to keep this girl, we might have to give you some pointers." Lincoln earns an elbow from Statler with that joke.

"Boys," Dad tries to sound stern, though I don't miss his chuckle. "If Wyatt walks over here and punches you for talking about his woman in that context, I won't stop him."

I can't help but rub my face; the two-day stubble reflects the frantic pace of the last few days. "Dinner," I redirect them, "let's focus on that. Make yourselves useful."

"Pizza?" Statler suggests, looking to Lincoln for agreement.

He nods. "I'll order the Lochlan special."

I chime in. "Add some barbeque wings. She needs lots of protein."

"You got it," Lincoln confirms, phone in hand, ready to place the order. The day has been long, but surrounded by family, I feel myself grounding.

With dinner plans in place, I head back upstairs, bounding up the steps two at a time. I worry that she might get cold if leave her in the water too long. I crouch down, nudging Cooper aside softly, and run my fingers through her damp hair. She remains still, undisturbed by my presence. Leaning down, I kiss her forehead. She shifts slightly, showing me a subtle sign of life, but doesn't wake. I reach for a towel from the rack and drape it over my shoulder.

Carefully, I slide my arms into the lukewarm water and lift her out. Instantly, she curls into me, shifting to curl her hands up by her chest, her face tucked into my neck, which makes me smile. I adore the way she snuggles into me as I wrap the towel around her and carry her to the bed.

Reflecting on the man I was before Parker entered my life, I believe I was decent. But now, striving to be the man she deserves, Dad's advice makes more and more sense to me all the time. My understanding of my dad has deepened, and I see his actions and my memories of him and my mom through an entirely new perspective. I can only hope to be the kind of partner he was, as I make loving Parker my life's work.

"It might take you a little more time to let me say it, angel, but I'm not going to live my life without you. I love you, Parker. That's my deal." I whisper this vow she's not ready to hear. I softly kiss her cheek and tuck the blankets around her. Retrieving my phone charger from the wall, I scoop up her phone, ensuring no calls or messages disturb her rest.

I gently use her hand to unlock her phone, then spend a few minutes adding my own fingerprint to its security. I don't want to wake her up, but there's not a chance in hell I'm going to stop monitoring her, Cooper's presence notwithstanding.

Turning to Cooper, I command, "Up," patting the bed. He's been attentive to my commands lately, at least the basics, seemingly accepting me quicker than she did. Once Cooper is settled at her feet, I leave the room, the door left ajar to catch any sounds of movement.

My family falls silent as I re-enter the kitchen, and I feel their concern for Parker. After ensuring her phone is charging and checking her glucose level, I report on her status—perfectly normal. Sensing there's something they know, I prompt them. "Give me the update."

"I talked to Cami, and she's on board with your idea of involving the media," Lincoln begins. "But we've got to play by the rules to avoid any legal action from him. Cami believes we should be choosy about who interviews Parker. She suggested a male interviewer to avoid perceptions of excessive sympathy. She's reaching out to contacts and expects to have a few options by tomorrow."

"Good. Statler?"

"I've spoken with Will. He's given us the green light. Just needs the details, and the plane is ours. I'm thinking the living room of the guest apartment will be perfect for the interviews. And no, they shouldn't stay overnight," Statler reports with a nod of agreement from me.

"Who's on pick-up duty for Cami and Mr. Mason tomorrow?" I inquire, already anticipating the logistics.

"Dad volunteered. He's taking my SUV, not a farm truck. He'll take the back roads for discretion," Statler confirms, and I nod in approval.

I take a moment to gather my thoughts. "About the interview—I won't tell her what to say or not to say, but she needs to practice. She shouldn't feel surprised or cornered. We'll work through that tomorrow." Emotion cracks my voice, and I pause before starting again. "I want you all to know I'm grateful."

"Wyatt, no need," Lincoln tries to interrupt.

I raise my hand for silence and press on. "You've all rallied to protect her, to protect a woman I love, without question. I'm aware I can be difficult, 'an arrogant ass,' as Parker might say," which elicits a chuckle from the group. "I love her more than I know how to describe, and I'm thankful for your acceptance and support when she's needed it most." I clear my throat, fighting the sting of tears, brushing away one that dares to fall. Today's events will stay with me for a long time.

Dad's voice is firm yet comforting. "We're all in this together, Wy, because when she became yours, she became ours too."

"Who would've guessed big bad Wyatt Lochlan would be the first to fall?" Lincoln's teasing voice breaks the solemn mood.

"Dickhead," I retort with a half-smile, standing as the gate beeps. We turn to the monitor, watching as dinner arrives, a momentary distraction from the day's emotional toll.

CHAPTER 59

Snacks

PARKER

Consciousness returns to me gradually, and the first thing I register is the familiar scent of leather and cedar, then the warmth of skin beneath my cheek.

Wyatt.

I'm nestled against him, our bodies fitting together in a way that has become second nature. I've never told him, but this closeness, limbs tangled and crossed, is my favorite way to sleep. My hand lies across his chest, feeling the steady rhythm of his heart, while my leg is entwined with his. My head rests on his shoulder, his arm across my back, hand resting on my hip. Each time I've awoken next to him, we were connected.

As I feel the rise and fall of his chest, I let my eyes flutter open. Observing him in this unguarded state fascinates me—he appears so peaceful and content. The steady sound of rain tapping against the window is comforting. The gentle drumming amplifies the room's stillness, only occasionally interrupted by Cooper's light snoring.

It's the kind of sound that makes the world outside this bed feel like an entirely different existence. The rain's lullaby, accompanied by a darkened sky, suggests it's somewhere in the dead of night.

I feel the softness of the cool sheets sliding across my skin and realize that I am completely naked. He must have lifted me directly from the tub and carried me to bed. Wyatt's strength makes me feel a million tingles, all of them good.

Taking advantage of the moment, I lift my hand, using a single finger and running it down his exposed chest, tracing the outline of his abs then moving to the line running over his hip, with its twin forming the sexiest V-shape. Arriving at the sheets haphazardly strewn across his hips, I move my hand slowly beneath until I feel the skin give way to the waistband of his briefs.

"Parker," he says, a warning tone accompanies the rasp in his voice as his hand moves from my hip over my ass. "You've only been asleep a few hours. Your body needs rest." He turns his body, laying on his side, kissing my forehead softly.

"I could argue that being touched by you is a form of rest. I am a doctor, you know." As my fingers dip under the waistband, his hand grabs my wrist carefully but firmly, preventing me from going any further.

"Is that so?" he mumbles, pulling my hand back up his chest. In one fluid motion I've never seen before, he shifts onto his back, one hand hooking under my thigh to pull it high against his hip, guiding me to straddle him. The warmth of his hands seeps into the skin of my hips as he pulls me forward. Taking advantage of the position, I roll my hips across him slowly, only for my second movement to be interrupted by Cooper's bark.

"Shit." Wyatt's voice cuts through the haze of lust in the air. His eyes clear of sleep immediately. He's reaching for the phone on the nightstand—*my* phone. His thumb presses against it, and to my surprise, it unlocks. I cross my arms, a mix of confusion and irritation brewing within me.

"Did you just use your own fingerprint to get into my phone?" I question, watching him shift his eyes from me to the phone screen and back. If he did what I think, he isn't going to live long enough to enjoy the fact that I'm naked and on top of him right now.

"Level first. Fight second."

The phone's glow casts light upon his stupid, gorgeous face when I see his eyes dart back to the screen.

"Too low, baby. No wonder since you slept through dinner. C'mon, let's get you a midnight snack." He sits up, bringing us face to face.

"No fighting, but we do need to talk." I uncross my arms. He lifts me off his lap so I can slide off the bed. "Can I borrow some clothes?"

He stands next to me, his body not yet catching onto the fact that we aren't finishing our previous activity just yet.

"One second," before disappearing into his closet. He returns swiftly, offering me an oversized T-shirt and sweatpants. His body's response is now under control, though I can't help but wish it wasn't. Quickly slipping on the soft shirt, then the pants, I tug the drawstring tight and roll the waistband over so they stay put.

"Food. Then a conversation," I concede, turning to find him in athletic shorts, his torso bare. I can't resist commenting, "It's worth mentioning that your abs make me want to take a bite out of you instead of whatever food is in the kitchen."

His eyes focus on mine, the intensity I see in them makes me bite my lip. "Dammit, woman, you're killing me."

With a shake of his head, he extends his hand. It feels natural to take it, even when he places it on his shoulder so I can follow him downstairs. As we approach the kitchen, he flicks on the light above the island, bathing in the space in soft white light.

"You've got a smorgasbord to choose from: pizza, chicken wings, or the remnants of your cooler," Wyatt announces, pulling me into his body with a slight tug. Before I can react, he sets me atop the kitchen island. The sudden shift in perspective is always a little disorienting, yet thrilling. Sitting eye-level with him, I have unfettered access to the curve of his neck. A neck I'd really love to have my mouth on right now.

Food first, you big ho.

"What kind of wings?"

"Lincoln wasn't sure, so he opted for unsauced wings with an assortment of sauces," Wyatt explains, his body angled towards the open fridge, his gaze flicking back to meet mine.

The fridge light casts an almost celestial glow around him, and I can't help but blurt out, "What are you, some sort of Greek cowboy god?" It's a genuine question, given the scene before me.

"Focus, baby," he growls—a low, primal sound that sends a shiver down my spine as my thighs squeeze together involuntarily.

"Right." My tone is playful, yet pointed. "Is honey mustard one of the options?"

"Yes, it is." He retrieves containers from the fridge, his arms full as he strides to the microwave. I watch, captivated by the fluidity of his movements.

As the microwave hums to life, he calls out, "Drink? There's OJ, your Dr. Pepper, or water."

"Water," I answer. He fetches a bottle, pops the cap, and hands it to me. "Do I get my phone back now, Wyatt?" The question hangs between us, a blend of jest and earnestness coloring my voice.

"Of course." Wyatt hands over my phone with a grin oozing charm and sex appeal. The emotional rollercoaster of the past week flashes through my mind—the breakdowns, the tears, the anxiety.

Way to really cross the emotional spectrum, Parker. But I'm independent and intelligent and not going to be steamrolled. I fought hard to find that part of me again, and I'll be damned if I lose it.

The microwave dings and brings me back to the present. Wyatt pulls out the loaded plate and slides it toward me. I take the opportunity to scoot back on the island, crossing my legs comfortably. As I nibble on the snacks and sip my drink, I can't help but take him in. He's sharing the wings with me, patient and silent, fully aware of the impending conversation but offering no preemptive apologies or explanations.

Finishing the last wing, I brace myself. "So, time to talk, Mr. Lochlan."

"I didn't hear the bell, but okay. What exactly are we fighting about?" He feigns ignorance.

"Not fighting. Talking. You added your biometrics to my phone without permission." I push the empty plate his way.

"Yes, I did." His shrug is casual as he disposes of our trash.

"Excuse me, but usually when someone does something they shouldn't, they apologize," I retort, fully expecting him to acknowledge the breach.

"That is true, but I don't see what I did wrong here," he calmly reasons. "You were exhausted and needed sleep. Cooper was with you, but I needed to monitor you from downstairs. Plus, your phone was nearly dead. Adding my fingerprint solved the issue of not having the app on my phone. The alternative was to call your dad every fifteen minutes, which, considering my first impression involved me holding you while you were unconscious, seemed like a bad idea."

His explanation is logical, yet I can't help feeling he's crossed a line.

"You didn't ask." My voice is losing steam, but I push forward. "Don't bulldoze me, Wyatt. I won't have what I want or think or feel just pushed aside. I won't be nothing again—"

"I'm sorry," he cuts in immediately, his voice stripped of any arrogance or ego as he steps in front of me, lifting my hands and putting them over his heart. "Parker, I never want you to feel that way. Not ever. I was worried. Terrified is probably more accurate. I saw a problem and a quick way to fix it. I wasn't trying to minimize your voice or bulldoze you. It feels a lot like you're mixing me up with him. That's not fair."

As I look into Wyatt's eyes, the hurt in them is evident, like a sudden storm clouding over a clear blue sky. His usually confident gaze is tinged with vulnerability, the kind that reaches deep into my chest and grips my heart. The corners of his eyes tighten ever so slightly, a physical manifestation of the pain my assumption has caused him.

Taking a deep breath, I concede, "You're right, you're not him. I'm sorry." I pull back my hands from his chest, clutching his hands in my lap. "I appreciate you apologizing."

"But," he begins, his grip firm on my hand.

"No. No buts," I interject with a whine, but he persists with a smile.

"But," he continues, "I'm used to solving problems, being in control, making decisions. I'm trying to figure out how to balance your strength *and* mine. Not an easy thing to do. Cut me a little slack while I figure it out, please."

His eyes search mine before he leans in for a quick kiss. Then, swallowing quietly as though the words make him a little nervous, he explains. "Wanting to protect you, to make sure you sleep and eat, to take care of you—I can't suppress that instinct. I am who I am, and I want you to be you, so we need to figure out how to ensure we don't have to compromise who we are. And just so you know, long monologues aren't usually my thing. According to Lincoln, I'm practically poetic these days. He thanks you for that." He rolls his eyes, a playful glint in them softening the seriousness of our exchange.

"I know you're doing a lot for me and that you care. I should be more grateful," I begin, reaching up to touch his shoulders, but Wyatt is having none of it.

"Nope. No way. Not happening," he asserts, pulling me to the edge of the counter. I have to unfold my legs to make room for him to step closer. "You're not caving because of the circumstance we're in, that won't work for me. I insist you fight with me, *try* with me, call me on my crap, and I'll call you on yours. No swallowing down feelings to try to be grateful or make the other person feel better. No avoiding what you think to avoid a conflict."

"Then, what *do* you want?" I throw my hands up in frustration.

"I want you to understand, not be sorry. I want you to say we'll keep figuring this out, not apologize. We can feel two things and both can be true. If you want to be grateful you can, but don't be kind to avoid being uncomfortable," he explains, his voice firm yet caring.

"Fine. I'm *not* sorry," I cross my arms defensively. "I do understand what you're saying." I soften, my shoulders relaxing under the weight of his smile. "If I agree to cut you some slack, can you include me in your solutions? Just please, no fighting. I freaking hate it."

"Deal," he agrees, laughing lightly, his hands gently coaxing my arms apart, wrapping them around his neck. "Now, you have options. You can let me keep my access to your phone or kick me out. I'd like to request, as it seems to be the easiest solution, you put the app on my phone too, regardless of what you choose." He leans in, sealing his request with a kiss.

"You can keep your access, Wyatt. I'd like to think about the app and decide tomorrow. Fair?" I return his kiss while lifting my legs to wrap them around his waist.

"Sounds good. Look at that, we had our first fight," he says with a hint of amusement.

"My god, Wyatt, that was like our millionth standoff," I retort playfully, poking his rock-hard bare chest.

"That's not fighting, baby," He slides his hands under my backside and lifts me off the counter, keeping me wrapped around him. "That's foreplay." His grin is disarmingly handsome, and without another word, he carries me back upstairs. When he lays me over him this time, there's no interruption.

CHAPTER 60

Mine

WYATT

My internal alarm wakes me, unaware of how little sleep we've gotten. Parker's skin is warm and soft under my hands, her body relaxed and tucked into the curve of my own.

Unable to resist, I kiss her shoulder, pulling her back tighter into my chest. "Good morning."

"Hi." Her voice is a delicately sleepy, as though she just left a dream behind. I let my hand trail across her stomach, hip, and finally thighs. She purrs, stretching and arching under my touch. "It'll be a great morning if you finish what you're starting, Wyatt." Her hips make a slow and intentional circle over me, aware of exactly what reaction I'm having to her as she hums.

"How would you like me to finish what I've started?" Softly, I scrape my teeth across her neck, over her pulse, feeling the thud pick up pace against my lips.

"Inside me." She tilts her head, giving me more skin, as she slips her hand behind her, running it down my hip. Rolling my hips forward, I show her just how ready for her I am.

"Deal." Keeping her back to me, my hands drive her up and over the first wave with my fingers. Her soft whimpers ignite a fire, and I crave more of her. Rolling her to her back, my hands catalogue every curve, appreciating them all the more for what this body has carried her through. As I move down, over her hips, I grip each leg and place it over my shoulder.

"Wyatt." Her voice, breathless, stops me. "You don't have to do that."

"Parker—" I pause, lowering my mouth to her inner thigh. "Does this make you uncomfortable?"

"No," she answers, her eyes clouded with hunger, muscles trembling.

"If that changes, tell me. Until then, I'm a cowboy, and I'm hungry. Do you know what that means?"

"No." Breathless, her eyes stare into mine, the darkness of the room no barrier to the connection that forms between us.

"Don't interrupt." I wink.

Taking my time, I build her up before sending her over the edge again. I kiss my way back up just to claim her lips in her favorite kind of kiss, letting my fingers slide through the silky strands of her dark hair before I lay on my side, propped up on my elbow.

"Told you that you were a whole meal," I lean over and whisper against her lips.

A tender smile curves her lips. She shakes her head with languid grace, her eyes closed as if to savor the moment.

"You know what else I was right about?"

"What?" She turns her head, humming lightly as I run my fingers through her hair again before she turns, cuddling into my chest.

"How good you look in my bed." I grip her chin, pulling back so I can lift her face. "I want to see your eyes."

There's a clarity in them when they open, a spark of happiness that brightens the blue even in the absence of light.

"There's my angel."

"*Yours?*" The spark of challenge twinkles in the blue around her irises.

"Do you need me to prove it?" Giving her no time to answer, my hand slides down her body, and she groans at the contact.

"Wyatt." My name on her lips resonates with the sacredness of a prayer and the urgency of a plea.

"Yes?" Smiling against her forehead, I feign innocence as I reach across her, aiming for the nightstand.

She locks her hand on my arm, eyes clear as they find mine. "Wait."

Halting immediately, I bring my hand back, wrapping it around her, hugging her to me instead. "What do you need, baby?"

"I'd like to be in charge this time, if that's okay."

"Of course it is." I kiss her cheek. "What do you need me to do?"

"Lay down. No touching me." A mischievous spark ignites in her eyes, and my blood heats to a thousand degrees in response.

Doing as she asks, I pull my hands back, resting them behind my head. Adjusting her position, she sits at my hip, leisurely running her hands over me. The touch isn't tentative, it's torturous.

She's not scared, she's confident, and I love it. Watching her is like being drunk on desire alone, a shudder working through me as her hands explore. My jaw clenches, fighting the urge to move my hands.

A groan breaks from my chest when her mouth joins her hands, and I can't stop myself from sinking my hand into her soft chestnut hair. She stops, pulling back from me. My eyes open instantly at the loss of contact. Eyes of pure blue flame find mine.

"I want to show you, Wyatt, to give you all the things I feel but can't say. So, if you'd be so kind as to quit touching me, I'd like to continue." Her voice is prim and proper, but what she's doing with her mouth is wicked.

Releasing her hair, I lift my hands, except all I can do is squeeze them into fists as I hold back, letting her lead, which pushes me to the edge of my very sanity. Heat floods my body, building at the base of my spine until my control threatens to snap.

"Parker." Her name is both warning and plea as it breaks free from my chest. "I need you, angel."

I feel her retreat, keeping my eyes shut tight to fight the pressure building inside me, until she lays her palm against my cheek. That beautiful, million-watt smile electrifies me.

"If I told you we didn't need anything between us, that I have an IUD, and I'm completely healthy, how would you feel?" Her whispered questions leave me breathless, understanding the gravity of that vulnerability, that gift, burns in my chest.

"You, Parker Lorraine Mason, are my greatest gift. I'll love you, in any and every way you let me. If you want to give me that, I'd be . . . honored, grateful, overwhelmed. Not sure I can pick just one thing. Tell me what you want."

Her eyes, endlessly expressive, paint a picture of her wants and needs in a vivid stroke that requires no translation. The energy shifts as she kisses me, pouring all her confirmation into that single moment. She breaks the kiss, looking straight into my eyes as she speaks.

"I want to belong to you, Wyatt Henry Lochlan, in a way I've never belonged to anyone."

Her words, simple yet profound, humble me.

"If that deal is on the table, I'll take it. As long as I get to belong to you, in a way I've never belonged to anyone." Closing my teeth over her bottom lip, I tug gently, bringing her mouth back to mine.

"Deal." She smirks, then pulls away.

"Can I touch you now?" I raise an eyebrow, waiting for her answer, wanting this to play out however she wants.

"No." Her smile is far from innocent as she raises up and settles over my hips.

"You're killing me." I groan but hold back my hands as she moves over me. This time, though, I don't close my eyes. I watch the woman I love take me as her own.

"Tell me, Parker. Tell me you're mine," I beg unashamedly.

"I'm yours." Her breath hitches as her eyes close, soft sounds accompanying each move she makes.

"Tell me who I belong to, baby."

"Me," she says confidently. "You're mine."

"Tell me I can touch you now."

"Yes." She opens her eyes, looking down at me, pleasure engraved into every feature of her stunning face.

I can't move fast enough, my hands automatically finding her. She collapses forward, braced on her hands, her hair falling like a curtain around us, as I speak words of praise into her ear. I feel her suck in her breath, and every muscle in her body clenches around me. Beyond the edge of reason, at the feel of her release, I follow her lead.

My arms wrap around her back, keeping her against me, as we each work to regain our breath. Her heart beats erratically, wildly, against my own. She shifts slightly, her back arching as she finds her place on my shoulder, inhaling deeply, every muscle relaxing against me as if she's home.

"I think we embarrassed Cooper." I gesture towards the closet where her dog has comically wedged himself, only his hindquarters visible. The sight is so absurdly endearing that it draws a burst of laughter from her, a sound that echoes with pure joy. She settles back down, her body draped across my chest, my heart swelling.

"Dang it, Parker, I love the sound of your laugh." She tilts her head, her eyes meeting mine, and there it is—that radiant, megawatt smile that outshines the brightest stars. My hand cups the back of her neck, pulling her into a deeper kiss.

"Wyatt?" She pulls back to look at me, both arms now crossed on my chest.

"Yes, baby." I run my fingers through her hair.

"I may not be a cowboy, but next time, I'm not letting you interrupt. Not even if you beg." She raises an eyebrow and smiles down at me.

"Yes, ma'am." As she slips away, heading toward the bathroom, my gaze lingers on her retreating figure. Her graceful steps own a quiet strength that completely captivates me. And when she glances back over her shoulder, a playful wink sent my way, my heart finds a new rhythm and beats contentedly.

In all my dreams, I never envisioned a reality like her.

CHAPTER 61

Pigeon

PARKER

Wyatt lies back against the headboard, his posture regal and confident, an embodiment of my earlier assumption—the Greek cowboy god indeed, carved from the very essence of the mountains he loves and dawn's first light. Smug satisfaction on his face is softened by the tenderness of his eyes. The morning slowly lightens the room, contouring his face and highlighting his strong jaw and the deep chocolate of his eyes.

He lifts his arm, an unspoken invitation, a silent declaration of my belonging. Crawling back into bed, the sheets cool against my skin, I nestle against his side.

"Now what?" I feel a surge of tranquility settle over me as I breathe him in, my body loose and relaxed.

"Now," Wyatt replies easily, "we shower, grab some food, and sort out the details of this plan. Or," he adds, giving me the power to choose, "we could eat first, then shower. It's entirely up to you."

I stare at him, feeling a knot form in my throat as emotions threaten to spill over. I look away, struggling to compose myself.

Wyatt's gentle touch guides my face back to his. "Give me something to hold for you, Parker."

"You undo me, Wyatt," I whisper, a single tear escaping despite my best efforts, only to be caught by his thumb.

"That's okay," he returns, resting his forehead against mine, arms surrounding me in a hug that's beginning to feel like home. "I'm learning how to put you back together."

I let out a deep breath and reach up, wrapping my arms around his neck to return his hug, wishing we could linger right here forever. But my stomach growls, a clear call to reality.

"What time is it?" I pull away from him, taking a cleansing breath, regaining my composure, tucking my emotions away for now.

Wyatt grabs his phone, then flips the screen to show me—six-thirty. He then unlocks my phone with his thumbprint.

"I love it when you look at me like you disapprove. It makes me think very dirty things." He arches one eyebrow, catching me off guard with my own expression.

"I'm not quite used to it. I also haven't decided about the app yet," I remind him, feigning challenge.

"Let me know when you do," he says, his voice earnest. "Preferably soon, as I'd like to solve my need to care for you and your need to maintain independence."

"I knew I was right the first night we met. You're used to getting what you want." I cross my arms with a mock sternness.

"I always said you were smart," he returns. Finding my ticklish spot, he elicits a squeal from me. Amidst my laughter, he takes the opportunity to check my glucose level—always the protector, even in our lightest moments. His care is a constant, a thread woven through every interaction, every touch, every look. It's what makes this moment, this morning, so profoundly ours.

"What does it say, pigeon?" I ask, trying to make sense of the numbers on the phone's screen from my upside-down view.

"Pigeon?" Wyatt questions with a hint of amusement.

"Yeah, you know," I reply with a nonchalant shrug. "Since you plan on watching me relentlessly and hovering over me, and they are the birds that kept saying 'mine' in that animated fish movie. Seems fitting."

Wyatt's laughter fills the room, a rich sound full of love. He runs a hand through my hair and pulls me closer for a kiss.

"Those were seagulls, but you can call me whatever you want if it means you're happy, healthy, and safe," he says, his breath warm but his tone serious despite the playful banter. He softly nips at my bottom lip, a teasing promise of care. "And your level is within normal, albeit on the lower side."

"Then, shower first it is," I declare, sitting up.

Pulling me fully into his lap, Wyatt stands from the bed, my legs around his waist, and walks us straight to the shower.

◇◇◇◇◇◇◇◇◇◇◇◇◇◇◇◇

WYATT

Parker stands staring at the toiletries I haphazardly packed last night while she took a bath. She's wrapped in a towel, her wet hair cascading down her back as she sifts the bottles and tubes I gathered.

"You're beautiful," I blurt out, unable to keep the awe from my voice.

She looks up, startled. "Where did that come from?"

"I've thought it at least a hundred times a day since I met you."

Her eyebrows lift, and a slight blush colors her cheeks. *Note to self—tell her she's beautiful every single day.*

"Thank you." A smile pulls her lips up as she turns back to her task, finding the bottle she needs and dispensing its contents into her hands. I watch her, feeling like a sentimental jackass, but I can't look away.

It's a rainy Saturday morning, and with visitors expected, I have no plans other than to stay by her side. I grab a pair of athletic shorts and head to the closet for a T-shirt, picking out one for each of us.

When I return, she's standing in underwear and a bra, both black. Her panties look like little shorts and hug her ass perfectly. *Those'll look great on the floor later.*

"What did you just say?" Parker pauses, her eyes narrowing slightly as she turns to face me. There's a playful suspicion in her voice that makes me pause.

"Didn't realize I said that out loud, honestly," I admit with a half-smile. "It's a little difficult to keep my internal filter working when you're half naked." I add, stepping closer to her. "You open to renegotiate that deal about keeping thoughts to myself?"

Reaching for the lotion bottle in her hand, I dispense a generous amount into my palm, warming it between my hands before gently applying it to her back. As I rub the lotion into Parker's skin, the sweet, comforting scent of vanilla rises in the air.

"What would the new deal be?" Her body stretches, responding to the way I work the tension from her back.

"How about I tell you what's in my head, and you tell me what you're feeling from now on? More like a trade." I seal the offer with a kiss on her shoulder.

"One addition." She turns to face me. "I get to wear your clothes whenever I want. Deal?"

"Deal." I agree immediately.

In one swift motion, she grabs the hem of my shirt, playfully peeling it off me and draping it over herself. She hands me the shirt I had picked for her, and I pull it over my head.

"You know, I would have let you wear whatever you want, anyway."

"I would have told you how I feel." Her smirk is a challenge. "Now, if you don't stop distracting me so we can eat soon, I can't be held responsible for Cooper waking up every living thing in this house with his alert or for whatever happens to you for standing between me and food."

"I'll feed you, baby." I lean against the bed and watch her pull on tights. "But it's good to know what your version of hangry looks like."

"Hangry? I'll show you hangry," she teases, advancing to jab me playfully, but I'm quicker, capturing her hand.

"Finish getting ready." I kiss to her knuckles. "I'll meet you downstairs."

Retreating to the door, I wink and vanish, leaving her with a promise of more to come.

CHAPTER 62

Awkward

PARKER

I make my way down the stairs, the fabric of Wyatt's shirt—a soft cotton that still holds the warmth of his body—comfortably loose around me. My tights hug my legs, and cozy socks cushion my feet against the cool wooden steps. My hair, now dry, is a wild crown of a messy bun. It's a makeshift look, but hunger is my stylist this morning.

The rich, smoky scent of bacon wafts up to greet me, and my stomach growls in anticipation. I'm definitely hungrier than I realized, and the thought of the crispy, savory strips makes my mouth water.

I hurry down the short hallway and hear the homey clatter of cookware. Statler stands at the stove, expertly flipping said bacon. Lincoln is absorbed in his laptop, fingers dancing across the keys, while Shep leans casually against the island, the steam from his coffee cup curling up into the morning light. Wyatt, however, is nowhere to be seen.

"Oh, hi." My voice breaks the morning routine as three sets of eyes shift towards me.

"Morning, sweetheart." Shep smiles. "How are you feeling?"

"Well—" I pause, then decide to let the truth lead even if it makes me a little nervous. "Like I spilled my entire messy, traumatic story about ten hours ago, dragged all of you into drama you didn't sign up for, and then slept with your son." Lincoln starts coughing, more like choking, while Shep's smile never wavers. "So, a little awkward."

"I appreciate the honesty," Shep responds, then lifts an arm invitingly. I don't hesitate to walk into the embrace, finding comfort in the hug that reminds me of my own father's. It feels like the most natural thing in the world.

"Nothing a little food and thinking can't fix," he reassures me, planting a kiss on my head before releasing me. I pivot back towards the kitchen, setting my sights on the fridge and catch Wyatt's smile from the doorway. Pure joy radiates from him. Clearly he witnessed me hugging his dad.

"You forgot to mention," Wyatt adds, "you flashed my brother with that tattoo. Now, I have to decide if he gets to live."

"I have a feeling the only thing you'd achieve is both of you being bloody," I say with a nonchalant shrug. Statler's laughter erupts, an infrequent display of emotion that makes me smile when it does. "Besides, he didn't see anything more than if I were on the beach in a bikini."

"First," Wyatt closes the distance between us with determined strides, "I might just have to spar with him to prove I still could. Second, we need to have a serious discussion about those bikinis." His words are light, teasing, as he tilts my chin up to meet his kiss.

In that moment, the world fades into a hushed stillness. I clasp his wrists, pressing closer, drawn by the magnetic pull of his presence. It's intoxicating—the taste of him, the firm yet gentle way his lips command mine. He eases back slightly, and our foreheads touch in a silent moment all our own.

"I should point out," I whisper, a tender edge to my words, "that no one but you can do *that*." I open my eyes to see him grinning. I breathe out slowly as he drops his hands. "Wasn't there mention of food?"

"I got ya covered, Doc," Statler calls out, not missing a beat.

"Statler," I approach him with a grateful smile, "thanks for the breakfast. It means a lot." His smile widens, and with a playful glance at his brother, he sticks his tongue out in mock defiance.

"You're welcome."

Seizing the moment, I address the room. "Just a friendly reminder—I'm a vet, not a medic. Any tongue-sticking out or other brotherly shenanigans to get under one another's skin, and you're on your own for cleanup." I see Wyatt's eyes smiling over the rim of his coffee cup and hear Lincoln laughing from his corner of the kitchen. I send a conspiratorial wink Wyatt's way.

"Doc, you might've missed your true calling as a lawyer," Lincoln teases, his own eyes full of light this morning.

"Nah, not nearly enough blood in law for my taste." I feel Statler's hip nudge against mine, a silent cue to take the plate of bacon. I scoop it up, then grab another plate full of fluffy pancakes, nearly colliding with Wyatt as I turn. His hands find my hips, steadying me.

"Thank you." I look up into his eyes.

"You're welcome." He's about to step aside when Cooper's alert cuts through the air.

"Sit," Wyatt commands, his face instantly serious as he relieves me of the breakfast plates.

"Losing sentence structure again, I see," I tease as I settle onto the bench by the window, crossing my legs comfortably.

"Drink?" Wyatt's brow furrows, his eyes intense and worried.

"Juice is fine. It's just his first alert. No need to panic," I reassure him in my calmest "doctor" tone, which seems to work on Wyatt as well as it does on my four-legged patients.

He shoots me a stern look, but I'm already biting into a strip of bacon. Wyatt places a glass of OJ and my phone in front of me. Watching him, I can't help but smile at the man who is so dedicated to me that he needs to check the app on his own. Thinking about it, I start to piece together his reactions over the months I've known him and realize he isn't asking for my app to monitor me because he doesn't trust me to take care of myself.

This man, who carries me up steps, adds his biometrics, and threatens me to consciousness, is scared. In that moment, I already know I've made my decision about the app.

"Two questions," I ask, causing Wyatt to pause, his stance casual yet expectant. "First, can I have your phone? Second, do you have peanut butter?"

"You've found Wyatt's weakness, Parker. He devours that stuff like crazy." Lincoln's voice rings out with a hint of amusement.

Wyatt turns to me, a hopeful glint in his eyes as he slides his phone over next to mine. "Crunchy work?"

I can't help but laugh softly, still nibbling on the bacon. "Of course. That's the best kind. How did I not know this? You told me your favorite food was steak." I light-heartedly accuse him as he disappears into the pantry.

When he reappears, he smirks. "My favorite food *is* steak. My second favorite food is peanut butter."

"Are you eating peanut butter with bacon?" Lincoln leans in, curiosity piqued.

"Nope, peanut butter and pancakes. Syrup isn't really a thing I can do too much of with a pancake. It tends to send me into a spike. I figured out early on that balance is key. Peanut butter became my go-to for pancakes, waffles, stuff like that. I don't know if you'll have the right kind. If not, no big deal, I'll just focus on bacon and eggs."

Wyatt returns, jar in hand. "What's the right kind?" he asks, his brow furrowed.

I take the jar from him, examining the label closely. A smile of relief spreads across my face. "This kind. Just peanuts and salt. Many brands add extra sugar and fillers that don't mesh well with what I need."

"Noted." Wyatt finally takes his seat, his movements slow and deliberate.

"Well, don't wait on me," I urge Wyatt with a nudge of my foot as I pry open the peanut butter jar and lavish a pancake with it. Folding it in half, I take a huge bite. Glancing up, I catch all four men watching me, their concern for my well-being evident as they wait for my levels to stabilize. I swallow the mouthful quickly.

"Gentlemen, I'm laying down a new law here." I infuse a firm, no-nonsense edge to my voice, fully calling on my "doctor persona," as Cami puts it. "You can't treat me—or this condition—like I'm abnormal. I get that yesterday was an intense introduction, and I regret that. But remember, there are a lot people out there like me. Feeling normal and in control is important to me. You've seen how Cooper's alerts escalate." I lock eyes with Wyatt, ensuring my point hits home. "And even if there's a reason to worry, panic is never helpful. We handle it. So, please, no more watching me. It makes me feel like a circus act." With the last sentence, my voice softens, and the vulnerability of my words hang in the air.

Statler's smile breaks the tension. "It's not that," he assures me, his amusement clear. "I've just never seen someone shove half a pancake in their mouth all at once, like a taco stuffed with a half-inch-thick layer of peanut butter. Reminds me of an army ranger I once knew."

Laughter bubbles up from within me, unbidden and genuine.

With the mood lightened, everyone digs into their breakfast. Wyatt's gaze lingers on my phone, but he's also eating. Cooper lies quietly under the table, no longer on alert. As my levels normalize, I continue to enjoy my unconventional breakfast. Between bites, I download my app onto Wyatt's phone, ensuring he has access to it, then slide the device back to him. He smiles like he just won another bull-dogging championship.

My appetite is a force to be reckoned with this morning, and I methodically work through the mountain of food before me. It's a hunger that feels like it could rival a ravenous teenaged boy. Eventually, my stomach waves a white flag, and I push the plate away with a satisfied sigh.

"I can't eat another bite." My gaze lifts to Wyatt. "I need to feed Cooper. I can run over and do that, and when I get back, we can talk about the plan. Sound good?"

"Almost. Except you don't have to go get Cooper's stuff. I brought it over last night. Laundry room. Why don't you do that, and we'll clean up. I can fill you in on what I'm thinking. Dad's going to run an errand, and when he gets back, the real party starts." Wyatt recites the plan with the ease of someone discussing mundane chores, his response practical and tone even.

I pause as a thought forms in my mind. "May I make an alteration?" My hand finds his, seeking the connection between us.

"Of course." His smile is mischievous, and I can almost read the unspoken additions he's entertaining in his mind.

"Not that." I squeeze his fingers. "I need to call and talk to my dad, and probably Cami. I need to fill them in. I need to work in a run at some point today too. Then, if we're going to talk about this all day, I need to do something with my hands. Is it okay if I check out the pantry and see what comes to mind and then make a giant mess in this beautiful kitchen?" The words tumble out, a mix of necessity and a plea for normalcy.

"Young lady, you can make a mess in this kitchen all you want. There are three men sitting right in front of you that know exactly how to clean it up." Shep's voice is stern and warm at the same time.

Wyatt rises, allowing me space to leave the bench. "Agreed. As for calling your dad and Cami, go for it."

"Thank you," I express my gratitude to him, then address everyone at the table. "Thank you—all of you." My voice wobbles, so I make my exit before they can respond, the weight of their kindness and acceptance presses warmly against my heart.

Getting Cooper started with his food and a quick walk means there's only one thing left. It's time to face the music.

CHAPTER 63

Baking

I find comfort in the big blue chair by the window; its oversized form offers a perfect place to sit. The deep navy fabric is soft to the touch and promises lazy afternoons spent lost in the pages of a good book.

I start with Cami, dialing her number, only to be greeted by the impersonal tone of her voicemail. Without missing a beat, I switch to text.

PARKER

Hi.

CAMI

Hello gorgeous. Anything exciting happening in your life lately?

You suck. LOL.

I've heard that before. 😏

I think Wyatt has a plan. It's a lot to text, but I'd like you to be here. Not just because we need your expert advice, but because you deserve to be here. I told them everything. And you were right, I feel better. I owe you an apology. I'm so sorry Cami.

I love you sweetie. I'm not fragile enough to let you being stubborn for a minute come between us. <3 I'm so proud of you. I'll only ever be proud of you. So, how's glasses, tats, and baseball hats doing after yesterday?

OMG. 💀 Glasses, tats, and baseball hats? I mean your rhyming is good. I'll give you that. They're great. How's Em?

I'm honestly not sure. she's been sort of withdrawn. Claims it's an artistic rut. I'm trying to give the artist space as requested.

hmm that's definitely odd. She hasn't been responding to our group chat memes either. She hasn't sent a joke in a while.

Yep. I figure I'll make a surprise trip soon or something, do the big sister bust-in.

After my attempt to reach Greg is met with the digital silence of voicemail, I shrug it off. It's slightly unusual, considering the events of yesterday, but Greg has his own life to lead. I suspect he's probably lost in his culinary world, phone forgotten. I rise, feeling a renewed sense of purpose, and head back down the hall.

The gentle clink of dishes and soft rush of water from the faucet are the only sounds in the kitchen. Wyatt stands at the sink, his back to me, hands submerged in suds. I approach, the scent of dish soap mingling with the lingering aroma of breakfast.

"Where did everyone go?" My voice breaks the silence as I come to stand beside him.

He answers without turning, focused on his task. "Errands, research, probably some ranch work squeezed in there."

I notice his casual attire, the opposite of his usual rugged jeans and boots. "Doesn't ranch work include you? You're not dressed." I tease, reaching for a towel to help.

"I'm taking the day off."

His statement is so out of character for him that it stops me in my tracks. I find myself staring at this man who embodies a tireless work ethic. He must feel my gaze because he turns to me, a question in his eyes.

"Parker—" he places the last clean dish on the counter. "Do you read the last page of a book first?"

"Yes. Always," I reply, my curiosity piqued.

He sets the last dish aside and faces me fully, his hands finding their way to my waist. "I figured as much. Well, let me tell you what the last page says, so that maybe on our way there you can keep it in mind." His voice is soft but firm, and I'm drawn in by the intensity of his gaze. "Being yours, only yours, means that I'm here with you. Without fail. Without hesitation. Every day. No matter what. Under any circumstance."

I reach up, my hands slide over the soft cotton of his shirt, the fabric warm from his body heat. I press my hands against his chest, feeling the solid beat of his heart, a rhythm that seems to echo my own. As I fold into his chest, his arms wrap around me, strong and secure. I rest my head against him, every fiber of my being relaxes, a silent exhale of peace and contentment.

"As someone with very clear abandonment and loss-based trauma, I appreciate the regularity with which you keep repeating that kind of thing. Also, I'll call my therapist and try to work on it. I may also need you to say it again, a few thousand more times," I whisper, my voice barely above a breath, yet filled with a weight of meaning that I hope he understands. His chuckle is a low, rumbling vibration that carries through his chest and into my soul.

"I'll say it whenever you like, Parker. And I'm glad you're going to talk to someone." His arms are a fortress, and I nestle deeper into his warmth.

I tilt my head up to him, the question on my lips more a formality than anything. "What's the plan?" The truth is, I could easily remain in his arms indefinitely.

"Well," he murmurs, his breath warm against my temple, "I wouldn't advise running outside, but I've got a treadmill in the basement if you want to work out. Or you can cook or bake, and we can talk. Or, my favorite option, we can go back upstairs and spend the morning in bed before everyone comes back."

The last suggestion sends a thrill through me, and I can't resist teasing him with a kiss to his chest. "I *want* the last option," I admit, "but it's probably not the most responsible choice. However, if you agree to keep that on the table for later, then I think that should count as my cardio for the day." I feel the curve of his smile against my forehead.

"Great plan," he agrees, his lips finding mine before grazing my throat, a featherlight touch that burns in my blood.

"We won't be productive if you keep that up." The words leave my lips, unconvincing even to my own ears.

"Can't have that." Cool air hits my face and neck, my body swaying without his support.

"Pigeon," I retort, no true heat behind my words. "I believe that leaves me with option two, which was making a mess in the kitchen and you cleaning it up." I barely manage a step toward the pantry when Wyatt's arms wrap around me from behind and gently squeeze.

"Sounds like a plan," he breathes into my ear, sending a pleasant tremble down my body.

I survey the pantry, my mind already crafting what I can make from the available ingredients. Deciding quickly, I grab what I need for hearty bread bowls and rich tomato soup, accompanied by sweet, citrus-infused orange rolls. Setting up my workstation beneath the windows, I start measuring and separating as Wyatt finishes the dishes.

The dough for the sweet rolls comes together under my hands, the familiar process comforting me. I leave it to rise, then turn my attention to the bread bowls, shaping them with equal care. With the bread bowls nestled in their warm spots, I glance over to find Wyatt tidying up, his movements methodical and quiet.

The kitchen is serene, the rhythmic patter of rain and the soft strains of music from the speakers creating an oasis. This peaceful silence tells me that the ease I feel with Wyatt is natural, and our coordinated movements in the kitchen echo that lesson. With the oven preheated, I focus on prepping the tomatoes and garlic for roasting.

"I haven't seen you measure a single thing," Wyatt observes as I slide the tray into the oven.

"I don't need to," I reply with a casual shrug, confident in the intuitive sense that guides my cooking.

"How do you know how to make all that?" Wyatt leans back against the counter, a dish towel casually slung over his shoulder. His posture is a mix of confidence and nonchalance, and it's ridiculously attractive.

"Baby, stop looking at me like that and answer the question, or we're going to let everything you just put in the oven burn." His words pull me back from the edge of my thoughts, and I push aside the tantalizing images flooding my mind.

"Fine." I exhale, a smirk breaking free before I focus on his question. "When Greg and Cameron adopted me, they insisted on family therapy. Given my fears and triggers, our therapist encouraged activities that fostered a sense of control and independence. Things that would make me feel like I would be okay if it all fell apart. Cooking became our thing. The restaurant always had family dinner on the weekends, before opening, where all the staff got together. We started with that, letting me learn in the big kitchen where it was just us before everyone got there. That evolved into cooking more and more, especially on rainy days." The recollection sends a wave of warmth through me, and I can't help but smile at the sweet nostalgia.

Wyatt pushes away from the counter, extending his hand to me. "Why don't we reverse roles for a bit. What questions do you have for me? I'm assuming we have a little time since that bread needs to rise."

"Yes, we do, and yes, I'd like that." I accept his hand, feeling the strength of his grip. "Can we go sit out there, though?" I gesture toward the living room, craving the comfort of the big chair by the window.

"Of course." We move together toward the living room, our fingers intertwined.

CHAPTER 64

Sharing

WYATT

As we enter the living room, Parker makes a beeline for the big blue chair in the corner. But I have a different idea. Quickly, I take a seat in the chair myself and pat my leg, inviting her to join me.

"You want me to sit in your lap?" One eyebrow arching in light-hearted challenge.

"Yes, Parker, I do," I keep my arms open, silently urging her to accept my invitation.

"You need a good blanket down here, you know. I should go get the one at the apartment that you got me." She turns to sit across my lap sideways, tucking her feet under my thigh and leaning back into the arm I have around her back.

"Nah. I'll get you one just for this chair," I brush her hair back from her forehead. "Now, what's your question?"

"Why does Riot train in Texas? And how did she become an elite gymnast? That's not exactly easy." Her curiosity is as endearing as it is relentless. I can't help but laugh, catching her hand mid-gesture.

"That's quite a story. You sure that's the one you want to start with?"

"We have time, right?" She smiles up at me with that shrug that always seems to say so much more.

I take a deep breath, ready to dive into the past. "She was three when our mom passed from breast cancer. Mom had a chemo buddy named Grace, who also had a daughter Riot's age, Bennett. They bonded instantly, along with Grace's mother, Willa, who we all call Mrs. G. We became close, like family. My mom and Grace died a few months apart."

Parker's gentle kiss on my cheek and her hand over my heart is a balm to the ache that never fully goes away. "I'm sorry that you lost them both," she whispers.

"Me too," I admit, intertwining my fingers with hers. It's tough to talk about Mom, but I want Parker to know everything, so she understands that she isn't the only one who needs to be vulnerable. "Mrs. G. ended up with a toddler to raise, just like my dad, and we all stayed close, becoming one big family. To channel the energy of two toddlers, Mrs. G. got them into gymnastics. Bennett wasn't keen on it at first, but Riot—she was a natural. She needed more than what our local gym could offer by the time she was nine. The coach here knew a coach in Texas. The coach in Texas saw her potential and reached out. Dad was proud as hell, and so was I."

"I can only imagine. That's an incredible opportunity."

"It was, but Dad wasn't going to leave us alone or the ranch or the business, so he was set to break Riot's heart. Then Mrs. G. volunteered to take Riot and Benny both to Texas. It took a bit to hammer out an agreement my dad was comfortable with, but basically in the off season they all come back here, and during training and competition season, she's there. She's been all over the world. She competed in junior division and then kept going when she was old enough to go into senior elite. She's aiming for the Olympics next year. She'll be nineteen then. She swears that's old in gymnast years."

"I don't know about old, but it's definitely impressive. It's a really tough sport from what I understand."

"She and Benny are a force to be reckoned with, though, and the Olympics has been their plan for years. Mrs. G. made them both homeschool so their education wouldn't suffer with all the training and travel, and they both ended up graduating early. Benny is into music, and man, she can sing. Both of them are convinced they're going to come back here and start a flower farm. It still sounds like a crazy idea to me."

"What's wrong with that?" she asks, immediately defensive for the two sisters she's never met.

"Baby, I'm not a farmer. I'm a rancher," I explain.

"You're still going to let them, aren't you?" she insists, ready to stand up for them without question.

"Absolutely." I wink and give her hand a reassuring squeeze.

"Softie," she teases.

"Riot's had me wrapped around her finger since the day she was born. I love all my siblings, but Riot's just different. Softie or not, I made them write me a business plan and include start-up costs and everything. They nailed it. They even came in with proposed locations and how to leverage our current business to drive sales. They're incredible. Incredible women seem to be a theme in my life," I say, looking at her with a raised eyebrow.

"Do they have a name picked out?" she asks, her curiosity piqued.

"Nope. They said they need to get through the Olympics first, then they'd decide."

"And if she makes the Olympics, will you be there?"

"Are you kidding me? Of course. At least one of us is at every competition and usually all of us are at the big ones, like Worlds. I'm the one who named her, you know."

Parker's fingers dance across my chest, before drawing invisible patterns in a gesture that's become familiar in the quiet moments we share together like this.

"How so?" she asks, her touch light and curious.

I chuckle softly at the memory that is as clear as if it were yesterday. "When we found out Mom was having a girl, we all started tossing around names. Dad said our job was to love her, make her tough, but also keep her safe. Mom laughed, saying Dad was going to have us all starting a riot over her if he wasn't careful. I blurted out that 'Riot' should be her name because that's what we'd do for her. My mom loved roses, and that's how she became Riot Rose."

"Can I ask—I mean, only if you're comfortable . . . you know what? Never mind." Parker hesitates, her next question dancing on the tip of her tongue.

"Angel." I capture her wandering hand. "Ask."

"Will you tell me about your mom?"

"Of course. Mom was beautiful, which is why I'm so good look-ing." Her light smack on my chest accompanies the roll of her eyes.

"And so humble," she teases.

"Never claimed that," I admit. "She was a bit taller than you, with short blond hair that had a natural wave to it. She was expressive, always talking with her hands—you had to be careful not to get too close, or you might catch a stray gesture."

"Who takes after her the most?" Parker continues her gentle tracing, this time with the chain around my neck. Her touch is comforting.

"Riot, without a doubt. Though Lincoln is the only one with her eyes. Mom was fierce, passionate about everything. She loved deeply and fought fiercely. She could stare down a troublesome horse, and somehow the horse would understand she was the bigger force. Her love for flowers—I think Riot inherited that. I got her competitive-ness. She wouldn't let you win at anything unless you earned it. The first time I beat her at Scrabble, it felt like I'd won a world champi-onship. But she was also someone you could sit with in silence and come away feeling better, even if you never said anything. I remember hearing about a story from Dad once that she won an abused horse in a game of pool. Dad just watched, and when she told him to get the trailer, he cut her off, saying he'd already hooked it up when she made the bet. It was waiting outside for her."

Sharing these stories with Parker, I feel a deep sense of connection, not just to my past, but to the woman in my arms who listens with her whole heart.

Parker's eyes search mine for answers. "He was that confident in her?" she asks, her eyes reflecting the depth of our conversation.

"Yep. Mom was like the sun of our family. She centered us all somehow, and we all had to figure out how to keep that sun within us while losing it when she passed."

"Thank you," she says softly. "For sharing her with me."

"You're welcome," I respond, turning to kiss her palm with a mix of gratitude and intimacy.

She traces the chain at my neck again, curiosity lacing her voice as she asks, "Can you tell me about this chain? It's the only thing you wear consistently besides a hat."

I nod, letting her pull the pendant from beneath my shirt.

I grasp the circular disc between my fingers, feeling the contours that have become a part of me. "It's the Lion of Judah. Mom gave it to me a few weeks before she passed," I start, the memory bittersweet. "My faith has been a rocky journey, Parker. I can't say I've figured it all out, but Mom—her faith was a rock, unwavering to the very end." I can almost hear her voice, feel her presence as I recount her words. "She believed lions are protectors, leaders—strong and fearless. She said this lion would be my strength to lean on when I needed it. She told me to follow the lion, because if I did, I'd learn to become just like one." My voice strains and Parker's gentle touch catches a tear before I can pull it back.

Parker's gaze is inquisitive, searching. "Have you? Followed the lion?"

I nod, a mixture of conviction and sentiment stirring within me. "I'd like to think so. I've been safe when I shouldn't have been enough times to know there's something bigger than me calling the shots. I have a feeling God has a soft spot for cowboys. The rest I'm figuring out along the way."

Her thumb glides over the pendant, tracing the lion's features. "I like it," she says softly. With a tender motion, she tucks the symbol of my mother's legacy back under my shirt.

"What else?" I prompt her, ready for more questions, but the repetitive dinging of the kitchen timer interrupts us.

"First, I've got to go back to deal with the kitchen, then I have a few more," she says.

"Let's go then." I stand, lifting her effortlessly into my arms.

"You know, I'm beginning to think you just like carrying me," she teases, her arms sliding around my neck.

"I have no idea what you're talking about," I play along, pressing a kiss to her forehead. It's becoming increasingly hard to keep my mouth off her.

In the kitchen, I watch her move with practiced ease, her hands dusted with flour as she kneads the bread dough. She's in her element, and I'm captivated by the fluid movements of her hands.

Once she's prepped everything for the soup, she grabs the other dough and begins rolling it out. When she's all done, I start cleaning the latest used utensils. She peppers me with questions, asking about my first kiss, when I lost my virginity, my time on the rodeo circuit, and my least favorite food.

"I can't believe you hate Brussels sprouts," she says, leaning on the island with a look of mock horror.

"Believe it. Never liked them." I shrug.

"You just haven't had them the right way. Greg makes them all charred with bacon and this fig glaze thing. They'll change your life."

I can't help but smile at her determination.

"If you still don't like them after that, then I'll make it up to you some other way," she winks.

I'm already looking forward to it.

The driveway alarm pulls my attention to the monitor. An SUV with blacked-out windows has arrived, and I feel Parker's tension rise.

"Wyatt, who's that?" Concern laces her voice.

I walk over, placing my hands on her shoulders reassuringly. "I have a surprise for you. Go open the door."

Guests

PARKER

Wyatt stands before me, his smile knowing and calm. With a deep breath, I coax my feet forward, curiosity winning over dread. This time, Wyatt lets me open the door. My fingers tremble as they grasp the doorknob, and I swing it open. The sight of Greg and Cami strikes me like a gust of sharp winter air, stealing my breath.

With each step toward my dad, I feel emotion rise, threatening to spill over. I had thought my tears were spent, but they prove me wrong as they trace warm paths down my cheeks. Greg's arms open and I step into them, once again finding a haven that's held me safe for most of my life.

"Hello, Snow," he murmurs, his voice a muted rumble against my ear.

"Hi, Dad." I can barely manage the words as I pull away just enough to see his face, the lines of worry and love inscribed in every line. I swipe at my damp cheeks, futilely trying to stem the flow.

"My turn," Cami's voice cuts through the moment, light and insistent. Dad steps back, and I turn to Cami, her vibrant energy lighting up the world around us.

"I love you, Cami," I say aloud, forgoing our usual silent conversation of signs for the weight of spoken words. She clings to me, her hug a lifeline that reels me back from the deluge of tears.

She pulls back, her hands dancing with a message that brings a reluctant smile to my face. *"If you don't keep this man, I will."*

My smile widens, and I sign back, the motion fluid and sure. *"I actually think I plan on doing just that."*

"Finally," she exclaims, her eyes rolling dramatically as she steps aside.

I watch Wyatt maneuver past us, suitcases in tow, Statler close on his heels. Dad's arm finds its way around my waist, a gesture of support as we cross the threshold into the house.

"Someone's making orange rolls," Greg says.

The warm, citrusy scent of orange rolls wafts through the air, mingling with the hearty aroma of tomato soup, and I can't help but add, "And bread bowls with tomato soup," as we make our way to the kitchen.

I'm giving them the tour without formality and pretense when Wyatt reappears. My eyes stop on him, and in that instant, a sense of rightness settles over me. Cami's words echo in my heart. I don't need to search for my bravery; it's embodied in the man before me, in the steadfastness of his gaze and gentle curve of his smile. Everything clicks into place, and I know, without a doubt, that no matter what happens next, everything will be okay.

Our eyes carry on a silent conversation in a room full of chatter. I'm drawn to him, my steps unhesitating, my hands reaching out to frame his face. I pull him close, pouring every feeling into our kiss. His hands draw me nearer, and in that embrace, my soul settles.

"Thank you." His smile is my reward, a curve of joy that lifts the heavy shadows from my heart.

Greg's voice, teasing and warm, drifts over my shoulder. "It would seem I should have packed my knives." Laughter bubbles up from deep within me, a bright sound that feels like the first rays of dawn after a long night.

"Sir, I respect the hell out of you, but you should know, there isn't a person in this room more powerful than the woman you raised. You won't ever need the knives." Wyatt's smile is unwavering as he addresses my father.

This man.

"Damn." Cami nudges Greg, her hand on his shoulder. "I don't think you have anything to worry about, Papa G."

"Might need to give me a little more time to quit hating you a little," Greg teases, and Wyatt laughs.

I shift, Wyatt's arms still a circle around me, but now I face my father. Our eyes meet, and in that glance, a world of understanding passes between us. I nod, a small gesture laden with meaning, and he returns it, a silent acknowledgment of the bond we share.

Shep's voice cuts through the moment. "Well, Son, we've gotten everyone here you requested. Why don't you tell us what's cooking in that brain of yours?"

Wyatt's actions speak louder than any words could. He's gathered together my tribe, my protectors, my chosen family. Standing here, surrounded by love and support, I realize he's brought me an army.

"I've learned a thing or two over the years. The first being, there's no court like the court of public opinion. Lincoln tells me that, so far, the asshole hasn't done anything strictly illegal except lie his ass off. I propose we play the game on offense. We find a media outlet—the more powerful and connected, the better so they aren't easy to discredit. We offer them an exclusive, one-on-one interview in a location of our choice. Then," Wyatt turns to me, "you tell the truth, without telling the truth. You'll need to be careful, so you don't open yourself up to legal action, but I think Lincoln has a plan for that. At this point, only we know for certain he has any connection to Parker's daughter, and we're going to keep it that way. When we're done, we let the public decide." He pauses, his eyes still holding mine. "That said, if you don't like that plan, we start talking and find another. Either way, we deal with this now—and together."

Wyatt's words hang in the air, a challenge and a promise combined. The court of public opinion—a battleground where perceptions are both sword and shield. Lincoln's legal counsel resonates in my mind, a cautionary backdrop to Wyatt's strategy.

Every eye in the room falls on me. I see their concern and feel their conviction. My glance shifts to Cami, and I arch an eyebrow in silent inquiry. Her response is immediate, fierce, and tinged with the kind of loyalty that can't be bought or faked.

"Honey, it would be my honor to use every connection I have to decimate this sorry excuse of wasted human DNA in an overpriced suit." Laughter erupts, a brief respite from the gravity of our situation.

"What connections?" Lincoln's question slices through the chuckles, and the room falls silent.

"My full name is Camilla Rae Lance. My father was an NFL legend and Hall of Famer. My mother was a well-known artist, as is my sister. We keep a low profile typically, for reasons not relevant to this discussion, but I'll happily leverage my name, my team, and anything else, anywhere we need it, Parker. That's an easy *yes*." She holds my hand, her grip as firm as her resolve.

"Can't say I saw that one coming," Lincoln says, his eyes shining brightly.

Words fail me as I stand before the people who love me, a collage of faces mixed with concern and determination. "Even a month ago, the thought of taking a stand like what you're describing was unfathomable. I know everything we're about to do is hard, and I'd be lying if I told you I wasn't outright terrified. I know I lied to him, but it was the right thing to do to protect her. Protecting her, reclaiming her, is what we need to do. If, for no other reason than that, I'll do whatever it takes. She's mine." The declaration is more than a statement of possession; it's a vow. Finally, I've drawn a line in the sand.

"May I?" Wyatt's gaze meets mine, a silent request that I answer with a subtle nod. He steps forward, assuming command with an ease that speaks of his determination. In that move, I see his mother was right about her son. This lion of Judah is protecting me, and he is mine.

"Let's start making calls," he says. His voice sets out everyone's tasks like a general. "Statler's been patching up our personal airfield, which should allow us to fly anyone in if needed. It has its own road to the house, so we can avoid the reporters at the front gate." His words paint a picture of preparation, of pieces falling into place.

"Cami, you're on connections," he continues. "Find us a media outlet. Then, figure out if there are any specifics we need to know about doing something like this." The gravity of his instructions is not lost on me; the stakes are high. "Key parts of this negotiation are that they cannot leak in anyway what they are doing this in advance of the interview itself. They cannot bring more people than they clear through us, and the interview takes place here, on our terms." His conditions are a fortress designed to protect us.

"On it," Cami responds. Her fingers dance the tango on her phone's screen and messages fly like arrows to unseen targets.

"Lincoln," Wyatt turns, "I need you to teach us how to talk about this without putting ourselves at risk. What do we need to avoid? What do we need to refuse to answer? All that."

"I'll have a brief for you shortly, then we can practice," he assures us. I can't help but feel a flicker of relief. His eyes flick to Cami. "Duchess, any chance we can negotiate that they have to clear their questions with us in advance and that we won't answer any questions that aren't approved?"

Her response is swift, a spark of defiance in her eyes. "Leave it to me, lawman." She winks, and I can't help but think of them as a powerful mix—fire and dynamite, ready to ignite at a moment's notice.

"Statler, I want you to get cameras up in the keeper's apartment now, and I don't want anyone to know they're there," Wyatt continues the instructions. "I want our own record of the interview, and I want to be able to watch them set up and see if there's anything shady. I want no surprises."

"Copy," he responds, a nod of understanding before he's off, his steps purposeful.

"Dinner's in about two hours!" I call out after him.

"Ten-four, gorgeous," he throws back, his voice trailing laughter. I roll my eyes; he's not one to be afraid of poking the bear, and Wyatt's his favorite target.

"Any jobs for me?" I look up at him, ready to take on whatever task he deems fit.

"If you think you're up for it, can you write down all the things you remember and how they occurred?"

"Oh, I don't have to. I keep a digital journal. I have for years. I have a record of every single day almost, minus the last few."

"Okay, check. Your job now is to hang with your dad and finish dinner." Laughter fills the room, a light moment in the midst of our serious endeavor.

"What will you be doing?" I ask, curious about his role in this intricate strategy he's built.

"I'd like to propose that you let me go get more of your stuff from your place at the clinic and move it here." His suggestion hangs between us, an offer of something more permanent, more real.

"You want me to move in?" I draw out each word, hyper-aware of the audience we've garnered. His father, my father, their gazes heavy on us. Lincoln and Cami's conversation skids to a halt.

"I'd love that, but if it makes you more comfortable to think about it like an extended vacation from your current apartment, I would understand." His understanding is a gift, his compromise is a soft landing, a cushion against the weight of a big decision, but I don't need it.

"I could certainly use more clothes, and I need a few of Cooper's things as well." I inhale deeply, steadying myself. "But if you're asking if I want to stay, I think I'd be happy to make that deal." The words are a bridge crossing into a future I hadn't dared to imagine until yesterday.

"To be negotiated later?" he teases, and I can't help but respond to the light in his eyes.

"Deal. Can I make you a list of what I need? I can go over to the arena apartment and grab what I need from there while you go to the clinic."

"Anything for you," he proclaims, with his hand over his heart in a theatrical display of devotion.

I roll my eyes, though affection tugs at the corners of my mouth. "I'll remind you of that the next time I want to win an argument."

CHAPTER 66

The Letter

PARKER

Cami's silence cloaks us as we make our way to the arena apartment. I've felt her eyes on me since the moment Wyatt laid out our tasks around the kitchen island. The click of the door shutting behind us feels final, and when Cami turns to me, I see she's ready to break her silence.

She signs, *"How are you? Really?"* Her eyes implore me in the dim light.

I draw a deep breath, tasting the dusty air full of anticipation. *"You are only the third person I ever learned to love,"* I begin, my hands moving with deliberateness. *"You taught me that strength doesn't need to roar, that love echoes louder than any shout, and that light—no matter how faint—cannot be smothered by darkness."* I see the shimmer of tears in Cami's eyes, reflecting in the sparse light like tiny stars. *"I'm sorry if I've never told you that,"* I add.

Her tears spill down her cheeks, and she brushes them away with a fierceness that speaks of her distaste for crying. *"You seem so different,"* she signs, her movements sharp with concern. *"I was just here, but today, it's different. Why? How?"*

"Wyatt," I sign back, the name a simple truth that seems to hang between us. *"I didn't mean to, but against all reason, I've fallen completely in love with him."* I pause, searching for the words to paint the picture of my heart's recent upheaval. *"It's like he found a way to stand beside me without a word, and instead of trying to strip me of my defenses, he simply added to them. It's hard to explain."*

"You don't need to," her big smile is genuine and knowing. "I'm so happy for you, but more than that, Parker, I am proud of you. Proud to love you, to know you, to stand with you."

Her hands find mine, and we embrace. "Now that we've sorted that through," she says, her voice a warm melody, "let's get your things. When are you going to tell him?"

A laugh bubbles up from somewhere deep inside. "I don't know how. I need to get this mess sorted out first, then figure out how to tell him. I'm not sure if saying anything now is helpful. When exactly *is* the right time to put all your cards on the table and leave your heart completely open?"

As we rummage through the fridge, she teases me. "Having never done that, I'm guessing you'll just know."

"Sounds as accurate as anything else," I admit, the laughter coming easier now. "He's used every deal between us to reveal some part of himself, to show his true colors. It's strange, but it's also precious. It's his way of honoring my voice, I think. And I love knowing he's a man of his word. Now, I have to figure out how to articulate my own deal."

"Just remember, I look good in jewel tones when you're picking out wedding colors." She winks, her humor a balm to my soul.

"Let's tackle these hurdles one at a time." I'm feeling determined to get past this mess. "Emotional interviews, exes who've overstayed their welcome in our lives, reclaiming what's mine—weddings are a bridge to cross later, and besides, he has to ask first."

"Agreed." Cami nods. "Let's bring this asshat down—a celebration I fully intend to mark by getting victoriously drunk." Her laughter is infectious, and soon we're both caught in a deluge of giggles; this time the tears stream down in joyous abandon.

"Ladies," Greg's voice echoes down the hall, a note of amusement in his tone. "What on earth is happening in here?" His smile is a beacon as he appears, and it triggers another round of laughter so intense that it leaves my sides aching.

Once the laughter subsides enough to resume packing, Greg's voice turns serious. "Cami, would you mind giving Parker and me a moment alone?"

"Not at all," she replies, her arms laden with bags as she plants a kiss on my cheek, then Greg's, before departing.

"Parker," Greg begins, and the gravity in his voice roots me to the spot.

"What is it?" My heart thuds in my chest.

"Cameron left something for you," he says, his eyes holding a depth of unspoken history. "He wanted you to have it when you found someone worthy of your love, someone you chose. I wasn't sure if now was the right time, but when Wyatt called, I went and got it from the safe." A lump forms in my throat, freezing me to the floor. "I was going to ask if he was the one when I arrived, but seeing you together, I think I already know the answer."

"How?" The question is a whisper, my breath tight in my chest. "I just figured it out yesterday."

"Because, my girl, I know you as well as I know myself. Throughout my life, there have been only three people I've looked at with an all-consuming love. The day I met Cameron, the day I met you, and the day I met Stella. That look of love is unmistakable."

The tears are there, just on the brink, as if they're waiting for permission to fall. "Why do you say it like you're letting me go?" The words come out choked with vulnerability.

"Oh, Snow," he says, and there's a warmth in his voice that feels like a soft blanket wrapped around me. "I'll never let you go. Not for a single heartbeat. Yet, here I stand, a father who has just come face-to-face with the man I'll have to share you with, the man you'll turn to first instead of me from now on." He chuckles then, which sounds out of place with the solemnity of the moment, and he wipes away a tear that dared to escape down his cheek.

"That sounds terrible. Why are you laughing?" I can't help but ask, even as a part of me understands the bittersweet joy in his eyes.

"Because I see myself and Cameron in him," he admits, and there's a pride in his voice that's both heartbreaking and comforting. "I'm not sure how you managed to find a cowboy in Wyoming who embodies two gay men from Boston."

"I have no idea what you're talking about." My tone is laced with sarcasm, an attempt to lighten the mood. It works; we both laugh.

"I'll always be here, Snow. I'm not going anywhere," he assures me, his voice steady and sure. "But I know when it's time to yield the stage." His eyes harden for a moment, protective and fierce. "Though if he ever hurts you, I'll kill him. He should know that. Make sure you tell him." He walks over then, and his hug is a stronghold. Eventually, he lets go, but not before running his hand over my hair in a gesture so familiar it aches.

Then, with a finality that feels like the closing of a book, he pulls an envelope from his back pocket and lays it on the counter. He doesn't say a word as he takes the rest of the items in bags and walks out, leaving me alone with the letter. My hands tremble as I reach for it, the paper slightly stiff under my fingers. I steel myself for the words I'm about to read, for the piece of the past that's about to become my present.

I let gravity claim me; I find myself sitting on the floor, pressing the letter against my heart like a shield. My eyes squeeze closed, a feeble effort to barricade the oncoming flood of emotions. It's as though each cherished memory plays like a film—our laughter, our talks, our silences, even our last day. The love I feel is a force untamed by loss, unbounded by the finality of death. I draw in a deep breath, and with it, I inhale a love that neither time nor distance can erode.

CHAPTER 67

A New Deal

The journey to her place and back was quick. We chose the path of least resistance, media be damned. Having dropped off her things in our room, I'm on the hunt, because I want my woman.

Cami's laughter, mingling with Dad's and Lincoln's, drifts from the kitchen, but I don't hear Parker. She must still be at the apartment. As I stride across the driveway, I spot Greg, his arms full of groceries.

"Need a hand with those?" I call out, closing the distance with a jog.

"No." He halts, his gaze piercing. "But there is something—what are your intentions with my daughter?" His question hangs in the air.

"Should we have this conversation now, or would you prefer to wait until your hands are free, just in case you don't like my answer?" I ask, my sincerity as clear as the determination I feel.

"Son, I saw the answer on your face. I need to know you know it too."

I meet his gaze, unflinching and unafraid, and lay bare the truth that has anchored me for weeks. "My intention is to love her every single day for the rest of my life. I want to be her home, her armor and sword, and anything else she needs whenever she needs it. I want to celebrate all the incredible things she's done and the ones she's going to do. I can only hope you think I'm worthy of that place in her life."

"Wyatt," he says, and there's a shimmer of tears in his eyes, a mix of sadness and relief. "In the kitchen, there's only one executive chef. That kitchen is their domain, and they're responsible for it. I hope you'll try to understand when I tell you, I can't give away the kitchen. I can, however, step aside and be a sous chef. And if you ever tell Parker I compared her to a kitchen, I *will* find my knives."

"I understand, sir." Holding back a smile is impossible. "Thank you."

"She's back there." He nods, and given the look in his eyes, that nod is more than a direction—it's a blessing.

I set off at a jog, my heart racing, not with fear this time, but with purpose. If I have to make a thousand deals to convince her, I will. I can't let her walk into this storm without knowing. Rushing through the door to the apartment, the sound of her crying stops my heart. It isn't a cry of injury, but it's a cry of pain all the same. As the hall opens up to the living area, I spy her sitting in the middle of the empty living room floor, clutching a piece of paper to her chest.

"Baby," I whisper, crouching down to her level, a desperate plea in my voice, "talk to me." Her eyes flutter open, revealing emotions that I can't quite decipher. It's like looking into a kaleidoscope of her soul—beautiful and complex.

"Help me up."

I grasp her hand and carefully pull her to her feet, and I wait for her to speak.

"You said our deal was to be negotiated later. I'd like to negotiate now." Her voice is confident, even though it's strained. She wipes away tears and steps back. I watch, in awe, as she takes a slow deep breath, her shoulders squaring. My strong woman, my warrior. Quietly, my hands slide into my pockets, controlling my urge to reach for her.

"What do you want, Parker?" The question hangs between us, charged with the potential of her answer.

"You," she breathes out, and though it's merely a whisper, it resonates with the force of a shout in the quiet room.

"What do you want from me?" I press, needing to understand what she's really asking for.

Her hands tremble slightly as she takes another breath. "I have loved exactly six people in my life. The first two taught me what love meant. The third and fourth taught me I had a greater capacity to love than I knew. The fifth taught me the beauty and the pain of love. And the sixth," she pauses, her gaze locking with mine, "is you. You taught me that love can heal. I've been trying to stop being so scared, trying to find my bravery. Today, I realized, I already found it because it's you."

She stands there, her hands no longer trembling, her eyes clear and bright, even rimmed in red, and she's never been more beautiful.

"I love you, Wyatt. I love you for the way you see me, how you never hold me back but never let me feel alone. I love that you push me as much as you protect me. I love needing you. I love arguing with you, which is surprising because I hate fighting." She laughs and sniffles at the same time, and I feel a smile begin to tug the corners of my mouth. "My deal is as follows: I'd like all my adventures and memories to be yours. I'd like to live here with you. I'd like to need you, to argue sometimes, and to love you until I can't breathe. I'm not sure I'll ever want more children," her voice falters slightly, "and you should know that now. But that's what I want."

A surge of emotion breaks through my carefully constructed barriers. I close the distance between us without thinking, my hands finding their way through her hair and fingers curling gently around her neck.

"I'm so glad you finally figured it out," I confess, "because I love you. I think I've loved you from the very moment you branded me an asshole."

A giggle escapes her, although her eyes are watery, her smile lights up the blue until they sparkle like glass.

"All my deals, all my days, every moment, every adventure, every memory, every fight—they're all yours. I am wholly yours, and the only future I want is the one with you."

She barely lets me finish my words before she's leaning forward, her soft lips against mine in a kiss that's more like a vow, a seal over a binding contract. It's not frenzied between us, not a devouring force. It's a kiss that binds, a kiss full of promises. Lifting her off her toes, I feel her arms wrap around my neck, her legs wrap around my waist—my perfect fit.

"Bed. Upstairs." She mumbles against my lips.

Turning toward the stairs, I ascend two at a time, aimed at the bedroom she's been using. As soon as her feet hit the floor, neither of us wastes time, making quick work of our clothes. As soon as she's bare, my hands glide along the gloriously perfect warmth of her skin, grazing over her scars, lowering my lips to the sweet vanilla-scented skin on her neck, drawing a quiet moan from her lips. Lifting her again, laying her under me on the bed, I pull back, burning this moment into my memory.

Her hands roam freely, driving me crazy as her nails drag over my back as I cover the landscape of her skin, the map of it sealed in my mind, curves I could follow even if I couldn't see. Shifting slightly, I slide a hand down to find her center. She whimpers under my hand's movements.

"Louder, Parker," I whisper in her ear. "I love every sound you make, but there's one that's my favorite." I watch her, my hands building her to the edge, giving her everything she wants.

"Wyatt." She gasps out a breath, groaning my name.

"That's the one." I change the angle just slightly to drive to the spot I know she likes, feeling her clench around me, going wild as release flows through her.

She collapses back, and I pull away from her just a fraction. She whines, making me chuckle, then wiggles closer to me, nuzzling into my neck.

"Open your eyes for me." As her eyelids rise, those soul piercing blue eyes find mine. Lowering my forehead to hers, I breathe her in. "I love you, Parker."

She smiles, lifting her hands and sliding them along my jaw before pulling me down to her lips. Her eyes are bright, a small smile lifting the corners of her mouth. Slowly, I slip inside her, ensnared in her gaze. Her thighs tremble against me as she tilts her head back and a quiet groan slips free.

"That's it," I coax her on.

"More." Her short nails dig into the skin of my shoulders, the pain nothing compared to the pleasure. Her demand courses through my blood, my control unraveling under her hands. Her eyes stay on mine until she breaks around me, head thrown back, voice rising, muscles clenching.

"That's my girl." My muscles burn as I feel every quake of her release.

She opens up those endless sky-blue eyes, her hands bracketing my face. "I love you, Wyatt."

Release slams into me at her words, heat spiraling, my breath catching in my chest. As I still, her arms and legs wrap around me, pulling my weight down onto her. She buries her face in my shoulder as her hips roll softly, drawing another groan from me.

"Now we're even," she whispers, nudging my neck with her nose. Her grip loosens, and when I look down, she's got a mile-wide smile.

Raining kisses over her face, I can't help but smile when she laughs. "I like the way you negotiate."

Quickly reversing our positions, I feel her settle on my shoulder. As I weave my fingers through her silky hair, trailing down the gentle slope of her back, she hums—a sound of pure contentment that vibrates against the skin of my neck.

"We should probably head back," she murmurs, her voice satisfied, every muscle of her being radiating relaxation. "They might wonder where we disappeared to."

"I doubt they're wondering," I chuckle.

The innocence in her eyes as she lifts her gaze to mine is priceless—as is the moment her eyes widen, realization dawning that perhaps our absence hasn't gone unnoticed. Her horror is endearing as the heat of embarrassment creeps up her neck.

She groans and buries her face against my chest, seeking refuge. When she dares to look up again, a blush paints her cheeks a delicate shade of rose.

"I love you," I confess. The words carry the weight of my entire universe. Words I'll never tire of saying as my chest squeezes with the sweetest kind of ache.

"I love you," she echoes back, her lips finding mine in a kiss that's a gentle affirmation. Her eyes, those windows to her soul, soften.

"We better gather up your stuff and head back. We have to finish off this chapter so we can start the next one."

Her smile is a sunrise, bright and full of promise. "That's the best thing I've ever heard," she says, her joy infectious.

"There's one thing that would sound better." I momentarily lose myself in those sparkling blue eyes.

Her eyebrow arches in curiosity. "And what might that be?" She pushes off my chest, sitting up across my hips.

I follow her up, leaning back on my arms. "You'll have to wait and find out." I wink.

We get ourselves cleaned up and dressed. Together, we gather the last of her belongings. I coax Cooper from his hiding place beneath the bed, his reluctant form emerging into the light. We approach the staircase, and I pause, ready to lift my hand, but she anticipates the gesture, her arm gracefully draping over my shoulder.

Reaching the foot of the stairs, she pauses on the last step, her hand squeezing my shoulder before she leans in and presses a sweet and tender kiss to my temple. She slides her hand from my shoulder before stepping around to my side and winking at me.

We collect the final few items from the kitchen, including a paper she folds with reverence before tucking it back into its envelope. Hand in hand, we step through the threshold, embarking on the journey toward what we *both* now call home.

CHAPTER 68

Five

PARKER

The last five days have swirled in a unique storm, each moment brimming with emotion and action. Yet, in the eye, I've found a deep sense of peace. Cami and Lincoln, with their uncanny synergy, selected the ideal media outlet on the very first day. They're formidable, almost unnervingly so for two people who didn't know each other until a few weeks ago.

On the second day, Wyatt declared that if I had to do something that scared me, like relive all these memories through questions, everyone else did too. So he did the unthinkable and asked me and Greg to make Brussels sprouts. It made Greg laugh, but by the end of the night, we had converted the Lochlan clan. Who knew a simple vegetable, when basted in a sticky, sweet sauce and adorned with crispy bacon, could become an object of unanimous adoration?

Okay, I knew.

The third day, after a tough morning of being schooled by Lincoln, I let Wyatt read Cameron's letter. I also shared with him where I've kept Stella's ashes. Then he declared the remainder of the day off limits to more questions, more stories, more memories. Instead, I spent all afternoon in his arms, a marathon of all the *Die Hard* movies our only job.

Negotiations with the media outlet were grueling, but we emerged with an agreement on day four. Cami's publicist, the queen maestro of spin, launched a social media campaign that painted my life in bold, new strokes—things that felt much more like the woman I'd become, strong and confident.

It was a revelation to witness the narrative shift in such a short time, thanks to social media. It was also empowering, taking back control of my own story. Sharing in that space felt a bit odd, but in doing so, it revealed an entire community of mothers and fathers who shared their own stories. People who'd been adopted came out in full force, in ways that felt overwhelming but also loving. Even when you know you're not alone, it's a peculiar feeling to sense support rise up around you.

The past two days have been an onslaught of questions, a relentless probing into the most intimate parts of my life as we prepare for this interview. As expected, it's been a little rough. Yet, amidst the chaos, Lincoln and I have deepened our friendship. He was right when he said he was who he needed to be for his family, revealing a side that's both strategic and fiercely protective. Unlike James, Lincoln's ferocity is tempered with compassion. He's ensured that I'm as prepared for the battle ahead as possible, advocating for me with a quiet, unwavering strength.

The light-hearted banter that usually fills the air in this house has been scarce lately. I find myself longing for the days when our routine returns and my biggest concerns are animal antics and midnight emergencies.

The start of bringing regularity back to reality is today. The news team's arrival this morning signals the rapidly closing part of my story and the opening of the next. Will, Statler's friend from the Marine unit, arrived shortly after Dad and Cami. He's a whiz kid, only twenty-two, with a mind that calculates at a much higher level of intelligence than most. His maturity speaks to a depth inside him; I sense a backstory behind his quiet smiles and demeanor.

He and Statler function almost without words at all, their connection more a brotherhood than a friendship. They've turned the apartment into a surveillance hub, cameras tucked away in every nook, all feeding into a nest of monitors elsewhere in the barn. It's as though we're staging a high-stakes drama, and in a way, I suppose we are.

As I add the final touches to my hair, I take my time, each stroke of the brush a small step toward bolstering my confidence. Though with Wyatt around, my confidence is about as high as it's ever been. Yesterday, as I blinked away the remnants of sleep, his voice cut through the haze, telling me I was beautiful, which he then proceeded to prove by covering me head to toe with kisses.

The rhythm of our days, going to sleep with him every night and waking with him every morning, has been an experience. Though he jokes about putting a mini-fridge in our room to curb our midnight snack runs, I know he enjoys those quiet moments in the barely lit kitchen, just the two of us.

The sound of the door swinging open breaks the silence, and without a glance, I know it's him. Wyatt has this way of entering a room that's all his own—no knocks, just presence. As he pivots into the bathroom, a wolf whistle slices through the air, sending a spiral of sweetness through me. I catch his gaze in the mirror, that familiar hunger in his eyes.

"Do I look interview ready?" I ask, giving a slow, deliberate twirl. The skirt flutters around my ankles. Cami and I picked this outfit together. It's more than just clothing today; it's armor. The navy blue of the shirt hugs my form, a contrast to the softness of the skirt, while the belt cinches everything together. Wyatt's grin spreads across his face, that boyish charm never failing to warm my heart.

"Angel, do you even have to ask?" he teases, motioning me closer with a crooked finger.

I wag a finger back at him, half-warning, half-invitation. "Don't mess me up," I say, only a playful threat in my voice.

"I wouldn't even consider it." The twinkle in his eye tells me he's lying through his teeth.

I take a moment to admire him—the way the dark jeans and boots complement the casual light blue shirt, the thin gold chain peeking out at his neckline. "You don't look so bad yourself, cowboy," I return. "You're just missing the backwards hat."

His head cocks to the side, a picture of genuine confusion. "Why does the hat matter?"

"I can't explain it, but the backwards hat really does something to me, especially when you have your sleeves rolled up like this and that chain around your neck. It gives me the urge to bite my lip," I confess with a wink, letting him in on one of the many little things that he does that just works.

"I'll be sure to abuse that knowledge." He smirks, eyes on fire. "You ready?" His finger hooks through my belt, a gentle but firm pull that draws me into his arms. We sway together, a silent dance to a rhythm only he hears, moving us seamlessly from the sanctuary of the bathroom to the bedroom.

"You remember the signal, if you need to call anything off or if you're uncomfortable?" The question comes, a soft echo of the dozens of times he's asked before.

"Yes, I remember. *Pigeon.*" I slide my arms around his neck while his arms circle me protectively like a shield.

His eyes fixate on mine. "I'll be watching the whole time, right outside." His hands chart a course down my sides, settling comfortably on my hips.

"I know. I can do this." The words are more than a reassurance to him; they're a vow to myself.

His lips press against my forehead, providing a final nudge of encouragement. "I don't have a single doubt about that."

With resolve, I intertwine my fingers with his and say, "Let's go."

CHAPTER 69

Wings

WYATT

She strides through the apartment door, a picture of determination, and every one of my instincts screams at me to follow. Our discussions about who should be with her while she completes the interview have been one big, endless argument. She was determined to face the interview alone, refusing to yield, even when I begged. So here I stand, huddled in the announcer's box, surrounded by a half dozen monitors that Statler and Will meticulously arranged, watching a live image of the room.

The preliminary bullshit of introductions and hooking up microphones has dwindled; the stage is set for Jack Malone. Camilla's strategy was to have a man conduct the interview. The publicist agreed that it was the right way to dispel any notions of excessive empathy. We'd selected this particular outlet, not just for its expansive and varied audience, but for its unflinching commitment to asking hard questions and digging for truth. Malone is notorious for his confrontational style. He takes no shit, and that was exactly why Camilla wanted him for this, and unsurprisingly, why I hated him. Though Parker fell on Camilla's side, she understood my worry, leading to the signal—a way for her to talk to me if she needed to.

Parker's beautiful, sitting calm and ready, not a hint of nerves in sight. Lincoln has done everything he can to prepare her for this. Camilla warned us that Jack wasn't happy about not being able to ask his own questions, which meant he'd absolutely try to do just that.

Under normal circumstances, this observation room is plenty big. Yet, in this moment, it contracts around me; the walls inching closer with each passing second. The persistent hum of monitors melds with the scrape of cables. The earthy scent of dirt, usually comforting and familiar, now makes the air feel heavy. No part of me wants to stand here, waiting and watching. Every muscle is coiled tightly, and I'm ready to bust through that door at the slightest cue.

A thousand invisible ants relentlessly march across my skin. The door before me is a barrier I am compelled to respect as I watch Malone start digging in. Jack's smile is a thin veneer, the kind that doesn't quite reach his eyes.

"So, Ms. Mason, you've gone through a lot of trouble to coordinate this interview. Can you tell us why you're speaking now?"

Her response is immediate, her voice rock steady. "First, it's *Doctor* Mason." The look she pins him with is one I know all too well—sharp enough to slice through steel. I've been on the receiving end of that gaze; it's not something you forget.

Jack's hands go up, a mock surrender. "I apologize." But his eyes, they're dancing with provocation. He's not sorry. He's a pit bull pawing at the edges of her patience, seeing how far he can push.

She doesn't flinch. "No problem. I realize a great many stories about me in recent weeks might suggest I haven't accomplished much, or that I have no respect for life. But I've worked tirelessly to be where I am, precisely because of the value and respect I place on life."

"Good job, babe," Camilla murmurs from beside me, her voice hushed yet full of tension. Her nails are caught between her teeth. Lincoln's hand is gentle but firm as he eases hers away from her mouth to prevent more chewing. Our eyes meet over Camilla's bowed head, and he offers a subtle shake of his head—a full paragraph in a glance.

"I can appreciate that," Jack concedes, and the dance continues.

For the next forty minutes, the interview weaves through the tapestry of Parker's life. Jack probes into her adoption, her professional journey, her childhood, but I feel the danger approaching, and I can only pray Parker senses it too.

Jack's posture shifts, a calculated display of casual curiosity as he crosses his legs and reclines. His eyes, however, betray the intent of a man about to delve into the real reason he's here.

"How did you meet James Perkins?" he asks, his voice a blend of nonchalance and precision.

PARKER

The moment stretches, taut as a wire, as Jack finally steers the conversation into the heart of the storm. The thrust and parry of questions and answers has frayed my nerves to their edges, but I won't stop until I've done what I came here to do.

"I met James in college." The memory surfaces like a photograph faded by time. "We were both at a party, and he stood out with his charm and humor. At first, that was attractive." The recollection is bittersweet; those traits, once so alluring, later revealed themselves as masterful illusions.

"What happened in the months after you met?" Jack's posture is a study in openness and invitation, but his eyes, sharp like a predator, betray the undertone of his question.

"We started seeing one another, until I decided I no longer wanted to participate at all. I wasn't overly fond of James's behavior. We parted ways."

"When did you find out you were pregnant with Mr. Perkin's baby?" Jack pushes.

"Paternity to my child was never established to be James Perkins. You've seen the paperwork yourself." My voice is firm, unwavering. "Let me be crystal clear—James and I were not together, and the question of my child's paternity has never been proven. Perhaps that causes some to see me differently. There's nothing I can do about that. Though some may see her as a mistake, an accident, to me, my daughter was a miracle, the most wondrous event of my life."

His next question is softer, yet it probes deeper. "Why do you say that?"

"She was like Haley's comet—rare and breathtaking, a once-in-a-lifetime phenomenon," the words flow from a well of profound truth.

"Why did you leave James Perkins?" Jack asks, his head tilting to the side like a snake, switching back to the drama of the story.

"James has a talent for veiled manipulation that, at first, I didn't see. His *advice* on my attire, his *suggestions* on when to speak or what to say. His praise when I did what he wanted, and his little punishments when I didn't, were handed out with calculated precision. Over time, it became less subtle and more cruel. His comments ranged from the food I was eating to my intelligence, my weight, and my history. He isolated me from friends and family, and when I finally realized the situation for what it was, I left."

"That's quite an accusation, Dr. Mason." Jack's response is measured, his tone betraying no hint of emotion, though the words hang between us like a challenge.

"A lived experience isn't an accusation, Mr. Malone."

"That may be, but you're suggesting that the son of the governor of Georgia was abusive, are you not?" He leans in, the question unapproved, unexpected, yet undeniably deliberate.

"I'm not suggesting anything. You're drawing a conclusion from my experiences, and there's nothing I can do about that. All I'm saying is that as time passed, I realized that a relationship with James was not what I wanted. While rejection may be difficult to stomach, I never imagined he would find a way to retaliate by trying to destroy my life with his accusations and edited audio clips." My body itches to fold into a defensive posture, to cross my arms and legs, to tremble under the weight of his gaze.

"Are you denying that's your voice in the recording?" Jack accuses.

"Not at all. It's my voice, but it's entirely out of context. As a mother, I'm not disclosing the location of my child. I'm not providing him with some story to win an election. My daughter is not a weapon to be used, she's mine. I challenge you to find a mother who wouldn't do whatever it took to protect her child, alive or dead."

Jack leans forward, the pretense of relaxation abandoned. "Is your child the biological child of James Perkins?" Jack's grin is sharp, a hunter's smile baring his teeth, the question meant to slice deeply.

"I have no proof that James Perkins is the biological father of my child." Lincoln was very clear about this point. By clear, I mean he drilled it in my head until I could say it in my sleep.

"Why not allow Mr. Perkins to complete a DNA test now? Why are you blocking James Perkins from accessing his child?" The casualness of Jack's tone stood in opposition to the spear of accusation in his questions' meaning.

"*My* daughter, Mr. Malone, is nothing more than a memory today. There's nothing to test, no big conspiracy. My daughter's life was never, and will never be, about James Perkins. Neither I, nor any mother in my position, would simply allow anyone who wanted access to those memories."

"What happened to this child?" Jack inquires, switching tactics, pulling back from the story.

"*My* child. She's not a 'this' or 'that' or 'his' or 'it.' She's *mine*, Mr. Malone, and I won't correct you again." The words escape my lips, a declaration of war over a line I refuse to let be crossed. My hands ball into fists, the blood roars in my ears.

"I apologize," Jack nods, feigning repentance. "What happened to your daughter?"

"At first, I thought everything was fine, but life has a way of taking your breath when you least expect it." The memory is a cold, sharp blade. "I learned during my daughter's anatomy scan that she had a rare congenital heart defect. She wouldn't live more than a few hours beyond her birth."

"And do you feel guilty for that, Dr. Mason?" The question, callous and unexpected, blows me away.

"Excuse me?" The word is a snarl, rage coursing through me like wildfire, and I no longer care if it shows. My patience has shattered, my composure blown away like ash in the wind.

Jack's posture, his lean forward, that silent assertion of dominance. "Do you feel guilty for the death of your child? Was it your condition, or perhaps drugs and alcohol that influenced her development?" His words are like daggers, aimed to wound.

"Listen to me carefully," I say, deliberately pronouncing each word. Lincoln's reprimands dissolve from my memory. Only a primal instinct to protect my child remained. "You are neither without the ability to research or call upon the knowledge yourself, but since you insist on behaving cruelly, I will answer your question, this question, only once. No one was at fault for the anomaly in my daughter's heart. I did absolutely nothing to cause this. Her condition has absolutely nothing to do with mine, nor were there any complications in her birth. To suggest that there was anything less than perfect about her insults and disparages her, along with every other parent in the world of a differently abled child or one with special needs. I'm not sure your viewers would appreciate you claiming that sentiment over their children."

Silence descends and thickly cloaks the room. Jack shifts, a restless motion betraying his discomfort as he crosses his legs once more. My gaze is unyielding, pinning him in place with a relentlessness that's risen from deep inside me.

"It is my job to ask the tough questions, Dr. Mason," he offers, but the words are hollow and devoid of true contrition.

"I'm sure you think that's true," I retort, and the impact is visible. He recoils, a physical response to the unexpected bite in my voice.

"Please, continue," he says, nodding to concede the floor back to me. I sense the power dynamics have subtly shifted.

"I went into labor at thirty-eight weeks and birthed the most beautiful little girl. She lived for thirteen hours and twenty-seven minutes. She passed away peacefully in my arms." The words fracture as they leave my lips. Each time I recount this sacred moment, it's as if the air is stolen from my lungs, her absence leaving me breathless.

Jack's voice is a slow drawl, heavy with implication. "Where is she buried?"

"She isn't," I assert, my tone resolute. "And I refuse to let those with malicious intent—like certain media outlets—know where her ashes were spread." My words break free from the script we've rehearsed for days. "The very same vultures who preyed upon my sealed adoption records, committing an act as invasive as it was painful. Countless adopted children across the globe can empathize with the profound loss and delicate nature of such experiences. It baffles me, Mr. Malone, that you and your colleagues fail to grasp this principle. It appears that the media's respect for life pales in comparison to mine."

WYATT

"She's way off book, but she's brilliant." In the hushed atmosphere of the room, Camilla's whisper is a subtle sound. She's squeezing my fingers tightly, and I can feel the small tremble in her hand.

"Badass wolf pack, right?" I whisper, though it feels like a shout.

"Damn straight," she affirms, her gaze lifting to meet mine, a spark of fierce loyalty in her eyes. "You better lock her down, Wyatt.

Don't disappoint me." Her words are a challenge, a dare to rise to the occasion.

A grin tugs the corners of my mouth. "I have no intention of disappointing you—or her," I vow.

Together, we pivot back to the screen.

PARKER

"Dr. Mason, what do you want people to know about you and your relationship with James Perkins," Jack asks, carefully backing down from asking further questions about Stella.

"When James flew here to visit me a few weeks ago, presumably after he researched where to find me and my phone number, he didn't even know my daughter had passed away. For five years, I've not heard a single word from him."

"What would you say to those voters considering casting their ballot for Mr. Perkins as your side of the story is very different from his?" Jack's baiting me. I hear Lincoln and Cami's voices in my head repeating their lessons on careful wording as I prepare to answer.

"I promised my daughter I'd do incredible things in her honor, and I've kept that promise. I thought that losing her would kill me, and I've spent five years carrying grief and pain that almost consumed me. But somehow, light and hope found their way back into my life, and I've been blessed with a future I'm excited for. Vote however you like, I have no stake in that game. Regardless of which way people choose to vote, I hope every person who watches this and hears the story of my daughter remembers that they can make it through their own hard moments. I hope what people hear from me is to keep going. The light will find you when you least expect it, and you'll find a future worth fighting for."

I've reached the limit of my patience. With a deliberate gesture, I cross my arms and tap my fingers three times against my sleeve—my signal for Wyatt.

"Mr. Malone, I think I've allowed you to ask more than enough questions, and I've said all I came here to say. Have a safe journey home."

Rising, I begin to disconnect myself from the tangle of microphones and cords, each motion a severing of ties. I was careful, following the line of truth, avoiding anything that would cause me to lie. Now it's time to stop talking. Jack's protests for "just a few more questions" fall on deaf ears as I stride toward the door, each step taking me closer to the future that beckons me from beyond this room.

WYATT

The moment her arms cross and her fingers tap, it's as if a starting gun has fired in my mind. I don't wait for another sign; I'm in motion, my feet pounding the steps with an urgency that echoes the rapid drumming of my heart. Reaching the apartment door just as it swings open, I'm there to catch her as she steps out.

Jack's voice, pleading for more questions, becomes a distant murmur. She leans back ever so slightly, her eyes locking onto mine with an intensity that speaks volumes more than words ever could.

"Do you think we could have hot wings for dinner? I'm starving," she asks, a playful lilt in her voice that represents nothing of the gravity of the past hour.

A laugh escapes me, bubbling up from a place of relief and adoration. "Angel, you can have whatever you want." It's a promise, a vow, as I lift her into my arms.

Together, we turn away from the chaos, from the probing questions and prying eyes, and step toward the life we're building.

CHAPTER 70

Races

Three days later . . .

Tonight, the interview will be public. The uncertainty of what made the final cut hangs in the air, but Parker's made up her mind; she won't watch it. The rest of the family is tuning in, ready to set the record straight if need be. It's an odd feeling, observing my brothers through the lens of this experience. We've always been a rowdy bunch, but beneath the teasing and joking, maturity seems to have crept up on us. Then again, sometimes, it seems we haven't matured all that much. Nothing could illustrate that better than the scene before me.

Greg's voice breaks through the anticipation. "Son, are you sure you want to race me?" His challenge to Statler evident in the stern lines of his face though the light in his eyes, so like Parker's, holds deep affection.

Statler stands tall, his reply earnest. "Yes, sir. Everyone needs to aspire to something. If you beat me, I'll be honored." There's a twinkle in his eye, a lightness to him that's been absent for a long time. The people we've added to our family in the past few months, Greg and Cami included, have found a way to bring something out in him that feels lighter and more like the man I remember before he joined the Marines.

"Alright. Rules," Camilla declares, her presence commanding as she leans against the kitchen island.

I'm drawn to Parker, my arm finding its home around her waist, pulling her close. She responds instinctively, stepping back into my chest, leaning her weight into me. I'll never get used to touching her, to feeling her soften in my arms.

"He knows he's going to get smoked, right?" I whisper, a playful taunt in the quiet space between us.

"Which one?" Her laughter is like a song, light and free. "Both of them have their ego on the line here."

"And who are we rooting for?" I murmur, my lips brushing the top of her head, my chin settling on her shoulder.

"I'm a daddy's girl, Wyatt, probably important to learn that now." Mischief colors her voice. "Besides, that man has been chopping onions for about as long as Statler's been breathing."

"Fair point," I concede, my lips finding the soft skin of her neck. The playful banter continues, and I can't help but soak in her warmth.

"Am I going to need a PDA deal for home too?" she teases, her voice a soft murmur against the backdrop of familial chatter.

"Afraid I can't make that deal," I whisper back, my voice low, meant only for her. "I know what you taste like."

Her elbow finds my gut in a gentle rebuke. "My dad's right there," she whisper-hisses, her playful scold laced with laughter. "Do you want to die?"

I muffle my chuckle in her hair, then turn my gaze back to the kitchen's island where the challenge is taking place.

Camilla takes command, saying, "The rules are as follows: Both gentlemen have to use the same knife, they will not know the other person's timing so no single competitor has a time-based advantage, and Lincoln will keep time as the official scorekeeper. If Papa G wins, Statler has to spend a week on the line in Chicago. If Statler wins, Papa G has to give up the recipe for burgers to someone other than Parker. Do all parties agree?"

The handshake between Greg and Statler is firm, a silent contract sealed with mutual respect and competitive fire. Statler's turn at the chopping block is a show of precision and speed, his hands a blur, the knife somehow an extension of his hands. The diced pieces fall into perfect cubes. He is the fastest I've ever seen him, which shows me he holds back more from me than I thought.

Then, it's Greg's turn. The air is thick with expectation, every eye fixed on the older man as he takes the knife. His movements are fluid, a show of experience and confidence. When the timer stops, it's clear—he's won by a full fifteen seconds.

"Looks like you get to come to the kitchen for a week." Greg's voice is warm with both pride and challenge as he claps Statler on the back.

"It would seem that way, sir." Statler's smile is broad and genuine. "I look forward to it. I'm going to win that burger recipe someday, though."

"If you get that good, young man, you'll have earned it," Greg replies, his smile matching Statler's.

The room's attention shifts as Camilla signs to Parker, a private joke that forces them to erupt into laughter.

"Dad, Cami says this calls for *the* song," Parker announces, a twinkle in her eye.

Greg's groan is half-hearted, his protest in form only. "Fine. One time. You girls are killing me."

"What's the story here, duchess?" Lincoln's new nickname for Cami seems to have stuck.

"We played it as a celebration when Greg won *Knifed* and it just stuck. It's his winning anthem!" Cami's eyes are shining with mischief.

Parker, ever the orchestrator, heads to the kitchen tablet.

As "Legend" by The Score fills the kitchen with its opening notes, the girls come alive with a burst of energy. The opening *"Nah, nah, nah"* is met with swaying hips and raised arms. As the chorus surges with "Bang, bang, bang, this fire's a weapon," they throw their fists in the air, punctuating each "bang" with a sharp movement.

The bridge, "Blood, sweat, I'll break my bones," sees them coming together, their movements synchronized as they use sign language in perfect sync. As the song reaches its climax with "Won't stop till we're legends," they're jumping, spinning, and laughing, their bodies moving freely. They sign the words with bold, exaggerated gestures, ensuring even those who can't sign don't miss a word. Greg, caught up in the moment, breaks through and joins their dance, his motions aligning with theirs. The song ends, and the high fives are a punctuation to the joyous moment.

"Parker, I think we have a date to go on, if everyone's done with us," I laugh, my gaze sweeping the room. The nods come, and the family disperses, leaving us in a bubble of our own.

"You plan on telling me what this date entails?" Parker's hands rest lightly on my chest.

"Not a chance." Sealing my words with a kiss, my arms wrap around her. "I get you all to myself for a while, and I don't plan to waste a single minute."

"Then why are you not kissing me?" she challenges, rising on her toes, her eyes alight with playful defiance.

"Great question." My hands slide under her arms, lifting until she wraps her legs around my waist and arms around my neck. Her laughter rings out as I carry her from the house, the promise of the evening ahead of us. The sunset paints the sky as we drive, and later, we finally break in the front seat of the truck properly.

CHAPTER 71

Next

PARKER

Four days later . . .

As the dust settled and my story found its way into the world, the backlash against James was swift and unyielding. Women emerged, voices strong with condemnation and shared experiences concerning his behavior, and in a flash, he vanished from the political landscape. His family cited shifting priorities, but the whispers Cami shared told a different story. Whether he resurfaces or fades into obscurity, he's become a ghost of my past, no longer a specter haunting my future.

The media circus finally packed up, leaving behind a silence that speaks of normalcy on the horizon. This interlude, settling in the house with Wyatt and Cami and Dad's comforting presence, has been a gift in so many ways, healing and beautiful even if it was painful to get here. Yet, I find myself ready for the mundane. Dad and I have filled the freezer to the brim, and the Lochlans aren't anxious to see him leave. He's promised, however, to return when the freezer is empty again.

With Cami's departure looming, I drift into the guest room, intent on helping her pack. Instead, I'm greeted by the furious clatter of keys—her focus unleashed. Hesitant to interrupt, I flick the lights to catch her attention, as I can see her external processor has been removed. Her hands pause, then dance with the news.

"Parker, I woke up this morning and the words—they just won't stop flowing. I don't know where this story will lead, but I can feel it—the magic," she signs, her eyes alight with newfound fervor.

"That's incredible! See, you just needed a change of scenery to clear your head." My heart swells with pride for her breakthrough.

"No, it's more than that. It's this place—it lets me breathe. Last night's walk was so quiet and peaceful. I love the city, but this place is so different. I understand, now, why you love it."

I can't help but smile. Cami's life is a whirlwind. While the quiet of the countryside might not hold her forever, knowing it's touched her soul is a gift beyond measure.

"Does this mean you'll be coming back soon?" I ask, gathering her belongings into the suitcase, eager to keep the conversation—and her inspiration—flowing.

"Oh, absolutely. I need to check on Em. I don't have a good feeling there. But once that's settled, I'll be back." Her determination is clear in her eyes.

"And the story? What's it about? Cowboys? Wyoming?" My curiosity is piqued.

"Monsters," she signs, a mischievous glint in her eye. *"And that's all you get—for now."*

My eyes roll in mock exasperation. *"Fine. You keep at it; I'll finish up here."*

But Cami's already closing her laptop, a satisfied spark in her eyes. *"No, I'm done for now. Plus, I've got farewells to say."*

"You mean to Lincoln and everyone else? You've been laying it on thick in that direction." I wiggle my eyebrows to tease.

"I flirt where it's welcome," she retorts with a wink. *"Besides, Lincoln's just having fun. It's not like he can flirt with you or your dad."*

"We'll see about that." I laugh, nudging her toward the door to make her rounds of goodbyes.

As I wheel her suitcase into the living room, I catch a secretive exchange between her and Wyatt—a whisper, a smile, a nod. Dad's there, too, his grin betraying his own part in their conspiracy.

"Cami, what's the whispering about?" I wrap an arm around her in a side hug.

"It's about you, obviously." Her eyes flick to Wyatt and back again.

"Alright, you all need to get going, or you'll be late," I chide gently.

Dad steps in, his arms enveloping me. "I'm going to miss you, baby girl."

"Miss you, too, Dad. But remember, you're welcome back anytime."

He nods, but there's a seriousness in his tone. "I know. But you need your routine. I'll be calling every day, though."

I pull back, a frown creasing my brow. "Why would you call daily, Dad?"

He lifts his hands to my face, and I find comfort in this familiar touch. "Because I won't be able to tell if you're still alive. I took the app off my phone."

"Why now?" The question hangs in the air, but he's already leaning in.

"Because I trust him," his voice a whisper meant only for me. The weight of those words settles in my heart. He steps back and kisses my cheek softly. "Just don't forget, you're a Boston fan, baby girl." Greg's voice booms, his playful ribbing echoing in the crisp air, a familiar soundtrack to these past weeks.

"I love you, Dad," I say, my voice soft, just for him. I wrap my arms around him, stealing one last moment of closeness. I repeat the gesture with Cami; her presence is a comfort that's hard to let go of.

As they descend the porch, Statler's SUV awaits. They conspired against me, insisting I go on a date with Wyatt instead of my planned airport run. Democracy in action, I suppose, and I'm outnumbered.

I stand there, waving until they disappear down the driveway, the road now a quiet promise of solitude. Turning back, I catch Shep and Lincoln making their own departures.

"Where are you all going?" My question hangs, a mix of curiosity and a faint sense of abandonment combining inside me.

Lincoln's answer is casual. "I haven't been home in a few weeks, so I'm sleeping in my own bed tonight." He gestures toward Shep, who seems to be leaving too.

"I'm off to Charlie's for dinner and poker. Looks like it's just you two tonight."

As they drive away, Wyatt's arms wrap around me from behind, an embrace that's as much a promise of the evening alone as it is protective.

Leaning back into him, I tilt my head to meet his gaze. "Did you coordinate that?"

"I have no idea what you're talking about." The twinkle in his eye tells a different story. "I've been busy with the ranch, remember?"

"Maybe I'm not the only bad liar around here," I tease, turning to face him.

"I haven't had you alone in weeks," he says, and in his voice, I hear the longing, the need for just us, no distractions.

"What's the plan?" My heart starts racing with the anticipation of his surprise.

"You'll find out soon enough," a mischievous edge laces his words. "Go change into the outfit Cami left for you, then meet me in the barn."

His instructions are an invitation, and I'm learning to lean into the adventure. As his lips meet mine, the world shrinks down to the sensation of his kiss, the warmth of his body.

"You better go," he murmurs. He leads me toward the door, our steps in sync as we ascend the stairs. I expect him to follow, but instead, he closes the door, leaving me with a trail of butterflies and tingling anticipation.

In our room, I'm greeted by an ensemble that speaks of Cami's impeccable taste—a long, flowing skirt paired with a backless bodysuit.

The note, a simple command from Cami, ignites a spark of excitement.

Put this on. Then go get your man.—Cami

Since when did our lives become a series of notes? I slip into the outfit, each piece a perfect fit, as if Cami wove it from my very thoughts. A few minutes at the mirror enhance the glow on my face and add volume to my hair—this outfit deserved the extra few minutes. Cami's never wrong about clothes.

"Okay, Cooper," I address my reflection, a playful seriousness in my tone. "We're dressed to the nines, and we're a vision. Now, let's do what the lady said, and go get our man."

With a final approving glance, I step out, ready to unravel the mystery Wyatt has laid before me.

CHAPTER 72

Love

***

WYATT

I knew Parker would take her time to get ready, and my intuition didn't fail me. Out here in the studio, I change into my chosen attire, each piece a deliberate selection for tonight's events with Cami's advice on what to wear at the forefront. Then, I begin the ritual of lighting hundreds of candles—no, not the flame-wielding kind that could turn a barn into a pyre. I'm many things, but stupid isn't one of them.

The barn transforms before my eyes, the overhead lights giving way to the soft glow of fairy lights that Cami, bless her, managed to conjure up in just two days. Her resourcefulness is something to behold.

The LED candles flicker gently, their light reflecting off polished surfaces and glinting through the gaps in the timber. The fairy lights, strung with care along the length of the aisle, add a touch of whimsy, which Cami insisted Parker needed more of in her life. Because I agree, I did everything Cami said. They drape from the rafters, a cascade of tiny, twinkling lights that mimic the starry sky. The barn's high ceilings are lost to the darkness, giving the space an intimate, cozy feel.

The sparkling pathway of lights lead from the door to an open circle in the middle. We've been stealthy, keeping Parker away from the barn to prepare for the surprise.

As each minute passes, a sense of calm washes over me. The man I was months ago would have been a bundle of nerves, stomach twisted in knots at the mere thought of this moment. But in his place stands someone who sees a future so bright, so full of promise, that fear has no place. I love her with a certainty that anchors me.

The creak of the door means she's arrived, and I cue the music on my phone. The sight of Parker's face as she steps into the barn, illuminated by countless tiny lights, is a vision that eclipses all others. For her, I'd light up a million more tiny lights, a billion times over.

"Hello, angel," I greet her, my voice a soft echo in the vastness of the barn as Taylor Swift's "New Year's Day" begins to play. Parker stands at the threshold, her hands covering her mouth, a portrait of awe.

"Parker, come here," I beckon, extending my hand to bridge the distance between us. Her eyes widen in surprise, and she takes that first tentative step into the transformed space. Cooper dutifully steps at her side.

"Wyatt . . . what is all this?" Her voice is a mix of wonder and curiosity. As she slips her hand into mine, I draw her into a dance, the world outside fading away.

"What does it feel like, Parker?"

She rests her cheek against my chest. "Big," she whispers back, her voice barely audible over the music.

"You could say that," I agree, the corners of my mouth lifting in a smile. "I made a new playlist. Thought we could dance to it for a while."

"What's it called?" Her body relaxes into the rhythm of our dance as the song continues softly.

"The Dr. Parker Lorraine Lochlan playlist," I confess.

She pulls back slightly, searching my face for confirmation. "Really?" There's a tremble of fear in her voice, but it's underscored by a swirl of hope in her eyes.

"Really," I affirm, pulling her close once more. "I've spent my life taking care of things, of people. When my mom passed, that responsibility grew. It's a part of me. But you, Parker, you challenged me."

"You were a jerk," she retorts softly, her words muffled against my chest, but there's no heat in them, only the warmth. Her gentle accusation draws a laugh from me, a sound that fills the barn and mingles with the music.

"Yes, I was, baby. And I might be again—just fair warning," I confess. "But that night, you sparked something. You made me think. I've always known my own strength, but you, Parker, you're the strongest person I've ever met. My dad told me recently that strong women— they don't need you, they choose you. And you made me want to be chosen."

I watch her, this force of nature, as I continue, "I learned how you needed me to love you, and what I learned was extraordinary. I learned you never needed a savior—you've been your own all along. You didn't need a hero. You're a warrior in your own right. What I discovered was that you needed my strength to be silent. You needed me to be your partner, to walk beside you, sometimes behind you, but never in front of you. Loving you is making me a better man every day."

She stands motionless, gazing at me as tears streak through her carefully applied makeup. I can't resist the pull to comfort her and kiss away the tears. So, I do, and then move on to her forehead, nose, cheeks, and finally, her lips.

"I promise you, Parker, I'm going to drive you crazy. I'm never going to be able to stop wanting to care for you, feed you, and argue with you. But I also promise to be your sanctuary, your safe place. I promise you that, every day without fail, I'll be your home—the place where you don't have to be strong unless you choose to be. A place for you to be quiet and still, adventurous and determined, soft and cuddly. And don't try to deny that you like cuddling." She laughs, a little breathless, as the words hang between us.

I release her only long enough to kneel and present the ring that symbolizes my promise to keep every word.

"Get up. Now," she commands, her voice firm yet laced with emotion. I can't help but laugh, as I rise to my feet.

"Okay, I'm standing," I assure her, even as I gently brush back her hair. "But this isn't quite how I pictured this moment unfolding."

"Only we get to decide how it's supposed to go. And I decide, right now, that you don't get to tell me all this, then let go. You have to talk from right here." Her words are a declaration of partnership. When she wraps her arms around me to squeeze, my wince is automatic.

"Why are you flinching?" Parker's touch retreats as quickly as it came, her eyes searching for an answer, immediately concerned.

"I had something else planned to show you later, but you're rewriting the script here," I say, un-tucking and lifting my shirt to reveal the bandage over fresh ink.

"Undo the bandage, Parker." Her fingers work the tape, hesitant yet compelled, and when the bandage falls away, she looks up, seeking the meaning behind the art.

"I hope you don't mind, I've already inked you onto my skin. It's your birth flower and Stella's," I begin, revealing the poppy and lily of the valley intertwined. "I know she's yours, Parker—"

"Stop." Her hand silences me, her touch gentle against the skin around the fresh ink. "I love it. I love that you thought of her. I love that I don't have to keep her from you because I really want to share her with you. She never belonged to anyone but me, Wyatt," she continues, her eyes brimming with love, "because I think she and I were meant to belong to you." Her words soothe the raw edges of my nerves. The gravity of her words leaves me nearly speechless.

"I'm honored," I whisper. "Any particular place you want to be when I ask this next question?" My voice is steady, but the anticipation thrums through me like a heartbeat.

She lowers my shirt, then steps back into my arms, her forehead finding its place against my chest. "Right here," she says, her voice muffled against my shirt. "Right here is perfect."

"Eyes, angel," I coax, gently tilting her chin up as my fingers weave through her hair, cradling her face in my hands. "Will you marry me?"

"Yes." Her voice rings clear and strong. Her radiant smile lights up her face, and her crystal-blue eyes shine more brightly than I've ever seen.

"Thank God," I exhale with relief, "because there's an entire party of people waiting for us in town."

"What?" She pulls away, surprise etching her features as I lean in for another kiss.

"I told everyone I was doing this days ago. Who do you think helped me get it all set up? They're all gone because they're waiting for us, along with a few other people we know. Your dad and Cami are flying out tomorrow, not today."

"You really thought of everything, didn't you?" she asks, her eyes a whirlpool of shock and joy.

"Probably not," I admit with a shrug, "but I've got a lifetime to learn, and that's a life I'm really looking forward to."

"Me too," she whispers, her lips meeting mine in a kiss that seals the words.

Today marks the best day of my life, but something tells me, with her by my side, we're going to craft a whole wall of best days—and I can't wait to start.

Epilogue

Three years later . . .

Three years have woven themselves into the fabric of our lives, and today, our home is ready for the arrival of family and friends. I hustle inside with an armful of firewood, shaking off the winter snow in the garage before stepping into the warmth of our home. The air is rich with the scent of oranges, cinnamon, and vanilla—a mix Parker insists is the essence of Christmas. It's hard to argue when the smell wraps around you like a memory.

We exchanged vows in the barn, surrounded by the fairy lights and family, just a few months after I proposed. I thought that day was the best day of my life, but life with Parker is a constant ascent—each day reaching new heights, and this Christmas is no exception.

Draping my jacket aside, I stack the wood in the hall before making my way to the kitchen, but it's empty. A smile tugs at my lips—I know exactly where to find her. In the living room, she's there, nestled in the blue chair that's become her favorite over the years, now adorned with the blanket she declared essential after our first Christmas together.

She's asleep, the fatigue of two days spent cooking and baking evident in the peaceful rise and fall of her chest. The brisket is smoking outside, and with the size of our family these days, she didn't have to do anything, but food is her way of saying "I love you," and we all speak her language fluently.

I lower myself in front of her, my hands finding the curve of her belly, the life within a miracle we've created together. "Mmmm, Wyatt." Her voice is a sleepy murmur, her eyes fluttering open. "I wasn't asleep."

"I would never think that," I reply, my thumbs drawing circles over the skin that stretches taut over our future. Leaning in, I press a kiss to the life beneath her skin. She likes to tell me I'm obsessed with our baby girl, and she's right. Witnessing Parker grow her day after day is a wonder that eclipses all my dreams.

"I just sat down for a minute, and she quit kicking, and I got warm." Her voice fades as my hands glide to her hips, massaging the ache that comes with being this far along in pregnancy. Her moan is a sound of relief I never tire of hearing.

"You can stay in this chair all day, all night, forever and I wouldn't care. If you're comfortable and can get some rest, do it. I can handle everything."

She chuckles, a sound that always seems to dance straight to my heart. "I can't stay in this chair because I need pants and mine don't fit." As she pulls back the blanket, revealing her bare legs, barely covered by the hem of my shirt. I can't help but think these small moments are the ones I never want to forget.

"Baby, no one is going to care what pants you're wearing."

"I care. Help me up," she lifts her hands towards me. It's a gesture full of trust, one that still catches me off guard sometimes, in the best way. I take her hands, feeling the familiar warmth, but as she makes to stand, I scoop her into my arms, bride style, and feel her body tense with surprise.

"Wyatt, I'm too heavy. You can't carry me upstairs," she protests, but I can hear the laughter in her voice, mixed with a hint of concern.

I stop, going completely still, looking into her eyes, wanting her to see the truth in mine. "Parker Lochlan, there will not be a day in this life I can't carry you. Besides, right now, I've got all my girls in my arms, and I'm not letting go," I declare. My heart swells with a love so fierce it almost hurts.

"When you say it like that, it's hard to argue." Her head finds its familiar spot on my shoulder. I can feel her breath, steady and warm against my neck. "What time is it?"

"You've got plenty of time. No one's getting here for at least two hours."

"Can I ask for something?" she whispers, her voice so soft it's almost lost in the creak of the stairs as I carry her up.

"Well," I start, trying to keep the mood light, "that depends on what it is. If you want me to solve world hunger, it'll take me a minute." I feel her smile against my shoulder, like a ray of sunshine breaking through clouds.

"I want to take a bath. But," her voice trails off again, and I can sense the frustration building within her.

"But what, angel?" I set her down gently on the bed, standing between her legs.

"I can't get out of the freaking tub anymore! I'm due in three weeks and I can't see my feet, and I can't get out of the tub. I barely made it out when I tested it yesterday, and that's because I didn't have water in there." Her words tumble out, a mix of annoyance and vulnerability that make my chest tighten.

"Why didn't you tell me this yesterday?" My hands instinctively move to her belly, where our future is making herself known with not so gentle kicks.

"Because I'm annoyed by it. It's dumb. I'm a freaking doctor, and I feel helpless," she admits, turning away from me, her arms crossed in a self-protective gesture.

"Eyes, Parker," I say softly. She turns back, and I can see the storm of emotions among the vivid blue that's become my favorite color. I cup her face, my thumbs gently stroking her cheeks, and lean down to kiss her, just the way she loves, the way she claimed all those years ago. "I think I know how to fix this."

"How's that?"

"First," reaching over my head, I grab the collar of my shirt, yanking it off, "we take a bath together. Second," my hands find the hem of another shirt she's stolen from me, sliding it up and over her head, "we'll get dressed and enjoy our family."

"I don't hate your plan." She smiles, eyes shining with emotion.

"Good. Because I love taking care of you."

"I love you, Wyatt." She leans in, kissing the center of my chest in a familiar gesture that spreads warmth through my heart.

"I love you, Parker." Pulling her off the bed, my hands slip under the band of her underwear, removing them slowly.

"You're wearing too many clothes, Wyatt." She traces a finger down the chain around my neck, then my chest, until she hits my belt buckle.

"I am, aren't I? We should solve that."

I may have a few more things on the list that I didn't mention, like her moaning my name.

PARKER

That was the best bath of my life. It didn't hurt to have Wyatt in it with me and maybe we did a few things that aren't strictly related to grooming, but what can I say, I've never been able to stop wanting that man. True to his word, he's helping me step into a pair of soft maternity leggings and one of his shirts.

"How do I look?" I step back from his arms, spinning in a slow circle.

"Absolutely stunning." His smile and the truth in his eyes tells me he means every word. It's not flattery or smoke; it's love.

He turns away, retreating into the closet, and I can't help but admire him in only his underwear, every inch of him golden, chiseled perfection. All I want is to bite him. *Okay, baby hormones, take a chill pill.*

When he reappears, the epitome of comfort in his sweats and T-shirt, my emotions surge like a tide I can't control. Tears cascade down my cheeks unbidden.

"What are you doing?" The words barely make it past the lump in my throat.

"I'm dressing comfortably. It's family, not a state dinner." His approach is gentle, his hands finding my belly. "Where is she?"

Guiding his hands over the curve of my belly, I feel her there, nestled beneath my ribs. I press his hands down gently until he connects with her, a father's touch that already holds so much love.

"Hello, little love." Her response is a flutter against my ribs, a tiny dance.

"She loves your voice. I think she gets that from me." Watching him with her fills me with a love so profound that, sometimes, I can only stare. I wasn't certain about having another baby, but I woke up one day and realized I didn't want to watch Wyatt as only an uncle. I wanted nothing more than I wanted to watch Wyatt become a dad—the love inside him so fierce, a lifetime of moments just like this one.

"Just wait until you're out here. I'll talk to you all you want." His smile is a promise, a future filled with words and laughter. "You ready?"

"Yeah, I think so." I feel a flutter of anticipation as we move toward the door. At the top of the stairs, I pause, a ritual as familiar as breathing, and he steps in front of me. My hand finds its place on his shoulder, a touchstone to one of our first deals.

"She's not going to be tall enough to do this for a long time. What's your plan there, cowboy?" I ask, a playful challenge in my voice. He pauses, turns, and we're eye to eye, a moment suspended in time.

"I plan to carry her for a long time, then I figure she can hold my free hand so you keep your spot on my shoulder. I've got it all worked out," he says, and I can't help but smirk.

"Sounds like it." My heart swells with love for this man who plans for our daughter's future with such care and tenderness.

Then, the sound of footsteps from the garage pulls me back to the present. We descend the stairs, and as we meet our family at the bottom, I see them—dressed in the comfort of sweats and T-shirts, a mirror of our own attire. Tears well in my eyes, not from sorrow, but from an overwhelming sense of belonging.

God, I love my family.

Making Deals Playlist

1. "Legend" by The Score
2. "Steady Heart" by Kameron Marlowe
3. "Porch Swing Angel" by Muscadine Bloodline
4. "Sun to Me" by Zach Bryan
5. "Fire Away" by Chris Stapleton
6. "Better Together" by Luke Combs
7. "To a T" by Ryan Hurd
8. "Nothin' on You" by Cody Johnson
9. "Dance Her Home" by Cody Johnson
10. "On My Way to You" by Cody Johnson
11. "Your Heart or Mine" by Jon Pardi
12. "Next Thing You Know" by Jordan Davis
13. "Worst Way" by Riley Green
14. "Wind Up Missing You" by Tucker Westmore
15. "Save Me The Trouble" by Dan + Shay
16. "5 Foot 9" by Tyler Hubbard
17. "Love You Anyways" by Luke Combs
18. "10-90" by Muscadine Bloodline
19. "Hard to Leave" by Riley Green
20. "Call A Cowboy" by Lainey Wilson

21. "Dirty Looks" by Lainey Wilson
22. "New Year's Day" by Taylor Swift
23. "Stand By Me" by Florence + The Machine
24. "Have A Little Faith in Me" by John Hiatt

Acknowledgments

First and foremost, I must thank God for giving me the chance and the drive to tell stories for a living. In a million different ways, I get to live out this purpose, and it never fails to be magical—even when it's terrifying.

The first person who deserves thanks here is my sister-in-law. Rachel, you read this story before I allowed any other single human to even know I had written it. You loved these characters, you loved me, and you didn't let me keep them hidden. Your joy and encouragement and edits all helped bring this world to life.

Next up—Daphne. You get all the credit for me being able to hold this book in my hands. When I was worried and overwhelmed, you told me my only job was to get the paper dirty. Without you, thousands of words and a world of stories would still be locked in my head. Thank you for holding me accountable and reminding me that a storyteller's only job is to tell a story.

To Erin, Lori, Sharon, Jennifer, and the host of humans that have held my hand through editing, a thousand questions, cover and interior design, blurbs, and dozens of tiny things (read: big things) that go into making a book—a book—you have my heart and gratitude forever. From my neurotic project plan to overly obsessive questions and the use of not enough commas and too many exclamation points, you are my heroes! (See what I did there?)

To Bailey, I can't say thank you enough. In a million ways, your friendship and words and laughter made this book possible. Also, thank you for our sweet Catahoula, who is the inspiration behind Cooper.

To Emily, I don't even know what to say. Words don't seem enough to express how grateful I am to have you in my life. From coffee to crying, you've stuck by me and journeyed this story of mine in ways that reminded me it was special and that I wasn't as big an imposter as I constantly feel (you're silently correcting me that I am not an imposter at all—I know).

To Haley, your thoughts and words and feelings and feedback were absolutely priceless to me, and I cannot wait until I get to hand you the physical copy of this book. You're one in a million!

If I started this by thanking God for making me who I am, I must end it by thanking my husband, without whom I wouldn't have seen any of the gifts in my life come to be. Thank you for sitting next to me while I sobbed and typed out words with earbuds in. Thank you for never commenting on how long I sit at this computer, or the entire days lost to the flood of words from a story deep in my soul. Thank you for being invested every time I turn to tell you about something my characters have done. Thank you most of all for loving every version of me over all our years together and making space for each of them to exist as I evolved and grew. The words here aren't enough, but I know for certain this book would still be sitting on my computer if you hadn't made me find my bravery. So much like Parker, I realized in this process, my bravery is you.

To those of you who stuck around to read this long—you're amazing. I hope Parker and Wyatt gave you everything you were hoping for and then some. You are magical, and in a world that can be anything but kind, thank you for the kindness of cozying up with these lovely characters. Your reading lets me keep writing, and I'm grateful to you for that.

About the Author

I vy Charles is an author—though if you ask her, that title still feels a little terrifying. Don't worry, she's panicking enough for everyone. When she's not tucked into her favorite chair, earbuds in, typing away on her beloved mechanical keyboard, she's busy chasing after the husband and kids who bring chaos, joy, and meaning to her life.

From baseball diamonds to bookstores, Ivy is passionate about storytelling—the kind that lingers long after the last page. She writes stories that sink into your skin, make you smile, maybe even make you kick your feet a little, and remind you to embrace your own brand of badass. And if along the way, she makes you fall a little in love? Well, that's just a bonus.

Learn more about her and upcoming releases at IvyCharles.com.

Ready for the next installment of the Maker series? Lincoln and Cami are up, and you know they are going to bring the fire, the banter, and a story with at least a few twists you won't see coming.

Sign up for Ivy's newsletter to stay up to date and receive sneak peeks, bonus content, and learn more about the world of the Lochlans.